DERRING-DO FOR BEGINNERS

DERRING-DO FOR BEGINNERS

THE RED COMPANY

BOOK ONE

VICTORIA GODDARD

PART ONE
IN THE CITY

CHAPTER ONE

IN WHICH DAMIAN FIGHTS HIS FIRST DUEL

I t was quiet in Ixsaa, in the hours before dawn. In the room he shared with his twin brother, Damian lay for a few moments in his bed, listening to his own heart beating. Alezian was breathing softly, and it was a windless morning at the tail end of summer. He could smell the herbs that scented their sheets, and a waft of less pleasant odour from outside the window. In the distance the baker's rooster crowed; it was always the first awake.

Damian knew the crows of every cockerel and rooster in the Greenmarket. He knew which houses had night-wandering cats, and whose dogs or geese could be counted on to stir. He knew the night tracks of rats, and the occasional secret visits of the wild foxes, the soft-winged owls, the night-flying geese.

He was training to be a swordsman, and he practiced early in the morning, before the city was awake.

People watched him if he started too late, which he found discomforting. As he was not willing to abandon the more extravagant elements—the hand-over-hand swing along the underside of the harbour chain, the climb across the face of the aqueduct, the circuit of the three walls of Ixsaa in their varying states of decrepitude—but he was not inclined towards display, either, he had moved his start time earlier and earlier, until he was able to do the whole circuit safely in the dark.

His twin brother thought him mad, but that was all right. Damian could not fathom Alezian's own interests in trade, for all Ixsaa was a city of merchants, not warriors. Alezian could follow the merchants, the ways of the city their mother had adopted; Damian could follow the narrow path of their quietly whispered family legends.

This particular morning he stretched and dressed, and glanced once at his brother in the bed beside his, who, as always, slept deeply.

Alezian had to be chivvied to exercise when he was on land, claiming —with some truth, Damian admitted—that the most successful merchants were always the fattest. The only thing that kept him from true corpulence was his love of sailing.

For the whole last year Alezian had been going back and forth between the Ixsaan navy, where he might start as an officer, or the merchant fleet, where he would have to begin as an ordinary seaman. Either way he needed to be able to climb the ropes and manage a cutlass. This morning he was legally able to decide; he would, Damian was sure, choose the merchants.

This morning Damian was legally able to duel.

He dressed in his practice gear, leather breeches supple with age and use, linen shirt with the sleeves bound at his wrist, leather jerkin. He pulled on the half-boots he always wore.

He was mocked for that habit, half-boots being entirely unfashionable, but Damian reasoned that any real fight would come either when he was expecting it, when he could dress as he wished, or when he was not, in which case he should be prepared to fight in his ordinary clothes.

Both Alezian and their mother sighed at this logic and tried to convince him he should wear something other than leather and old, worn linen for his ordinary clothes.

Damian snorted softly. Let his brother yearn after silk and velvet and rare furs and all the trappings and trinkets of wealth. That was not *his* concern.

He slipped out of the room as silently as he could, practicing stealth as a matter of habit as well as courtesy.

He, Damian Raskae, might have chosen the way of the sword from the earliest possible age, but he had chosen it for its beauty and its challenge, not its violence or its power. He did not want to be a boorish fighter, the sort his mother had always dismissed in her stories.

His mother was in the kitchen. Damian was startled to see her, for though she was an early riser, an hour before dawn rarely saw her out of bed. He had intended to do no more than pass through on his way to the locked shed where they kept their weapons, but she gestured to the seat next to her.

"Good morning," he said reluctantly.

"Good morning, Damian," she replied, not in Calandran but in their own language, Tanteyr.

They rarely spoke it nowadays, though it had been the language of his childhood. Most of the other Tantey in the city had moved on, seeking a place they could form their own community.

Damian hesitated, his curiosity pricked, though he responded in Calandran to show that he was a man now, not bound by her rules. Alezian had been very firm about that. He was always much clearer about the way things were done than Damian was. "What is it, Ema?"

"It is your sixteenth birthday today, Damian," she said, still in Tanteyr.

"Yes, Ema. Can we talk about it later? I want to get to the grounds before dawn."

She regarded him steadily. He met her gaze, refusing to back down. This was not the mountains, not the old country of her stories, where she had been a queen. This was the city, and in the city a man was expected to be strong and resolute.

He was just turned sixteen. In the city he was a man now, able to join the navy or run for office or own a business or fight a duel. He was by some minutes the elder over Alezian, and under Ixsaan law was now technically the head of the household. He did not need to submit to his mother any longer.

He opened his mouth to say that, and caught himself.

Every story she had told him of the old country, the one high up in the mountains, had ingrained that youth should bow before age, child before parent, prince before queen—and that women were the equal of men.

Did he not pride himself he was not a boor, not *only* a fighter, but also (if secretly) a prince of the Realm, one to whom courtesy ought come as easily as skill at arms? Was he not proud that his mother had been a warrior, was a better archer than most, was one of the best riders in the city?

She was still watching him, her expression faintly sad. Did she think he had forgotten all their own language? He thought Alezian might have, or pretended to.

Alezian wanted to be accepted, to become a merchant prince, to live in one of the big houses on the Crescent and look out on his ships coming and going up from the Delta. Alezian was embarrassed by their mother's refusal to do a proper feminine job, that she had hung out her shingle as a public notary, and that she trained the horses she bred up in one of the feeder valleys herself.

Damian bowed to his mother and then sat down. "My apologies, Ema," he said in Tanteyr, fumbling a bit with the words. "It is yet early, and I was not anticipating this audience."

The more formal language and pacing made him feel grander than the small kitchen seemed to warrant. He straightened his shoulders, trying to feel like a prince of the old country.

"What is it your desire to speak of?"

She paused, watching him. He bore her scrutiny as patiently as he could, imagining her a queen, crowned with silver as she had once been.

Then she shook her head. "No, go on, Dami. I don't think this is a good time, after all. I don't think you're ready to hear what I wanted to tell you."

He knew well enough not to press after such a flat statement, and so he took his leave, kissing the hand she held out in the Ixsaan custom.

He puzzled over her words as he went around the fountain in their tiny courtyard to the shed on the far side, wondering if he'd misunderstood something.

Possibly he had spoken incorrectly. He really did not speak Tanteyr often. As Alezian said, there was no need to. Their mother had left because of a civil war in the old country, and almost all of those who had initially stayed with her had gone off to found their own colony somewhere far away from Ixsaa.

It was not as if Damian or Alezian were ever going to become *king*. He had paid enough attention to know that was not how succession worked up there in the mountains. And anyone who came this far to trade would have learned Calandran as a matter of course.

His heart beat faster, as it always did, as he undid the locks on the shed.

He did not need to see to know what was inside: his mother's bows and quivers on the left, her swords and spears. On the right, his brother's sword and cutlass.

And in the middle, the swords and daggers and other weapons Damian had scrounged, bought, and been given over the years.

He reached for the sword in the middle, hand closing on the tooled leather of its scabbard, and smiled in simple joy to have the rapier in his hand.

As he belted it on his hip all thought of his mother's apparent quibbles left his thoughts.

She was a warrior queen; he was almost a warrior prince. Surely that was more than enough.

She was probably a little emotional that her two boys were becoming men today, and she did not like showing emotion, his mother. Another way she was not like the women of the city.

He relocked the shed, excitement surging as it always did when he had his sword at his side and the morning before him. He did not bother with unlatching the gate but instead leaped up and swung himself over the top of the wall and off lightly into the still-sleeping city.

Inside the house Kasiar Ounlalin sat in her kitchen, the sword she had intended to give her elder son laid on the table before her, and missed her late husband terribly.

Damian was running easily by the time he left the last houses of the city behind, though his heart was beating much harder than was usual.

He could not see anyone as he approached the duelling grounds, but it was still very early; the sky behind the mountains was barely tinted with red.

The air was fresh, smelling good with some sort of herbal or flowery scent. He noted the direction of the wind and the small likelihood of clouds, and did not distract himself with questions of what the wind smelled like.

He also did not look too often at the pale falcon riding high above him. That was a secret he was unwilling to share with anyone outside of his family.

It occurred to him that perhaps it was some piece of knowledge to do with that portion of their heritage that his mother had wanted to tell him. He glanced up at the falcon.

It was too early for him to chase its shadow, the falcon's usual challenge.

Perhaps it, too, was acknowledging that this day was a special one.

He slowed to a walk when he turned off the main road north to the lane leading to the duelling grounds. He did not want to seem *too* eager. That was considered a fault by both his mother and the fraternity of swordsmen he was finally about to join.

The crumbling stone walls of some ancient edifice from the long-vanished Calandran Empire provided a sheltered and private place for the duels, which were sacred to the god of war and only to be seen by men.

As a boy he had been permitted to watch from the inner fence marking out the circular grounds, never to cross the threshold and set his sword against a man's.

That would change this morning—if one of the swordsmen were willing to meet him. It would be humiliating to find no one there.

He was not worried about humiliating himself on the grounds. He was here to learn.

Torches burned either side of the door, indicating someone, at least, had come.

He took a breath, settling himself, looking up at a flicker, but a soft cooing told him it was a pigeon moving in the niche over the door, not some uncanny movement of the blurred carving of the ancient god contained within.

He raised his right hand to part the heavy curtains, leather dyed red, that blocked the door, and ducked through.

His heart was beating steadily now, his breath easy. He was ready to meet what the fates had in store for him.

There were five men there. They stood around another torch, this one thrust into the ground by the gate of the inner enclosure, speaking quietly among themselves. When Damian walked up they stopped and ranged themselves to look at him.

He regarded them in the uncertain light, taking in their silhouettes and their stances.

Two he knew from watching at the staging grounds where the cara-vans gathered, though he did not know their names: a red-haired man from the Delta, tall, barrel-chested, with arms whose muscles were like clusters of river rocks, and a black-haired and black-bearded Calandran, as tall as the red-haired man but lean and quick as the narrow bastard sword he was known for.

A little apart from them were two young blades from the Crescent, severn or eight years older than Damian himself.

They had nothing in common with the first two but the respect given to those who bore a certain degree of mastery; the young blades between them had won all the prizes for fencing in the war-games held each summer for the past five years. They had the usual proud surnames of the Crescent's wealthy families, but went by Erios and Faros when out and about in the half-masks that marked them as members of the Fraternity of the Crescent Blade.

The fifth was a stranger. He stood easily, the silhouette of his clothes slightly foreign: his breeches did not cling close but billowed out slightly before being bound into his tall boots, and he wore a half-cloak in some dark colour, as if the cool air was winter-cold. It moved restlessly in the light wind, swirling over the sword belted and chained at his hip.

Damian had watched the duellers for the past several years. He knew the ritual. Once he came to the waist-high stone between door and fence he stopped and bowed.

"Who approaches the duelling ground?" asked the black-bearded Calandran.

"One seeking to prove himself," Damian replied—at last, at last! His heart was beating too fast again, as if it wanted to match the guttering of the torch in the breeze. The stranger's cloak moved in the wind, like a restless shadow.

"Only men may stand upon this ground, which is sacred to Arkhos, the god of war."

"I am of age this day, and I willingly bring my blood and my blade as an offering to Arkhos," Damian said truthfully, though he had to suppress a pang that he so easily denied the teachings of his mother.

It was not as if making an offering to one of the Calandran gods meant he no longer believed in his own, he told himself.

It was not exactly forbidden, anyway.

And no one really *believed* in the hundred gods of Calandra.

"Come, then, and test your blade and your blood in the cold hour before dawn," said the black-bearded Calandran. "I am called Horchus."

Horchus! Damian bowed again in acknowledgement and followed him into the duelling grounds. Horchus was famous for his cool head and the length of his reach and for his luck. It was said any caravan he refused to join went to the soothsayers to beg charms against disaster, for he had an almost uncanny knowledge of what would be a good job and which end in landslide or bandit attack.

They paced out the distance. Horchus took the side nearest the gate, as was traditional, and drew his sword.

Damian hastily followed suit, nearly catching his blade in the scabbard in his haste. He was glad it was still the dim blue pre-dawn. He knew his pale skin showed every least flush; Alezian had teased him about it enough.

Once he had the hilt in his hand he steadied, emotions leaching away from the surface as they always did.

"First blood only," the Delta man said.

Damian saluted with his blade. Ixsaan law was very clear on the constraints required for a duel to be legal. And he was not violent by nature—not bloodthirsty. He did not want to *hurt* other people.

It was just that he wanted to be the best, and to do that he had to fight against those who were better than he until he could learn no more from them.

"Begin," said the Delta man.

Damian was not much of a reader. He found it tiresome to decode the squiggles and smudges of letters, and was bored by the texts themselves.

In school he had hunted out the stories of battles and tactics, and there were few of those in the heavy histories of Ixsaa, a trading city to its core.

He was even slower with the Tanteyr lettering, frustrated by his inability and never sure of the meaning of the words so laboriously deciphered.

Half the time he got to the end of a passage that seemed to be about war only to find it was some stupid metaphor about philosophy.

He did not, therefore, know all the names of the moves he was performing, and he didn't care. He knew them, knew at a level below conscious thought what he should do to meet each of Horchus' movements. He had not trained for hours every day, with and without a sword in hand, if not for this.

Each parry and thrust came without thought or effort.

He was surprised at how quickly the duel was over.

Horchus made what Damian was sure was a feint, but the accompanying thrust never came, and Damian's own sword slid through the circular parry as if through his own shadow.

He had worked hard on precision, and he touched the sharp point to the Calandran's shoulder exactly as hard, and no harder, as was required to draw forth one drop of blood.

The light was paler now, if still more blue than gold. It was bright enough to show the surprised respect in Horchus' bearing as he backed off to make the final salute. "First blood to you."

Damian saluted, tucking away the feel of the movements, the variants Horchus had used, the rhythm of this duel over all the ones he had ever witnessed before.

Later he would take the memory out and work through the duel again, playing both sides against his shadow, until he had absorbed all that he could learn from it.

His mother had taught him everything she could, and he had cadged the odd lesson from whoever would give him one, but there had never been any money for a tutor such as the Crescent blades would have, so he had learned to make do with his shadow and his memory.

The Delta man came next. "I'm Ghanau mir Aviroth," he said briefly. "Ready?"

Damian saluted. He knew nothing by repute of Ghanau mir Aviroth, but he had watched many of his practice fights at the staging grounds. He knew the Delta man was preternaturally strong, nearly as fast as Horchus, and had travelled far and learned many unusual styles. The rest, he supposed, would come in the fight.

Two minutes later he lowered his sword, moved nearly to tears by the beauty of the Delta man's skill, by the delicate control that focused each of those heavy-handed blows, and the sheer strength required to shift from move to move so quickly when so much force lay behind the strikes. Not actually to tears, of course: he was a man now, and men of Ixsaa did not weep for beauty, or for anything else.

Ghanau looked at the line of blood on his forearm, which he wore bared in the Delta fashion. Blue lines of tattoos ran back from his knuckles to disappear into his sleeves.

He turned to display his cut to Horchus, who shrugged slightly.

Ghanau clenched his fist so that the fine line of blood beaded and ran down the channel of his knuckles to drip onto the hard-packed ground. "Blood to the mother of blood."

"I'm next," said Faros, leaping down from where he sat on the fence.

As he stalked forward, sword already drawn, his mask seemed appropriate. It was made of leather, with a beak like a bird of prey, the face sewn all over with green and black sequins that glittered faintly.

Alezian had gone on, one day, about how the fashion for sequins for the Fraternity's masks had made some tin-merchant rich.

Faros's dark eyes were emphasized by the shaping of the eye-holes, his mouth shadowed by the beak. Damian had always thought the Fraternity of the Crescent Blade's masks looked ridiculous, but that was before he had ever faced one across the duelling grounds.

No, he decided, even in the flickering torchlight and the solemn atmosphere it still looked ridiculous.

Faros did not wait. He tossed off a salute that became an attack as soon as his sword left the vertical.

Damian had studied the war-games with all the interest he did not give his books or his mother tongue. He had watched Erios and Faros as they came up out of the gangs of young noblemen, watched them as they distinguished themselves in fencing and riding, watched as black-and-green and red-and-blue became the banners that decorated the plazas each year.

He had a memory for such things: he could go home and review what he had watched intently, almost as if he stood there before it once again. He had translated those memories into practice routines, learning the ways of the fencers he saw by repeating their own moves over and over again until they became his own.

Horchus and Ghanau had both fenced in the style of the caravan guards, which had developed out of the old Calandran army's infantry training. Even though the swords used now were longer and heavier than the ancient Calandrans', their motions, however quick, were those of a foot soldier who would have a shield in his other hand and many others fighting at his shoulders.

The Fraternity of the Crescent Blade used the noble style, which had been developed from the cavalry officers who had ultimately proven the downfall of the Calandran Empire, back in the days when their gods were still seriously worshipped.

Damian had managed to gather that much out of his schooling, at least.

Their name came from their neighbourhood rather than their straight sabres, and they used them to slash more than thrust.

Faros was not expecting Damian to be able to switch so easily to the noble style.

He was disarmed within three moves, and Damian had to think where to prick him to win the point.

Finally he flicked his sword in the difficult maneuver he named to himself the Fly-Bite, snapping the blade so that the tip curved over his opponent's neck and pricked him on his shoulder blade.

Faros stepped back, clasping his shoulder, his whole body slack with surprise before being tensed again with chagrin. Damian knew that Alezian would say that he had made an enemy: but what was he supposed to do, pretend to a lack in the one skill he had?

"Point," said Erios, grinning maliciously at his friend and striding over to take his place before Damian. He saluted with exaggerated precision.

Erios had not won the prize last summer, but the rumours had it—and Damian saw no reason to doubt them—that this was because he had been spurned by the girl he was courting just before the war-games began. She had been touched with the evidence of his love and he was now happily engaged to be married and, apparently, back in his finest form.

Erios had been paying more attention, and this bout lasted a full five minutes. The light was gold and glittering fiercely on the red and gold sequins of his mask when Damian found his opening and executed a perfect thrust to the heart. He stopped, of course, when his blade touched skin.

It took a moment for Erios to gather himself to make the final salute, which he did with an air of malicious enjoyment the mask did nothing to disguise. Damian was a little puzzled, but did not worry about it, for he was never very good at understanding other people's emotions and he had much to store away in his mind to go over later from these four duels.

And then—there was still the last man to consider.

He turned to the stranger.

The sunlight was breaking through the passes now: the sky above them was streaked with pink clouds, and far off to the west odd clumps of trees on the plains west of the river were illuminated as if dipped in rose pigment.

In the fresh breeze the half-cloak was shown now to be a deep red. The breeches were fawn cloth, as was his shirt; he wore a wide green sash around his waist. He had curly dark hair and a close-trimmed beard, like most Ixsaans, and he was much older than Damian, perhaps as old as thirty.

His sword hung from a silver-chased belt. He wore an earring with a jewelled drop in his left ear: the gem caught the sun in a blaze of red fire as he pushed his tall black boot from the fence and sauntered over.

Damian lowered his sword to a less aggressive position. "Good morning, sir," he said, assessing not the details—Alezian would be calculating the cost of each item of clothing—but the shape and tenor of the stranger's body. Every motion indicated strength, and skill, and confidence.

This was someone Damian very much wanted to know. "Would you care to meet my blade?"

The stranger hooked his thumbs into his belt and rocked back on his heels. "Not this morning, I think."

Damian nodded in acknowledgement, though he also acknowledged to himself a sharp pang of disappointment. He looked around briefly, to make sure there wasn't anyone else waiting to fence, and saw that Erios and Faros had taken themselves off, as had Ghanau mir Aviroth, leaving Horchus leaning against the fence.

"In that case, then," Damian said, sheathing his sword, "I thank you, Horchus, for the gift of your time and skill today."

"We're not the only ones who've been waiting for you to come of age," Horchus grunted, "but not everyone wanted to meet you this morning. This is Rean, by the way."

Damian nearly stumbled at this casual introduction of the most famous swordsman on the length of the river from Escarpment to Delta. Rean laughed. "Don't worry, young man. I'll meet you another day."

"I'll hold you to that, sir," Damian said quietly.

Rean laughed again. He had the kind of laugh a person could come to like, Damian thought, robust and rolling. "I expect you will at that. Come, walk with us back to the city."

CHAPTER TWO

IN WHICH DAMIAN CONSIDERS ENDS IN THEMSELVES

Rean invited him out that evening. Damian was uncertain, but Alezian was going out with his friends, and it was so good to be invited *himself* that he met the older man at the appointed time and place. It was just the Rose and Phoenix Inn, in the Greenmarket, which was owned by his mother's great friend. Damian had helped Pelan Cadia any number of times when she needed help moving crates and the like, though he'd never visited as a patron before.

Damian did not like the taste of wine, it turned out. He drank what people bought for him ("The lad's just turned a man!" Rean had cried to all his friends. "Treat him royally, boys!"), and managed, he thought, not to embarrass himself. He didn't say much of anything, but Rean didn't seem to expect him to. That, too, was something of a gift.

The evening ended with Damian returning home, slightly dizzy from the wine and disliking how it made him feel, but well pleased at having been able to speak of fighting with someone who understood. All in all, he thought, it had been a very successful birthday.

The next morning he returned to his usual routine. After tending his mother's horses, he returned briefly home, to find Alezian on his way out to ready himself for his maiden voyage—he had, indeed, chosen a short run around the Middle Sea with a merchant ship—and decided therefore to spend the afternoon in his secret practice place in the reed plains, going over what he had learned from the duels the day before.

He ran home lightly through the gathering dusk along the narrow game-trails. He was familiar with their twists and turns, the places where the herons waited, the places where the marsh foxes marked their territories, the places where he had to run silently as a shadow so as not to disturb the singing frogs.

It had taken him years of concentrated practice before he could pass through the game-trails without disturbing the wild animals; now it was habit. Their deep silences did not mock him; their knowledge was unwritten, their thoughts unspoken, their ways economical, gracious, beautiful. In the hidden meadows of the reed plains where the tiny anxo deer grazed, Damian felt enveloped by the world, not apart from it.

He came home and listened to Alezian describing all the trinkets he had acquired to sell along his voyage. Damian sat a little away from the table where his brother had spread out his wares, where he could watch his mother and brother in the pool of golden candlelight.

Their faces were richly coloured in the light, wavering with brighter highlights cast up from the glittering trinkets. He listened to their voices, the eager anticipation in Alezian's, the warm approval in their mother's.

He felt as privileged to watch them as when he had crouched, unmoving, for the hours it took a clutch of swan eggs to hatch into grey puffs of cygnets.

"What do you think, Dami?" his brother asked, turning to hold up some silvery ornament whose gemstones glittered like dewdrops in the candlelight. "Will I do well over the water with these?"

He knew his brother understood such things; and their mother's enjoyment of the wares suggested they were pretty. "Yes."

"A benediction indeed!" cried Alezian, laughing, and turned back to the table.

Damian let his mind dwell on the shape of Ghanau's movements as they had duelled, drawing in the beauty he had found there.

The rippling conversation of his mother and his brother ran on, like the voices of the rivers, neither demanding nor rejecting his attention, but part of the shape and beauty of the world, a mystery to which his only answer was to shape his own motions as echo and reflection.

~

Damian knew he was not a swift thinker. He plodded along far behind everyone else, having to disregard all the glittering surface they loved so much in order to find any least solid idea to hold onto. At the guild school the difference between him and his twin was marked, for Alezian gravitated naturally to the successful and the popular, as adept with people as he was with money or words. The boys he liked best were the ones (he confidently predicted) who would go on to the university and the inns of court and become lawyers, merchants, bankers, and judges.

They spent every minute of every day, it seemed to Damian, arguing about the most ridiculous things: what this accent or that did to the meaning of a word, the word for a sentence, the sentence for a paragraph, the paragraph for an entire school of philosophy. Alezian kept them from outright mockery, but Damian knew well enough what they were thinking as he toiled away whole volumes behind them.

Excellence, he read in one of his schoolbooks, *is its own prize: to be good at something worth doing is an end in itself.*

By the time he had worked his way to that part of the text the others had long since moved on from their debates about whether something could truly be good in its own right or only for what it could do for something—which always seemed to mean some*one*—else.

He had not attended much to the arguments, needing to concentrate ferociously to make the squiggles and streaks on the page turn into words, and the arguments had been dizzyingly complex, fearsomely witty, and liberally powdered with quotations drawn from books Damian had not even heard of. But he did remember that Alezian had won the day, as he usually did, with his argument that goods were always relative to their usefulness, not to themselves.

Excellence is an end in itself, he read, and having spent so monstrous an effort to decode the words, he thought about them.

He did not have all the arguments Alezian and his friends did. He could not array quotations or authorities or witty puns or any of the rest either in support of his thoughts or against them. He had only his own experience and his own ideas to go on.

He watched the caravan guards and took his mental pictures of their work off to private places where he could separate out all the parts of their moves and make them his own. He swam in the many streams to the north of the city, learning the currents and ways of each in turn, from the placid Little Pink to the robust Goldtree. This summer he had begun to turn his thoughts towards how he could master the width and strength of the Greenwater and Redwine Arms themselves.

He ran and climbed and dashed and ran again, until he could run at full speed the whole long length of the Stair of Ten Thousand Steps, from the Temple of the Sea Goddess at the lower tip of the Crescent all the way up to the Temple of the Sky God at the very top of Mount Zahar.

Over time his mind settled solidly on the truth that he loved it all for its own sake: that he might have begun in order to keep himself from envying his brother, but that he continued because he thought it was good to do.

Not good *for* anything.

He could conceive no reason why it was more useful to be able to run up the Stair two stairs at a time (his newer challenge, and did he feel it) than it was to be able to run it at all. The fact that no one else either could or bothered to do it made it clear enough that it was not *useful* in the least. It was just ... good.

It made Damian feel good to feel his body responding to his demands of it. It made him feel pleased to realize he had mastered something, then spend the hours or days it might take him to devise a new, more difficult challenge, and then the weeks or months or even years it took to master that.

He did not mind his dull wit or clumsy understanding or inarticulate tongue when he ran through the floodplains keeping pace with his falcon's shadow.

He was not sure he learned anything else so solidly from all the years at the guild school as that simple statement that no one else thought was true, but although Damian could not present any arguments that his brother could not easily have demolished, he held it all the more tightly to himself.

Excellence is an end in itself.

He did not need anything, he said to himself, but that truth to strive for.

He had chosen his art (though he knew Alezian, lover of all things beautiful, would laugh at him to hear him call it so), and with all the devoted attention Damian could bring to bear he strove to master it.

He would never be the warrior-poet prince of his mother's stories, never have the sworn companion whose friendship was valued as an end in itself, because each believed the other an end in himself, never have the glorious adventures facing gods or monsters or seemingly insurmountable odds.

But he could strive to be the best swordsman in the world.

The next day Alezian boarded his ship. Damian saw him off, carrying his trunk of wares down to the quays for him. Alezian had already made friends with one of the other new sailors, a young man whose carriage proclaimed him from the Crescent.

Damian watched his brother greet this friend, glad (if also, as always, a little envious) that Alezian had found his place so easily, and made his way back up to the Greenmarket and out of the city to the staging grounds where the caravan guards camped between tours.

Horchus nodded at him when he took up his usual position along the fence that separated the horse pickets from the open area where the guards sparred. Damian nodded back.

That was the difference the duels made; he was no longer the anonymous boy, but a known man, here to observe.

Most of the caravans had already gone for the spring trading season, so there were only a dozen or so men practicing, and no other observers.

He reflected that there rarely were observers from outside the community of guards. They had tolerated his presence, because he had always taken great care not to get in the way, nor to interrupt them with questions or comments. He did not see that there was any need to change; had he not learned from them all these years all the same?

He was considerably surprised when Rean—whom he'd watched carefully instructing another guard how to respond to movements in the noble style—finished his training and came over to him. "Damian," he said, saluting with a slightly mocking fillip to his motion.

Damian nodded politely. "Rean."

Rean sheathed his sword and hooked his thumbs over his belt. He regarded Damian for a few moments, rocking slightly on his feet, his shirt and breeches moving in the breeze where they were loose, accentuating his silhouette where they were bound tight about his wrists, the tops of his boots, his sashed waist.

Damian bore his regard patiently, unable to guess what Rean was interested in. He matched Rean's clothing up with what he had seen other men wearing the day before, and decided that the guard was at the forefront of a new fashion amongst the guards and perhaps some of the more daring of the younger men in the city.

Finally Rean laughed. "You are a quiet one, aren't you? A dark horse?"

Damian had not heard that phrase, but he recognized it as an allusion, or perhaps a joke; he was fair of skin and hair, impossible to mistake for a native Ixsaan. He shrugged.

Rean laughed again. "Or perhaps a lamb. I think I like you, my lamb. Why don't you come inside and show us what you can do with that sword of yours outside of the duelling grounds?"

That, at least, was something he understood. The training exercises were never as solemn as the duels, did not require the offerings to the god of war or the secrecy of who met whom. In practice the guards laughed and joked and swapped stories along with their moves.

Their humour was one of the things that Damian did not quite understand. He was aware that there were currents of unspoken communication passing between these men, who were a close-knit community that was slow to let outsiders into their midst.

Damian had been coming to observe them for years, but he had never been invited within the precinct of the fence, never acknowledged by so much as a nod until today. But now he was a man, and had fought four duels, and Horchus had nodded to him, and Rean had spoken with him.

Damian decided that on this momentous occasion he would match himself to those he faced. The point here was to improve, to learn, not to win.

He focused.

The afternoon flew by. Apart from practice with his mother (and, very occasionally, his brother) and the duels he had never actually crossed swords with anyone. He had to keep an intense degree of focus on not turning the friendly sparring into serious fights.

He knew the men he faced by the shape of their movements, knew before they moved their habitual choices of feint or parry or thrust, their favoured stances. He had fenced them in his mind's eye over and over again, closing his eyes to visualize them before him, growing strong enough and precise enough to stop his sword where he imagined it touching their blades.

It was odd in the extreme to open his eyes to see the real men there, their motions like parodies of themselves, always slower and more obvious than Damian had made them in his memory.

They seemed to be moving through honey, and he sighed inwardly at this evidence that he was, as he sometimes forgot, not all that smart. He should have been able to hold their true speed in his mind; but like the letters that did not stay there, this, too, had fallen out.

The control required to cut his usual speed by a third or more was a good lesson to learn, he told himself. He was dripping with sweat from the afternoon heat when he stopped to drink from a waterskin Rean came up to offer him.

He also had a thunderous headache from all the concentration required. Another sign of his general lack of acumen, he realized glumly, when Rean said enough was enough already.

Fencing with his shadow was all very well and good but it was nothing like practicing with real people. He did not end up with ferocious headaches after two hours with his shadow.

"Come along with us tonight," Rean said casually as they washed themselves at the horse-trough. Damian had just dunked his head; when he looked at the older man the sunlight glared brilliantly in his eyes. He blinked, hoping he did not look too stupid. Rean went on, "We'll be at the Greenmarket Inn to start with. Sunset."

Damian pondered the possible reasons for this invitation. At length he nodded. Rean clapped him on the shoulder, a wet slap. "Good lamb. We'll see you later, then."

That was a dismissal. Damian nodded again, making them all laugh as water sprayed from his hair, and put on his damp shirt, his worn belt, his sword. He blinked against the dazzle still in his eyes and walked off, not caring that the laughter quieted and then rose again as he exited the grounds. He had much to think about from the sparring matches.

Damian did not like the wine any better the second time. He told himself Alezian would be proud that he was making an effort to meet people who might be important to his future career; certainly his mother was. When he had told he was going out with Rean again she had told him to take care.

She had always told him to take care, to be careful, before trying any other new thing. *Take care* was the fundamental lesson she had taught her sons: to pay attention, to work hard, to not shirk the effort required.

He nodded, a little impatient at the repeated advice, a little nervous that he would ruin this opportunity. Alezian would have known exactly what to say to make himself belong. Damian could only pay attention to what everyone else said and did and do his poor best to conform and be unobtrusive.

When they spilled out of the Inn after a few drinks and Rean took him by the arm, therefore, Damian neither freed himself nor stated how little he liked being touched by strangers, but instead went along. When Rean and the other guards started to sing, Damian listened and joined in on the chorus and hoped he was not blushing too fiercely at the ruder words.

By the time he realized they were going to the greyhounds he could not think of a way to withdraw without giving offence. He had almost determined to leave anyway when Rean suddenly said, "Have you been to the races before?"

"No," Damian admitted, which made all the others roar with laughter.

"A lamb indeed," Rean said. "You stick close with me and I'll make sure you're right."

"Thank you," Damian said politely.

This was part of the men's world, he told himself. He'd heard the older boys talk among themselves about the greyhound races and the fighting pits.

Alezian had gone with a party of friends whose older brothers had taken them, had come back full of enthusiasm for the crowds, the speed of the dogs, the atmosphere of electric excitement, the enthralling sense of being part of a crowd all cheering on the same thing. Perhaps being at Rean's side would give Damian the entry into that world, too.

The races were held at an abandoned ochre working in the northeast of the floodplain, left dry by some change in the Greenwater Arm's course. The entry went down a steep slope, through a narrow defile between cliffs worn smooth by the water and the passing of many men.

Even in the midst of the small crowd from the Inn Damian could taste the faint acrid tang in the back of his mouth that said this was redearth ochre, the most common type. Half the city's houses had stucco whose plaster was coloured with it.

Rean tugged him along, his eager laughter muffled by the crowd's noises. Damian followed, concentrating on not losing him, hearing the sounds of a large crowd of men and the more distant snarls and yaps of the dogs.

The whole was much louder than he'd expected, voices raised with drink and enthusiasm and to be heard over the steady rumble of the Greenwater on the far side of the racecourse.

"First we need to wet our throats," Rean bawled in Damian's ear. "Then the bets."

Damian had no time to say he wasn't thirsty. Rean had his arm around his shoulders, and was introducing him to people Damian could not easily distinguish in the dark: the torches set around the perimeter of the course cast more shadows than light this far back.

He did not know whether to be offended that Rean's introduction was usually along the lines of: "My new lamb, with a fine touch. You'll know him one day."

The men they met seemed to think this a good enough introduction, laughing and buffeting Rean on the shoulder and answering with obscure comments as incomprehensible to Damian's ear as the guild scholars' debates.

He bought one of the skins of wine Rean collected from a man who stood with them piled all around him, as that seemed expected and he had to repay Rean for his invitation some way or another. Rean gossiped with the wine-seller for a few minutes as other men came up for their skins.

Damian stood to the side, watching the dark figures moving in and out of the light, wishing Rean did not keep pointing at him. How was he ever going to learn the ways of these men if he was not left in peace to observe them? They were worse than the huge flocks of migrating birds in the winter when an eagle or a fox disturbed them.

He had learned how to pass through the midst of the birds, he told himself with gritted teeth. Not even the nervy wood ducks flushed up when he came among them now. He could learn to be a man.

The wine-seller went back to his skins. Rean led Damian along the edges of the crowd to where another man sat on a stool of some form, torches placed on either side. He was huge, taller than Rean and fatter than Alezian's dreams. His long merchant's gown rippled as he moved, the waves of reflected light suggesting that the fabric was fine silk.

The man spoke with heavy pauses between his words, as if it were an effort to get the air out, but Damian, hearing no sound of broken wind or other true affliction, thought it might be an affectation.

Their mother's stories were full of people who feigned to be less than they were to reach their ends, like a killdeer pretending to a broken wing to draw predators from her nest.

The fat merchant was talking about names and numbers, odds and bargains. Damian watched as men formed a short line before him, waiting their turns to speak. The merchant responded, sometimes lifting his hands for emphasis so that jewelled rings flashed. Before each petitioner left someone from behind the torchlight would step forward and exchange money for a mark on a slate.

"Want to make your bets?" Rean asked.

Damian shook his head silently. He knew nothing of the dogs, or of the ways of betting on them. He had also spent enough time with his brother to know that the fat man held all the power, and that if it were possible to be a merchant of information, this man was; and that he was very successful at it.

"I'll tell you what to put your money on. Come on, it will be fun."

Damian shook his head again. He planted his feet against Rean's gentle tugging. After a few more cajoling words the older man laughed and shrugged and went to speak to the fat man. Damian held the wine-skins and watched as the coins exchanged hands, the mark on the slate was made, and Rean came back rubbing his hands gleefully with the expectation of reward to come.

Damian handed him back his wine and decided not to ask why Rean bothered, when it was so obvious that the fat man would win. He would not be so fat or so well-dressed if he did not know how to turn those petitioners' coins into his own profit.

Rean drank a long slug from the first wineskin. He handed it to Damian, who stoppered it for him and slung it back over his shoulder with the others. "Now for a spot to watch. Come!"

Damian went, concentrating first on not losing Rean—easy enough, as the man was hailing everyone he met with loud and excited whoops about the dogs he had just bet on—and on not bumping into other men.

Some stood with lurking menace, their stances stable, their hands free, their senses alert. He marked them as predators, and passed them by.

No one seemed to mind Rean pushing through, nor Damian in his wake. They ended up right at the front, alongside the fence, next to a cluster of men Rean obviously knew well. They traded stories and wine-skins, names and ideas flying through the air, laughter and curses cutting out any sense Damian might have made of it.

He tried to keep his attention as alert for trouble as the predators he had passed, his stance as stable, his hands as free. This last was difficult, for Rean kept pressing the wineskin into his hands and trying to draw him into the conversations. Damian passed the skin back to whoever's hand was closest and wondered why they found so much pleasure in the rough acidic taste and the rougher stories of conquest.

After an interminable period he felt Rean's hand heavy on his shoulder, his breath hot in his ear. "The first race is about start, my quiet lamb," he said. "Eyes front on the dapple-grey dog."

Everything was dappled grey in the torchlight, but he turned obedient to the pressure to see the two greyhounds straining against their handlers in the distance. A man walked out with a covered basket. The dogs leaned against their leashes, their whole attention forward.

They knew what was in the basket, Damian thought, and were eager for it.

Someone blew a whistle. The man with the basket opened it and dumped out a hare, which landed awkwardly, froze, saw the now silent hounds, and then streaked off the opposite direction, directly towards the stands. The whistle blew again and the handlers unleashed the greyhounds.

They should have been beautiful: their speed, the hare's agility, the dogs' ability to turn at high speed after the hare's zigzagging course, the sudden final leap by which one caught the hare.

Around him men were screaming and cheering, shouting and jeering, drinking and talking over the form of hare and hound. Damian stood there, stunned by the savagery he heard in their voices, the slaking of lusts he did not understand.

He thought back to Alezian's excited account of the coursing. He had not mentioned the urging on of the dog lapping the blood of the hare. His brother had been fully immersed in the crowd, part of it, not crushed against the fence wondering what he was missing.

Alezian never stood apart from the crowd, wondering what he was missing.

Damian concentrated harder.

The next race was a repeat of the first, except that the men around him were growing drunker with every passing minute.

Damian wondered dolefully if he should be drinking, but he had not liked the heaviness of the morning after the evening at the Greenmarket Inn, the feeling that his mind was slower than ever.

He pressed up against the fence, watching the handlers whip the winning dog away from the dismembered hare, Rean leaning heavily against his back but talking to his friends beside him.

Damian had no arguments to put forward against it. He was not even sure what it was he disliked so much. The dogs were obeying their instincts; the hare its. He had seen worse violence done by predators hunting in the marshes, had himself (to his regret) inflicted worse in the early days of his own hunting. He regretted that clumsiness that had not resulted in clean deaths.

He did not think the dogs were wrong in running after the hare, nor in killing it once they had caught it. As much as say the falcon should not stoop, the heron not strike.

"You're a hard one to please," Rean said in his ear after the third race, draping his arm over Damian's shoulder again. He was half-way drunk: Damian could smell it on his breath, hear it in the slurred edge to his words. "You should be betting—that would spice it up for you. No better spice than that."

Was that what he was missing?

But one thing he had learned at the guild school was that money very definitely was not an end in itself, but a tool to be used.

A wave of noise swept through the crowd, loud as the approaching front of a storm. Rean clutched at his shoulder. "Here comes the Tyssan bitch," he said, breath hot and stinking. "She's the one to put your money on ... say, I should double my bet on this race. And my skin's empty. Come then."

Damian followed him willingly, past the silent menace of the predators, back to where the fat man watched the crowd like a heron its pool and the wine-seller had a much-diminished pile of skins.

"I'm off to the bushes," he said vaguely to Rean, who waved at him as another friend loomed out of the darkness to exclaim about some cock-fight he'd seen upriver. "See you later."

"You'll miss the race," Rean said, but his attention was all for his friend, and Damian was sure there was no further need for his own presence.

He slipped quietly behind the line of torches marking the betting merchant and the wine-seller, ignored the rank bushes where other men had relieved themselves, and followed the dim line of the ochre-working's walls to the entrance.

His ears rang from the noise. He walked down the lane, feet scuffing against the packed surface. He felt disturbed in a way he could not articulate.

As he always did when his feelings overwhelmed his ability to think about them, Damian sought relief in physical exertion.

Up here the wind was from the west, blowing away the noise of the Greenwater Arm and the crowds jeering at the hounds alike. Instead of the stench of too many men and too much wine it brought the muddy tang of the reed plains and beyond it something else, something thin and spicy and alluring.

Damian felt his heart lift and his feet start to move faster of their own accord. He ran into the wind, following the cool pressure on his face, that scent of far places and the unknown.

CHAPTER THREE

IN WHICH DAMIAN ATTAINS A POSITION

Kasiar was a solitary woman by nature, by inclination, and by her status as both an outsider and a woman working in a man's job, but she had two close friends among the other professional women in the Greenmarket.

The innkeeper, Cadia mir Daniroth, was a Delta woman who had inherited The Inn in some odd sequence of events that Kasiar had never fully learned, and who kept a tight house there just on the edge of the law for both taverns and women business owners.

The Greenmarket had once been a separate village from the rest of Ixsaa, and jealously guarded some of its ancient rights. These efforts formed the bulk of Kasiar's own work.

Their other friend was a true foreigner, from far to the west of the river. Maude Shayana owned a small stationery store located across the alley from the Inn.

Kasiar liked her accent and her no-nonsense way of looking at the world, and if both of them occasionally wondered what secrets the other was hiding, well, that was their prerogative as friends and fellow conspirators in the quiet resistance against male domination.

They usually met a few times a week, for midday or a light meal after siesta, before the Inn grew busy with its usual custom, taking turns bringing the food. Both Kasiar and Maude preferred their own cooking to anything the various sequence of cooks at the Inn ever provided them, but they did not have the heart to tell Cadia that excellent though her wine might be the food was terrible.

About a month after the twins' sixteenth birthday Kasiar received a letter from Alezian before she went to meet her friends. Damian, of course, was out. He'd given her a careless kiss to her hand and a shrug in reply to her asking where he was going and when he would be back.

He might be back for supper; but then again he might come back at midnight of the second day, smelling of wine and horses and crowds, and sleep until he rose again to do his exercises and leave.

She had been hoping he would make a friend for years. She should not be so disappointed now that he had.

In Alezian's carefully neat hand—he had been proud to overhear the guild teacher praise his writing once, and wrote ever afterwards with a copybook perfection that Damian had never once even approached—he wrote:

Dear Ema and Damian,

We have reached our first port of call, Yrio, and will spend the next three days here loading cargo. I have exchanged two of my small trinkets for ones that I believe will do well further along our circuit. We shall see if my estimations are correct.

Damian will be pleased to know that the crew practices at arms for an hour each day. We drill with cutlass, dagger, and grappling hooks in case we meet with pirates or enemies of our flag. It is all very exciting, but I am given to understand there is almost never any need for action on this run. The longer journey out to the Spice Islands and back is the one where corsairs are more often met.

I am already planning which ship to sign on for such a journey: and not as an ordinary seaman, let me tell you! One could never be a successful merchant from such a lowly position. I shall have to be sure of being a petty officer at the least by the time I take to the high seas. It is well enough being an ordinary seaman around the Middle Sea, where we stop every week at a tiny little port to share the news and make our trades, and will be home again before the season is out, but the food would not keep me happy three months at a time at sea.

I have made a friend among the other 'greenhorns' (as they call us who have signed on for the first time this passage). Barios is what he calls himself: he is from the Crescent, and if he had not fallen in love with the sea he might have been one of that Fraternity that Damian knows. He can see that I am not one of the common sort, and will insist on calling me Alezios! I do not mind, however, for he and his family connexions will be useful to me one day. Until then, I enjoy his company, and, of course, it is good to learn from one born to it how one ought to behave.

With fondest regards,

Alezian (Alezios!)

"Something the matter?" asked Cadia, filling her cup with red wine.

Kasiar had gone to the Inn seeking comfort, but now she found herself sipping from her cup instead of speaking. She shrugged.

"Come," Maude said gently, "you can tell us. Is it something to do with your sons? Or better, to do with Alderman Coster?"

Kasiar shrugged again. "Not the alderman, at least not today. He wants to shut you down, you know, Cadia."

"Let him try," the innkeeper replied blithely. "Don't change the subject unless you must?"

She appreciated the acknowledgment that she might not actually be able, or willing, to share a secret with them. "It's not a secret," she said, sighing, though it felt like one. "I had a letter from Alezian today."

"And that's not good news? Has he fallen in love with a girl in some foreign port or fallen afoul of some disease?"

She laughed weakly at the thought of the prim and fastidious Alezian losing control of himself to such an extent. "No, nothing like that. No. Perhaps it is something like that."

She met Maude's eyes, then sighed and looked away.

"I suppose I realized today that I'm losing them ... that I think I've already lost them. Perhaps it's just part of the transition from child to adult, and I'm clutching at them to keep them from leaving me. But I realized today that Alezian had left me behind in his heart long before he left in the ship."

"You still have Damian," Maude said after a moment.

"Damian." Kasiar rolled her cup around the table, watching the wine slosh in it, wondering if saying aloud what she'd been thinking would make things better or worse. "I have been coming to the conclusion that I've been wrong about him."

"How so?"

Kasiar kept her eyes on her cup. "His father was a brilliant man. Damian looks so much like him that I have always thought him the same, but … I have been realizing that that is perhaps a little unfair. It hurts that Alezian wants to leave everything behind to become one of the merchants in a big house on the Crescent, but he at least has set his eyes on a goal and is working towards it. Damian …"

"Damian is one of the most gifted swordsmen anyone has ever seen," Cadia said firmly.

"He is a superlative swordsman," Kasiar agreed quietly. "But that is all he is."

Maude took away Kasiar's cup. "You don't mean that, Kasiar, surely. He has so much to offer."

"Does he? Look at the facts, Maude! He is uninterested in anything but fighting. He was barely able to attend the guild school. I have never *once* seen him pick up something to read on his own. Give him anything physical to do and he can do it and willingly, but ask him to use his mind and you might as well be speaking another language—one he has no interest in learning!"

She shook her head, regretting her words already. "I have been realizing that perhaps it is that he *cannot* learn it. He is appallingly ignorant of anything outside his chosen field. I thought that perhaps he needed a friend to open up his mind to the rest of the world, but now that he has finally made one all I hear is Rean thinks this and Rean thinks that. If I ask what he, Damian, thinks, he just looks at me and repeats whatever Rean has put into his head."

"I don't know anything against Rean," Cadia said thoughtfully.

Kasiar made a gesture of frustration. "That's good, because Damian appears to be completely willing to follow him without the slightest hint of critical thought. Critical thought is one of Damian's many closed books." She could hear the bitterness in her voice, and repented. "Oh, I shouldn't be so disappointed. He does work hard at his fencing. I can be proud of him for that."

"You can be proud of him—you *will* be proud of him—for other things," Maude said, leaning to embrace her. "He's still very young, and Rean is handsome and charismatic. Hero-worship is a powerful force, you know—and to be honest, probably the attention of an older man is something he has been craving without realizing it. Not that you have not done a splendid job raising them on your own! But he is coming to be a man now, and he does not have many men to look towards for his model. Rean is a symbol of what Damian wants: it's no surprise that Damian is full of enthusiasm for everything he says at the moment."

"It wouldn't be such a problem if Damian had *any* other influence in his life," Kasiar said helplessly. "He doesn't listen to me any longer—that's not the Ixsaan way, of course—and who else is there but this Rean?"

"Alezian—"

"As if he's ever had the least influence on his brother. Or the other way around. One only cares for money, the other only for fighting."

She sighed again, thinking of her husband, the artist and philosopher who'd been also a skilled warrior, the ancestral tales she had told her sons, hoping they might emulate them, of princes equally skilled in courtesy, poetry, dalliance, and daring.

"Perhaps a time at sea will have woken him to the more athletic pursuits," Maude said.

But nothing, Kasiar thought dolefully, seemed able to wake Damian's mind to the world around him.

The three friends looked soberly at each other. Then Cadia said, "Something comes to mind."

Maude and Kasiar waited, knowing Cadia sometimes took a while to gather her thoughts together. After a few moments Cadia nodded. "Yes. That's it. Damian's been coming to the taproom with Rean this past month."

"Yes," said Kasiar, who didn't much relish the idea of Damian becoming a hardened drinker but much preferring the Inn to any of the various other taverns outside the city walls he might have been going to.

"He doesn't drink very much, your Damian. Only enough to be polite."

"Probably realized it'd affect his fencing," Kasiar muttered. "That's the only thing he'd be thinking of."

"Every time someone's tried to start a fight when Damian's been there he's stopped it. I always notice when they've gone on or nights they don't come. I was thinking that I might ask him if he wanted to work as a bouncer for me. Give him something to do, some responsibility, some money of his own. He'd meet more people, too."

"If it wouldn't be too much trouble for you ..."

"He'd hardly want to work for *me*," Maude the bookseller said, and made them all laugh.

Rean thought him working at the Inn was a great joke.

"You'll hate it, Damian," he said when Damian told him. "Never able to drink, to gamble, to come out playing with me ..."

"You know I don't like drinking or gambling," Damian pointed out. A month of outings had only underscored his initial distaste. But still ... it was the closest he'd ever been to belonging, and it was worth the tiresome evenings to be have that acknowledgement from the caravan guards, that willingness to practice on the part of Rean. Damian cast around for an argument that would sound better to his friend. "And even I did, I'd need money for it."

Rean continued to look downcast, long enough that Damian became apprehensive he was actually hurt. "Rean, you know we'll still have all the day to practice together. And I won't be working *every* evening. Eleven days a fortnight, Pelan Cadia said."

"I only wish you'd talked to me about it first," Rean said, reaching out and ruffling his hair.

Damian did not like this but did not know how to ask him to stop without sounding foolish. He moved away to shake out his sword hand. "Another bout before we go in?"

"No, I have something to tell you, too, though I suppose it doesn't matter so much now."

"Oh?"

"Yes, I'm taking a position on a caravan."

Damian was conscious of a hollow sensation in his stomach, as if something had just dropped. He turned his sword in the light, squinting along the edge to see if it needed to be polished.

A faint brownish smudge might have been from the dust—they were in the Umber Bottoms, practicing fighting on irregular ground—but it might also be incipient rust spots.

After a moment he managed to say, as if it didn't matter to him, "I thought you didn't want to go out on the caravans any longer?"

Rean had been talking about other ideas—nothing concrete, but hints of something different, something new, something exciting. Damian had not yet dared to ask if those ideas involved what the old stories would call adventure ... or if they might possibly involve him.

He did not want to join a caravan, be a hire-guard, hemmed in by other people's orders.

Rean's voice was fervent with some inner vision of splendour. "This caravan's going *west*. West, Damian!"

"Over the river?"

"Over the horizon."

Rean pointed grandly at the purple distance. Damian was conscious of a slight disappointment that Rean did not point true west, but somewhere off to the south; he should have known that the Redwine meandered along this stretch.

"West to the sunset—west to the Golden Empire—west to *magic*, Damian. Just *think* of what there might be that direction. Whole new worlds to explore ... You should come with me."

Magic was in his mother's stories, a beautiful and a perilous art. In Ixsaa no one talked of magic as anything other than a despicable, dangerous sort of vice.

Damian—no. He might want adventure, might want the kind of magic that was in his mother's stories, might want to see the Golden Empire (except was there not some ancient tale about why his mother's people had retreated to their mountain fastness, hidden away from the world ...?)—but—

He said, firmly, "I've already accepted Pelan Cadia's offer."

"What of it? Bouncers are two a penny. Just think—all the new people we'll meet—all the new fighters we'll meet—all the new styles! And the opportunity to prove yourself in real fights, not duels at dawn or breaking up stupid bruisers' arguments. Westward over the horizon, into the sunset, where magic is common as water. You could make a *real* name for yourself out there, you know."

"But I promised," Damian said.

"So?"

Damian expected a laugh and an apology to follow, but Rean was looking at him expectantly. "I'm not going to break a promise, Rean."

"She's only a woman. What does a promise matter, anyway, when it's your entire future at stake?"

Damian realized he was still holding his sword out, and to cover his confusion he wiped it with the edge of his shirt and sheathed it. He walked over to where they'd left their other things, and drank from the leather water-skin. It did not help him sort out his thoughts.

He re-stoppered the skin slowly. He could not think of any argument to put forth against Rean's laughing refusal to accept that a promise was a promise, no matter who it was made to. But—surely—surely a promise *was* a promise? If he'd made it to Rean, Rean would expect him to keep it. Why should it be any different to keep a promise made to Pelan Cadia?

An arm over his shoulders startled him. He jumped, and Rean laughed, squeezing him tight. "Oh, lambkin, have I shocked you? I got carried away with how wonderful it would be to have you at my side, under my command, *with me*, out there in the West. Things are different Over the River, you know."

Damian wormed out from under his arm. "So I hear," he replied coldly.

"It's your whole future," Rean said.

"I won't start my future with a broken promise."

"I shouldn't have put it that way. I didn't mean it. Look—the innkeeper knows you have ambitions—practically everyone in the city knows you want to be the best! I wouldn't be surprised if she *encouraged* you to go. Look, I'll help you find a replacement to cover the position. Yes, that's what we'll do. We can stop by the camp on our way back to the city."

Rean looked so happy to have come up with this solution that Damian wavered.

He could imagine how delightful it would be to work at Rean's side—even under his command, for of course Damian himself did not have any experience as a working fighter—and how wonderful indeed it would be to learn from all the new fighters he would meet along the way—

"I'm captain, of course, so all you need to do is sign the contract. You're of age, after all, and I already know you know one end of a sword from another."

He squeezed Damian's shoulder as he said that, the tone of his voice strange. Damian felt flustered and uncomfortable, and latched on to one thing he thought he knew.

"You mean, there's no need to talk to the caravan overseer? I thought they liked to know who they were hiring?"

"Oh, Norlos knows me, and knows anyone I recommend *personally* will do fine. The only time it's iffy is if it turns out an underage boy wants to join."

Damian registered a tinge of distaste. "Does that happen often?"

Rean laughed dismissively. "The glamour of life on the road, you know. But I know when *your* birthday was. Come on, Damian, what do you say? We'll go by the staging grounds and sign the contract, then go get you properly kitted up for adventure. Find someone to take your spot, if you really think you need to, though to be honest I find women respond better to a note."

"A *note*?"

"Didn't you go to the guild school? Never mind, I can write something for you. You can make your mark on the contract. I'll tell you the important parts."

Damian might not have been a keen scholar in any regard, but his mother was a lawyer and his brother a budding merchant prince. He had been raised on stories of the unscrupulous fleecing the gullible and unwary by way of contracts. He took a step back.

He might still have gone with him if Rean hadn't chosen that moment to wave off towards the south again and say, "Just think of the West, Damian, waiting for you."

Damian opened his mouth to correct his direction but was interrupted by the scream of a falcon. He looked up to where the gyrfalcon was slanting across the brilliant blue sky, feathers blazing white in the midday sun, motion smooth and powerful and glorious, image of everything Damian had ever wanted to be.

Rean said, "That's a fine bird. Wish I had my bow with me." Then he laughed, rich, rolling, uncaring. "Too far for a clean shot now, anyway. Waste of an arrow."

"You'd shoot a falcon like that?"

"Why not?"

Damian was once more flummoxed. He could not say that that particular wild falcon belonged to him; that was betraying a secret. He had no intention of saying that he found it beautiful, for after the weeks of cockfights and dog races he knew that Rean cared nothing for anything so weak and womanish as that.

He was not even sure why he himself thought it a bad thing to destroy beauty, or even simply wantonly to destroy, unless it was some teaching his mother had instilled in him through her stories and legends of the old country.

He knew Rean would laugh and dismiss any poor argument he might try to put forward. He wasn't Alezian, able to make arguments line up and be persuasive.

At last he shrugged, feeling it a betrayal of some nameless part of it him that that was all he did.

"No matter, I suppose," he said, even as his stomach seemed to curdle. The falcon hung in the sky, ablaze in the sunlight. He took a breath. "But I won't be going with you, Rean. Not this time."

"Not ever, if you refuse this opportunity," said Rean, and walked off.

PART TWO
SOMEONE LEAVES TOWN

CHAPTER FOUR

IN WHICH JULLANAR IS EXAMINED

Jullanar Thistlethwaite glanced around surreptitiously, worried one of the proctors would think she was cheating but too curious not to look.

The grand hall of the university was off-limits to anyone except students, faculty, and invited guests. The only time ordinary people ever saw its interior was on this occasion, the annual writing of the Entrance Examination.

The fifty or sixty other young men and women bent over their desks seemed oblivious to the atmosphere, the history, the *weight* of what they were doing.

Jullanar looked at them, their intent faces, their furious concentration or smug certainty or anxious fortitude, and felt blank.

The room smelled of dust and a faint acridity she thought was from the old-fashioned ink they were using for the exams.

She looked dubiously at her feather quill. It had not occurred to her that they were serious about doing this the way it had always been done, all the way back several hundred years before the Empire had ever come to Alinor.

Three hundred? Four? She should know. They must have studied it.

The hall had been built at some point in those hazy pre-Imperial days.

Jullanar was sure she'd been taught when the University of Fiella-by-the-Sea had been founded, but she couldn't think of it just this moment.

Once upon a time, way back in those days when the Charter of Universities was written, Fiellan had been an important duchy. The hall supposedly reflected that ancient status. Its high ceiling with the many carved beams crisscrossing its length was supposed to be a great architectural feature.

Jullanar wished it was not so dim and cold in here. That was probably traditional, too, not to use magic to heat the space, only the cavernous inefficient fire pits down the middle of the room.

A servant dressed in an old-fashioned smock and leggings tiptoed in with an apron full of peat logs. Jullanar watched as she laid logs on the coals and prodded them until the flames rose.

That was another way ordinary people got to see inside the walls of a university.

Her parents would not be impressed if she ended up a serving maid, after everything.

All around her was the unfamiliar scrape of quills scratching across parchment. Jullanar had read in a book that parchment was still used for official proclamations, because it was tougher than paper and harder to burn.

She admitted to herself that she didn't understand why the imperial wizards would not just enchant libraries against the threat of fire.

Perhaps there was another reason for it.

Quills were much messier than proper pens with metal nibs.

One of the proctors was pacing up and down the lines of students. Before she turned down Jullanar's row Jullanar turned hastily to her own parchment.

It was not as if she hadn't studied for the exams. She had. Madame Clancette had told them—everyone had told them—that this was one of the most important things they would ever do.

If you were not rich enough that such things didn't matter, placement on the Entrance Examinations determined everything about your future: whether you could go to university, and if so, what university you could go to.

And that in turn determined likely course of study, and what class of person you would meet (and, therefore, probably join), and who would become your friends, future allies, possible spouses.

Jullanar had to wonder if this had been the intention of the people who had first set these exams. Had they had any intimations that their work would in future centuries still be used to sort and categorize the young people of Alinor?

Everyone was supposed to take the Entrance Examination in the spring of their eighteenth year. Or at least everyone who didn't leave the kingschools at sixteen and go directly into apprenticeships or the army or ... farming. That sort of thing.

The top students were usually those from the best families, of course, who had gone to the best schools and had the best tutors.

But the chance was there—and every once in a while actually came true—that someone from another level of society altogether made one of the coveted top places.

Place in the top ten in your year and you could go to one of the Circle Schools, whose names were known and respected across the whole length and breadth of the Empire. People on other worlds knew the names of Tara, Stoneybridge, Morrowlea.

No one Jullanar knew had ever attained so high, but four years ago her eldest sister had come twelfth in Fiellan and thus been able to choose a school on the Golden List.

The proctor walked past her, turned back, and stood behind her shoulder. Jullanar flushed and focused on the questions before her. She knew these. She did. They were not so very difficult, not to start with.

She wrote, the quill scratching across the parchment and spattering black ink here and there. Her fingers were stained at the tips—both hands, from when she'd sloshed the ink a little trying to open the cap of the inkwell.

She wrote, imagining herself back in the days of old when outside the grand hall was not placid prosperous Fiella-by-the-Sea, seat of a minor duchy in a minor country of a large province of the vast Empire of Astandalas.

In those ancient days she would have been wearing—she didn't know. Maybe a smock and leggings like the servant. Not a student's or Scholar's long robes, that was for sure. And outside the square would not have been full of revellers drunk with the free celebrations of the Emperor Eritanyr's twenty-fifth Accession Day.

She was not the only one slightly distracted by the shouts and horn-blasts and various other noises filtering into the room. At one particularly loud blast she looked up to see that half the other students were also looking around, most of them frowning at the distraction.

"Eyes down!" the head proctor barked. "Ten minutes!"

Jullanar obeyed, quill moving faster as she tried to be complete if she could not be elegant. She was never very good at being elegant. Scholarship was her only hope, everyone from Madame Clancette to her sisters had told her.

The addendum that Jullanar was not, in point of fact, very studious went unspoken.

"Five minutes!"

Two questions left. Jullanar frowned at the second-last, a mathematical problem she remembered vaguely that she'd decided to study on another occasion (which occasion had not, she remembered rather more acutely, ever materialized), and skipped it for the very last. *Describe in your own words the role of the university in society.*

Was that even mentioned in the books? No matter, that wasn't a hard question. It was even a nice sop, there at the end of the examination, something easy.

Jullanar was in the middle of an exhortation of the role of the freedom of intellectual pursuit when an iron bell clanked, seemingly in her ear.

She jumped, knocking the desk with her knees and elbow. She caught the inkwell, but black ink dripped from her hands, down the slanting surface of her desk, onto the lap of what had been her second-best dress.

She stared at the streaks and blotches and spatters across her parchment.

She looked up helplessly to see that all the nearer students were staring at her in horror and pity. The head proctor hastened towards her, his face set into deep creases of disapproval.

For a moment the only sound was the ink dripping onto the floor, and then Jullanar started to laugh.

~

The day the examination results were posted was not officially a holiday, but anyone with children who had sat it was expected, even encouraged, to take the day to celebrate.

Jullanar's father was a physician, and the posting-day fell on one of his regular surgeries. He had apologized that morning that he did not want to chance harming his patients by not holding his hours as usual.

She was the fourth daughter. She knew he'd only taken the day off for Maudie, the eldest, the one who had come twelfth. It was pure coincidence that Nelly's and Lavinia's posting-days had landed on his free days, and Jullanar's hadn't.

She came late to the wall where the results were posted. The main body of eager and apprehensive young men and women had already dispersed, leaving those, like Jullanar, who were shy, to approach quietly, by themselves.

She hesitated at the corner of the town hall, looking across the square at the ducal palace with its four—no, three flags.

At the top, the Sun Banner of Astandalas, white and black and gold. Next down, the lavender, green, and white flag of the Imperial Province of Northwest Oriole. The unicorn was invisible at this distance as anything but a white smudge. Third, the striped green-and-orange banner of the kingdom of Rondé.

Jullanar wondered why they did not fly the flag of Fiellan itself. She turned the question over in her mind, thinking of what it might mean. In a novel it would probably mean that the duke was not in residence.

The palace was another building whose interior she would only see on a special occasion. She might make a friend at university of good enough family to sponsor a presentation to the duchess, if … if, well, such a friend with such a family were so inclined.

Jullanar did not easily make friends, not the way her sisters did. She did not know why it was so difficult, why she had no one to stand with her as she went up to the posting wall to see what fate had in store for her.

She could have asked one of her sisters, she supposed, but she was closest to Maudie, and Maudie had not come home from Vaunton for the long vacation, as she had been offered a summer position helping her tutor catalogue manuscripts or something before going on to her second degree.

It was not until the letter had come that Jullanar had realized how much she had been counting on Maudie's presence.

Maudie was the smart one in the family, the one who had done well enough on the exams to go to a school on the Golden List, the one who was going to become a Scholar. Jullanar had been expected to be left behind, but not so soon.

She hung back until she felt stupid and self-conscious and far too exposed for the coward she was. Everyone else would already know the results by now. It was possible someone would even have gone home before her with the news of how Jullanar had done.

They were not expecting much, her family, not after she had come home with her hands and dress coated in black ink. You could still see the marks on her hands from where the ink had yet to fade. She nibbled at the spot on her thumb.

Finally she could bear the dread no longer. It couldn't be as bad as she feared, surely. She wasn't *stupid*—she had *known* what the answers were, to everything except for that last mathematics question. And the ink hadn't covered *all* the parchment. Most of it had gone on her dress.

At the top were the names of the ten best scorers. She barely glanced up there, curious only to see whether Jullanar Hestin from Madame Clancette's had made it high enough to achieve her ambition of going to Oakhill.

Not quite, though coming eleventh would have been a triumph for anyone else.

There were five *Jullanars* in her year at Madame Clancette's, and what few like another dozen from other schools in the region. Jullanar's eye caught on each of them

11. Jullanar Hestin.

17. Jullanar Viergagne.

24. Jullanar Woodhill.

She moved over a step as someone else came up beside her, reading the second column intently.

28. Jullanar Eelbarrow.

41. Jullanar Brooks.

45. Jullanar Smith.

The person beside her grunted softly, with a faint hint of triumph, and turned away with quicker steps than on arriving.

Jullanar moved over another step, so she could read the third column.

79. Jullanar Foster.

And then, heart sinking, the fourth.

Surely she hadn't failed? No one from Madame Clancette's Finishing School for Girls had ever failed the Entrance Examinations.

No—there it was—her breath caught in her throat when she finally saw her name.

99. Jullanar Thistlethwaite.

She stood there, staring blindly, barely aware of the people coming and going behind her.

A familiar trill of laughter came in one ear and went out the other; even as she thought, slowly, *Clara*, her younger sister tripped up to her and took her by the elbow.

"There you are, Julie! Everyone's waiting to hear how you—oh." And after a moment, "Well, it's not the end of the world."

Jullanar turned to stare dumbly at her. Clara seemed to take this as an encouraging sign, for she laughed gaily and squeezed her arm. "Though you might have to go to university there!"

"It's not a complete disaster, surely," said Jullanar's middle sister Lavinia, who had just come home from her second year at Yrchester, comfortably in the middle of the Silver List. "Jullanar was hardly going to net a lord, anyway, even if she had made the top ten and landed a spot at one of the Circle schools."

"Top nine," Nelly said, putting a decisive stitch into her current pillowcase. "Morrowlea only takes one from all of Rondé."

"It'll have to be Firkin, I suppose," Clara said practically, but spoiled it by giggling. She was the youngest of the five sisters, and this meant that her results next year could hardly be worse.

"Oh, darling," her mother said, "she's below that."

In the end only four universities remained open to her choice.

Each of Alinor's universities held a scholarship for one student from each of the regions in the ancient Charter of Signatory States.

If one had the money for tuition, accommodation, books, and so on, one could, of course, apply anywhere, but for everyone else one's placement on the Results List governed one's choice of schools.

Jullanar's options were Nimmer, Lower Quillon, the Outer Reaches, and Galderon.

Nimmer, at the farthest southwestern Border between Empire and outworld, had only joined Astandalas the year before and consequently remained an occupied city.

The Outer Reaches was at the farthest northern edge of the map, known for barbarous magic and strange customs.

Lower Quillon had just resurfaced from a decade-long siege by rebels.

Galderon was so far away they had to consult the *Illustrated Atlas of the Peoples of the Empire* to determine if they spoke Shaian or some barbarian tongue like the Nimmerites.

"Galderon, hmm?" said Clara. "Is that even a real place? Do you think they have any amenities yet, or is it all tallow candles and, er, peat fires?"

"That's the Outer Reaches, silly."

Jullanar listened to her family argue over her future, attention wandering to the *Atlas* before her. She could not quite bring herself to task.

She knew she should be arguing for her own life, but she had nothing to put before her family besides vague and unarticulated dreams of she-knew-not-what.

She had no vocation, no major goals, no strong desires, unless they were the simple ones of wanting to see with her own eyes the feather and shell garments of the Wide Sea Islanders of Zunidh, the diaphanous silk veils and snakes of a high-ranking Voonran priestess, the golden splendour of Astandalas of the Emperors itself.

"—Julie gets seasick on the ferry, how could she possibly spend two months on a ship?"

"—Better a little *mal-de-mer* than a half-ruined city lined with cruci-fied rebels."

"Papa!"

"Those are the wages of rebellion, girls. The peace we enjoy comes with its cost."

"Don't be absurd, Ben," Jullanar's mother said firmly.

But Jullanar, half-listening as she flipped through the *Atlas*, wishing she had paid more attention in Geography, in History, in—well—noticed that her mother quietly dropped both Lower Quillon and Nimmer.

In the end Galderon won, because it was marginally cheaper for her to go overland with the stage-coach than it was to go to the Outer Reaches by sea.

A major consideration was that Dr. Thistlethwaite had been wanting to send his sister, Jullanar's Aunt Maude, a parcel, and had been fretting over making sure it got to the outgoing caravan safely; and the stage-coach company was willing to cut a deal to have Jullanar along to see to the parcel.

Aunt Maude lived even farther away than Galderon—quite outside the bounds of the Empire, in fact—but because she had come first in her year's Entrance Examinations and had consequently gone to Morrowlea, she was considered an eccentric genius and an object of familial pride for going off on sociological expeditions into the barbarian outworlds.

The staging post for the caravan of merchants licensed to leave the Empire on that Border was just outside of Galderon. The merchants left some month before the autumn term would begin, so Jullanar set forth on her journey in the summer doldrums when no other students were travelling.

In a letter whose cheerful tone did not quite hide how disappointed she was in Jullanar's lack of scholarly acumen, Maudie gave Jullanar instructions for how to be at least marginally successful in her classes and with her tutor.

Be prepared was obvious; but what did *Work to your tutor's preferences* mean?

Lavinia and Nell gave her strict and copious instructions regarding the criteria and potential techniques she should use for finding a suitable husband at Galderon.

Jullanar quailed at the suggestions for how she should dress and comport herself, which she had been failing to perfect ever since Lavinia first started noticing the male sex and accordingly discovered just how embarrassing her next-younger sister was, and felt a gnawing dread at the not-exactly-jesting comment that if she married lower than 'the best in trade' they would never speak to her again.

Clara told her that if she couldn't land a husband or become a Scholar she should at least try to have an adventure, but since she tittered incessantly while saying this, Jullanar gave little heed to the otherwise-encouraging advice.

She was also given strict and copious instructions for conveying the parcel safely to the staging post, with only belated notice given the logistics of travelling so far on her own.

Listening to first her mother and then her father and then her mother again tell her in excruciating detail exactly how valuable the parcel was and how important it was that she not lose, drop, manhandle, or otherwise damage it, Jullanar received the strong impression that the box was rather more precious in their eyes than she was herself.

Only her father added advice on any other subject than how Jullanar —blessed as she was with a plump physique, mousy hair, and little personal charm—might go about landing a husband (for she was certainly never going to make it in a profession, let alone as a Scholar, if she failed so abysmally in the Entrance Examinations). He came up to her as she sat on her trunk awaiting the gig to be brought round from the stables.

"Come now, my girl," he said, as she tried to smile eagerly.

"Yes, Papa."

She wondered despite herself where the dye for the remarkably vivid green paper cover the book he was holding had come from.

"It will be very hard at first, no doubt, to be so far from home, but one day you'll turn around and discover that the year has flown by. You'll meet people, learn new things, and—and the Lady will help you find a road to walk on. Not everyone knows from childhood, Julie."

"Thank you, Papa."

He worked his moustache a moment, then spoke a bit more softly. "You'll find friends of your heart, my dear, one day."

If there was one dream Jullanar had articulated to herself, it was that. She swallowed hard. "Thank you, Papa."

He cleared his throat. "Don't cry yourself into a headache. Drink lots of water, eat sparingly of new foods at first, and make sure you get out to stretch your legs at every halt. Don't lose your aunt's parcel—"

"And here's the gig," Jullanar said, giggling at the familiar lecture, which, minus the part about her aunt's parcel, had formed the late-summer refrain for four years now as her sisters went off to their own, much nearer and more prestigious schools.

Her father kissed her, handed her into the gig and her trunks after her, kissed her again, then pressed the green book into her hands.

"Good-bye, Jullanar. Stay safe, my girl. Write to tell us when you arrive. May your year be full of new knowledge and new friends—and a few small adventures. But not big ones, mind you! Nothing dangerous."

"Of course not, Papa."

The coachman shook the reins, the horse started to trot, and Jullanar waved once to her sisters and her mother in the upstairs window, and turned her attention firmly to the present, and not the uncertain and distant future.

CHAPTER FIVE

IN WHICH JULLANAR COMES TO THE GATES OF THE CITY OF KNOWLEDGE

The bright green book was Maude Thistlethwaite's *Ethnography of the Painted City: an Account of the Culture, Language, Religion, History, and Architecture of a Barbarian Conurbation (Volume I)*, and it occupied Jullanar for the whole first week of her journey.

She occasionally looked out the stagecoach window as the undulating patchwork fields and orchards of North Fiellan became the flat marshes of northern Ronderell.

The marshes in turn gave way to the steep pastures of the Ronderell uplands, home to sheep, snaking stone walls that climbed at improbable angles up the faces of the mountains, and wide mats of purple heather and yellow gorse and dull-green bracken.

Through the mountain pass, and down into the uplands of Lind, where the sheep were black-faced but which otherwise looked exactly like Ronderell, but which was another country altogether.

Lind was still part of the Empire, so the border was the merest formality. The unfamiliar flag of Lind faced the familiar flag of Rondé under the great banners of Astandalas; bored and fat soldiers in regional dress waved the coach through without bothering to look at papers.

There was only Zauber of the Circle Schools in the kingdom of

Rondé, though in the far-off pre-Imperial days of the Charter of Signatory States the three duchies (and one earldom) of Rondé had warranted their own seats in the Entrance Examinations.

Jullanar did not like to think what her place would have been had she been competing against all those her age in Ronderell, Erlingale, and the Farry March as well as Fiellan.

Lind was home to Quance, first on the Golden List; to Orlem, which was second; and to Oakhill, which was the seventh of the Circle Schools.

Jullanar resolutely read about the rich mineral deposits around the Painted City, which coloured earth and water and gave the city its name.

She read about the great river Oonar, whose many mouths were a mystery even to the city set just above it.

She passed the sign to Orio City, capital of the Imperial Province of Northwest Oriole and home of Tara, oldest and foremost of the Circle Schools, and she sighed and tried to memorize the short glossary of words in the Painted City's language her aunt had seen fit to include.

On the other side of Orio Bay she gave up on the Painted City's flora and fauna, exotic as it was, and pulled out her favourite prose romance.

The deeds of disguised prince Tzu-Tzên saw her through the endless peach and almond orchards of south Tarvenol, past Zilberburgh, Vaunton, West Lorin, all on the Golden List, all proudly flying their own flags under the Sun Banner of Astandalas, all visible from the Great Eastern Highway.

South of Tarvenol the land grew drier, grey-brown and scrubby in the late summer heat. Dusty vines marched along the hillsides, and there were goats grazing where there had been cows.

There were more passengers along the edge of the Lesser Arcady, but Jullanar, who had rebelled against her father's advice and tried a piece of what turned out to be incorrectly prepared octopus, was far too miserable to do more than stare at the low grey hills they were approaching. The cheerful conversation of her fellow travellers was, she told herself, something she would feel when she got closer to Galderon.

They passed a dozen schools of varying note and name in the scattered wealthy communities along the coast of the Lesser Arcady, whose southeastern border they were skirting, and one by one the other students departed for their new lives.

At last she came to the twin ports of East and West Noon facing each other across the Surge.

For two centuries the Surge had marked the eastern Border of the Empire on Alinor. West Noon, on the Northwest Oriolese side, was heavily fortified, with thick stone walls, many towers, and the long low barracks of a permanent army encampment.

East Noon had fallen a hundred years before Jullanar first saw it across the Surge, but she could see the differences in architecture. West Noon's graceful columns and recurved roofs were faced by square constructions and few windows, all painted an uncompromising flat white that hurt her eyes.

The last conductor of the Northwest Oriolese stage handed her out of her coach, handed out her trunk and the precious parcel, and nodded at the flat barge some twenty yards away.

"There you are, miss," he said. "Be mindful of them foreigners, now."

"Thank you," replied Jullanar absently. Her heart was racing a little with the excitement of leaving province and continent behind, and because the ferryman was wearing the yellow cummerbund and red comma-shaped hat that the *Atlas of Imperial Peoples* claimed was the traditional garb of East Oriole.

East Noon was very quaint and picturesque—which was to say, small —and after a small lunch of flatbreads stuffed with salty cheese and spinach Jullanar was ready for the Eastern Oriolese stagecoach and the last three days of her journey.

After she had settled herself in her seat, along with two other passengers who seemed entirely disinclined to conversation, being a courting couple much engrossed in their own affairs, she discovered that the other side of East Noon consisted of a flat plain subdivided by a rigidly symmetrical arrangement of irrigation canals.

These formed neatly square ponds filled with geometrically arranged clumps of grass. The only thing to spoil the symmetry were some white-and-black ducks scattered across the water.

Jullanar asked, and received the answer from the astonished courting couple, that these were rice paddies owned by the Imperial Duke of Zborowanda.

Abashed at their astonishment, quailing at the endless squares and the one straight line of the road causeway, Jullanar delved into her valise and found there the little packet of information she had been sent by Galderon after she had written to accept her place.

She was intrigued to discover that Galderon had made a small but notable contribution to the history of political philosophy, in the form of the 'Plumbing' Theory of Social Change. It was to her disappointment that the booklet did not explain what exactly this entailed, and made her contemplate taking a course in Political Philosophy solely to find out.

The university was otherwise dedicated to Hydrology, Aquaculture, and related topics, including water magic and plumbing design.

Jullanar read through the booklet twice, looked out on the continuing symmetrical paddies, and was not altogether comforted by the reflection that the rice fields of East Oriole fed one-fifth of the Imperial Armies.

It was the first week of August when Jullanar finally arrived at Galderon.

Or rather, at the covered bench that appeared to be the coach-stop for the university. Jullanar stood there, her valise and the Precious Box for Aunt Maude at her feet, still clutching her latest novel, and thought that perhaps she should have enquired a little more closely as to why the coachman seemed to find her attendance at the university so hilarious.

For a wild moment she wondered if the whole thing—the very idea of a university here—was a joke.

She turned around in a slow pirouette.

The flat fields stretched out in their geometry all on this side of the road.

On the other side of the road, directly opposite the covered bench, was a turnstile gate. A wooden sign on the gatepost pointed away to 'Galderon Village: 1 mile', and sure enough, a mile or so away along a double-hedged lane was a cluster of trees and buildings.

The second sign on the post pointed to a gravel path that meandered through gardens and artful tangles of bushes and trees. This said 'University Entrance Lodge'. But between sign and distant village there were no buildings at all.

Jullanar looked back at the covered bench. Yes, it said GALDERON on the wooden signboard, in clear black lettering.

Someone might be pranking her, but the coachman seemed to be of good faith, if indubitably in on the joke.

Jullanar was not in on the joke.

She stood there a while, taking in the heavy humid air, the distant mews of wheeling gulls, the definite lack of wind. There was a strange smell hanging in the air, not exactly unpleasant but odd, like too much sage or rue. It made the back of her nose prickle.

When she stopped sneezing she decided this was the beginning of her new life, her new *self*, and the new and improved Jullanar was not timid or distracted or *wet*.

She could not do much about her appearance—various acquaintances and sisters at Madame Clancette's had, to their credit, tried—but if she could not be as popular as Lavinia, or as smart as Maudie, or as accomplished as Nell, or as pretty as Clara, well, at least—Jullanar had decided this at some point in the past day of endless geometric fields—at least she could be a woman of *character*.

She put her book away in the pocket of her dress, picked up her valise and the Precious Box, and set off across the road to the turnstile with a set chin and determined shoulders.

She did not look either way as she crossed, and was therefore severely startled when a cyclist careened out of nowhere and crashed into her.

"Oof," said Jullanar with feeling. She'd landed flat on her rear with a solid thump and a cloud of white dust.

The valise had gone flying but she'd managed to cushion the Precious Box with her own body. At the moment she rather begrudged it. *It* was hardly going to bruise as she suspected she would.

"Oh, I am so sorry—so very sorry!"

Jullanar looked up from considering the palm of her right hand, which was skinned, and what she thought was a tear in her skirt half-disguised by a smear of grease from the bicycle. They were very uncommon in North Fiellan, and only the most daring young men rode them.

This cyclist was a pretty girl of about her own age, all heart-shaped face and cornflower blue eyes and curling hair the colour of honey done up in an artless jumble Jullanar would not have been able to imitate with a book and several days' notice.

She wore a split-skirt riding habit in a light green muslin printed with tiny white flowers, and was just now picking up a straw bonnet in a style entirely unfamiliar to Jullanar but obviously the height of fashion *somewhere*.

For a wild moment Jullanar could only think that perhaps *she* could get a bicycle herself, and be, for once, just that little bit daring.

"Are you hurt?" the girl went on, disentangling herself from her bicycle and hurrying over to help Jullanar up. "I wasn't looking where I was going at all! I wasn't expecting anyone to be *here*, you see!"

Jullanar struggled back to her feet, cursing her body's unwieldiness and the Precious Box's weight. She set the Precious Box down on the ground, after a wary glance to make sure no one else was coming post-haste around the corner—and that made her frown at the bicyclist.

"What do you mean? This is the main coach stop for Galderon, isn't it? Surely the coach comes by at a regular time?"

The girl giggled. "Of course, but hardly anyone's coming now, are they?"

"Why not?"

That caused the eruption of yet more giggles. "Well, the university is closed, of course. No one's expecting anyone this year, and most everyone else will be going to Lingron over the other side of the canal. That's where most of the Army are bivouacked—I say, are you all right? Did you get off at the wrong stop? The coachman along this route's known for not correcting people if they do!"

Jullanar was not paying much attention to *that*. Not when—dear Lady, had she heard this correctly? She couldn't—it couldn't possibly be true!

She licked her lips and winced at her own nervousness, then coughed as the dust settled around them and in the face of the girl's apparent concern she could only say, weakly, "What do you mean, the university is closed?"

"Yes," the girl said blithely, gesturing at the empty field. "They turned themselves invisible, the sillies, you see." She giggled. "Or don't see, actually! But until they figure out how to turn themselves back, they'll be closed."

Jullanar stared at her apparently guileless, even earnest, face, and then back at the field on the other side of the stile. The girl did not look mischievous or malicious. Jullanar was all too familiar with the many ways the pretty and the popular—and everything about this girl suggested she was both—asserted their superiority over the merely ordinary. It was nevertheless galling to be dismissed so easily.

Unless—perhaps the girl was being honest?

Jullanar considered the strange disposition of shrubberies, the way the gravel and stone-flagged paths seemed to stop at random points, the rectangular or circular plots of grass with no visible reason for their orientation, and had to conclude that the whole place *did* look very much like a university might if all the buildings weren't there.

The sign pointing to the 'Porter's Lodge' decided her. Unless the whole community were in on the joke, which was surely absurd (a thought that would recur to Jullanar on later experience as a sign of her present innocence), it did look very much as if the University of Galderon was invisible.

She set down the Precious Box, weak-kneed with shock. "But what am I to do?" she said aloud. "Is it truly closed?"

The girl nodded sympathetically, leaning back against her bicycle. "I'm afraid so. I was supposed to start this year, too. They're saying in town that they'll have to ask the Lady of Alinor to come sort them out, and *she's* at Court, naturally."

Jullanar dismissed questions of the Lady of Alinor or the Court of Astandalas, presumably what the girl meant. She shook her head again, trying to come up with something rational. "What are you going to do, then?"

"My parents had planned to go travelling for the year, so the house is let, to a lovely family from Tukcheng. He's a captain in the Army, so it's not as if the university being closed will affect that. They'll still have to be here, for the Border rotation." She sighed gustily. "Here we are, with an entire regiment billeted across the parish, and nothing for it but my parents must pack me up and send me to my grandmother's in Dorne!"

Confused by these unfamiliar place-names, Jullanar tried to latch on something certain, but all she could think was that this was *exactly* her luck.

"Have you a long way home?" the girl asked suddenly. "You're very early, even if the university were open this term."

"Two weeks' journey," she replied glumly.

Even if she could not imagine what to do in the immediate predicament, she could well imagine her reception once home.

She would be sent to Great-Aunt Claudia, no doubt.

It was unlikely her father would permit her to go to Galderon the next year; not when the first year was always the most expensive, and with Lavinia due to be married next autumn and Clara also to start.

"So far!" The girl breathed. "You must be from Northwest Oriole, then, are you? Or from—ooh, are you from one of the other parts of the Empire? Are you very keen on waterworks? You must be, to have come so far to study here. Oh—where *are* my manners? First I knock you down, then I don't introduce myself! I'm Marianne, Marianne Faraday."

"Pleasure," Jullanar replied automatically, performing the polite curtsy Madame Clancette had drilled into her. "Jullanar Thistlethwaite, of Fiella-by-the-Sea. That's in Rondé."

"Not Ysthar, then," Marianne said, sounding disappointed, but then brightening. "How very remarkable a name!"

"You may call me Jullanar," said she hastily, knowing how poorly 'Thistlethwaite' fared on most tongues, even those from Fiellan.

Marianne Faraday's accent was not so strong as she'd been expecting—and indeed, her colouring and features was much more like what Jullanar knew from home than she'd seen out the window looking on the locals, who seemed to run to tan skin and shiny straight black hair—but still, it never hurt to avoid that embarrassment.

"And you must call me Marianne! Shall we be friends, Jullanar? I feel certain you are a kindred spirit, and it was certainly fate that we met like this."

Jullanar had never had someone express an immediate desire for her friendship before. All her previous experience called of her to be doubtful of this offer.

It had happened before, at the kingschool and at Madame Clancette's, that someone had responded to her overtures of friendship only for it to wither and die when it became clear Jullanar was the butt of the jokes and the lowest in the pecking order.

Why this was the case Jullanar had never quite been able to figure out.

She was, she suspected, neither pretty enough nor charming enough nor smart enough nor well enough accomplished.

She was the fourth of five daughters, the one expected by everyone to be her parents' stalwart support in their old age, and, in the meantime, the best chaperone anyone could want for their daughters.

But this was a new place, where no one knew her, and there was no Jullanar Forester to start the gossip nor Lavinia and Clara to ensure she heard it. Instead there was pretty, amiable, friendly Marianne Faraday, who bore every visible sign of one comfortable in her skin and her place.

"Thank you. I'd like that very much," Jullanar replied shyly. "I don't know anyone else here."

"You're so brave!"

"Not really, I don't think."

"You've travelled weeks to get here, all by yourself! You must have had so many adventures along the way!"

Jullanar tried to think of one, and failed dismally. Fortunately her new friend was much more at ease in carrying on a conversation.

"I don't know so many people here either," she confessed. "We moved here from Dorne a year ago—my father was replacing the local sheriff while he recuperated from an illness, as a favour to the Governor, who's a family friend—and I've been home being tutored for the Exam. My brother is in the Army, we're expecting him home any day now."

"Is that where you were going?" Jullanar asked, indicating the bicycle.

"The mustering grounds are over on the other side of the village. I was looking for ribbon, but the stores are closed today. Some sort of local holiday. I was on my way home now—I say! You must come with me. Unless you have lodgings already arranged?"

"I was hoping the Porter might have a suggestion."

Marianne giggled again. "Nothing doing, unless you want to be turned invisible as well! No, come with me. It's the least I can do, after knocking you over like that. Here, let me help you with that box. I think it'll fit well enough in my basket."

She put action to words before Jullanar could do more than stammer her thanks.

"It's about a mile, I hope that's all right? If you've been on the stage for weeks I imagine you want to stretch your legs. ... Is that valise very heavy?"

"No, it's not bad."

"Well, let me know if you need a rest. I'm sure you must have some books in there."

Jullanar smiled. "A couple."

"And what are they? Please say they're not all weighty tomes on hydraulics and water management. I only read romances for pleasure. It is the despair of my mother, but not all of us are in love with natural history, are we? 'Twould be a dull world if we were."

"Definitely," Jullanar replied, once again not stating outright that she was not at all interested in waterworks, and instead asked after Marianne's favourites.

This topic made her forget the weight of her valise, her ignominious arrival, and the increased uncertainty of the year ahead.

With a friend, a true friend, she thought, surely she could do anything.

CHAPTER SIX

IN WHICH JULLANAR DOES NOT CORRECT OTHER PEOPLE'S ASSUMPTIONS

Mrs. Faraday was as trim and pretty as her daughter, and just as pleasant.

She didn't bat an eyelash when Marianne announced she'd brought home a guest to stay. She merely clucked in sympathy when she discovered that Jullanar had come all the way from Northwest Oriole only to find Galderon closed.

"Oh, you poor dear!" she cried, looking (to Jullanar's private surprise) genuinely distressed. "After you've been travelling for so long—and by yourself? Oh, my poor, brave darling! Marianne, ring for Betta. We *must* get you a bath and a change of clothes and a proper meal."

In short order Jullanar found herself in a pretty bedroom, all white furniture and light pink upholstery, while a maid drew a great enamelled bath for her and then shyly asked after clothing. Jullanar had kept one gown ready for her arrival in Galderon, and gladly handed over her travel-stained garments to be cleaned.

The bath was utterly divine. She stretched out and, daringly, washed her hair. When she emerged she found Betta had set out soft cotton towels and had even brushed out the creases from her dress.

Dressed, she put her hair up in a coiled braid. It was the only even remotely fancy hairstyle she could do herself; the Thistlethwaites had one lady's maid, who attended to her mother, but with four sisters there was never a lack of assistance for such pleasant activities.

It was one of Jullanar's great secrets that despite everything, she truly enjoyed fussing with her hair. Her hair did not cooperate in return, but still she brushed it smooth and used a pale green ribbon that matched her dress to tie it into a coronet.

That done, and the Precious Box safely set into a corner where it wouldn't fall nor be struck by opening doors or unwary feet, she went hesitantly downstairs to find her hosts, who surprised her immensely.

She had never felt herself so welcome, so unhesitatingly accepted, in her life. Both Marianne and her mother were the sort of people she would have expected to be disdainful of her essential ordinariness.

But instead the opposite was true: Marianne acted as if Jullanar—Jullanar!—were the friend of her heart she'd always longed for, and Mrs. Faraday even said that she'd always wanted a second daughter.

Marianne agreed. It was breakfast on the second day, and the household was eagerly anticipating the arrival of the brother in the Army. He was not due home for another fortnight at the earliest, but that didn't stop his female relations for talking over his coming visit.

"But a sister," said Marianne wistfully. "Oh, how lucky you are to have four! You must miss them terribly."

Jullanar did not quite know what to say to this. Certainly she missed Maudie, and had since her eldest sister had gone off to Vaunton. But Lavinia and Nell and Clara?

"I was sorry Maudie hadn't come home before I left," she temporized. "I had to leave so early, you see, and she had a summer internship assisting her professor ..."

"How wondrously accomplished you all must be," Mrs. Faraday said in approval. "And you so brave, darling, to come all this way to study your heart's desire!"

Once again Jullanar didn't want to disappoint them by saying she hadn't exactly *chosen* hydrology as her life's ambition.

They seemed so very pleased with the idea that she was studying what was apparently usually a very *masculine* sort of subject, as if she were a great champion of women's rights.

And ... it wasn't *necessarily* a lie, was it? It wasn't as if she *couldn't* decide to study hydrology, next year.

"It's a pity I missed their letter," Jullanar said, "though I am glad to have met you, Marianne, and Mrs. Faraday."

"Why are you so early?" Marianne asked, passing her the teapot. "More tea, Jullanar? Papa's brother in Astandalas sends it to us specially."

It was excellent tea: rich, subtly smoky, with a hint of something almost floral. "Thank you."

She accepted the scones Mrs. Faraday passed her as well, and the pots of the new year's strawberry jam and butter.

All of this was food very much like at home, not anything like what she'd tried at the rest stops, but she couldn't complain about its quality or flavour.

And she was, she admitted, so *pleased* to be in a house, and welcome to boot, with a new friend, that was half-familiar, after all the uncertainties and anguishes of travelling across the continent to Lady-knew-what.

"I came early on account of Galderon being so close to the mustering grounds for the trade caravans heading across the Border," she explained. "My aunt is a sociologist—she went to Morrowlea—and is studying the customs of a city in the Outlands. My father gave me a box to see safely there."

"To the Outlands?" Marianne asked, eyes wide with amazement. "You are so very brave!"

Mrs. Faraday was frowning in calculation. "I suppose you *might* have been able to get there and back again before classes started, though it would have been a bit tight. How very intrepid of you indeed!"

Jullanar blushed, but she had just taken a bite of her scone and she couldn't swallow quickly enough to protest that she had only been tasked with seeing the Precious Box to the merchant caravan, not all the way to the Painted City itself. By the time she had managed to clear her throat, Marianne and her mother were discussing the best way for her to get there.

"Does she need a passport?" Marianne wondered. "Do they even have guards on the Border?"

"I'm sure you know what your brother's company does, my dear!"

Marianne blushed, far more becomingly than Jullanar knew she ever did. "Oh, of course, Mother, I wasn't thinking! My brother—Captain Faraday—"

Her pride was clear in her voice; her mother smiled indulgently, obviously equally proud of her son's accomplishments.

"My brother's company has spent five years on this Border, mostly on the other side. It's perfectly safe, don't worry," she added hastily. "We don't have any problems with the barbarians."

"Which side is your aunt, darling?" Mrs. Faraday asked. "On the other side of the mountains, or on the other side of the river?"

Jullanar hesitated. "I ... I don't know what you mean, ma'am? She's in the Painted City, which is not on Alinor at all. I think it's called Daun ..."

"Oh," breathed Marianne. "The *true* Outlands."

"Those who have to do with the Border call that *Across the River*," Mrs. Faraday explained.

"That's what my brother Reynard always says! Oh, Jullanar, you must meet him! He will be able to give you all the advice you need, even if he isn't going back on duty immediately. He has some months of leave, does he not, Mother?"

"Indeed, I hope he will be able to escort you to Dorne, Marianne," Mrs. Faraday said. "Well, girls, this is splendid news."

"What do you mean, Mrs. Faraday?" Jullanar asked timidly.

"Why, you shall be able to spend a goodly amount of time with your aunt, whom you must love dearly to go all that way for. It's a pity it's difficult to pass letters *Across the River*, but with Reynard on that side I'm sure he will be happy to deliver missives between the two of you over the course of the year before you can return to Galderon. I believe the passage between the worlds can only be attempted certain times of the year, but Reynard will keep you apprised if the situation with the university changes and I'm sure he will be most able to escort you back."

Jullanar was briefly taken with the dispiriting notion that *of course* no one would worry about their son escorting her places, and once more missed her opportunity to clarify matters.

〜

Marianne was not, perhaps, the smartest girl Jullanar had ever met, but apart from her physical attributes she was blessed with a sunny disposition and great friendliness.

Quite how she did not have half a dozen bosom companions flocking around her at all times Jullanar did not understand at all. It wasn't until that afternoon, when Mrs. Faraday suggested they take the gig to 'town', that she began to have an inkling of why.

It started with calling for the 'boy' to ready the gig. The person who answered the summons was fifty if he were a day, and Jullanar frankly thought that at first that he had come instead of whomever they had intended.

But Mrs. Faraday gave him instructions in a distant, cool voice. He kept his eyes down and his shoulders slumped, his face slack, but there was nothing hesitating about his movements.

"It's so hard to get good staff out here," Mrs. Faraday said, sighing, as he sloped off. She and Jullanar were standing on the front verandah of their house, waiting for Marianne to come down after changing her garments for the trip.

"Oh?" Jullanar replied curiously. "None of the locals like the work?"

"They *like* it well enough, I suppose," Mrs. Faraday admitted. "It's just that they're not very well *trained*. They're so insolent and *proud*. It's as if they don't understand what a benefit it is to everyone that we are here to govern them."

Jullanar considered this. Surely the amiable Mrs. Faraday could not mean what that sounded like, could she? She ventured, "What do you mean, ma'am?"

"You're so polite, child. You know that Galderon has been part of the Empire for fifty years, of course—certainly long enough to be properly integrated, if you ask me, though it *is* so close to the Border that I suppose it's not entirely strange that untoward ideas come through. The people here still consider them kin, you know, the folk Outside."

The capital letter was quite clear. "But Galderon has been a university for centuries, has it not?" Jullanar was quite certain that that had been in the information package.

Mrs. Faraday made a dismissive gesture with her white-gloved hand, peering under the broad brim of her bonnet to see if either the gig or her daughter had arrived.

"It's been a centre of learning of one sort of another, I suppose. It used to be a temple complex, I believe, in the old days, though I'm sure I don't understand the religion here. It's only been a university proper for a century—I understand that the administration was a strong proponent of the coming of the Empire, which just goes to show how sensible they are. It draws on the elite from across East Oriole. Dorne really doesn't have the same reputation, I'm afraid."

Which explained why it was permissible for Marianne to go to Galderon. Jullanar wasn't quite sure how a semi-monastic centre of learning fit into what she knew of the Charter of States who adhered to the results of the Entrance Examination, but it wasn't something anyone was particularly interested in.

The List was the List, and Galderon was ninety-seventh on it, after the Outer Reaches and before Nimmer, and therefore it was Acceptable.

But Jullanar could not help but be a bit disquieted with the utter dismissal the Faradays made of 'the locals'.

They arrived at 'town'—not Galderon, which was a mere village, but neighbouring Lingron, where the army was bivouacked—after perhaps an hour on the gig. It was on the far side of the University of Galderon from the Faradays' home, and in the usual run of things apparently took only half an hour or so to reach.

"But because of the situation with the university," Mrs. Faraday said disapprovingly, "we are obliged to go *quite* out of our way."

Jullanar thought the drive was lovely. They trundled along a well-made road between a hedgerow and a sluggishly flowing canal. Great fish were visible in the shadows, not silver or dark grey as she would have expected but dramatic orange and white and black and calico.

There were more of the black and white ducks, and great patches of a plant like an erect water lily. Both the leaves and the flowers stood high above the water, and the developing seed-pods were like strange pepper-pots. The flowers themselves were a subtle range of pinks and whites.

"What are those flowers?" she asked Marianne.

"Lotus," Mrs. Faraday replied.

"They're a sacred flower here," Marianne put in. "They represent purity and rebirth."

"The roots are edible," Mrs. Faraday added, as if that made the flowers respectable.

Jullanar looked at the patches of circular leaves, all tumbled about on the surface of the canal like Marianne's artful curls, and the exquisitely shaped blossoms, and wondered how anyone could ever have borne to dig them up to try.

Lingron was a town of perhaps three hundred houses. It was located on the edge of a lake that Jullanar had not noticed on the maps.

There were a few quays with small fishing boats tied up to them, but most of the waterfront seemed oddly desolate despite the fine old buildings lining it. Mrs. Faraday drove the gig at a sharper pace along the road, seemingly determined to get away from the water as quickly as possible.

Jullanar frowned at the lake. She couldn't see the far side because of a strange silvery shimmer, not quite a mist, that hung over the water and extended to the left and right as far as she could see.

"What's that shimmer?" she asked Marianne quietly.

Marianne gave her a blank look. "What shimmer?"

"Out there, over the lake."

Marianne shrank back, casting an anxious look at her mother's back. Mrs. Faraday's shoulders stiffened, but she didn't say anything. Her daughter leaned to whisper in Jullanar's ear, who leaned back, curiosity roused.

"That's the edge of the Empire," Marianne breathed.

Jullanar gave it a further perturbed glance and then set her eyes resolutely forward.

That was the edge of the Empire? That blank shimmer hiding whatever lay beyond?

She desperately wanted to ask questions—what caused the shimmer? What lay on the other side of the lake, on the other side of the Border?

Why was it so obviously a taboo subject?—but it *was* obviously a taboo subject, and so she held her tongue and asked Marianne instead where they were headed.

To a friend of Mrs. Faraday's, apparently, the wife of a colonel, to ask when Captain Faraday might be expected home.

From Marianne's bright eye and flushing cheek, there was also a chance they might see some of the other young and dashing officers of the army. And indeed, when they arrived at the officer's residence they found one of "Reynard's good friends" visiting with the wife of his colonel.

He stood up to greet them, and with a warning smile to Jullanar (who knew immediately she was being assigned the role of chaperone), Mrs. Faraday introduced her to the colonel's wife, Mrs. Bethwell, and the young captain.

Tom Gidiron was perhaps thirty, regular of feature and utterly dashing in his uniform. He wore tall gleaming boots and really quite resplendent pale-fawn leggings, both of which showed off his shapely calves, and a rich bottle-green tunic with a scarlet-and-silver sash to show his rank and company. His curly black hair was not regulation length, being down past his collar, and a certain pallor to his jawline suggested he'd recently shaved a beard.

Marianne and Mrs. Faraday exclaimed over his hair. Jullanar waited awkwardly off to the side. It took her a few moments to realize that Captain Gidiron had dyed his hair; Marianne was mourning his guinea-gold locks.

Did people actually use words like that aloud?

Marianne Faraday did, it seemed. Captain Gidiron laughed.

"The beard grows fast enough not to worry," he said, rubbing his jaw, "but I *do* need to keep the hair for when I go back Across the River. Don't fret, Miss Faraday! When I'm done my mission I'll shave it off and it'll all grow back as it was, never you fear."

"But why do you need to dye it, Captain Gidiron?" Marianne asked.

"It's all in the interests of blending in with the natives when I go," he said carelessly. "Wouldn't want them to think me *too* foreign! And I refused to go ginger."

Jullanar wondered what on earth was wrong with ginger hair. Her own was definitely on the mousy-brown side, but she had always liked the auburn sheen certain lights gave her hair.

"Now, what's all your news?" he said, sitting down and then jumping up hastily when he saw Jullanar. "Oh, you brought a guest! My apologies, miss!"

"Oh, Captain Gidiron, this is Miss Jullanar Thistle—"

"Thistlethwaite," Jullanar said hurriedly, curtsying.

Captain Gidiron bowed politely. "How do you do."

They all sat down, Jullanar on an uncomfortable chair by the window and Marianne on the sofa next to the captain. Mrs. Faraday and Mrs. Bethwell gave her another speaking glance and withdrew to the far side of the room, where they spoke quietly together.

"Jullanar will be attending Galderon with me," Marianne said. "She came early this year as she has a mission to deliver a package Across the River, and missed the university's letter saying they're closed."

Captain Gidiron gave Jullanar a rather close examination when he heard of her 'mission', but he turned with an enquiring air to Marianne. "What do you mean, closed?"

Marianne explained about Galderon's folly and then expounded on Jullanar's bravery in coming so far to study her heart's desire, and wasn't it grand how she was going to cross the Border on her *mission*.

"Indeed, you must be quite remarkable," Captain Gidiron said, with the kind of smug flirtatiousness that Jullanar knew was entirely in practice, and not at all in earnest.

She smiled demurely at him, ignoring the compliment, and asked him to tell her more about his life as a soldier of the Empire.

Men always liked talking about themselves best, she had found, every time she'd been obliged to sit and talk with one of her sisters' suitors. And they particularly liked it if they got to do so in front of the pretty girl they liked best.

Captain Gidiron was no different in that at all. Jullanar wasn't sure whether that boded well or ill for her plan to become a woman of *character* in Galderon. She hadn't managed to stop seeming the perfect chaperone, that was clear.

Well ... there was always next year.

CHAPTER SEVEN

IN WHICH JULLANAR DISCOVERS SHE HAS A MISSION

The caravan of merchants who were licensed to cross the Border—or perhaps more accurately, who were licensed to *return* from over the Border—consisted of a dozen covered wagons drawn by sturdy, tall mules.

According to Marianne, the mules were a specialty of the region near Dorne, where her grandmother lived.

"Oh, how I wish I were going with you!" she cried, sighing extravagantly, as she and Jullanar hesitated at the edge of the mustering grounds. "You're so brave, Jullanar!"

Jullanar wished she could go with Marianne to the grandmother in Dorne. From Marianne's accounts the old lady would be about as likely to welcome her as Jullanar's own Great-Aunt Claudia, but at least it wasn't Kingsford.

Well, neither was the Painted City. She smiled, almost as falsely as she had when talking to her family. "That would be nice, but we'll have our own adventures and then be able to tell each other about them next year, when we're at Galderon together."

"Perhaps we can share lodgings," Marianne said brightly.

"That would be lovely."

Not that Jullanar expected this to happen, but it *was* nice to think that when she came back next year (she resolutely did not ask herself how she would afford such a thing) that she would already know one person here.

"There!" Marianne cried. "I see Mrs. Hawthorne. She'll be the one to talk to—her husband's the head merchant. Come on, Jullanar. Adventure awaits!"

Jullanar followed her down the line of wagons to where a tall, slim, dark-skinned and dark-haired woman, perhaps in her late forties or early fifties, was looking over a collection of baskets and wooden crates, referring often to a small notebook in her hand. Marianne waited deferentially a few feet away, Jullanar trailing reluctantly behind her, while the woman finished up counting over her stores.

At last she turned to them. Her glance took Jullanar in without evident approval, before she turned to Marianne with a thin, absent-minded smile. "Miss Faraday." Her voice was cool and pleasant. "Who is your friend?"

"Mrs. Hawthorne, may I present Miss Thistlethwaite? Jullanar, Mrs. Hawthorne is the headwoman for the caravan."

Jullanar curtsied promptly. Back home in Fiellan such association with *trade* would not be considered anywhere near respectable enough to associate with a family like the Faradays. The Thistlethwaites might, because her father's wild younger brother was a ship's captain, but it would not have been a connection to be *sought*.

Perhaps things were less stratified here at the edge of the Empire. Or Mrs. Hawthorne had married down. Or Mr. Hawthorne was very, very rich. But in that case, why would he still be going off on trade expeditions himself?

"Mrs. Hawthorne is in charge of the scholarly side of the expedition," Marianne went on cheerfully. "There's so much to discover Across the River!"

That made much more sense. Jullanar smiled shyly as the woman softened, as everyone seemed to, in the face of Marianne's blithe good humour.

"Jullanar has a mission Across the River herself, Mrs. Hawthorne. She needs to deliver something to the Painted City."

Mrs. Hawthorne raised her eyebrows in silent inquiry.

"My aunt Maude is a Scholar herself—she's on an, er, a sociological mission there," Jullanar added self-consciously.

There was a pause, before Mrs. Hawthorne's expression cleared. "Maude Thistlethwaite, of course. We have conveyed parcels for her in the past."

Marianne giggled. "This time Jullanar *and* her parcel need conveying, Mrs. Hawthorne! You can arrange that, can't you?"

Jullanar could not imagine she looked so winsome, but she tried to look as if this were necessary and normal and something she, too, desired.

Perhaps Mrs. Hawthorne didn't want to disappoint Marianne Faraday, either, for after a long moment spent considering Jullanar with pursed lips and suspicious eyes, she nodded. "Very well. Have you much baggage, miss?"

Jullanar had half-hoped Mrs. Hawthorne would refuse. (Great-Aunt Claudia in Kingsford couldn't be that bad, surely?) She shook her head, unable to muster speech.

"Just a valise and the box, Mrs. Hawthorne," Marianne put in helpfully. "You'll hardly notice her."

Jullanar felt she should say something marginally helpful. "I'm good at being quiet and discreet, ma'am," she said, perhaps too meekly.

Mrs. Hawthorne gave her a nearly amused smile. "Indeed. Something of an underappreciated art, hmm? Well, let me not stand in the way of your ... mission. I'll ensure the supplies you'll need for the passage across. You'll need something to pay the merchants on the other side—we don't go all the way to the Painted City."

"Not *yet*," Marianne said loyally. "My brother says it won't be long now."

"Indeed! He would know." Mrs. Hawthorne stared at Jullanar for a moment longer before recalling herself. "We leave in three days, miss. Be here the night before—six o'clock, Marianne—with whatever you need to take. I'll have food, but you'll need your own bedding and so on."

"Thank you, ma'am," Jullanar said, as Marianne gushed her own gratitude.

"I am always happy to assist," Mrs. Hawthorne proclaimed, picking up her notebook again in a meaningful gesture. As Jullanar turned away, she heard the woman mutter, "But what use sending a *girl* is, I'm sure I don't know."

You and me both, thought Jullanar dismally, even as Marianne chattered on about the other officers they might as well call on before they were to meet her mother.

The following three days passed in a kind of dream-like state for Jullanar, who was growing increasingly terrified of going with the caravan across the Border. She and Marianne spent a considerable amount of time walking, exploring the neighbourhood.

They went back to Lingron to acquire the requisite 'bedding', which consisted of two blankets, one a medium-weight woollen one and the other waxed canvas to use if the ground 'should happen to be damp', Marianne said blithely, adding that her brother always bought from this chandler when he was adding to the official gear.

Jullanar had thought chandlers were for outfitting ships, but didn't contradict Marianne.

It was very difficult for anyone to contradict Marianne, she found. The pretty young woman darted around the shops and officers' bivouacs with gay laughter and vivacious conversation, charming everyone she met. Jullanar felt even more clumsy and colourless than ever in comparison, but conversely also very much enjoyed her company.

On the third day, Mrs. Faraday had a sumptuous luncheon prepared for her 'last day'. Jullanar had not been granted such a present by her own family, and was struck speechless by the Faradays' thoughtfulness.

"Now," Mrs. Faraday said after she had stammered her thanks for their hospitality over the past week, "I'm sure you know what you're about, my dear, but I wanted to give you something useful."

"I've got a gift for you as well," Marianne put in. "Mama, may I be excused to fetch it?"

"Of course, Marianne," said Mrs. Faraday, and waited till her daughter had left before fixing Jullanar with an intent eye. Jullanar straightened automatically, setting her hands in her lap and looking attentive.

Mrs. Faraday sighed and shook her head. "You're so young," she murmured. "And yet so determined …"

Jullanar had spent the morning feeling queasy and trying to hide her nervous trembling, and did not feel *determined* in the least to do anything but not make an utter fool of herself. Not that that resolution ever particularly worked for her! But at least there was no ink here to spill all over herself.

Mrs. Faraday finally nodded decisively, and reached into the pocket of her fancy apron for a small cloth bag, which she passed to Jullanar. "There," she said. "A little assistance, should you need it.—No, don't open it now! There's Marianne coming back."

Jullanar tucked the little bag into her own pocket, as her North-Fiellanese gown did not come with the fancy outer apron that Mrs. Faraday's style did, and smiled as her friend came bouncing into the room holding several books and another cloth bag, this rather larger than the one her mother had given her.

"Oh Jullanar, what an adventure you're on! I thought coming here marvellous enough, but to go all the way to your aunt … Oh! I am envious of your courage, you know."

"Now Marianne," said her mother indulgently.

Marianne tossed her head so her curls bounced. "Mama, you know I shall behave most circumspectly at my grandmother's house. I am not running away with Jullanar, much as I should wish to!"

"You wouldn't wish to sleep on the bedding I have," Jullanar pointed out gently, not saying that she didn't think *she* wished to, either, but she was too far committed to this course of action to back out now.

She was too far committed to the false supposition that she was panting to study hydrology, too, to do anything but thank Marianne for the introductory textbooks on the subject her friend gave her so she could *study ahead.*

"You'll show all those *men* when you come back," Marianne proclaimed stoutly.

Jullanar blushed and did not contradict her.

After the luncheon, Jullanar returned to her room and performed one final inspection of the pretty space that had been such an unexpected comfort to her here, at what had been supposed to be be the end of her journey but was, it turned out, only the beginning.

She still had a few minutes, she thought at the end, and so turned to the bags the Faradays had given her.

The one from Marianne contained a fine silver hairbrush, a small hand-mirror made of silvered glass set in an elegant brass frame, and two packets of silk ribbons in various colours, lengths, and widths.

Jullanar was just turning them over in her hand when someone knocked on the door and Marianne came in, biting her lip and flushing when she saw that Jullanar had opened her gift.

"Oh! I thought you would open that later," she said, then giggled nervously. "I thought ... it's always nice to have something pretty, isn't it?"

"It is," Jullanar said, forcing a smile over the lump in her throat. "Thank you for everything, Marianne."

"When Reynard goes back on his next mission, I'll send him with letters for you," Marianne promised. "You'd better pack that away—my mother has called for the gig. You don't want to be late for Mrs. Hawthorne!"

"Certainly not!" Jullanar laughed and quickly set the ribbons and other items back into the bag, and tucked that, the books, and the little pouch from Mrs. Faraday into her valise. Her new blankets were neatly rolled, the waxed canvas on the outside, and tied with leather straps.

It really was not very much equipment for going anywhere, let alone out of the Empire and to another world, but then again, Jullanar had already crossed much of two continents with less.

⁓

They left before dawn.

Jullanar had been given a place in Mrs. Hawthorne's wagon, which was in the lead of the caravan. She sat beside the older woman, upright as if Madame Clancette would be coming around with her yardstick at any moment, her valise and the Precious Box immediately behind her, and felt an utter fraud.

Mrs. Hawthorne said nothing. In the dark, everyone seemed hushed, coming in and out of the intermittent lights with silent, purposeful movements that held no relation to anything Jullanar understood. She felt as if she were floating, detached from herself and the scene.

It was the last time they would use the magic lights, Mrs. Hawthorne had said last night. They were part of the benefits of living within the Empire, and as of sunrise tomorrow they would be *outside*.

Jullanar shivered and pulled her shawl closer round her shoulders. It had been so hot along the stagecoach ride that she hadn't pulled it out of her valise before last night.

The shawl smelled of lavender and sweet woodruff and cedar, from the herbs and chests her mother used to store winter clothes, and the sudden, surprising hint of *home* had nearly made her cry.

She bit her lip and was glad for the darkness and the fact that Mrs. Hawthorne made a single, sharp whistle. The signal was picked up by someone in front—her husband? Jullanar had yet to meet Mr. Hawthorne, supposed leader of the caravan—and with a creaking grumble and a single whinny from of the mules the wagons set off.

The caravan consisted of some fifteen wagons, each drawn by either two or four muscular mules. The wagons themselves were broad, high-wheeled, and had arched canvas coverings to shelter the merchants and their trade-goods.

They had slept last night amongst the hessian sacks and wooden chests that were Mrs. Hawthorne's cargo, Jullanar at one edge and Mrs. Hawthorne at the other, with her maid between them.

Most of the wagons had two or three people associated with them besides the merchant himself. Along with Jullanar, Mrs. Hawthorne had her maid and a manservant, who had slept on the ground and now rode on a pony, leading the mules. The maid sat in the back, guarding Mrs. Hawthorne's supplies.

Jullanar had tried to make friends with her last night, but the woman —probably ten or fifteen years older than her, and very prim and far more neatly put together than she herself—had merely given her a supercilious, condescending smile, and said that it wasn't for the likes of her to associate with *her*, and that surely Jullanar would prefer the practice for when she got to the other side, wouldn't she?

She was still puzzled by that comment. There had been the suggestion
that it was Jullanar who was not respectable enough for the maid, not the
other way around.

While last night she had assumed it was because she was being over-
familiar, in the tedious way her older sisters and mother had always chided
her for, in this cold light before dawn it seemed to take on more ominous
meaning.

A clatter of hooves swept up the outside of the column, startling her
until she remembered the soldiers who were accompanying them as
guards. They would take them to the border, she understood, where they
would meet a company who had been exploring the other side.

The road was hard-packed and smooth going. She was a little
surprised at how wide and well-maintained it was, for the direction
outside. Across the River, Over the Mountains—such simple phrases for
such a complicated, terrifying reality!

To leave the Empire behind; to leave the very world behind as well, for
one where the name of Astandalas was almost entirely unknown and the
only Astandalans any of the people on that side would have met were the
handful of traders going to the Fair, Jullanar's Aunt Maude, and the
soldiers who were, she guessed, half spies.

The motion of the wagon, the darkness of a close night before dawn,
the cool air in her face, her anxious and mostly sleepless night—all served
to send her off into a doze.

And so it was not until the guards came galloping back on the other
side of the column, with a shouted cry to Mrs. Hawthorne that the border
was nigh, that it occurred to Jullanar that all that emphasis and odd looks
she'd been given when her *mission* was mentioned was because Mrs.
Hawthorne and Captain Gidiron and all the rest thought *she* was a spy.

The Border, from the inside, looked like a faint silvery curtain.

They halted a few dozen yards back, where a guard post held a dozen
soldiers. Their own soldiers rode forward to speak with the ones at the
post. Mrs. Hawthorne's wagon was in the lead now, and so Jullanar had
an excellent view.

The gravelled road continued up to the building. On the other side of it was a horizontal pole set across the road, painted in black, yellow, and white stripes: the colours of Astandalas. The Sun Banner, the imperial flag, would no doubt be flying bravely over the guard post once the sun rose.

On the other side of the pole was the silvery curtain of mist, like a sea-squall blowing in that never quite arrived.

Jullanar thought perhaps she could see faint shapes in it, dimly moving. She could smell that same odd scent from Galderon, all rue and sage and prickly static-electricity, and sneezed as quietly as she could.

It came out in a pathetic little squeak and she huddled into herself, embarrassed, as Mrs. Hawthorne gave her a glance and the unfriendly maid sneered.

How anyone could even think for a moment she was a spy!

But perhaps, she thought dismally, they thought her a *very good* one. A good spy would be unobtrusive, and unassuming, and easy to overlook, wouldn't she?

All the better to receive confidences or be ignored as she went about the household business, which men always disregarded or outright forgot. Jullanar had been called in to serve her father and his friends at times, when the maids had their half-day, and if she were quiet about it she often heard snatches of stories and news her father would never have let her hear on purpose.

A soldier came out of the post carrying a bugle, followed by another one with a folded cloth: the flag, of course. They paced ceremoniously out of the mage-lights illuminating the building's entry, though the heavy blackness was starting to give way to a dim blue morning.

The flagpole was before the building, this side of the border-crossing. The soldier with the flag carefully worked to fasten the banner to the ropes; the noise of the tackle seemed very loud in the stillness. He looked to the bugler, who lifted his instrument but did not yet play.

Two other soldiers came out and stood on either side of the pole. Then they all waited, while the air lightened and lightened again. The silver curtain was brighter now, lighter in colour and more metallic in gleam, and it was definitely moving, like cobwebs caught in a breeze.

Then there was a sudden flash of golden light. Jullanar cried out softly and turned her head as it blinded her, even as the bugler began to play a reveille and the flag-bearer ran up the banner. Another rattle and thump, and then Mrs. Hawthorne whistled again, and the wagons started forward.

Jullanar blinked the tears from her eyes. The rattle and thump—that was the pole being lifted out of the way. Now it was lying on the ground to the side of the road. The two soldiers saluted as they passed by.

Their own guards were six ahead and six at the rear, with outriders usually on either side but keeping close for this passage.

Jullanar strained forward, eager to see what was on the other side, but the silvery curtains still obscured more than the sense of trees and open space and the rising sun.

The mules shook their heads and brayed loudly as they passed through the curtain, but they kept going.

Jullanar braced herself but was nevertheless astonished by the feeling, that she could feel the air sliding across her skin, something invisible yet viscous, honey-thick but yet effervescent, utterly foreign but yet familiar—and then they were through, and she was almost gasping at the fact that the air tasted differently on this side.

She swayed in her seat and put her hand on the edge of the wagon, gripping the wooden rail tightly. She couldn't help but turn around to see what the Border looked like from this side, but of course the canvas roof of the wagon was in the way, and all she saw was the maid smirking at her.

Jullanar straightened her back as Madame Clancette said to do when nervous, blinked away the tears from the sun, and looked around curiously.

The first thing she saw was a wide blackened plain, with tree stumps here and there. It was scarred and unpleasant, and she shivered. The air seemed thinner on this side—or was it richer?—she couldn't tell, but it was strange and she was not at all sure she liked it.

Mrs. Hawthorne was regarding her with a knowing smile. "Your first time leaving, I take it."

She nodded, unable to make herself speak.

The trees she had thought she'd seen were spindly silver dead ones, tall and leaning all askew. Far in the distance—at least a mile, she thought haphazardly—was the edge of a proper forest.

The forest swung around in a wide arc about them, meeting the lake —which looked much the same as it had on the other—to the left, the north, and extending off into the haze to the south. The sun had risen just enough to be obscured by some thin clouds, and it was now bearable to look ahead of them.

The burned plain was wider than she'd realized, she discovered after they had spent a good half hour or more slowly plodding across it.

At one point she ventured to ask Mrs. Hawthorne why it was burned, only to be told it had been done by their own soldiers, to ensure the Border could not be secretly attacked.

Jullanar looked around. Apart from flakes of ash or burnt grass stems, nothing moved in the wasteland. No birds flew over the ash, nor any insects. There was no sign at all of any other people. Only the road, hard-beaten earth, ran straight ahead.

"Where does the road go?" she asked after another silence. Mrs. Hawthorne was staring at the approaching woods with a vaguely irritated expression, which she turned on Jullanar, who flushed in embarrassment.

"It goes," Mrs. Hawthorne said slowly, "to the passage we are taking."

"Did ... our people make it?"

The older woman gave her a flat stare. "Who else?"

Jullanar remembered that Galderon had been a place of learning for at least five hundred years before the coming of the Empire to Alinor, for it was one of the Universities on the Charter—even if it had not been permitted to participate with those schools within the demesne of Astandalas until it, too, had joined (*been conquered*, whispered a voice in her mind)—which must mean, at the very least, that it had had enough population nearby to support it.

And when the Border was pushed back from the Surge between East and West Noon, past Kiroon and Bamong, past the River Fouyen that meandered eventually down to Dorne, past the endless rice paddies now belonging to the Imperial Duke of Zborawanda, it had swallowed Galderon and encompassed Lingron, and there stopped.

There were two whole Armies of Astandalas on this Border, guarding the length from where the mysterious Mountains of Desire (who named them that? why?) entered the Northern Ocean all the way south to the farther side of the great Bay of Wharalan.

The Province of East Oriole was large, according to the *Atlas* in Madame Clancette's library, but it was not so large as Northwest Oriole, and the continent surely extended much farther, past those mountains and past that bay.

There were no rice paddies on this side, and no villages, but once they entered the woods Jullanar was certain hidden people were watching them.

~

They stopped when they crested a hill to water the mules and stretch their own legs. Jullanar was mortified to be informed by Mrs. Hawthorne's maid that she ought relieve herself behind a bush while she had the chance.

Jullanar pushed quite far back into the woods before she felt securely hidden from anyone, or at least anyone she could see.

As she made her way back, she got a little lost, and came out above the road on a rocky outcropping. She spent a good few minutes searching for a way down before it occurred to her to look out and around at the visible landscape.

To the east and south and north were wooded hills, rising ever more steeply in the distance both north and south. To the east they were crossing against the grain of the hills, and the road clearly went down into valley and up over pass again and again. Each valley seemed thickly wooded, though there was something odd about the trees in the valleys ahead.

Perhaps they were willows, she thought, peering at the verticals, the slashes of what seemed to be long fluttering lance-like leaves. Certainly it seemed wetter here; the cut of the road was lined with streams and rivulets leaping gaily down and running in gullies on either side.

Behind her, to the west, the forest stopped abruptly at the burned plain.

The blackened ground stretched out into the distance, a crescent-shaped scar on the land. From this height she could see the curve of the Border, running parallel to a bend of the mountains. To the north was the valley of the river that ran into the lake by Lingron, or so she assumed.

From this side of the Border, you could not see into the Empire.

What was a silvery curtain from the inside was from here a great golden dome extending across half the visible horizon.

On that side was all that Jullanar had ever known; on this side, barest rumour.

She looked as long as she dared at the blackened no-man's-land and the magical Border, before she slipped and slid down to the road, fearful suddenly that Mrs. Hawthorne would leave her behind if she didn't hasten back.

But Mrs. Hawthorne only raised an eyebrow at her and gave her an apple and a pastry stuffed with herbs and cheese, and told her they still had a long ways to go before they reached their destination.

CHAPTER EIGHT

IN WHICH JULLANAR LOOKS THROUGH A LANTERN

They spent that first night in an encampment surrounded by long-needled pine trees.

The pines swayed and whispered all night, their branches scratching across the covering of the wagon.

The merchants had drawn the wagons in a circle around a bonfire, where there had been music—a few of the men had instruments—and singing for an hour or so before the dark drove everyone to their sleeping arrangements.

Jullanar was once again given the outside edge, the maid beside her and Mrs. Hawthorne on the inside, closest to the fire. Past her were the mules, and past the mules was a perimeter line of sentries.

And beyond the sentries, there was the part of East Oriole that was Outside.

The stars seemed so much brighter than any Jullanar had seen before, but then again this was the first time she'd ever been anything like outside a town's walls at night.

She did not think she liked it very much. She felt horribly exposed, chilled in a way that had little to do with the weather.

Nevertheless, as she had no other remedy she pulled her blanket closer about her and pretended its tight cocoon was enough.

After a day of going up and down over the ridges, each one more thickly forested with increasingly foreign plants, they went over a pass and descended into a bigger valley.

This one had a river in its heart, and for the first time incontrovertible evidence that there *were* people here—besides the road itself—for another road joined theirs, and there were cleared fields with small black cows grazing in them.

They passed one village. The houses were few in number but each large, four or five storeys high, with steeply angled thatched roofs. There was smoke coming out the chimneys of two of the houses, but there were no people visible.

The Astandalan merchants rode by quietly, ignoring the village. Jullanar asked Mrs. Hawthorne what she knew of the place, which was —nothing.

"They're not our concern," the headwoman said, lips pursed as she looked at the house they were passing.

They were near neighbours, Jullanar thought, and yet their architecture was so different, and the plants they grew in the vegetable plots beside the road were not the ones she knew from her week at the Faradays', let alone from home.

What were those vining plants with smooth green fruits, three or four feet long, each with a pebble tied to the end? (To keep them straight?) What colour were those irises when they bloomed in the spring, and why were they growing in shallow square pools?

There were more lotus, these ones flowering a paler pink than the ones she'd seen in the canals on the other side. It was a damp, moist day as they passed the village, not quite rain but with fine water droplets in the air, and the lotus-flowers shimmered like paper lanterns at a fair.

Gorde, one of the soldiers was riding close to the wagon, and he laughed at Mrs. Hawthorne's non-answer. He was only a few years older than Jullanar, brown of hair and skin, and he had told her she reminded him of his sisters, *back home* on Ysthar.

She'd accepted the qualification of his interest without unhappiness (it wasn't as if she really *wanted* to practice flirting with strangers, when she had no one but the coolly disapproving Mrs. Hawthorne at her side), and reciprocated with questions about his family and his home south of Astandalas the Golden.

"This is an active Border, remember," he told Jullanar. He gestured at the silent village, with the shutters closed on all the houses but the sense that people were inside, watching them pass by. "They know this isolation won't last much longer now."

Jullanar thought of East and West Noon, facing each other across the narrow Surge. A hundred yards apart, maybe, and for centuries that curtain had separated them, silver on one side and gold on the other, hiding what lay beyond.

"Do you know why the roofs are so steep?" she asked Gorde.

"They get a sh—er, a great deal of snow in the winter. That's one reason why the Border's where it still is. You see those trees, there?"

He pointed at a small grove of well-pruned trees. "Those are white mulberry trees. The people here raise silkworms, upstairs in their houses. Barbaric, isn't it? But their silk is highly prized."

Jullanar looked again at the houses. It did seem disgusting to be raising worms indoors, but then again, was it so different from any of the streets in Fiella-by-the-Sea where the shop was downstairs and the artisans lived up?

She didn't have the opportunity to ask any further questions, for Gorde was called forward, and he was the only one who was remotely willing to answer her questions. Instead she settled back on the hard seat, glad she'd thought to sit on her tarp for some cushioning but still wishing they had arrived.

Or failing that, that she could get out and walk for a while.

But that was not *safe*, she understood, and truly she was frightened of being lost in this strange and foreign land.

They kept up the river valley, following as it wound back into taller and taller hills. The day after they passed the village they entered into a bamboo forest.

Jullanar had learned what bamboo was in Galderon, for the Faradays had a clump in their garden. It was a kind of grass with hollow stems—culms, they were called—and fluttery leaves. The clump in the Faradays' garden was about six feet tall, the culms the size of her thumb and a deep, shiny green-black colour. They swayed gracefully in the breezes and generally seemed a tidy, decorative sort of plant.

The bamboo in the forest was their wild cousin. Instead of six feet the stems were thirty, even forty feet high, and the culms were like tree-trunks. Jullanar could not circle them with her two hands, when she got the chance to try on one of their infrequent rest halts. The surface of the culm was smooth, shiny under a faint dust like the bloom on a plum, ridged horizontally where the leaves joined the stem.

The bamboo swayed and creaked and clacked as the culms knocked against each other, but it all happened high above them. The ground between the culms was thick with dead leaves and broken stems, and it was very quiet and dim.

There must have been animal and bird life somewhere in the forest, but whether it was from the noise of their passage or her own lack of knowledge or some other reason Jullanar did not see anything that whole day.

They climbed steadily, if slowly, through the forest. The river was still running beside them, much smaller now and noisier as it tumbled whitely over mossy rocks. The only sunlight came through the open space above the river, beside which the road ran. On the left, and on the far bank of the river to their right, the bamboo forest stretched still and solemn.

The close proximity of road and river caused certain problems. From time to time there were streams coming in from the side, which necessitated bridges. These were made not of wood, but of the bamboo trunks. The wagons rumbled over, the mules' hooves slipping on the hard, rounded surfaces.

Other portions of the road were muddy from where the river had overrun its banks. A few times the last wagon would get stuck after the rest of them had churned up the mud, and they would have to stop while the men worked to loosen the wheels. Their progress was much slower, and the mules seemed restive.

The soldiers rode more closely now, a dozen of them in three ranks of four a hundred yards ahead of Mrs. Hawthorne's wagon. Their bright green uniforms and yellow sashes were a comforting sight to Jullanar, reassuring her that no matter how alien this side of the Border was, she was still under the aegis of the Emperor and all his power.

One of the lead soldiers called out, pointing up at something around a bend in the road. The front rank spurred their horses to join him, and the others fell back until they were only just ahead of Mrs. Hawthorne's mules.

As they made the bend, the air seemed to lighten and brighten. They were coming out of the bamboo forest, Jullanar realized belatedly, even as she tilted her head to feel the fresh air and sunlight on her face.

She had to blink back sun-woken moisture when she looked down again, and blushed at Mrs. Hawthorne's silent disapproval. Jullanar straightened her back and regarded her surroundings carefully.

They had entered a rough clearing at the base of a rocky cliff that seemed to jut out from the mountain whose flank they had been slowly angling across all day. The cliff was perhaps twenty feet above the road, which curved around its base and then followed the spur back towards the mountains proper. It faced another spur, shorter but with a steeper cliff.

On top of each cliff was a stone watchtower with a shiny black roof like the back of a beetle. Below the roof was a parapet; and on each parapet were guards.

The guards wore clothing not so dissimilar to what she'd seen amongst the locals in Lingron and on the road to Galderon: loose cloth trousers and thigh-length tunics with wide sleeves.

The peasants working the rice paddies had worn their trousers and sleeves tied back, whereas these guards had some form of armoured breastplates and shin-guards and helmets. All of these appeared to be made of wicker, or perhaps split bamboo.

They were all holding cocked crossbows, which they held in readiness though not pointing directly at the caravan of merchants.

Jullanar looked up at the cliffs, the two watchtowers, the narrow pass, and knew without having had to study any form of warfare at all that this was the sort of bottle-neck that could make or break an army's passage.

If those men wished for this caravan to fail, it would take only a few men to slaughter them. If some of their people went back into the bamboo forest to lift up the bridges, there would be little way for anyone to escape to tell the Empire what had befallen them.

And yet ... when neither the caravan nor the soldiers sent with them returned, what would the local garrison commander do, but retaliate?

Jullanar thought of that burned plain on this side of the Border, and the road that surely had not been built by the Empire, not with this mud and muck and those bamboo bridges, and this pass through guarded and nearly hostile territory, and wondered very much what *active* really meant, for those on either side.

Pretty Marianne Faraday, grumbling over ribbons and flirting with the officers bivouacked there, on rest leave from the Border rotation ...What would she do if these folk decided to follow the road the other way?

The Empire was full of magic, Jullanar reminded herself. That Border was not just a pole across the road, not just a curtain of mist in the air. She didn't know what that mist could do when roused against an invading force, but she had learned enough history at Madame Clancette's to know that it was very rare indeed for any lands that the Empire had fully claimed to successfully rebel.

(In this Jullanar was at the mercy of a biased history, and an education that had not been particularly inclined towards criticism of authority; but it was true that the Empire had seen few *successful* rebellions since the College of Priest-Wizards had finally mastered weather-working.)

None of the caravan soldiers said anything, but their hands were not far from their swords and lances.

Mrs. Hawthorne drove the wagon as easily and calmly as she had the whole time since leaving Lingron, but when Jullanar glanced at her she saw that the headwoman's jaw was clenched.

She was sure she didn't breathe properly until the watchtowers were out of sight and they were deep in the bamboo forest again.

But now every creak and clatter and whisper suggested danger, and when they slept that night in their circle, the mules were on the inside, and her dreams were full of tiptoeing men in wicker armour coming to lean over her sleeping form and stare.

~

Their road dwindled to a cart track, and occasionally the soldiers had to stop to clear fallen culms out of their way, while the mules balked at invisible dangers, ears flicking and eyes rolling with nerves. Their speed slowed again, until Jullanar was sure she could have walked faster than the mules were going.

Then the road stopped.

Mrs. Hawthorne gave her man the reins, and while he watered the mules the headwoman climbed down and went to speak with the captain of the soldiers accompanying them.

Jullanar sipped from her own water flask, watching Mrs. Hawthorne. There was a suffocating sense of heat and humidity, though the air was conversely cool on her face. A mist seemed to be rising all around them, so that she couldn't see very far into the bamboo forest at all.

The road had twisted and turned in the bamboo forest, for no reason Jullanar could decipher, but going ever deeper into a valley that ran back into the mountains. The ground here was vibrant green with moss under the layers of dead leaves, and their road seemed to be almost unused but for the soldiers' passage ahead of them, which turned up clots of a thick black mud. There were an excessive number of mosquitos.

About thirty feet in front of her, the narrow ribbon of road opened up into a wider pool of green moss. In the middle of this was a stone construction consisting of an open-sided box on top of a pillar.

The top of the box had a curved roof like the watchtowers had possessed, though this one was carved of the same grey stone as the rest. The whole thing was encrusted with lichens, grey, orange, and a strange greeny-yellow, and looked very old and somehow uncanny.

Mrs. Hawthorne came back to the wagon and told Jullanar to get down. She did so, shaking out her skirts as best she could and feeling frumpier than ever next to the headwoman, who seemed as coolly elegant as when Jullanar had first met her.

"Come here," Mrs. Hawthorne said, leading her to the stone object. "You should know the route, just in case you need to travel by yourself for some reason."

Jullanar suppressed an hysterical giggle at the very *thought* she would be making this trek by herself on any occasion. She was supposed to be some excellent spy, she reminded herself, nodding obediently at Mrs. Hawthorne.

"Look through the windows in the lantern," Mrs. Hawthorne said.

"Lantern?"

"That's what it's called."

Mrs. Hawthorne's voice had the same brisk, dismissive tone she utilized whenever speaking of those barbarians Outside the Empire. Jullanar remembered her saying that *of course* this route had been discovered by an Imperial explorer; who else?

Who else, indeed, but whoever had built this lantern in the same style as the locally manned watchtowers, and who had lived here uncounted years before the coming of the Empire.

Uncounted by the Empire, anyway. There were still a few universities on the List that had not yet come within the protection of Astandalas.

Jullanar bent down so her head was level with the 'windows' in the stone lantern. Though she had not seen it when she looked over the lantern, when she looked through the windows she could clearly see a second lantern ahead of her.

"Do you see it?" Mrs. Hawthorne said.

"Yes, ma'am."

"Keep your eyes on it, and walk towards it."

Jullanar wanted to look at her in disbelief, but she *did* feel happier knowing she knew how to get home again, and so she obeyed. To her astonishment, as she lifted her head from the window she could still see the second lantern clearly, on the other side of the clearing where there hadn't been anything but bamboo stems before.

"Walk towards it," Mrs. Hawthorne said. "We'll follow."

The headwoman whistled, the shrill cry that set the caravan in motion. Jullanar did not look around, even as she heard the hooves of the soldiers' horses, the mules, the rumbling and creak of the wagon wheels. She kept her eye on the second lantern and walked across the clearing, Mrs. Hawthorne at her shoulder.

When she hesitated at the second lantern, Mrs. Hawthorne said, "The same again."

This time, looking through the window, the third lantern visibly stood at the mouth of a tunnel formed by arching and interwoven bamboo stems. It seemed both built and natural, as if the bamboo had grown into the arches on its own, but that was impossible, surely?

Nearly as impossible as the way Jullanar walked forward, eyes firmly on a lantern that had not been there, the green moss soft as velvet under her feet, the mist washing over her feet and ankles in visible eddies.

"And again," Mrs. Hawthorne said as they approached the third lantern.

Jullanar hardly had to bend for this one, though it had not looked larger when she'd first seen it. This time her eye found not another stone lantern, but instead a pair of white columns, slender and arched to form a X.

"Keep walking," said Mrs. Hawthorne, her hand coming to rest on Jullanar's shoulder.

Jullanar was too amazed at what she was doing to think of the hand as anything more than a comfort. She walked towards the white archway in the distance, along a path that slowly dwindled from moss to gravel, though she only knew that from the changing sound and textures underfoot.

The white mist rose thickly around them, billowing like egg whites beaten into meringue, almost solid to the touch.

There was one moment, halfway along, when a gust of wind blew from the side. Jullanar caught a scent of something intensely familiar—was that the sea?—and turned her head.

There, in a gap between the uprights of the tunnel, was a valley drenched in sunlight. A pale castle of many towers stood there, its windows and pennons glittering, and birds wheeling around.

She would have stopped to look more fully, had Mrs. Hawthorne's hand not been on her shoulder. "Don't stray!" the headwoman warned. "Haven't you heard any of the stories?"

And was that then—could it *possibly* be—Fairyland?

But Mrs. Hawthorne's hand was hard on her shoulder, and whatever tantalizing glimpse of adventure lay to the side, that was not the way the safe road led.

Jullanar perforce walked out of one world and into another.

CHAPTER NINE

IN WHICH JULLANAR TRIES TO LOOK ON THINGS AS AN ADVENTURE

Mrs. Hawthorne taught her a smattering of words in the language of the Painted City after they left the passage between worlds behind and began the approach towards the fair.

The language was called *Calandran*, and it was used throughout the region, Mrs. Hawthorne had told her. Jullanar had listened intently, written down the words phonetically in one of the notebooks she had been supposed to use at Galderon, and practised the sounds carefully when she could.

The week it took to travel from the passage to the Fair was enough to gain a grasp of *Please* and *thank-you* and *yes* and *no*, and a handful of verbs and nouns. Jullanar had a vague idea that making a sentence into a question did not work the way it did in Shaian, but she had not yet learned any way but to inflect her voice inquiringly.

On this side, the otherworldly side, the passage was marked by two white birches growing in a forest of trees whose bark peeled off in long blood-red strips.

There was a kind of stone landing—really just a natural outcropping of the bedrock (or so it seemed; but *someone* had found this passage, and made those lanterns, after all)—this side of the birches, so the wagons and horses left little trace of their passage.

She had asked, and Mrs. Hawthorne had told her that if she entered between those two birches, she would come at length to the first of the stone lanterns, and could—by the same means by which she had found the route—thus retrace her path.

Once more, Jullanar could only wonder who had devised this path, and how, and why. And indeed when.

The new road left behind the red-barked trees to pass through a forest of oak and ash and holly, almost identical to any of the ones Jullanar had seen near home in northern Fiellan. The road was not paved, but was a solid, well-beaten earth, dusty rather than muddy, and seemingly well-travelled. Mrs. Hawthorne said that there were towns to the west, fishing villages and small mines along a coast whose seas no Astandalan had ever sailed.

It was to the east that the Astandalan merchants travelled, to the Great Tyssian Fair in the small town of Fovisse.

The Great Tyssian Fair was, Jullanar admitted, something of a disappointment. She knew hardly any of the language, and the merchants in her caravan were all immediately concerned with their own business.

The soldiers guarding them still guarded the merchants, but also mixed with the guards brought by other caravans, chatting and talking away in that language she did not know. They seemed to be acquainted with many of the people here, having met the same merchants and guards time and again.

Mrs. Hawthorne negotiated her passage to the Painted City for her. Jullanar did not know what the headwoman had said she was doing, and could only hope that the merchant from the new caravan—*Pelo Aviroth*, she thought his name was—was honest and trustworthy.

This next stage of the journey cost her another two gold sovereigns to Mrs. Hawthorne, and the hand mirror Marianne had given her in trade to Pelo Aviroth. Her valise was feeling very light by now, and she could only hold on to it and the Precious Box for the last leg of the journey.

There were no other women in the new caravan. Jullanar tried not to be frightened at this, but it was hard. She kept remembering all the whispered warnings and horror stories from the other girls at Madame Clancette's, her older sisters, the gossip at her mother's sewing parties.

No one was ever explicit, of course, but somehow that made the nebulous fears worse. She looked sidelong at all the men, the merchants and their guards and grooms, and ... feared.

Yet this was one occasion when she could be glad she was plain, and plump, and a natural chaperone. No one was looking sidelong back at *her*.

All the way along the journey from the Great Tyssian Fair to the Painted City, Jullanar heard the wind.

It blew steadily from the west. The journey led the caravan through fields of grain, wheat or barley Jullanar couldn't tell and didn't know the words with which to ask. The grain was knee-high, by which she assumed it was spring, here in this strange other world she had come to. It rippled in the wind like the waves of the sea.

She'd been given a seat in one of the wagons. Everyone else was either walking or driving, with the exception of two guards on horseback, who seemed to be outriders of some form.

The wagon horses were stocky and short to her eyes, more like ponies than the farm horses of her admittedly limited experience. The mounted guards rode taller, obviously faster horses.

Jullanar watched them curiously. She had never really had anything to do with the animals, for her father's practice was entirely within the bounds of Fiella-by-the-Sea, and horses were an expensive luxury in a town.

The first half an hour or so, leaving the Fair and its associated tent city, was exciting. It was a whole new world, one where very few of her fellow Imperial citizens had ever stood.

Going on from the Fair itself was almost unheard of—the merchants had not, yet, for some political reason Jullanar did not quite understand when Mrs. Hawthorne mentioned it. She'd asked one of the maids, but the woman simply looked at her with pity in her eyes. Jullanar did not know why the pity was there, but it stung her pride, and she did not ask again.

Again and again she went back to the interlude with Marianne Faraday, and the one spontaneous friendship that had ever come her way. Even though she had only known Marianne for a week, she missed the other girl fiercely, and wished she had been able to accompany her to her grandmother in Dorne. But that had been impossible.

Jullanar reached out to settle the Precious Box after a particular bump made it jump out of place. They had started out on what looked like a proper stone-laid highway, but the cobbles it was made of were nowhere near so even as those at home.

All she could see were the wagons in front of her—hers was somewhere in the middle—the clusters of guards marching to the sides and rear, and beyond them, the young grain. The sky above them was a clear blue, with beautiful puffy white clouds. At the edges of the fields were flowers, orange and blue and a clear red poppy just like the ones at home.

She tried sketching the horses, but the wagon bumped and jostled too much. That left reading, which *did* garner some astonished looks from the merchants and their guards. She wondered what was so unusual about seeing her read. She had certainly not been the only passenger attempting to read on the stagecoach across Northwest Oriole.

Marianne had called her *brave*, and even though her friend wasn't there to witness it, Jullanar wanted desperately to prove her right.

It took a full ten days to reach the river. Jullanar had exchanged words with several men from the caravan, particularly the friendly middle-aged merchant driving her wagon. He was willing to point out objects and name them for her, eyes twinkling merrily at her efforts to repeat the words back to him.

He was *Pelo Camios*, it seemed, by which she learned that *Pelo* was probably not a name—not unless it was as common a name here as her own Jullanar was in Fiellan—but rather a title, like *Mr* or *Sayo*.

The grain was *huv*, and it was *balas*, which either meant *green* or *young* or perhaps both. Jullanar made note of her thoughts, glad she would be able to ask her aunt for assistance once she reached the Painted City.

O *Lady*, she prayed, please let her aunt not be angry she arrived so unexpectedly.

Pelo Camios made sure she had food and water whenever the caravan stopped. They rested the horses frequently, though there were no clocks in any of the villages they passed to indicate the hours.

There were no communities much larger than a village, which Jullanar found unfathomable.

On the stagecoach across Northwest Oriole there had been villages at least every few hours, a town once or twice a day, a city every other day or so. Even down along the coastline of the Lesser Arcady, the city-states had been no more than fifteen or twenty miles apart, all the land that could easily be held and farmed in that rugged landscape by people more interested in the sea.

Here, they passed out of the agricultural lands near the Fair the first day. The road led up a long hill. By the end of the afternoon the fields had turned to pastures and then to woods.

They were still climbing the morning of the second day, though not steeply. The road seemed to angle a little south as it went along the face of the slope.

The uplands were airy despite being wooded, with trees that seemed some form of oak. Some had strange pale scars on their trunks, too regular to be natural. Jullanar made a note about those, too.

It was incredibly frustrating to be in a new place, with all these new things around her, and be unable to ask any questions or have any hope of a reference book.

There didn't seem to be any acorns yet, so she added that to her tally of indications that it was spring. The oak forest stretched all the way along the uplands and down a fair way on the other side, though as they still seemed to be angling along the face of the slope, rather than going straight down, it was difficult to tell.

They were definitely going south as well as east, she thought, pleased at this small determination. She'd never been particularly good at directions before, but then again she'd never really had to try.

She'd learned the basics because Madame Clancette had felt a solid knowledge of imperial cartography was an important attribute for her girls; and of course it was usually on the Entrance Examination.

Jullanar had always loved maps, as it happened.

She had spent many happy hours matching up the people in the *Atlas of Imperial Peoples* with the maps in the *Atlas of the Empire*, which was an entirely different and much more expensive publication. Indeed, the library at Madame Clancette's was the only place she'd seen it.

She hadn't realized how much she'd internalized of those maps, how they had oriented her journey to Galderon, until now, when she had no maps at all and no way of getting one. If the merchants had maps they were not sharing them.

So she was pleased to use snippets of adventuring details from her books to determine direction from the sun. It was really not a very big thing, figuring out that south was the direction perpendicular to the sun's path from east to west; perhaps it was the smallest possible discovery, apart from that the sun rose in the east and sank in the west.

But for Jullanar, who had spent all her life but the past months of travel within the circumscribed limits of her small town, it was a minor triumph indeed.

They eventually descended out of the oak forest, which petered out into a kind of aromatic scrubland. It was rather similar to the landscape along the edge of the Lesser Arcady, in fact. She thought she identified the scents of thyme and sage on the air, at least.

The leaves seemed greyer here, and scraggly, but the wide slopes were also awash in blossoms. The most prominent was a gangly shrub with bright yellow pea-like blooms, scented like honey and something else she couldn't name, but rivers of little purple flowers, their bell-shaped blossoms in tiny clusters, were there too, and white one like goblets and pink ones like stars and all sorts of red and orange ones like trumpets or daisies or chalices.

She was so drunk on the colours that it took her half the day to look up and realize the land was empty.

At the edge of the Lesser Arcady, along the stagecoach route, there had been cities and universities and roads angling off up into the strange magical country in the highland valleys.

There were goats and vineyards, almond orchards and irrigation canals, dovecotes and chicken coops, farmsteads and tiny villages and even tinier hermitages. Terraces marched down hillsides, and the many ravines were bridged, shrines tucked under the arches. Smoke rose from more distant habitations to the inland side, and fishing boats with yellow hulls and white sails were visible in the bay to the other.

Along the highway itself there were always people walking, riding, leading laden donkeys or mules or pony-carts, herding sheep or goats or ducks or geese, making way for the carriages of the wealthy or the wagons of the well-to-do.

Even in the uplands of Ronderell and Lind, stone walls writhing across mountainsides and the multitude of sheep with occasional accompanying shepherd and sheepdog were clear evidence of people.

Here, though, only the road and themselves indicated human presence.

No, that wasn't quite true, Jullanar realized as she started to pay more attention. There was the evidence of ancient and now ruined buildings all around them. Tumbled-down stone walls suggested a village; they stopped at springs that had once been channelled into shaped stone basins. Blurred carvings on squared-off stones along the route had perhaps once been milestones.

It must have been a long time since people lived here, she thought, looking around at the way the vegetation had engulfed the stones. It was only when she really looked hard that she could see suggestions of human workings.

Now there weren't even goats or pigs that seemed to belong to anyone: just birds, and rabbits or other small creatures, and a few times she saw what she thought were deer. None seemed particularly wary of their passage, and indeed she saw one of the guards catch a pair of fat pheasant-like birds with a well-thrown stone.

Jullanar shuddered at seeing him kill the birds so competently. She knew that it was hard to have a real adventure if she was squeamish about hunting for food, but then again, this was likely all the adventure she would ever had.

She puzzled for the next several days over why no one lived here. The land on the other side of the oak forest, around the Fair, had been richer, judging by the plant life—though the flowers here made her doubt that first impression, except that there *were* a lot of stones just laying around on the ground. Still, there were the springs along the road, which were good, clean water, and an abundance of game.

(She forced herself to smile and thank the cook when she was given fried rabbit and flatbread for supper. It was tasty, thankfully, once she got over herself.)

The wind remained at her back. Sometimes it gusted, and she thought she smelled *home*, but that made no sense at all.

Even if the wind were blowing from the edge of the Border—and she supposed there was no impossible reason why it could not be—it was not as if her home was anywhere near the other side of that strange misty woods.

But she could not deny that sometimes she turned her head and was sure she smelled the familiar mixture of woodsmoke and brine and bread baking.

Altogether she was relieved when they crested a low rise, which had already done good work (she felt) by breaking the monotony of their steady, gentle, downwards slope, and saw before them the great valley of the River Oonar.

They paused for their midday break at the crest. Jullanar was able to walk around a bit, stretch her legs. She found a secluded spot to relieve herself—something she had become much better at since she started on this journey, when going out-of-doors behind only a shrub had been a matter of utter mortification—and looked out at the wider landscape.

The road slashed down through the scrubland to a small cluster of pale buildings, barely larger than a blot, some miles away. On the other side of the buildings the land changed, from grey-green spotted with colour to a much more uniform rich gold, which extended into a blue haze in the distance.

For a wild moment she wondered if they'd come to the sea. South the sun was too bright, so she looked to her left, north, where the gold faded into a darker shade before disappearing into a blue haze. Above the haze white peaks hung in the sky, almost as if they floated in midair.

The sound of feet scuffing on stones alerted her to company. She turned, not nearly as warily as at the beginning of this trip, to see that Pelo

Camios had brought her a flatbread wrapping some sort of meat. She thanked him as she took it, though her eyes strayed to the vista in front of her.

"*Esra Oonar,*" he said, gesturing widely at the valley. He then pointed in a direction just south of their obvious immediate destination at the edge of the river, to a point where the sun was catching on something minuscule but bright in the distance. "*All'okra* Ixsaa."

Not the sea, then, but the great valley of the River Oonar, which her aunt said in her book was called, in a children's story of the city, the River that Ran Away to Paradise, and came back dressed in every colour of the rainbow.

Pelo Camios regarded the prospect happily. She could see that he was enjoying her awe at the sight, and perhaps that he, too, was looking forward to arriving in the city and trading on the goods he had bought at the Fair.

"Two days," he said, perhaps the only phrase she had actually understood immediately from him.

Jullanar ate her flatbread and cold meat, whatever bird it was today, her eyes on the Painted City in the far distance.

It was as if her whole understanding of time and distance had swung around, so that *that* vast expanse of water was no inland sea, no ocean, but a river, whose valley they had spent the past seven days descending.

The merchant caravan arrived at the edge of the river around the middle of the next day. This lowest part of the river-basin was much richer ground than higher up: the ruins here seemed half-rebuilt, though only in little circles of buildings.

It didn't seem as if people liked to live in separate farms here, as she'd seen through most of Northwest Oriole. It was much more like East Noon in that regard, though without the strict geometry of the rice paddies.

The highway ran straight to the edge of the river and stopped at a jetty there. Jullanar had been expecting a bridge, at least until she'd seen the vastness of the Oonar, and now wondered exactly what sort of ferry she could expect.

Before they got close enough for her to see, Pelo Camios stopped so he could talk to a tall man who came out of one of the buildings and seemed to be taking some sort of record of who was there. He eyed Jullanar suspiciously, but Pelo Camios smiled easily and explained something. The man stared hard at her for another moment, then nodded brusquely and went on to the next wagon.

"Thank you," Jullanar said softly. She had no idea what sort of laws they had here about strangers coming, but she had no paperwork that would have been acceptable in the Empire for her to leave its borders, let alone arrive anywhere else.

It struck her then that this was perhaps a little strange—surely the merchants from Lingron, who had to be licensed to trade with the outworlds, should have been more strict about requiring her to have permission?—but she did not have time to think about that, for Pelo Camios had clucked to his horses and was guiding them to the jetty, where a boat indeed lay berthed and waiting.

Jullanar eyed it dubiously. It was a large flat-hulled sort of boat, not too dissimilar from the wherries she'd seen in the harbour of Fiella-by-the-Sea, though it had different rigging, with numerous triangular sails well near the front of the boat.

She frowned at it thoughtfully, but had never cared enough to pay close attention to the niceties of ship design. The sails were each dyed a different warm shade, from red to orange to a mustardy yellow. The boat itself was painted white.

The effect was very bright, especially as the water, to her surprise, was a deep milky plum in colour. It seemed to have a lot of sediment suspended in it, for she couldn't see down very far, only enough to see that the white colour of the wherry continued under the water line.

Pelo Camios directed her to wait to the side, where she'd be out of the way, and she stood in the shadow of the wall to watch while he and his men loaded the boat with his cargo. She still wasn't sure how many of the men in the caravan were the merchants themselves and which their underlings. Whichever it was, Pelo Camios oversaw the transferral of four different wagonloads of goods. These seemed to fill most of the hold.

She sat down on her trusty box and waited. It was truly amazing how much waiting around travelling involved. She had had no idea. Pelo

Camios was now talking to the various other men who had been driving the wagons.

They were nodding, frowning, smiling, shrugging—she had noticed many of the men had extravagant gestures, with which they punctuated their speech. One man jabbed his hand downward, fingers spread out; the rest laughed. Pelo Camios was laughing too, and then he pulled out a leather bag and started to hand over money to them.

Ah. He was paying them for their work, of course. One by one the men took their wages, then went back over to the horses and wagons and led them out of the docking area. Pelo Camios looked over at her, smiling, with a gesture that she took to mean 'keep waiting, I'm coming back in a minute', and disappeared after them.

She was tempted to get out her book, but felt someone—her aunt, maybe—would be disappointed if she let this opportunity to observe the locals go unobserved.

There hadn't been much about the western bank of the river in her aunt's book, which was focused on the city itself and its immediate environs.

Somewhere over there the river split into many channels, all of them with fanciful, colourful names. Jullanar looked down at the plum-coloured water again. Well, she had thought them fanciful.

The suspicious man was back, this time walking up and down outside the building opposite hers. He looked at her from time to time, frowning, but made no move to come over and interrogate her, for which she was grateful. There was no way she'd be able to answer more than the very simplest of questions.

There weren't many birds here, she noted idly. A few gulls, white and grey and seemingly identical to the ones she'd left behind in Fiella-by-the-Sea. In the water were some ducks, possibly, though not quite the same as her familiar mallards. Jullanar was pretty sure there were a lot more kinds of duck than mallards in the world—there were domesticated ones, too— there had been those black-and-white ones in the rice paddies—let alone on another world.

She wondered how people knew it was actually another world, and not just another part of Alinor. Magic, presumably.

It didn't seem fair that so many questions boiled down to that one answer. So what if she wasn't herself a wizard or a witch or any other sort of magic user? She still had questions.

She caught herself scowling at the suspicious man, and hastily looked away. Back along the road there was a bit of disturbance, dust raised up. She watched it come down the long slope, far faster than they had. One of the outriders, maybe, rejoining them.

Pelo Camios came back at that point. He spoke to the suspicious man for a few minutes before handing him another, smaller, leather bag. Jullanar wondered if that were payment or a bribe.

She had absolutely no way of knowing, and felt bad for thinking that the kind and friendly merchant was bribing people.

Yet she didn't know what else to call that forced gift of a hand mirror to the caravan leader—and what had happened to him? She hadn't seen the rest of the merchants or their wagons since they'd come to the jetty.

Yet another question for which she had no way of learning the answer. She put them out of her mind, as she must, when Pelo Camios approached her and offered her a hand up. She stood and brushed out her skirts as best she could, smiling apprehensively at him.

"Good," he said, and a few other words she did not know. Then, "Come," and when she nodded, picked up her valise for her—she had not been willing to relinquish the Precious Box to strangers—and helped her onto the gently moving wherry.

The three men who had been lashing down the cargo on the boat emerged from below and started to fuss with the sails and ropes. One directed her and the merchant to a bench placed near the middle of the boat, back from the mast and out of the way of the sailors. There was a kind of awning overhead, which provided some relief from the shade, at least. The sun on the water was very bright despite its colour.

With a soft snap the incessant west wind caught the orange and red sails, and with a slight lurch the wherry began to move.

Jullanar looked back, to see another wherry, this one with green and yellow striped sails, sliding down from a berth just upriver. Another cluster of wagons was being led up to the jetty.

A flight of gulls riding the air currents angled out to follow their wherry, as if they were a fishing boat back home, and Jullanar settled back

against her seat with a sigh, hoping her sisters' prophecies about her
tendency to seasickness would be unfounded.

She felt acceptable—hardly *good*, but not actually *sick*—for the first half
hour or so of the journey. They were heading more or less downriver with
the current, though tacking over as well under the influence of the wind.

The fresh air blowing against her face helped, as did the fresh water
Pelo Camios brought her. She had learned not to grimace at the animal
skin of the flask, one of the many things she tried to face bravely.

She was *longing* for a bath.

It was truly astonishing how big this river was. Aunt Maude's book
said it was enormous, perhaps the biggest river in its world, perhaps one of
the biggest rivers in all the Nine Worlds. Jullanar had had no reason not to
believe this, but she had not truly understood what that meant.

Half an hour into the journey and the cluster of buildings by the jetty
they had departed from was a white blotch—just as it had been from the
edge of the last slope down into the valley—while the bright spot that was
Ixsaa on the other side looked not a smidgeon closer.

Pelo Camios pulled out the wooden tablet she had seen him use before
and was going over it intently. She hadn't had the opportunity to look at it
closely, and had been a little puzzled by what it could be. The closest she'd
come to was a school-child's practice slates, but the sound he made with
his wooden stylus was totally different than chalk.

Now she could see that it was some tough but malleable substance,
wax perhaps, that he could write on with the pointed end of the wooden
stylus.

He seemed to be going over figures, from the vertical columns and
spacing, with frequent reference to a little leather-bound book he'd pulled
out of a pocket. Perhaps he was pricing his goods, she thought, now that
he'd paid off the waggoneers.

The sailors did something to a bright yellow sail, and the boat began
to move more decisively eastwards. The current was stronger here as well,
and Jullanar found her thoughts derailing as she tried not to let herself

become too queasy. The leather aftertaste of the water was thick in her mouth.

Pelo Camios looked up when the wherry rocked over a particularly large swell. He did not seem alarmed, rather the opposite in fact, for he smiled broadly and put away his books. He tapped Jullanar on the shoulder, making her focus on him instead of the way her stomach felt.

"Come," he said, "see" *something*. He stood up, offering her one hand; his other held onto a railing on his other side.

Jullanar didn't think that moving would help, but perhaps it wouldn't harm, either, and in any case she'd be closer to the edge of the boat. Even she knew that was a better place to be if you were sick.

She stumbled after him, attention between her nausea and her balance, and was grateful to reach the railing running around the top edge of the boat. There was some sort of wooden rung here, maybe to attach ropes to, and she gripped onto it firmly before she dared look up.

They were slanting across the current of the river, as she'd guessed from the bumpiness. What she had not expected at all was to be able to *see* the current, not just in the form of eddies and little whirlpools, but in a totally different colour of water. Running down the middle of the wide expanse of plum was a clearly demarcated stretch of clear blue-green water.

"*Oonar Farnvo*," Pelo Camios said, pointing to the plum side, and, indicating the clear stream, "*Oonar Onartha*."

Two names for two colours of water. Jullanar stared at the way that the waters ran alongside each other, not mingling at all as far as she could see.

Was this, too, to be answered by magic? Did some strange force keep them apart? Yet looking down she saw a long lithe silver shape—a fish?— come out of the murk and into the clear without any evident difficulty.

The clear water was much more attractive looking, bright and glittering and clear down many feet. It was also much more turbulent, which seemed unfair.

Jullanar gripped the railing and tried to look into the water, but the motion of the boat and the motion of the ripples were not in synchrony and she found herself starting to heave.

Pelo Camios made a startled noise and backed away. When she realized, several minutes later, that he had abandoned her to her lonely post, she could not find it in herself to be annoyed.

She was on the leeward side of the boat, which was a small mercy. She had also not eaten much that morning, which might or might not have been, as her stomach did not seem to care.

Eventually they crossed out of the turbulent clear water and back into the much more staid and solemn plum, and Jullanar was able to stand upright for a bit and breathe.

The eastern bank was visible now as more than simply a blue haze. It seemed green and gold to her eyes, before the blue haze took over and hid the knees of the mountains behind.

They were clearer than they had been, their white peaks floating serenely above it all. Jullanar would have liked to emulate them, but she felt much more akin to the jaundiced-looking seagull perched a little down the railing from her.

Pelo Camios came over with a wet cloth and another skin of water. She smiled at him gratefully, wondering if he had daughters himself, that he was so kind to her. Wiping her face was a gift from the Lady, to be sure. She was also glad to be able to keep a few small sips of water down.

He watched her cautiously, then pointed towards the still-distant bank. Something was five something else away. She nodded, though her incomprehension must have been obvious. It was so frustrating not to understand.

Was this how long it always took to learn another language? She had never had the opportunity, or the need, before. The whole Empire spoke and read Shaian; most countries had long since lost or abandoned whatever tongue had been used before the coming of Astandalas.

She had learned a smattering of Old Shaian at Madame Clancette's, because it was considered part of a proper education to know something of the Classical poets. But Jullanar realized she wasn't even sure of the name of the language that had been spoken in Fiellan before the Empire came. There must have been books written in it, for the universities were centuries older than the Empire, but no one had ever mentioned a thing about it in Jullanar's memory.

She frowned out at the purple water. They were drawing nearer the bank now, in calmer waters, once again heading almost due south with the current. Or not quite south; the river was curving in a wide arc. It looked as if it were marshland on the bank: the green and gold stuff were tall reeds. There still didn't seem to be many birds except for the gulls. It was hot, though. Perhaps they were all down in the vegetation.

They swept downriver, faster now, and Pelo Camios came back to stand beside her. She gripped the damp cloth in one hand, the rail in the other, but she didn't feel nauseated now, just sick with nerves. What *was* her aunt going to say?

Pelo Camios was smiling. He seemed to be pleased to be going home. Jullanar watched the reeds march past them, and then they were suddenly past the tall reeds and into an area of lower growth, wild purple and white irises everywhere and some sort of greenish-grey heron standing solemnly amongst them.

The bank was getting higher, almost cliff-like; the soil was layered orange and red, almost as bright as the sails.

High above, a white falcon hovered, as if watching their arrival. Jullanar chose to take its presence as a good omen.

The sailors called to each other, and did things with the ropes, and the boat slowed a little as it curved around a headland and into a backwater of the river, and there—oh, there ahead of them was the Painted City at last.

CHAPTER TEN

IN WHICH JULLANAR ARRIVES IN THE PAINTED CITY

They were heading towards an area of wharves with many ships and boats of all sizes tied up.

It didn't look all that different from the harbour at Fiella-by-the-Sea, though Jullanar was sure that if she'd known more about boats they would have looked foreign, too. Since she didn't, however, she lifted her eyes to the city proper.

Fiella-by-the-Sea was a city of stone and slate and wood. The local stone was a dark grey, and the slate a deep bluish-green; the wood was usually painted white. People tended to put white window boxes along each window, full of flowers through the summer and greenery in the winter. The yards were small and usually full of vegetables and herbs, intermixed with flowers and miniaturized fruit trees. The city, as a result, looked neat and tidy and sober and respectable, much like its citizens.

In sharp contrast, Ixsaa was fantastically exuberant.

Jullanar stood at the rail, staring, her eyes lifting from the bright-sailed boats and ships (even the largest ships had bright sails, many striped or chequered in dizzying display), to the almost brighter buildings above them.

There was one white stone building at the bottom, right in the middle of the wharves—it looked, in fact, as if it might extend right into the river itself—and behind it rose a single white staircase, up and up and up to the top of the high hill on which the city seemed to be built.

Another white building, a temple or a palace or a university, stood up there, keeping proud watch.

To the right of the staircase, the south, the buildings were large and little-windowed. They were probably warehouses, close to the wharves where trade goods were offloaded and reloaded, but Jullanar had never seen such artistic attention paid to a practical building of that type.

Their lower levels were pink and orange horizontal courses—bricks? —and above that a line of white stone, and above that several storeys of bright-painted material in simple, graphic designs.

The building currently before her was diapered in green and yellow and pink diamonds. The one next to it had wide red and purple stripes with large round yellow spots sprinkled across it.

The one next to that was orange and white and purple chevrons. And they kept going, these buildings that in Fiellan would have been plain brick and stone and slate with maybe a few ornamented window frames, maybe an interesting door.

Jullanar tore her eyes from the warehouses before their colours could make her feel nauseated again. Above them was a tower, striped black and white—surprisingly calm, in the circumstances—and then behind the commercial buildings a great jumble of colours, solid whites and greens and purples, and a thousand shades of orange and yellow and red, all the way up to that one white building on the crown of the mountain.

A yellow wall started to her left, she had a brief glimpse of greenery waving from its rough-tumbled top, and then the wherry tacked around to come in at one of the wharves, a little below the orange chevron building, and Jullanar saw her first glimpse of the great Aqueduct across the neck of the *Kisalos* branch of the river—water green as jade, pouring into the plum-red water of the main channel without mixing or mingling any more than the clear stream at the centre had.

The high stone arches of the Aqueduct were a soft pinkish-brown, striped with white and yellow, and at the far side a waterfall poured down into what her aunt's book had said was a deep cistern in the heart of the richest neighbourhood of the city, the Crescent on the Isle of Doves.

A whole flock of doves, white and cinnamon and grey, raised up suddenly into the sunlight, and cut through the wheeling seagulls yammering overhead. Jullanar felt overwhelmed by everything, by the sun and the colours and the newness of it all, and only noticed the sudden jolt that said they had reached the dock.

Pelo Camios came over to her and saw her solicitously onto dry land, her valise and the Precious Box at her side. He showed her to a large squared-off stone set to the side, just at a reasonable height to sit on, and indicated she should wait there. Jullanar was deeply grateful to have a few minutes to sit still on dry land, and to be more or less ignored by the people around her.

After a little while she caught her breath and more or less her composure. She lifted her chin and straightened her shoulders, which always made her feel a little more in command of herself.

Once again she remembered Marianne speaking in such admiration of her cleverness and bravery.

Jullanar did not feel very brave at all, and she knew she wasn't particularly clever, but she had made it here and she refused to be intimidated by crowds of strangers, no matter that they were all speaking a language she didn't have more than a bare few words of, all of them were men, and all of them were busy and hard at work and wearing odd and discomforting clothing.

No. She was a citizen of the greatest Empire of the Nine Worlds, and she was a woman Of Character, and she was having An Adventure.

She looked around. The wharves were bustling, as any commercial dock she had seen. West Noon's solitary ferryman had been the exception, but even there she had overheard someone saying that the main docks were to the south. Pelo Camios was talking to a cluster of men over to the side, all of them gesticulating happily as they spoke.

She could see now that Pelo Camios was ethnically of the city, with dark, curly hair and somewhat swarthy complexion. She saw a couple of dark-skinned men, who might have been ethnically Shaian from their colouring, though they were too far away for her to see if their features and hair were similar as well.

A handful of people were as light-skinned as herself, most of them seeming short, stocky, and red-haired at the same time. Her combination of mousy brown hair and pale skin was nowhere in evidence; back home it was very common indeed.

Clothing was different, too. Here the men doing the actual work of unloading were dressed rather like the sailors on the wherry, with bare legs and knee-length sleeveless tunics in a variety of colours tied with a kind of belt usually made of rope, as far as she could see. The tunics were perhaps a uniform, for most of the boats had men wearing the same colours—all green, or one shade of orange, or pink. She turned her gaze hastily from the bare calves she could see, blushing as she realized what she was looking at.

The sailors went barefoot; the dock workers had some sort of open shoe, both of which struck her as being a little unsafe given how many heavy and sharp things there were around. Neither wore hats, which she thought very odd.

The merchants and their clerks were obviously set apart by their clothing. They wore tight-fitting hose and ankle-high leather boots, the hose as brightly coloured as their buildings and in as many conflicting patterns.

Their tunics were white—which *must* have been expensive to keep clean—and quite close-fitting, with long sleeves; the tunics reached to just above the knees on most of the men, and were tied at the waist with a wider leather belt. Over the tunics they wore an open surcoat of sorts, with wide sleeves to show the inner tunic and contrasting colours on the outside and inner lining. That reached to the knees and was often but not always left open to show off the lining.

There seemed to be two sets of the men wearing these: one, like those Pelo Camios was speaking to, wore the whole lot and seemed, on the whole, middle-aged or older and also wealthy.

Next down were younger men looking attentive and busy, many of them with the waxed-wood tablets she'd seen Pelo Camios use. They were probably clerks or perhaps apprentices. They wore the same sort of garments but in less extravagant colours and designs, and their outer tunic or surcoat was not as elaborate and usually worn closed.

There was one further group of young men, who appeared not to be doing any work at all but were just observing everyone else. They wore the coloured hose and leather shoes of the merchants, but their white tunics were much shorter and sleeveless, like the dockyard workers, and instead of leather belts they wore bright-coloured sashes. Their surcoats were longer, sleeved, and brilliantly coloured.

They were farther away from her and she couldn't see more details than that, but as she watched one walked a little apart from his group to speak to one of the sailors from her wherry, and as he turned the surcoat flared out and revealed that he had a sword belted at his hip.

Pelo Camios left the group he was speaking to and came over to her, rubbing his hands together happily. As he dodged around a coil of wrist-thick rope he nearly tripped over a young boy, who couldn't have been much more than ten. He grumbled at the boy, who called something back, and then seemed to have a thought and beckoned the boy to come along with him.

Jullanar watched this curiously. The boy trotted along, apparently quite happy to be distracted from whatever he'd been doing before. He had the dark curls and tan complexion she'd seen as native to the city, and wore a dirty smock over bare legs and feet. An urchin, she guessed, hanging around the dockyards for little errands.

Pelo Camios had apparently decided he'd had enough of carrying her valise for her, and promptly gave it to the boy. Jullanar picked up the Precious Box, suddenly nervous. "This way," the merchant said, smiling reassuringly at her. "Not—" something. *Not long now*, maybe? She hoped so.

She followed him as he wound his way out of the dockyards and onto the gleaming white stair she'd seen from the boat. She sincerely hoped they were not going to climb the whole thing; it must have been thousands of steps up to the top of the mountain.

The flight was broken here and there by flat places, gathering spots for markets perhaps. They went up three of these—Jullanar was gasping for breath by then—before Pelo Camios, who was also breathing a little hard, decided to rest. The boy was eyeing both of them derisively, but stayed close.

Up here were more merchants, and—finally—other women. They were dressed not too differently from the merchants, though Jullanar was glad to see both tunic and surcoat were much longer for the women, even if still significantly shorter than what she was used to.

She had to admit the way the skirts flared at calf-length was rather pretty, showing off ankles and low shoes, almost slippers, in pretty colours. The bodices were shaped by lacing, and while some wore some manner of head covering, many did not. Their hair was usually worn long, in braids or sumptuous loose curls. Jullanar saw many of them looking curiously at her, but no one stopped them.

Pelo Camios led her along a street that stayed at more or less the same level as the plaza where they'd stopped. It curved along the face of the slope, bright-coloured houses on both sides—no spaces for gardens, here, just great terracotta pots containing trees or vines climbing up the facades. The doors were wooden, bound with elaborate ironwork hinges, often studded. They gave no hint of what was behind them.

The street turned into a staircase that went down, though not as far down as the docks had been. They passed a small green space around a fountain, where several young men and women about her age were lounging about in the ineffable attitude of students and their friends. One called out a question, to which Pelo Camios only laughed and shook his head.

Jullanar felt a pang that she would not be part of the students' number.

Not here, and perhaps not at all, unless she was able to earn enough money here to pay for next year at Galderon. The money from her father was nearly all depleted by the expenses of the journey, and she had only the small savings she'd brought from home, the gleanings of birthday and Winterturn gifts over the years.

She had not always been as thrifty with those as she probably should have been.

They came to the yellow wall. It must have been imposing at one point; it was still impressive. It was made of huge blocks of a rough-textured yellow sandstone, crumbling at the edges and much colonized by plants. The most obvious were a kind of orange wallflower, clashing horribly with a clove-pink of some form; there were also great sheets of a purple bellflower and cataracts of something with white and pink and red particoloured daisy flowers.

The road led them under the wall, through a tunnel that must have been nearly ten feet in length. Jullanar wondered how much higher the wall had been in its prime, when surely it had enclosed the city in its entirety.

The city sloped away from them on the other side of the wall. Jullanar caught her breath at the sight, and stopped despite herself. The boy rolled his eyes, but Pelo Camios smiled at her.

She was again much taken by how much he was enjoying her reactions to seeing his city, and thanked Mrs. Hawthorne back in the Astandalan caravan for being so careful to find him for her.

The yellow wall was about halfway down the slope of the central hill. The land went down quite steeply—there was a series of stairs here, and it came to her mind that she hadn't seen any horses or carts anywhere in the city, all loads being carried by hand or barrow—before rising up again to a lower height.

There was another wall there, that one of a reddish stone, and beyond that a cluster of pale buildings. Beyond that was yet another wall, this one tall and square, with open gates and pennons flying; and beyond that wall the city stopped quite abruptly, and the green and gold plains and the numerous waterways of the River that Ran Away to Paradise her aunt had described began.

And beyond all that, the white mountains rising up against the sky.

"Come," said Pelo Camios, and she blushed and murmured an apology, knowing he was a merchant and his time was therefore money.

Down they went, between bright coloured houses—red, orange, glaring white—past more huge terracotta pots, and here and there what were clearly shops, doors open to passersby and carved wooden signs hanging from metal poles above them. She tried to look at the signs and nearly tripped herself, only just barely being kept from falling by Pelo Camios' hand on her arm.

What a foolish kind of an adventurer was she!

She was going to be here for some time, for Mrs. Hawthorne had said the trading caravan crossed the Border only twice a year, and whatever her aunt thought of her unexpected arrival would surely have to extend to six month's accommodation. Jullanar could help her with her research, perhaps, organize her notes.

She would still have time to look at these shops, find out what the signs meant—they did not seem to have writing on them—and what they sold here. Tantalizing smells came out of some doorways, and less pleasant ones from others. She sneezed at a whiff of something sharp.

They reached the bottom of the dip, and climbed up another stair on the other side. Jullanar was tired and footsore, and had a stitch starting in her side. She wished she hadn't felt so protective of the Precious Box, and had let someone else carry it. Though she would have felt bad seeing the little boy haul it around.

Finally they reached the red wall, which seemed to be covered in plaster; it was flaking off in places, revealing old brown brick underneath. Strange material to use to build a city wall, Jullanar thought, and then they were through and into the pastel-coloured cluster of buildings.

There was light ahead of them, which turned out to be an open space. A huge building took up most of one side of the square, rambling and disjointed of architecture in a way that Jullanar's sisters would have thought unfortunately picturesque but which endeared itself to her immediately when she saw the sign hanging over its door, a fiery red-and-yellow bird holding a red flower in its claws.

That Aunt Maude had described in one of her few letters, finding it strange and wonderful that the insignia of Ysthar—a world under the dominion of the Empire for many centuries—should be the sign of an inn here in the Painted City of Daun.

And if that were The Rose and Phoenix Inn, then somewhere in sight should be her aunt's place.

Pelo Camios crossed in front of the inn to the lane on its other side, which was half obscured by a tree with hauntingly beautifully scented flowers.

(A lemon tree, Aunt Maude had said; and Jullanar thought she caught a glimpse of yellow amongst the dark green leaves, though she was past it so quickly she wasn't quite sure.)

Jullanar found her heart in her throat suddenly, for the next doorway was open, and there was one of those strange wooden signs hanging from a pole over it, and the merchant was calling out a greeting and going in.

She resettled the box in her grip—her arms were painful after such a long haul—and thought of how she would write to Marianne, whenever her aunt said a letter might be sent, and describe this arrival.

Then she took a deep breath and followed the merchant inside.

Much like her niece, Maude Thistlethwaite did not precisely dislike her surname, but did find it both inconvenient and irritating that almost everyone found it difficult to pronounce.

Unlike her niece, Maude had found this to be the case even with ostensibly well-spoken gentlemen and women from her own part of the world. She had, therefore, made the determination that she did not wish to be tied to her name, and began plotting from a very early age indeed to leave it behind.

Most of her class and generation would have chosen to do this by means of marriage, but Maude had never met any man she could stand the thought of sharing her living space with.

Becoming an eccentric scholarly spinster aunt and haring off on sociological expeditions to the Outworlds, where they spoke strange languages and did not have any idea what her true name ought to be—yes, that was much more her line.

She had, after some thought, chosen 'Shayana', which sounded plausibly West Ertyssian and also neatly denoted her linguistic heritage. It had not even been all that difficult to get used to being called by it. Certainly by her second year in Ixsaa—and it was now her fifth—it was hard to imagine ever returning to *Thistlethwaite*.

It was growing increasingly harder, in fact, to imagine ever returning at all.

Her house in Ixsaa was small, but it was her own. She was considered a wild eccentric, but as a foreigner she would have been one anyhow, and as a foreigner and a wild eccentric *here* she could live just as she pleased.

She had never imagined she would actually enjoy running a shop—it was something her parents would have been aghast at the idea of, for they had ideas of what station their children should aspire to, and Maude, who had come First in the Entrance Examinations in her year and was the Rondelan Scholar to Morrowlea, should have ended up a Scholar at one of the schools on the Golden List at the very least.

There had been a time when she had planned to return, publish her full scholarly monograph on the Painted City—the little book she had sent back to her alma mater to be published was only to ensure that no one thought her dead or totally failing at her work—and take her pick of the positions that would surely be presented to her.

There would be civilized teas, and conversations about politics and scholarship and fashion, and sumptuous academic gowns of antique cut, and the disciplined, orderly, beautiful life of the mind. And no one would think it odd for a Scholar to be unmarried.

She had more than enough material for her monograph. She had almost enough material for a full dictionary of Calandran to go alongside it.

She should, by all rights, be planning to go home on the next trading caravan going Over the River, a journey almost as emotionally fraught for Ixsaans as going Out of the Empire was for Astandalans.

Still, she had her store, which was finally doing better than 'just enough', and that in itself was a triumph of sorts she wished to continue enjoying. She had not expected a stationery store to be such a strange and unwelcome concept, in this city noted for its paints and pigments.

At first she had thought the cool welcome was because she was a foreigner, and a woman, and had chosen the edge of the Greenmarket (no matter that that was the only place a woman, and a foreigner, might be able to own property!—though it was true, also, that it was one of the most interesting parts of the city from a sociological perspective).

Later she had discovered that it was the idea that books were, or could be, accessible to the general public, that had occasioned such astonishment.

Fortunately for her she had managed to arrive at a moment of social change. About a generation before, the merchants and lawyers of the Crescent had finally, and probably permanently, edged out the war-lords and priests of the Old City for control of the city's offices. There had been any number of canny marriages, and a few discreet deaths, and suddenly the sons of those merchants and lawyers were the ones who had wealth and leisure and the promise of power.

It was her error not to realize that movable type had never been invented here, and all books still had to be copied by hand. Still, she made reasonable money on students up from the university and the guild schools coming to take a *pescia* or two of the major texts for copying.

She had made certain her copies were as clean and correct as they could be, and charged a little less for all parts of the transaction than the Apothecaries in the city proper. As she was in the Greenmarket, which had its own bylaws, and was friends with the one lawyer in the city most intimately familiar with those special bylaws, so far the Apothecaries' Guild had been unable to do anything but grumble at her.

She was doing well enough financially to put a bit aside every week, although she had yet to think what she might do with that money one day.

And she had friends, two women as dissimilar from herself or anyone she had ever known back home as she could imagine, who were smart and capable and *stronger* than anyone Maude had ever met. Every time she met up with them, with Kasiar who made her way as a lawyer in a man's city, and Cadia who ran an inn with an iron hand, she blessed the good fortune or fate that had brought here.

She did miss being able to speak her own language, sometimes, and get books in Shaian.

She missed the baths and running water of home, and the good lights —they used oil lamps here, which were dim and smoky things, or tallow candles; beeswax was too expensive except for special occasions.

She missed certain foods, and certain people, and certain quirks of weather or custom.

But above all of that, she *liked* Ixsaa.

It was late afternoon and she'd just opened the doors after a lazy siesta, a day or so before she could expect any of the spring traders to return from Over the River. She had spent the siesta puttering in the kitchen, trying a new bread recipe to bake in the community ovens at the back of the Inn for supper, and was now sorting through a stack of paper samples imported from further along the coast to see what she needed to order as replacements.

When Carleos Camios hallooed her from the doorway, Maude jumped in surprise before jumping up to greet him. He was one of her few allies amongst the Apothecaries' Guild, and also one of her staunchest friends amongst the merchants.

He travelled farther than most, still going Over the River with his men, and always made sure to take her letters and bring her back anything from Out West, as the Ixsaans styled the Astandalan merchants.

"I thought you weren't due until tomorrow at the earliest?" she said, turning to smile at him. "Can I get you anything, Carleos? Lemon water?"

"In a moment, Pelan Maude, in a moment. I have a surprise for you first."

She stopped at the doorway to the private part of the house, for both his expression and his voice were full of amusement. "Carleos," she said warningly, for kind-hearted as he was he was not immune to the odd practical joke. He was not immune to the odd proposal of marriage, either, but took her repeated refusals in good spirits.

"Nay, I jest not," he said, with one of the great shrugs she admired in Ixsaans. She could never learn to be so loose with her motions, so free with her hands. Not though the secluded women of the upper merchant classes *were*, but those a rank or two down, shopkeepers and their wives, had more leeway in their deportment.

He turned to beckon someone behind him. First through the door was a small boy, carrying a leather valise of disconcerting familiarity. While Maude was still goggling a bit at that—for it was the spitting image of the one she'd taken to university, her first year at Morrowlea—a quiet step heralded the arrival of a most unexpected young woman holding a familiar square box.

Half-aware of Carleos paying off the boy and sending him on his way, Maude examined the girl, rifling through memories to determine which of her various nieces this one might be. She hadn't seen them for six years, after all, and the difference between nine to fourteen and seventeen to twenty was considerable.

Not her namesake, safely at Vaunton—unless she'd already graduated? —and not the next one down, who was a simpering miss by all accounts and her own memory. The third one—what was her name? Lavinia?—no, she was the most straight-laced and particular of the five. This one wasn't young enough to be the youngest, and that left—

Maude sighed inwardly. That left Jullanar, the one who always had her head in a romance novel.

The girl curtsied as best she could while still holding the box. "Good afternoon, Aunt Maude," she said politely, though there was a tremor in her voice that belied her apparent calm. "I'm—"

"My niece, Jullanar, isn't it?" Maude said, taking sudden pity on her.

The girl was flushed with the heat and the sun (she was wearing cotton muslin, thank goodness, but otherwise entirely overdressed for the weather here), and her eyes were bright with unshed tears. Her face, which had seemed calm at first, was desperately trying to be resolute.

"I—yes, I am. Please—I know this is so unexpected, but—please, may I stay? I was going to Galderon, you see, only it was closed when I got there, and Papa had given me the box for you and I just decided—"

"To come along with it?" Maude said, beginning to smile, as she realized there had to be a great deal more to this girl than she had ever suspected.

It was no small thing, to decide to leave the Empire behind, let alone to persuade merchants to transport her safely to another world.

"My dear, how could I turn you away now? Come, come, set down that box here on the counter—you must be so tired!"

"Thank you," Jullanar said with heartfelt relief. She set the box down very carefully, turned to Carleos Camios and curtsied to him with all the painstaking effort of a recent finishing school graduate. "Thank you, Pelo Camios," she said, in quite reasonable Calandran. "Thank you so much."

He beamed at her. "It was my pleasure, young lady. You were an excellent travelling companion, all things considered. Maude, could you please tell her she has nothing to worry about? We could barely communicate but she was most polite and accommodating the whole way along, despite everyone else ignoring her entirely."

"No one offered any trouble?" Maude asked him sharply, surveying her niece carefully. She was pretty and young, very foreign to any Ixsaan eye, and travelling all alone.

Carleos shook his head hastily. "Not under my watch, Pelan Maude!" He winked at her. "Of course, I might have put it around the caravan that she was a dedicate novice of the Western Hearth coming to visit her aunt before she took her final vows as a Maiden Oracle ..."

Maude laughed outright at that. "Get away with you, you sly merchant!"

"I shall, I shall, now that I have seen your relation safely to your door. She truly was good company. It did my heart good to see how much she enjoyed the scenery. Not a good sailor, mind!"

"Very few in my family are," Maude replied dryly, knowing he was quite well aware of how she was not one of them. "Stop by again once you have your business settled?"

"Of a certainty, Pelan Maude. I've missed those almond cookies they make up here." He nodded to the both of them, winked again at her, and took himself off.

Maude turned to her niece, intending to question her more of her journey, only to find the girl with silent tears running down her face.

"Oh my dear," she said, and embraced her.

It didn't matter how inconvenient her arrival was or how little Maude had wanted anything to do with any of her young relations.

(That was one of the negative sides of being an academic; one was expected to teach.)

"You're here now, safe and sound. Come have a wash and a lie down and we'll talk later."

"Thank you," Jullanar whispered tremulously.

Maude had to admit that the familiarly accented Shaian sounded sweet in her ears.

CHAPTER ELEVEN

IN WHICH JULLANAR LEARNS OF SERENDIPITY

Aunt Maude was everything, Jullanar realized quickly, that she had ever wanted to be. She was intelligent, obviously, and observant, as she had to be for her work, but also kind, and welcoming, and seemingly unflappable. Jullanar's mother would have been prostrate with nerves to have a guest come unexpectedly to tea, let alone a niece come unexpectedly to stay.

Aunt Maude, however, spoke with Pelo Camios and sent him cheerfully on his way, seemingly entirely unintimidated by the man. Not that he was intimidating, really, he had been so kind, but this whole city was a *man's* city, and yet ...

And yet Aunt Maude had a store here, her very own, and her own house. It wasn't entirely unusual for women to have either back home, but it wasn't *expected*, either.

Aunt Maude, Jullanar decided very quickly, defied expectations. She did not carry on or complain that Jullanar arrived: she closed the outer door, ushered her and the Precious Box to the back room (where she then abandoned the Precious Box to look after her!). Jullanar was led through what seemed to be a kitchen and into a tiled room with a tub on the floor and a spigot with an ewer below it. A wooden rack to one side held a wide towel.

"Now, my dear, wash yourself here while I fetch you some clean clothes. You'll do fine with just a shift for now, I expect you'll want to lie down, won't you? You're still looking flushed from the heat. I'm afraid the baths are not what you are used to—that's a tale for later. I'll lay out a change for you through here, on the bed."

"Is it yours? Aunt, I could hardly—"

"Hush, my dear, you taking a rest on my bed will let me take the time to arrange the other room for you."

To her mental tally of her aunt's excellencies, Jullanar added 'efficient'. Within a very few minutes she had stripped off her dusty, sweaty clothes and washed herself in blessedly tepid water. Cold would have been too much like the sponge baths along the road. At least this time she could take off all her clothes and wash herself properly, except for her hair. She hoped there was a bath somewhere, or her aunt would show her how to wash it in just a basin.

The towel was quite large enough to go around her, though she felt daringly exposed as she crossed the hall to the door her aunt had indicated earlier. The walls were all creamy white plaster, the floors tiled in smooth red terracotta.

This room, her aunt's bedchamber, was small but airy, with a wooden chair, two deep chests, and the promised bed. Jullanar put on the shift which was hung on the back of the chair—it was too large for her, but all the more soft and cool on her skin for that—hung her damp towel in its place, and collapsed on the bed.

She had had no idea how tired she was and how much she was longing to be clean and safe and *there* until she found herself crying with relief.

She really was *not* a Great Adventurer, at all.

Maude ducked into her room to see that her niece was fast asleep on top of the bed. The girl looked very innocent and very young, her hair in a tumbledown braid all frizzed around her skull in a halo from the sponge bath's humidity.

And she had brought so little with her! A valise and the box from

Maude's brother, the girl's father, undoubtedly part of the reason why she'd been sent to Galderon.

There was a story there, to be sure, and Maude could admit to herself that she *was* undeniably curious what had brought the girl to this spot. Ben was not their father, no patriarchal tyrant, and his wife was hardly the sort, Maude had thought, to drive her children a world away. But then again no one had expected *Maude* to go until she had finally gone.

She set the girl's valise down quietly by the door and ducked out again. There were things to be done for any unexpected houseguest, including finding the notes towards that dictionary of Calandran that Jullanar was sure to need immediately.

What *was* she going to do with the girl until she learned enough of the language to be useful?

She was still bustling around with the lemon water and a plate of cut fruit when the door opened and her friends came in bearing their offerings for what Maude would have called 'tea', back home, and which took the place of the noon meal here where the sun caused everyone to aestivate.

Maude welcomed them, shooed them into the back courtyard, and returned to check on Jullanar. Knowing Carleos Camios, the girl would have been as well-fed as he himself was through their journey, and if she were as bad of a sailor as Maude was herself, well, she probably wouldn't be up to stomach any food for another few hours at least. Maude decided to leave her to her rest, and went back to her friends.

Kasiar accepted the glass of lemon water with an appreciative groan. "I can't believe I'm saying this, but I'm sorry Rean's gone. At least when he was around Damian had one interest outside of fencing. Now all he does is exercise and sulk."

Cadia spooned a handful of olives onto her plate. "Grim and silent is perfectly acceptable in a bouncer. Everyone is terrified of him. I've never had so few problems."

Kasiar laughed reluctantly. "Oh, my poor dear. I think they must have had a fight before Rean left, but he won't talk to me about it." She considered, and added. "To be fair, not that he's ever talked about anything but fencing."

"And what Rean thinks," Maude said.

"True enough. He's not even interested in what his brother's doing. I read him Alezian's last letter and all he said about it was that he hoped this Barios proved as a good a friend as Al thinks he is."

"Poor Damian," Maude said, meaning both the first experience of a rupture in friendship, and the wider poverty of his emotional life. She did not quite understand how the sons of such a loving and generous mother could be so narrow—but then, look at her own family, which she loved (more or less) but which she was also glad lived on a totally different world. Or had done, until that day's unexpected arrival.

And—that gave her an idea for what to do with both of them. She smiled slyly at her friend. "I might have a small solution for you."

"Oh?"

"My niece has just come for a visit."

"And?"

"She has a handful of Calandran words, but no more than that, and doesn't know anyone here but me. Perhaps Damian could be persuaded to teach her."

"My Damian?" Kasiar retorted, as if there were anyone else of that name in their acquaintance. "My glowering, sulky, silent, brainless swordsman of a son?"

"He's not that brainless," Cadia replied. "He can smell out a burgeoning fight and stop it before anyone quite knows what's going on."

"He's got good instincts, I'll grant him that," his mother said. "It's not as if I'd fear for her safety. Even if I didn't trust his sense of honour, he's shown no interest in the fairer sex at all."

"I would trust him, if Maude thinks her niece can be sensible. He *is* very good looking."

"Perilously so," Kasiar agreed mournfully.

Maude flicked a drop of water at her. "Enough of that! Carleos Camios was the one to bring her from the Great Western Fair, and he told all the men of the caravan she's a temple-dedicated virgin intending to devote herself as a Maiden Oracle."

"And is she?"

"I very much doubt it, but it will keep others from talking. No one would be surprised that Damian could respect that."

"True," Kasiar replied, seeming to brighten a little at this idea. She added, a little more softly, "I would love for him to make friends his own age ..."

Maude had spent perhaps five minutes with her niece since she arrived, and very little with her when she'd been twelve. What did she remember?

The girl had always had her head in a novel, and was considered overly prone to daydreams amongst her more practically-minded family.

She would have been raised, however, with strict morals and stricter prudery, and Maude was fairly sure she'd be able to impress upon the girl the fact that it would not be wise to develop anything beyond a friendship with Damian.

She knew it was asking too much, youthful passions being what they were, for the girl not to form some sort of idealized romantic idea around him, for he was of storybook beauty; but Jullanar was not, herself, and Maude knew that she would have been taught to look to the attainable.

She began to have second thoughts, but in the few moments her attention had wandered, Kasiar and the Innkeeper had already hashed out a new schedule for Damian that let him have plenty of time for his sword practice—for he was never going to give that up—and also to assist Jullanar with her language lessons.

By the time the two women took their leave, an hour later, Maude had a plan in place. If this didn't work—well, learning to deal with heartbreak was part of growing up, and if Damian (miracle of miracles) reciprocated, well—there were worse possible matches.

(It is possible that contemplating what Damian Raskae might be like as a son-in-law to her brother and his wife gave her enough joy to decide that nearly anything was worth the mere potential of it one day happening.)

When Jullanar awoke in the late afternoon, she was refreshed. She still felt a bit queasy, but wasn't sure if that was due to nervousness or lingering *mal-de-mer*. At the thought of the boat she shuddered a bit before forcing her thoughts away. Unfortunately, the only other pressing matter for consideration was her aunt's real response to her unexpected arrival.

"What *was* I thinking?" Jullanar murmured to herself in faint horror. She had been so focused on getting here that she hadn't truly thought through what *being* here would entail.

Here she had foisted herself onto her aunt without so much as a by-your-leave or a letter of warning, certainly no form of an invitation.

Jullanar felt tears starting, and cursed her proclivity to weeping at any moment of extreme emotion. It was so *wet* of her.

A light tap at the door heralded her aunt's arrival. Jullanar swallowed hard and brushed her face with her hands, hoping the tears weren't obvious.

"Good afternoon, Aunt Maude," she managed, standing up to curtsy as best she could in the shift. Madame Clancette had been very keen on the merits of constant politeness when facing adversity.

Aunt Maude surveyed her with a slight purse to her lips that Jullanar couldn't read. Her aunt vaguely resembled Jullanar's father, but she was a lot younger than him. Jullanar wasn't very good at guessing ages, but she thought her aunt couldn't be over forty, a good decade or so younger than her father.

"Good afternoon, Jullanar," was the eventual reply. "Are you feeling better?"

"Yes, Aunt. Thank you."

"Why don't you get dressed, dear, and then come through to the back *faila*—the courtyard, that is—and you can tell me why you're here."

"Yes, Aunt," Jullanar replied, and curtsied again in the hopes that her panic wouldn't show. Her aunt went out, and she sagged against the bed for a moment in anxious relief, before going to her valise and finding the crumpled round gown that she had, once again, kept for her arrival.

Maude surveyed her niece when she came out again, dressed now in a pink gown that was not entirely unflattering, in the Fiellanese style that looked so odd to her eyes now. The dress went down in several layers of petticoats to ankle height.

It had a corseted bodice, though not the extreme kind (in vogue with the richer sort of aristocratic ladies when Maude was at Morrowlea, derived from Astandalan court fashion) that had required assistance to get into and out of. This one must have laced at the front, though its ties were hidden by the dress. The neckline was high, and the sleeves slightly puffed above the elbow.

It gave Jullanar some definition to her curves; the girl still had some growing into herself to do.

Jullanar curtsied again when she entered the courtyard. Maude indicated that she should sit at the chair opposite her (not long vacated by Kasiar), which she did with the upright carriage—spine well away from the back of the chair—that was considered *de rigeur* for a gentlewoman. Maude herself had largely given up on that particular practice.

"Thank you," Jullanar said shyly, face pink with embarrassment. "I'm so sorry for arriving so unexpectedly, Aunt Maude, but I couldn't think what else to do."

Maude was deeply curious what had led to this arrival. "Have a glass of lemon water, my dear," she said, "and tell me what happened exactly to bring you here?"

Jullanar hesitated briefly, before she visibly steeled herself and began her account with her poor showing in the Entrance Examinations.

Aunt Maude's courtyard garden might have become Jullanar's favourite place, bar none, at first sight. It was a tiny place, perhaps fifteen feet square —a reasonably sized room indoors, but outside practically an inglenook. It was surrounded with plastered walls painted a deep cobalt blue, except for the frames around the doorways (there were two) and an arched aperture, which were all white.

There was a narrow earthen bed around the base of the walls, which was overflowing with flowers, vegetables, and vines all jumbled together. Several of the huge terracotta pots stood on the yellow sandstone paving, and those were full of flowers, too, most of whose names Jullanar didn't know in Shaian, let alone Calandran.

The centrepiece of the largest blank wall was an apricot tree, espaliered in the shape of a fan, and in the middle of the yard was a round wooden table and four comfortable wooden chairs. There was a parasol on a pole in the middle of the table, to protect against the already-bright sun. It was made of a heavy canvas with each of the triangular segments dyed a different shade of red, from cream all the way to a deep plum even darker than the river.

Jullanar sat there, sipping the lemon water her aunt had given her and nibbling at a crumbly, not too sweet, almond biscuit. Her aunt surveyed her thoughtfully after she finished her tale.

"So, to summarize," Aunt Maude said, "you are here due to taking advantage of serendipity."

"I beg your pardon, Aunt?"

"Serendipity is the quality of finding something you are not looking for, and the knack of realizing you have found it when you do."

"What a wonderful word," Jullanar murmured, turning it over in her mind and saying it aloud as well. "Serendipity ..."

"And serendipitous, perhaps, here as well," Aunt Maude said. "You didn't do so ill on the Entrance Examinations, my dear."

Jullanar flushed. "I nearly didn't pass at all."

"Anyone in the top third of the results has *passed*, you know. If you had the money, anywhere would have taken you as their student. But to choose Galderon, out of the ones you could have a scholarship to ... an interesting choice, indeed."

Jullanar thought of Marianne's assumption that she must be *most interested* in plumbing, hydrology, or water magic, and smiled weakly before endeavouring to change the subject. "You mentioned it might be ... serendipitous ... here, as well? Does that mean there is something I can do to help you?"

Aunt Maude did not immediately reply, regarding her instead with a serious eye. Jullanar tried not to fidget while under the inspection.

"I have a friend, a notary, who has a son a little younger than you. He is a bit of an odd duck, rather out of step with modern Ixsaan life."

"Would he do better somewhere like home?"

Aunt Maude laughed. "I very much doubt it! He would have done well in the age of heroes, I expect, where he could wield his sword to find glory. He's no soldier or caravan guard, that's for sure, but no scholar, either. His mother is a little worried about him, that he has no interests outside the old legends and his sword."

Jullanar tried, and failed, to think how she might be of any use whatsoever to a young man who loved the old legends of heroism and swordsmanship. She herself did like such tales, of course, but *as* tales. Her Grand Adventure was coming here, to this city outside the Empire, where she could live and learn with her aunt.

"Yes, Aunt?" she prompted, when nothing else seemed forthcoming.

"His mother and I were talking earlier, while you were resting, and we thought that it would do him good to have someone new to talk to, and *you* would be well served having someone to teach you the language and customs here." Aunt Maude paused and looked suddenly doubtful. "Admittedly, I'm not sure young Damian is quite the person to teach you the customs. He is ..."

"An odd duck, you said."

"He's far too young to be eccentric."

Jullanar laughed, then blushed at this display of vulgarity, not knowing that her aunt was secretly relieved that there was more to this would-be prim and proper young lady of Fiellan than appearances suggested.

"Now," her aunt said, "shall we see what's in that box you brought so carefully for me?"

Along with half a dozen books, several packets of letters, a box of tea, and a smaller wooden box that Aunt Maude squirrelled away without showing her, the box held half a dozen pairs of spectacles with lenses varying from those destined for the extremely near-sighted to one pair for someone, Aunt Maude said wryly, with Xharos' eyes.

"What do you mean?" Jullanar dared to ask.

"Xharos is the ancient Calandran god of archery and healing. He's called 'farsighted Xharos', by which really they just meant he had keen vision and could see a long way, but always makes me think of him needing spectacles like these. I can't think what your father was thinking about my sight. Not that I'm not grateful for the variety, but he *must* know by now that I'm nearsighted!"

"Oh," Jullanar said, watching as she carefully rolled the spare spectacles in the felt pouches they'd come stored in. (And wasn't she glad they had been wrapped so carefully! Despite all her caution, there had been that time Marianne knocked her over ... and a few times when the stagecoach jolted ... and that time when the wagon had tilted so alarmingly ...)

She suddenly realized that her aunt had said something further. "I beg your pardon?"

"No matter," Aunt Maude said easily, waving away her blushing apology. "Let me put this away, and then we'll have something to eat before we go see Kasiar and ... young Damian."

~

It was safe to say that 'young Damian' was not at all what Jullanar was expecting.

After she had eaten a cold white soup (made out of almonds and garlic and breadcrumbs, apparently; it tasted utterly foreign and quite delicious), Aunt Maude led her through her house to the store, and through that into the alleyway between her and the Inn.

Instead of going left, into the square, they went right, back towards the wall and the inner city. It had just occurred to Jullanar that she could start asking her list of questions, and was deciding which was most pressing, when her aunt turned in at a wooden door set into a peach wall.

Aunt Maude knocked once, then opened the door without waiting for a response. "Kasiar is expecting us," she said by way of explanation. "Come through here, my dear."

She led Jullanar down a cool hallway very similar to her own, though this one was tiled in green and blue rather than terracotta red. The walls had tapestries on them, like centuries-old ones in Fiellanese buildings. These showed a many-towered white castle, something out of a fairytale, on an island in a bright blue lake, and knights and grand ladies riding horses, eagles and falcons on their wrists.

Something about the style of the castle teased at her memory. Where had she seen something like that? It wasn't long ago ...

"Pelan Kasiar," Aunt Maude said quietly when she noticed what Jullanar was looking at, "is not from Ixsaa, but a place upriver, in the mountains. She hasn't told me more than that, but then again I haven't told her all that much about where I—where *we*—are from, either. As you learn more of the language and the culture here, we will talk more about that."

"Yes, Aunt Maude," Jullanar replied, guessing (after a moment's confusion) that this had something to do with her aunt's sociological studies.

Aunt Maude knocked lightly on another door, this one a light-coloured wood, and when a woman's voice called, "Come," in Calandran, ushered her in.

Jullanar followed obediently, finding herself in a square room with a few seats—a bench and several wooden chairs, some with cushions and the others with woven rush seats. There were more hangings on the walls, as well as some other curious objects on several side tables and bookcases.

Standing in the middle of the room was a woman of such presence and beauty that Jullanar instinctively curtsied when their gazes crossed.

Aunt Maude put her hand on her shoulder and squeezed gently. "Pelan Kasiar, Damian, this is my *uzra*, Jullanar. Jullanar, this is Pelan Kasiar and her *yzon*, Damian."

Jullanar curtsied again and knew she was blushing.

Pelan Kasiar was tall and light-skinned, though her hair was a rich chestnut brown. She wore it up in a crown of braids, with silver hairs spiralling through the plaits. That was the only real indication of age; otherwise she could have been anything over thirty. She had large, luminous grey eyes, a thin, regal nose, and an oval face that Jullanar swore to herself would always henceforth be her standard of female beauty.

Her son, 'young Damian', the odd duck, looked like an incarnate god.

Jullanar blushed merely looking at him, and stood there, eyes cast down, aghast that her aunt expected her to be able to function in his presence, a little pleased to be trusted to behave herself, a little chagrinned to know that a young man such as this one would never look twice at *her*.

He was fair, with hair out of a storybook—*blond* did not seem to convey its tousled golden glory, the way it was at once pale tow and glowing gold. He wore it shorter than most of the Ixsaan men she'd watched down by the docks, but then again he was clearly not Ixsaan, not with that pale skin and that hair and those eyes, as large and luminous a grey as his mother's.

He was frowning as he observed her in turn, and her heart sank a little, knowing that he could only be looking at dowdy, dumpy, plain Jullanar, with her mousy hair and her freckles and her deplorable lack of poise.

He had surprisingly prominent eyebrows for how pale they were, but perhaps that was because he had drawn them together. His mouth was sulky, and he stood like the dancing master at Madame Clancette's had, one leg forward and one leg slightly bent and back.

Pelan Kasiar had said something in Calandran to Aunt Maude, to which Aunt Maude nodded. She smiled at Damian, who gave her a short, abrupt nod in return.

Aunt Maude then turned to Jullanar. "He'll come fetch you from my store tomorrow morning after breakfast for your first lesson, if that's all right with you?"

All Jullanar could do was nod helplessly and thank them.

CHAPTER TWELVE

IN WHICH DAMIAN HOLDS HIS FIRST LESSON

Damian watched Pelan Maude take her strangely dressed niece back after an excruciatingly boring half an hour's stilted conversation over cold mint tea.

He did not usually stay while his mother and her friends visited, for the simple reason he had no interest in their conversation nor they in his activities, but he knew this was a necessary preliminary to his agreed-upon task.

He didn't participate much in the conversation, leaving it to the women to talk about Greenmarket gossip. He observed the niece, Jullanar, instead.

To begin with: Jullanar was quite a lovely name. It sounded almost Tanteyr, which his brother would not have liked but which Damian found pleasing. It ended properly, with an *ar* sound. He found it made him already better inclined to this duty.

The girl herself was obviously shy, as befitted a prospective Maiden Oracle, and dressed in strange garments that he hoped were not necessary to her vocation, because they were not very appropriate or convenient for going out into the reed plains. He couldn't think of a way to ask that in front of her aunt, however, so resolved to broach it with his mother after their guests had gone home.

So: shy, and very polite—she curtsied on seeing his mother, which also pleased him. She was a little clumsy, and perhaps a little plump, too.

He frowned at the thought, wondering if Maiden Oracles were like merchants, and the fatter the better. He hadn't seen many priestesses outside the quarterly processions, and of course no one saw a dedicated Maiden Oracle apart from the priestesses and petitioners requesting a blessing or a direction of the future.

Still, she wasn't a cloistered priestess *yet*, and he felt a prickling unease that she might not know how to properly defend herself. Even Alezian could defend himself, when he wasn't surprised by too many footpads.

He nodded to himself. He could share the wild places with her, and it would make everything go much smoother—he would feel much better— if he also made sure she could handle a knife, and maybe a bow, and perhaps the small sword wouldn't be too heavy for her—

Oh. They were leaving. He got up with his mother, surveying the girl's motions as she went out behind her aunt. Perhaps the clumsiness was all to do with being amongst strangers whose language she didn't speak.

That couldn't be easy at all.

~

In the morning, Damian thought about his planned first lesson as did his routine—along the Flood Wall to the edge of the Pigmenters Vats, along their side wall to the New Wall, along its irregular and broken top all the way around Mount Zahar until he reached the aqueduct.

Afoot along the narrow parapet of the canal until he reached the bridge to the Isle of Doves.

In a bid to increase his shoulder and arm strength he now went both out and back hand over hand along the undergirding of the bridge until he came back on the city side a jump away from the Harbourmaster's Tower.

Down the Tower's curving face to the docks, lightly across the beams of the riverboats to the Sea Goddess' Temple, then all the way up the Stair of Ten Thousand Steps, though he was still only able to take them two at a time for the first two flights; he managed an extra five steps this morning.

As a cool-down he walked the ceremonial spiral road from the Sky

God's Temple down to the northern stair, and arrived back at his mother's house as the sky shifted from grey to gold and pink.

He washed in the trough, then joined his mother for breakfast before she went to her work and he went to fetch his student. He had decided to bring both his usual sword and the lightest of the short swords for her, along with a set of daggers. That way he could break up the drudgery of memorizing words with something much more fun.

His mother crossed his path as he was closing the door to the weapons closet in the yard.

"Are you expecting to meet anyone, Damian?" she asked as he tucked a third dagger into his sash and slung the baldric of the short sword over his shoulder.

"Pelan Maude's niece Jullanar," he replied, suddenly unsure. "There wasn't anyone else, was there?"

His mother paused, but he couldn't see her very well in the still-shadowy courtyard. He heard her shift a bit on the stones, her skirts rustling. "Not as far as I know, no."

He nodded, reassured. "Have a good day, Ema."

She sounded somewhat bemused. "You too, Dami."

He loped easily down the lane to Pelan Maude's store. The door was ajar, and he knocked once before going in. Pelan Maude was standing by the counter, her niece next to her looking much more proper in an Ixsaan-style green dress with a flaring skirt and light leather shoes. He nodded approvingly at the shoes. It was good she hadn't worn city slippers intended for nothing more arduous than an evening's promenade.

"Good morning," he said clearly, to both Pelan Maude and her niece.

"Good morning," they both replied, Jullanar half a beat later. Her aunt continued, fixing Damian with a stern stare. "What time do you expect to be back, Damian?"

He considered. There had been a discussion, yesterday afternoon, that Out West they usually ate around noon. "By midday," he decided. That gave him plenty of time to do a practice this afternoon. It had been a while since he pushed himself in the heat, and he didn't have an evening shift at the Inn for a couple more days yet.

"May I ask where you're planning on going?"

There was a faint tremor in Pelan Maude's voice. Damian looked dubiously at her, but couldn't decide if she were concerned or trying not to laugh. He decided to assuage the concern, if that's what it was. He might still not be able to find any adventures, and his one attempt at a friend seemed to have failed dismally—he really wasn't good at following Alezian's lead—but he could still be as honourable as any prince in his mother's tales.

"We shall go for a walk into the commons and along the Pink," he said. "Into the reed-plains for a bit, out of the heat, then perhaps back along the Goldtree, if we get that far. I shall take good care of your niece, Pelan Maude. No one will give her offence in my presence!"

Pelan Maude inclined her head. "Thank you, Damian."

She added a few words in whatever language they spoke Out West, and Jullanar, who had been standing politely and patiently to the side, stepped forward.

Nervousness was evident in every angle of her limbs and motion of her body, and Damian decided at that moment that he would make sure that this prospective Maiden Oracle, who might have to do deal with *anyone* as a potential petitioner and certainly would have to deal with temple politics, would learn what he could teach her of self-defence.

Damian arrived approximately half an hour after dawn, glower in place and sulky look still curving his mouth. Now that she had warning of what to expect, Jullanar felt more able to look at what he wore.

Since this included two swords and at least three daggers this morning, it was not nearly as comforting as it should have been. He wore clothing rather like the young noblemen she'd seen down by the dock, except that his white shirt had longer sleeves and was looser.

His sash was red and he wore the surcoat open. His seemed to be made of linen, and was a dusky blue on both inside and out. It should have seemed plain and dull after the brilliant outfits, but the way he moved, with a lithe grace almost like a prowling cat's, the breadth of his shoulders under the surcoat, the svelte swing of his hips, precluded any such idea.

She followed him out of Aunt Maude's store. He stalked more than walked, the sword at his hip swinging back and forth. It had a thin chain angling back from the tip of the scabbard to his belt, which kept it from hitting the ground or his legs.

After a moment of mesmerized attention she realized she had dropped back too far and hastened to catch up, just as they entered the open square in front of the Inn.

"The *Kistaron*," he said, gesturing at the space. *Kis* was some sort of colour word, she thought—green, maybe.

So this was the Green-something.

Nothing seemed particularly green; it was paved in yellow sandstone slabs, with a few areas of small reddish-orange cobbles. There was a fountain in the middle, made of white stone quite elaborately carved, where a few young women were chatting as one filled an ewer with water.

They broke off their conversation to watch as Damian led her at angle across the square. They were visibly intrigued, but didn't say anything. Neither did he; he nodded once, shortly, but ignored the eruption of giggling that followed his acknowledgement.

Opposite the Inn were a few smaller buildings, pale yellow and pink and orange, hard up against an imposing wall. Damian led her into a tunnel through the wall, which had neither gate nor guard in it that she could see. The cobbled road continued ahead of them for a while, across a grassy field.

There didn't seem to be any people around, though in the middle distance she thought she could see a cluster of huts or a building of some kind—orange against the green—where the road seemed to meet a hedgerow or something similar.

It was already quite hazy and warm. Jullanar was glad her aunt had found her an Ixsaan-style dress to wear, though it felt scandalously daring to have her ankles and calves bare, and only one layer of petticoats beneath her outer skirt. She was also grateful for the straw hat to shade her face, even if that was not something she'd seen any other Ixsaan women wearing.

Damian led her purposefully, strides long and certain, across the first field, but before they reached the building cut off to the left along a beaten-dirt path. This was nicer to walk on, almost springy underfoot, and she smiled at a flash of yellow and white as some small bright bird darted across the path away from them.

She stole a glance at her guide. He had relaxed a touch, his frown easing, though his expression was still quite solemn and a touch sulky.

Perhaps it was just the cast of his face, Jullanar mused, as their path met up with another one at the edge of a canal half-choked with irises in full bloom. They were scented almost like ripe plums with a hint of violet. "A purple sort of smell," she said aloud, amused at the idea. Damian glanced at her, visibly startled.

She blushed, forgetting for a moment that he could not understand her silly notions, and gestured at the irises. He looked slowly from her to the flowers and back again, the furrow between his brows becoming more pronounced again, before his expression cleared and he smiled at her with a sweetness and joy that quite literally took her breath away.

Oh, she thought in confusion, one hand lifting unconsciously to her throat.

"*Orala*," he said, though whether that was the word for irises or something else she didn't know.

"Orala," she repeated haltingly.

He nodded, his expression returning to the solemn, sulky look, and started walking again without further comment.

He led her silently for another half an hour or so, by which time she was becoming tired of walking. They hadn't passed anyone else in all that time. After a while they came to two planks laid over the canal, which Damian took without pause. When Jullanar hesitated a little at the rickety bridge, he graciously turned back and offered her his hand for balance.

On the other side of the canal they passed through a belt of trees that looked like poplars except for being tall and narrow, like a quill. On the other side of that was another field, this one with a few scraggly animals grazing in it. They looked like a cross between sheep and goats, with spotted fawn and reddish-brown wool. Damian called them *lopomai*, which didn't help her much. Her aunt's book had not included very many animal names.

Whatever they were, they seemed entirely unbothered by her and Damian's presence, barely moving even as they came quite close to a few. Jullanar observed them curiously, assuming they were more for meat than wool given their short coats. There were no lambs or kids, which did confuse her as to what season, exactly, it was here.

That field was bounded by larger stream, this one quite an extraordinary shade of flesh pink, which Jullanar (who had started reading Marianne's books on hydrology out of desperation) presumed came from the silt suspended in its water. There did not seem to be a bridge, and Damian, after a considering glance at her, led her off to the left again along its bank.

The path was narrower here, still visible but obviously less travelled than on the other side of the grazing land. The other side of the stream was full of the reeds she'd seen from the river crossing: taller than her head, vertical green stems rising up to sprays of greenish-bronze-gold flowers. There was a scent to the air here, a little like old books, a little like a breath of cold air, a little like the plum-scented irises of earlier.

Behind a thicket of some sort of aromatic shrub with large five-petalled white flowers was a wooden post to which was tied up a little wooden rowboat.

Like everything she'd seen so far in Ixsaa, the boat was brightly painted, this time aquamarine on the outside and yellow and white on the inside. Damian handed her into it. She settled nervously onto the bench seat in the prow, and untied the rope before jumping in himself to take up the oars.

He rowed her downstream, the same way they'd been going, for a few minutes, until they encountered another stream. This one was larger, with water of a limpid sort of brown; Jullanar could clearly see down into its depths, where the bed seemed to sparkle with what looked like bubbles. As she had seen in the main river, the two waters did not seem to mix at all except with the odd curlicue of colour, like a drop of ink on first landing in a glass of water.

"*Niora Fal,*" Damian said, pointing at the pink stream, and, "*Niara Axhiniar,*" pointing at the brown one.

Jullanar nodded, then, when he looked at her expectantly, repeated the words carefully. He nodded once, then took up the oars again and rowed them smartly into the current of the Axhiniar. Jullanar marvelled at the fact that he seemed to find this just as easy as rowing downstream.

He was a very good rower, barely making any noise at all.

The day was warm but pleasantly shaded down here with the reeds rising up above them. She would have expected midges or flies, but there didn't seem to be many of those, either. As they went deeper into the reeds, the water seemed to lighten in colour until it looked like the amber jewelry her mother wore on special occasions.

A breeze came up, rustling the reeds high above them. As the flower-heads swayed light splashed down, like water cast from a fountain, flakes of white and gold catching on the water, on Damian's bright hair, on the sword he'd set carefully at his feet.

Jullanar relaxed under his obvious expert care and the feeling of being cocooned in a place far away from all the cares of the world.

Damian's face was a study in serenity, his slight pout no longer a distraction, his eyes wide-open but looking past her, his shoulders and arms moving smoothly, easily, as if he were a bird on the wing.

This, thought Jullanar clearly, *this* must be what it meant to be happy.

Damian was quite pleased with his new student. She was terribly unfit, as bad as Alezian ever had been, but she made no demurrals or difficulties about leaving the road and heading into the reed beds.

And ... she was alert to the beauty of the day, in a way he hadn't ever seen anyone else be, and he was glad in a way he hadn't been except in that first flush of friendship with Rean.

Except ... even then he had been aware, always, of what Alezian called the *transaction*.

Damian had admired Rean's reputation and skill with a sword and liked that Rean thought him worth talking to, worth taking about with him, but he hadn't actually liked anything they did together except for the fencing.

Perhaps, he mused as he rowed up the Amberwells Brook into the midst of the reed plains, it was because this relationship had started out quite deliberately as a transaction, a favour. He glanced briefly at Jullanar's face, insofar as he could make it out in the dappled light falling between the reeds. She was smiling dreamily, her whole demeanour relaxed and appreciative. The nervousness had subsided, and he nodded inwardly.

Yes, he could take her to the quiet places. He would wait and make sure she was what he thought before he took her to his secret places, but she had looked at the water and the land and the light on the water and the fragrance of the purple irises rising up and blushed for their beauty, and Damian was so, so glad, for Alezian did not look outside the city for beauty, and Damian had never been able to understand what his brother saw in his trinkets and treasures.

He tied his dinghy up to the post he had hammered in to mark the edge of the inner marshes. If one continued upstream, as they would on leaving, the Amberwells would lead eventually to the pools from which it took its name, where people came to catch ducks and snipe.

No one else came downstream this far, because between the pools and here was a complicated system of branching waterways. Damian knew their routing backwards and forwards, as one must when rowing. He supposed no one else really cared for the wild things except as a resource, and did not pursue them farther than necessary.

He helped Jullanar get out of the boat, slinging the short sword back over his shoulder once he made sure she was steady on the bank. There was a little hint of a path here, leading from his post to the glade where he most often practiced fencing. He was always much more careful not to leave any signs of his passage in any other direction.

Jullanar stayed close behind him. Her steps were fairly light, though she crunched on dried stems and made enough noise that the marsh creatures fell silent as for any hunter or ochre collector. Damian resolved that he would teach his student how to walk quietly, too. She appreciated the wild lands, and would surely appreciate its inhabitants once she learned to see them.

But that would come. First he had to be sure she could defend herself. *Most* people would leave a prospective Maiden Oracle alone, but there were always those who had no decency or care. He had promised her aunt that he would see her safe, and he had meant it.

They reached the glade, which was a circle about twenty feet wide. He wasn't entirely sure what had made it in the first place, but he had widened it carefully over the years, cutting down reeds and laying them crosswise on top of brush and logs on the moist earth at the edge of the streams, layering that with mud and with more reeds until the mud dried firm and secure.

He had brought a few things to use in his practice: a log to sit on when he felt like resting or to practice balancing on at other times, a dead snag he had pounded into the ground to use as obstacle and target, various items to make smaller targets, another piece of dead wood to hang water-skins and extra weapons on.

Jullanar looked around curiously and then stood in the middle, waiting for him. Damian cleared his throat nervously, then handed her the short sword. She took it with a doubtful expression, her hands uncertain on the scabbard and hilt, her posture stiff and hesitant.

He walked forward and showed her how to draw it, then named the parts of the sword—hilt, crosspiece, blade, edge, point—and the sheath or scabbard. He made her repeat the words, then point to the same elements of his longer rapier.

He decided he quite liked her accent, a stronger lilt than Pelan Maude had.

Then he showed her how to hold the hilt, and how to stand, and the first three positions of the classic style. Once he was sure she had them down, he asked her to name the parts of the sword again, and then she looked tired so he sat her down on the log, ran back to the dinghy for the clay bottle of water he kept cooling in the stream by the mooring post, and after making sure she drank her fill told her the names of all the things he could think of in the glade.

She seemed interested in the sword, once over her initial hesitation, so he showed her one of his shorter practice routines, one he thought even a raw beginner could learn.

They spent a few minutes discussing body parts, adjectives, and a few basic phrases—he demonstrated various verbs, making her laugh several times, but never in an unpleasant way.

Then, as a reward, he took her through the whole fencing routine, one move at a time, getting her to mirror his actions and correcting her.

The morning passed amazingly quickly, he thought, rowing her to the Amberwells so she could admire the white swans swimming there, and then all the way to the Goldtree and back to the North Bridge, where he left his boat so they could take the road back to the city.

Really, he thought happily as he saw her to her aunt's door and then loped home, swords jingling pleasantly in their scabbards, this wasn't so bad at all.

Inside her aunt's house, Jullanar contemplated her answer to the obvious question of how the morning had gone.

She wasn't sure she could describe the quiet beauty of the place Damian had taken her to, or the care with which he had positioned her hand on the sword, her feet on the ground, her arms in the air. He had corrected her pronunciation and frowned thoughtfully at her and acted out motion words, and she was tired and footsore and her arms were aching, but she had held a sword for the first time and, secretly, adored it.

Aunt Maude was waiting expectantly.

She smiled at her aunt. "I now know the names for all the parts of a sword, and three different types of dagger. I fear I shall have the most martial vocabulary of any young woman of Ixsaa in short order."

"That is a danger with young Damian," her aunt said, laughing fondly. "He is noticeably focused in his interests."

CHAPTER THIRTEEN

IN WHICH THERE IS MUCH PRACTICE

Damian, Jullanar discovered, was very keen on the merits of repetition. The second morning, when she personally felt rather sore and distinctly disinclined to do much besides lounge around her aunt's courtyard reading a book, he arrived bright and early (so very early) and with a disgusting amount of energy.

When she stumbled out to the door, yawning and with the unfinished end of her braid in her hand, he also gave her a glimmer of a smile, which was entirely unfair.

He led her in the same direction as before. No longer quite so nerve-wracked, and to be fair, less sore the longer they walked, she was able to take in more of the surroundings.

She didn't have enough words to hold a conversation beyond 'good morning', which should have been frustrating but for how restful Damian's company was. She had the feeling that he would have preferred the silence even if they could have communicated easily.

They passed the stand of purple irises, even more fully in bloom today. "*Orala*," she said carefully when they approached, stopping gratefully at the excuse for a rest. At Damian's glance, she touched one of the flowers and made a questioning noise.

"*Oralan*," he said, which might have been the singular. Jullanar touched one and repeated his word, then gestured broadly at the patch. "*Orala?*"

"Yes."

She touched an iris leaf. "*Kis,*" and her scandalously short green skirt, "*kis,*" and then the flower again. "What?"

Damian squatted effortlessly. He stroked the leaf. "*Kiston endon,*" and, gesturing at her skirt, "*Kista vela,*" and the flower, "*Maran oralan. Marna orala.*"

Jullanar wished her aunt's book had been clearer about the existence of declensions.

Once in their clearing, Damian held up his hands, fingers spread. He lowered each one as he recited the numbers.

Jullanar repeated them, smiling, then had a thought—for Damian was so earnest, and she had no way to thank him for his time but to be an attentive student and try, perhaps, to teach him something in return. And so she replied with the Shaian words for the numbers.

One golden eyebrow arched up in elegant surprise. A little hesitantly, Jullanar repeated the numbers again, enunciating clearly. Damian sighed, but there was a hint of a smile in his face when he repeated them back to her, only stumbling once.

And then he handed her the short sword from yesterday. With a severe look ("No more mischief now!" she could hear Madame Clancette saying, which only made her stifle giggles), he got her to recite all the parts of the weapon again, correcting her when she mixed up the parts of the hilt.

(Really, when would it ever matter to her to know the difference between *pommel* and *quillons*?)

"Good," he said. "Now, *erkhe.*"

Erkhe meant *practice*, Jullanar knew, but the way Damian said it made the word seem freighted with significance.

"*Erkhe,*" she repeated dutifully.

"Here," he said, drawing a line in the ground with his booted heel. He positioned her behind it, one toe on the line, the other foot back at an angle, her whole body tilted so that one shoulder was forward, the other back. Eventually he was satisfied with where her feet were and how she was holding the sword. She could feel hot spots on her fingers and thumb from yesterday.

"Good," he proclaimed again, and drew his own sword with a smooth motion "Thus." He lunged forward, front knee bending to a right angle, back leg long and straight, torso upright, sword extended with the point out.

He repeated this ten times, counting out loud as he went. Jullanar watched him, enjoying the play of his muscles, and only belatedly realized she was supposed to be paying attention so she could copy the motion.

"Now," he said, when he had finished his ten. "You."

It took her more than ten tries before he was satisfied with her basic form. She could not get anywhere near so low down as he could, her bent knee refusing to lower into a right angle, but he was happy with her posture.

("Upright carriage at all times, girls!" she heard her mother say, and again had to suppress giggles, for her mother would certainly not appreciate her learning how to hold a sword.)

"Good," he said at last, and retreated ten paces across the clearing so he faced her. He lifted his sword up vertically before his face in what she could guess was a kind of salute, which she hastily copied. "Now," he said again, "*erkhe.*"

He lunged. "One."

It warmed her considerably that he said it in Shaian.

She lunged and spoke in Calandran. "*One.*"

"Two."

"*Two.*"

Practice. Right.

Jullanar could not, of course, spend *all* of her time with Damian. He was busy doing whatever else he did with the rest of his days, and so Jullanar occupied her time assisting her aunt around her house and to a limited extent in the shop.

Jullanar had been taught, like her sisters, all the basic tasks of running a small household. The idea was that she would have a housekeeper and a maid of all work and a husband who could afford all the small magics that made living in the Empire so pleasantly civilized.

Actually, personally, manually scrubbing the floor was not a task she had ever done.

Jullanar found herself cheerful in the face of this unpleasant task, for her Aunt Maude was hardly a stern taskmaster—her joy in being able to hand over the task to Jullanar was so obvious as to be quite endearing, really—and Jullanar was very mindful of the fact that she had landed upon her aunt as a dependent without any warning.

If life in the Painted City required scrubbing, well, Jullanar couldn't truthfully say she was *glad* to do it ... but she didn't mind, either.

It would have been almost soothing if she hadn't had to go fetch water from the fountain for nearly every task. Her aunt had a cistern collecting rain water, which she used for cooking and drinking. Watering the pots in the back courtyard, cleaning, and bathing was all done with water from the fountain. This was another task her aunt gladly let devolve to her.

The first few days Jullanar could not do much besides smile shyly at the other women and girls collecting their own ewers of water. Most of them regarded her with a speculative expression that was not exactly unfriendly but was not particularly welcoming, either.

"They are still trying to figure you out," Aunt Maude said placidly when Jullanar hesitantly reported this, one afternoon when she was assisting hanging sheets to dry. She then winked. "To be honest, they're still trying to figure me out."

"I thought this was the part of the city where foreigners lived?"

"It is, to be sure, but it was its own village as well, long ago, and the Greenmarket still holds strongly to its ancient identity and traditions."

"That's why you, a woman and a foreigner, can own a shop here."

Aunt Maude smiled. "Exactly."

Jullanar pegged out the next sheet thoughtfully. (She was rather tired, washing bedding having been much more onerous a chore than she had ever realized. She promised herself she would never take launderers or maids of all work for granted again, even if in the Empire they had those useful charms for heated water to assist with the process.)

She had started to wonder a bit about what story her aunt gave to people. "Have you not said much about where you are from? Do they know you're here studying their culture?"

Her aunt laughed. "Certainly not! That's not the way to get objective results. No, they think me come here to the city because it *is* the city, where there are opportunities. My friends know I come from Over the River, from a small town far away from here where they speak another language, where the new trade-goods come from. Other than that? We all have our secrets, Jullanar."

Jullanar's secrets were few, but precious for all that. "The new trade-goods ... From the Empire, of course. When did they start coming here?"

"Lord Eidan discovered the passage through to Daun about twenty years ago. After the wizards did a preliminary anchoring of the route the first merchants came through, oh, about fifteen years ago now, I think it would be. That's when I started to hear about the goods coming back the other way, at any rate. The paints from here are spectacular, much higher quality than anything we can get at home."

Jullanar thought back to those three stone lanterns, encrusted with lichens like the oldest grave-stones in the cemeteries back home. They had looked much older than twenty years.

"It surprises me they don't have equally great paper or visual arts."

"There are a few good fresco painters down in the Crescent. Now that there's a university—it's only a generation old, can you believe it?—there are more educated people who in turn want more lovely things, and have the money for it. Of course, if the Empire comes, there will be plenty of opportunities for artists of all sorts."

Jullanar glanced at her, remembering what the Faradays had said. "Do you think that's likely?"

"Not while you're here," Aunt Maude said comfortingly. "It's still only trade-goods. Once the merchants start coming across the River I wouldn't be surprised if an army came soon after."

"And ... wouldn't you mind?"

Aunt Maude looked at her seriously. "This is a fascinating place, Jullanar, but it holds no candle to the Empire. Imagine how much more art, trade, scholarship—everything!—there would be once it's part of the Empire. It would be the start of a great renaissance for Ixsaa."

Jullanar said, "I suppose," and valiantly tried to imagine it. A month ago she would never have hesitated in saying that it was far better to be part of the Empire than not; and after thought she still came to that conclusion; but she did have to think.

A week after Jullanar's arrival, one of the young women her age greeted her at the fountain.

"Good afternoon," Jullanar replied in surprise, smiling back at her.

In general, she thought the citizens of Ixsaa were all considerably more attractive than the equivalent back home in Fiellan. They tended towards a deep tan skin, with shiny black hair quite often curling into ringlets. Men in the Greenmarket wore their hair in bowl-shaped crops, while young women had long hair and older women usually headcloths.

They were shorter than she was used to—here she was resolutely average, rather than short—the young people slim and active, the older ones tending towards comfortable plumpness. All in all, Jullanar felt herself still plain in comparison, but making up for that with her exotic colouring, so it didn't seem nearly as hard to bear as back home.

Even so, the girl who had greeted her was beautiful, all flashing dark eyes and red lips and dark curls tied back with a red ribbon. Her skirt was red, too, with an orange sash, her bloused top white linen embroidered with red and black patterns.

The girl said something else, too quickly and too strongly accented for Jullanar to catch. "I'm sorry," she said, "I am only learning Calandran."

"You are from far away, then," the girl said, enunciating carefully, "if you do not speak the *something* language."

"Over the River," Jullanar agreed, as her aunt had told her.

"How then do you know Damian?"

Ah.

Jullanar smiled in sunny imitation of Marianne and asked them to show her their style of spinning.

Damian had thought, on first being offered the job at the Inn, that it was a poor replacement for a man's work. Yet, as he grew accustomed to the addition to his schedule—the *two* additions, including the lessons with Pelan Maude's niece—he found that it was satisfying to stop other people from fighting.

His job was to assist with fetching and carrying as required by whoever was at the bar, which wasn't very often; most often it was to carry the money-box to the locked box in the office whenever it seemed to be getting too full, which it did once or twice an evening. Otherwise he was supposed to stand where he had a good view of all the patrons, and stop them from fighting.

He found himself a handful of good observation spots: one next to the bar, where he could see a good three-quarters of the room without having to move his body; one over by the door to the kitchen, which showed everything but the side hidden behind the back of the bar; and one a little away from the front door.

He liked the spot by the bar best, because he could easily see the front door and everyone who came in.

Pelan Cadia often worked the bar herself, and had a couple of other women who took turns of an evening. There was a constantly rotating handful of staff in the kitchens, which were notoriously bad.

Damian did not understand why it was so hard for Pelan Cadia to keep a good cook, but everyone knew one didn't go to the Inn for the quality of its food. Nevertheless, the food was cheap and plentiful, as was the wine, and the Inn itself was centrally located for anyone taking an evening promenade around the Greenmarket Square.

He stood in the shadows of his chosen corners, watching people come and go, learning the way they held themselves when they had had too much to drink, or just enough that they became convinced of their own invulnerability. Then he would come forward, silent and precise as the marsh fox, the heron at its pool, the falcon dropping down, and fix his chosen target with a cold, disapproving glare.

After the first few times he rarely had to use any physical strength to break up the fights. The first time he came forward, he had been a little nervous in his authority, and hesitated before interceding.

The two men had started to brawl, rolling over the table and sending beakers and trenchers flying. Other patrons were cheering them on or trying to rescue their own drinks, and no one was listening to anything he might have said.

Damian thought that Alezian could probably have argued the men into stopping, but he had no such silver tongue. He was strong, and precise, and knew exactly how to hurt someone: it took him two well placed blows and one herculean jerk to be able to seize both men by the backs of their tunics and pull them apart.

He stood there, angry at himself for letting them get to the point of property damage when Pelan Cadia was trusting him to keep the peace, and glowered the two blustering fighters into silence. He knew one of them, Miko, a tanner's apprentice who had been at the edge of the circle around Alezian; the other was a stranger.

"Enough," he said, trying to make his voice low and commanding as his mother had said was most effective. He could feel the strain of holding the men apart and off the ground, and reflected wistfully to himself that he had thought he was strong.

The two men seemed to have calmed down, he thought, so with one final glare he dropped them onto the ground, where they sat gasping and staring at him.

"Pick up your mess," he ordered, and—anticipating a complaint, for Miko had never liked cleaning up after the games, which Damian privately thought was probably the reason only the tanners had been willing to hire him—he added, "Fight again, and you're out."

He meant for the evening, for as far as he knew Pelan Cadia had never permanently turned away custom, except for one man who had done something to a girl in the kitchen (but rumour had it Pelan Cadia had seen to it he wouldn't bother *any* girl any more, so no wonder he hadn't come back to the Greenmarket at all, let alone the Inn). As he stalked back to his observation post he could feel the other patrons' eyes on him, and wondered if they could see how nervous he was.

After that, he had to break up a few fights, but always with people coming to the Inn for the first time, or after a reasonable absence. Sometimes his attention would sharpen on someone, only to find the person's neighbours hastily policing his behaviour themselves.

Damian did not understand this development, and could only hope it did not mean that Pelan Cadia would find him unnecessary after all, for even if people remained as much a mystery to him as ever, it *was* nice to feel he was part of the community, in his own small way.

Without Rean he did not like to go to the caravan guards' practice grounds, which anyway were pretty near deserted with the trading season.

That left the duels, but those were only once or twice a month—he had been fortunate his birthday fell on one of the days—and were anyway very thinly attended, since the Fraternity of the Crescent Blade were starting to focus on the war games held in the summer.

And so he was back to fencing with his shadow, and refining his skills in the wild lands, and trying to learn how to be a part of his city.

And—teaching Jullanar. Not that he could *fence* with her, not yet or anytime soon, but she was losing her fear of the sword and starting to show some distinct improvement. He was proud of how well she was doing.

He still did his morning routine, despite the late nights at the Inn, though in deference to the latter he sometimes rested during the afternoon siesta, which he'd never bothered with before.

He felt physically better for focusing on increasing his upper body strength and for not going out drinking (even as moderately as he had dared) with Rean and his friends. It was good, too, to see his little store of coins start to grow.

He came loping back into the Greenmarket late one afternoon after a long, solitary run through the reed plains. The girls at the fountain giggled as he passed them by, their drop spindles whirling up and down as they gossiped together.

Damian nodded shortly to them. Alezian would have stopped to talk and flirt, but Damian did not understand how he always knew what to say to make the girls laugh and respond warmly.

When *he* spoke to them, as sometimes happened if he were sent to get water for his mother, they always seemed to be muffling the kind of laughter that was aimed at him, not the kind that he could participate in.

And Jullanar wasn't there to help bridge the gap. She didn't have many words yet, but she was beginning to be able to hold a simple conversation—even with the girls at the fountain—and yet, instead of drifting away from his company, she'd instead started to add to it. When she was sitting at the fountain with the young women, she would greet him and they would exchange a few easy, unthreatening comments, about the weather or the bakery's offerings or the like.

One of the young women there now giggled, and Damian hastily strode on. Jullanar must be with her aunt. Perhaps he could visit with her, talk for a bit.

It was one of Pelan Maude's open days, he saw as he entered the street between the stationery store and the Inn. A cluster of young men stood there, laughing and talking over their books.

Damian assessed them. His heart sank as he took in the rich, deep colours of their knee-length open vests, the velvet caps, their shoes with the upturned toes. These were students at the university; more than that, he recognized at least two of them as Alezian's friends.

You had to be wealthy to attend the university, able to afford the clothes, the tuition, the materials. You also had to be smart, able to read and write fluently, able to memorize long arguments and replicate them in vigorous debate. The two who had been at the law guild school with Damian and Alezian were the sons of the leading barristers of the city, the ones who argued cases for the richest merchants.

It would be obvious if he turned around now, and he had no reason to. It was not as if he were *afraid* of them.

They saw him, nudging each other with their elbows, all falling silent and turning to watch his approach, like a row of squabbling seagulls seeing a sudden threat.

(What sort of threat could he pose to them? They could talk him in circles, as they all well knew.)

Damian slowed down into a deliberate saunter, shoulders back and loose, just as if he were in the Inn watching a potential fight brewing. Jullanar was nowhere in sight, unfortunately.

"Damian," one of Alezian's friends said.

Damian stopped, as was polite. He nodded his head. "Liro."

"This is Alezian's brother," Liro said to his friends, waving his hand in the air. "He's mentioned him."

The friends made interested murmurs. Damian could feel their attention sharpening on him, but couldn't read their expressions. He nodded again. What was he supposed to say to that? It wasn't as if Liro had actually introduced them.

"We're up to rent the next term's books," Liro said, as if he thought Damian would care. "It's all classical philosophy, of course. Bisus and Vanobios. You might remember we read *The Order of History* at school."

His voice was teasing, edged with sarcasm. Liro had always enjoyed needling him, as if Damian's slowness was a personal invitation to him, or some sort of affront to his understanding of the world. He'd been vocal in his opinion that Damian had no place in the guild school, that he was holding the rest of them back, that he was an embarrassment to the teacher.

Damian had agreed, but his mother had not, and so he went along with Alezian, straining to make the least sense out of the pages set before him, to scrawl something the teacher would accept as writing.

Even Alezian had laughed sometimes when Liro got going.

Someone else came out, setting Pelan Maude's door-bell to jangling, but it wasn't Jullanar, so Damian took advantage of the sudden bubble of conversation to nod again and keep going.

Behind him, he heard Liro's loud laugh. "Him? Oh, he's always like that. Thick as two planks, that one."

That night, Damian decided he needed to do something with his evenings when he wasn't at the Inn. It was obviously inappropriate to ask Jullanar if she wanted to do anything, and anyway she would want to spend time with her aunt before she entered seclusion on taking her final vows. Damian couldn't assume she would be there all the time, whenever he wanted to—and it wasn't as if he needed company *all* the time. It was just that he had been brooding over Liro's comment all afternoon, and could not help but come to the conclusion that his brother's friend was right.

Damian had tried, over and over again, to read, but no matter how much he tried, how much he practiced, the marks on the page refused to turn into words without the greatest of exertion.

It had taken him three years to be able to run up the whole length of the Stair of Ten Thousand Steps, but his mother had started teaching him and Alezian to read when they were five or six, and Damian still couldn't get through more than a page for an afternoon's effort.

He tried that afternoon, pulling out one of his schoolbooks from the dusty shelf where he'd put them so thankfully after he was finally permitted to leave the guild school. He got out his wax tablet and stylus, too, but even with the stylus to help him mark his place on the page he received nothing better than a headache.

He was short with his mother over their early meal, and felt guilty when he left afterwards.

He ran into the night, but the reed plains were no refuge from his own thoughts.

He tried to dissolve into physical exertion, but the shame would not lift.

After a while he decided that what he needed was a legitimate reason to fight someone.

He turned east, cutting across dykes and streams to the higher land where the greyhound races were held. There was no race tonight, but beyond the track was another abandoned quarry where the cockfights happened. Damian slid through the shadows, silently and sure, until he came to the edges of the crowd.

He watched the predators, those men who stood with their central core of menace. They waited for someone to become prey: someone drunk or unwary, separated from his fellows, with a full purse just ready for the taking.

There. That big man had seen something. His attention had sharpened on the plump student who had stumbled off towards the bushes where people relieved themselves. The student (was it one of those who had been with Liro at the store? No matter that; Damian was not doing this for him, for them, but for himself) fumbled with his breeches, staring into the darkness and whistling.

The big man had drawn only a knife; he was twice the size of the student, and his intent was unmistakable. He didn't even wait for the student to finish pissing, and Damian felt his lip curl in disgust at the idea that the big man enjoyed the sight of the student with his prick hanging out, his mouth wide open with shock and fear.

The big man didn't even have to ask for the purse for the student to reach for it. Damian chose that moment to step out of the shadows past the edge of the torchlight. He held his sword, point low, drawn because the big man held his knife.

Damian stepped deliberately into his vicinity, back to the student as he edged the young man over. The big man's stance shifted, muscles gathering at this interruption.

The fight was over in three seconds, two thrusts of the dagger and one stroke with the sword. The dagger fell to the ground and the big man cursed and retreated. Damian watched him go, noting the direction so he could follow afterwards and ensure the man wouldn't be returning with company.

He picked up the dagger, which was of reasonable steel and worth keeping, and turned to go.

"Wait," said the student. Damian looked at him steadily. The student was still holding his purse out, and angled it towards him. "Are you— don't you—"

Damian felt like telling him that he would never succeed in life if he just gave up the moment anyone looked at him, but there didn't seem much point. The student had come alone to the cockfights, or at least left his friends behind, and that was a stupidity he had to learn to correct himself.

The student seemed to see something in his face, for his tone changed to one of puzzlement. "Why ...?"

As if that was a question anyone ever needed to be answered. Obviously he hadn't wanted to see the student lose his purse, no matter how foolish he was being; and also he wanted to fight.

Damian scoffed silently, placed the dagger into his sash, and slid off into the shadows, looking for more trouble of a sort he *could* decipher.

PART THREE

SOMEONE COMES TO TOWN

CHAPTER FOURTEEN
IN WHICH A MONTH HAS PASSED

After a month of daily lessons, Jullanar had progressed to being able to hold a simple conversation. She could expand somewhat more fluently if it were about swords, daggers, or other weaponry.

(She was somewhat curious to know if Shaian had as many words for types of dagger as Calandran did, but Aunt Maude didn't know.)

She and Damian could both count to one hundred in both languages, and she had managed to get to one hundred lunges, once, with pauses between sets.

She had also reached the point of being able to do the whole dance-like pattern Damian insisted she learn without mistakes, though not at all quickly. Damian informed her solemnly that this would come with time, and started to make her repeat certain movements until she was nearly dreaming of doing them.

(Those lunges.)

Damian seemed to be pleased with her progress. He rowed her along various streams and small rivers through the reed plains north of the city, and began teaching her how to move silently.

She had thought she was being quiet, until he had taken her to a distant, secret part of the marshes and made her sit on a dead log and wait.

If he hadn't proven himself always so courteous and (face it) uninterested she might have be been afraid of the solitude and silence. As it was, she had learned to trust him out here, far from the city and the speculative, suspicious glances that followed them everywhere they went together.

In the marshes Damian was kind and even patient, though he switched off to physical lessons frequently enough she was quite sure he was more bored than he showed. In the city, he scowled silently and retreated to a kind of blank glowering disinterest that was rather distressing to observe.

But out here it was different. When he set her on the log and said, "Sit still," she hesitated and then nodded firmly in agreement before arranging herself as comfortably as possible.

Behind her the reeds rose up as high as a city wall, rustling softly in a gentle wind. In front of her was a small open space of shorter grasses and flowering plants, and past a stand of irises (on the cusp of finishing flowering) the limpid golden-brown water of one of the numerous branches of the Axhiniar.

On the other side of the water was a stretch of empty land, almost a meadow, the grasses and herbs tangled about knee-high interspersed with clumps of sedge, cattails, and a few small stands of the tall reeds.

She sat, trying to see what Damian had wanted her to see, to hear what he wanted her to hear. Probably not the flowers. He was not very interested in them, and could rarely tell her what they were. She looked at the white daisy-like things, and purple-red clover, and something with clusters of purple three-petaled flowers, and knew she would have to wait for someone else to give their names.

She knew Damian as well as one could know a stranger in two weeks: his patience and his impatience, his kindness and his flaring temper, his utter devotion to the grace of the sword.

Sometimes he would do his own exercises while she rested. She did not know how to describe what he looked like in those moments, except that he seemed to move with ease and joy and almost the unconscious, unself-conscious ability of an animal. There was something extraordinary, epic, about his skill, even without taking into account his beauty.

She was staring dreamily at the ripples in the stream when she realized the birds were singing.

The lack of wildlife in the marshes had never failed to surprise her.

Her first instinct now was to exclaim and move, but Damian had told her to sit still, and after one unconscious shift she forced herself to do so. There was a slight hitch in the birdsong, but then it returned.

She sat there marvelling as the sound grew louder and louder. She could hear at least half a dozen different birds. Something going *plik-plik-plik*, something else trilling lustfully, another that sounded like a depressed foghorn, something like an abrupt cackle turning to a swallowed chortle. A few piercing, plaintive notes in a falling scale, repeated once, twice, then the same bird caught some avian inspiration and transported its scale into variations on an arpeggio.

Jullanar sat there as the air filled with sound, jaw slack with astonishment, hands gripping the fabric of her skirts. The sound was as deafening as the dead silence had been before.

Movement caught her eye next. She hardly dared turn her head, but did so slowly, trying to find again what motion had drawn her attention.

There, on the other side of the stream: a sparrow launched itself onto a clump of sedge, pecking busily at something she couldn't see. Another motion, farther away: three, no four—no, six—seven?—a whole *flock* of ground-feeding birds, grey and rust and speckled brown of plumage, some sort of partridge or quail.

A clucking trill made her look up. There on the clump of tall reeds nearest the bank was a group of yellow-and-blue titmice performing acrobats along the stems.

A plop drew her eyes down: a frog, two frogs, and then what she had thought a dead stump in the grasses at the water's edge made one sudden stab before returning to stillness, and was instead what she thought from one of her father's books was a notoriously shy bittern.

Another one sat beside it, its beak pointed straight up at the sky so that the striped feathers on its long neck blended with the shadows and grass around it.

She had no idea how long she sat there. Long enough for her posterior to feel numb and tingly from the hard log. Long enough for the birds to sing in full throat. Long enough for a herd of tiny deer, hardly bigger than spaniels, to pick their way out of the tall reeds and graze fearlessly on the shorter grass on the meads in front of her.

Jullanar sat there gripping her skirts, a little thirsty and a little full of the headache and trying not to cry, but also fiercely, desperately glad that everything she had thought about these places was wrong. How could she think there was nothing here?

She looked up and out, to see what else she could see, and was rewarded with the sight of Damian loping towards her. He was running, or that was the only word she could use to describe his motion, but he seemed to be barely touching the ground. Certainly he made no sound.

She held her breath, watching him draw near her. The wind was blowing into her face, bearing with it those scents of honey and snow and plums and something strange and different that she had learned to identify as belonging to the marshes. If the tiny deer and the birds caught his scent, they seemed unconcerned with it, as if he were one of them.

He ran towards her, surcoat flapping softly, feet skimming the ground. Each step brought him closer to the deer, the partridges, the foraging sparrows, the large crested orange-and-white bird that had landed on the dead snag ten feet from her to preen itself.

She held her breath, but though he passed within inches of the birds, they did not move, and his foot landed between one deer and the next, and they only shifted a few steps over, as they did for each other, and when he reached the edge of the stream he set one hand on the topmost branch of the snag, six inches from the orange bird, and with one powerful thrust of his legs he vaulted the stream to land in front of her, it didn't even cease its busy preening.

On the other side of the stream the orange bird gave a self-satisfied sort of chortle and flew off again.

"Hoopoe," Damian said, his voice barely louder than the wind, fitting in to the birdsong as easily as his steps had carried him through the wild marsh creatures.

"Hoopoe," repeated Jullanar almost as softly, but at her voice everything fell silent once more and the deer scattered into invisibility.

It was late afternoon: Kasiar was done her work for the day, and was cooking a light meal, making, as usual, enough for Damian, and wondering, as had also become usual, whether he would be there to eat it.

With Alezian gone and Damian so often out she had returned to the habits of her youth, eating as the sun set and then enjoying time to read or work on her new project of translating the central histories of the Tanteyr into Calandran.

She had decided enough was enough, and if she wanted to make sure her sons did not lose all hint of their culture, she would have to compromise enough to make it feasible for them to do so.

Alezian was never going to learn to read Tanteyr. And Damian seemed to have given up reading altogether as soon as he'd left the guild school behind.

So she cooked foods from the old country, and worked on the histories. On the rare evenings when Damian was home he made no comment about either the timing or the nature of the meal. It was not until Alezian had gone that Kasiar realized how little Damian cared for what he ate except insofar as it was fuel for his activities.

For experiment she tried a series of stews and cold spreads that were uniformly unappealing shades of brown and puce but which were exquisitely delicious. When she took them to lunch with her friends they exclaimed over the colours and shape, and then laughed with delight at the flavours. Damian simply ate.

And if he stayed in rather than going to the Inn or his other pursuits he sat there staring blankly at the wall.

She confessed she preferred it when he was out to seeing that bovine indifference.

Even if it meant he was falling into the rough crowds of the racecourses and cockfights. She held on to the knowledge that he never failed in his obligations either to Cadia at the Inn or to Maude as her niece's tutor. Indeed, both felt he was doing a fine job; Jullanar was slowly becoming able to hold conversations, and was tanned and healthy from all the long walks with Damian in the countryside.

Whatever Damian did on the nights he was not at the Inn, he was not letting it affect his practice or his obligations. Kasiar could be pleased with that, could be *proud* of that, that no matter what else he was, Damian was responsible.

She had not had much opportunity to talk with Maude's niece, who appeared to be shy as well as inarticulate in Calandran. And yet—

And yet she clearly *liked* Damian, and that odd friendship was a balm to Kasiar's heart.

She thrust her rolling pin against the dough, rolling out a round for her pie.

At least their changing lives meant that she felt free to cook what she liked, to recover her sense of her own identity.

She could not depend on her sons to carry forth their ancient culture with pride and glory: well, if that were the case, then it was up to her to salvage what she could of her own sense of pride, of glory, of worth.

Alezian swaggered in—there was no other word for it—as she was folding the crust over the meat pie.

At home in the old country she had been a queen: she had not been a cook. She had had to learn that skill, as so many, after she had exiled herself to stop the civil war. Without cookbooks or cook she was using her later experience to try to recreate those old dishes.

Damian did not care if what she put before him was imbalanced or used the wrong spices or had some strange combination of ingredients. He ate until he was sated and then sat staring at the wall until he was ready to exercise.

She looked up from her crust at a motion in her periphery, flour all over her hands and her apron, and saw in the doorway a stranger.

Alezian grinned at her and swaggered over, slinging his sack down to the floor as he came. He was dressed a new outfit, a fine white tunic and loose trousers, with an open surcoat in violet-blue raw silk.

"Alezian!" she cried, brushing her hands together to knock off the flour, extending them both to embrace him. He, fastidious as always, skipped back away from the flour, then laughed and took her right hand to give it a kiss.

"Ema," he said. "What are you baking?"

"Taroves," she said without thinking, saw the faltering dismay in his eyes, and added swiftly, "Meat pie, that is. Oh, my love, how are you? How was your voyage?"

He needed no further urging to tell her, sitting down at the table to unpack his treasures, explaining how he had taken his small hoard of trinkets and turned it into a small fortune.

Kasiar asked him questions about the ports he had visited, the people he had met, the countryside he had seen, and received answers that—well, showed how he was training his eye to be a merchant's.

At least, she consoled herself, he had a keen eye for beauty, no matter how quick he was to price it.

He was a man now, as much and as little as Damian was, and it was to be expected that at this stage of his life—just spreading his wings for the first time—he would choose his new career first. And he'd only been gone —what? Two months? Hardly that.

Damian came in before the meat pie was finished, sulky and frowning as ever, but seeming, for all that, to be fairly pleased his brother had returned safely. He sat down in the third chair at their little table, looking over the treasures Alezian had already unpacked, picking up odd items to weigh them in his hands.

Something was still missing there, Kasiar thought sadly; something Damian could not articulate. And yet ... he *was* a fine young man, step by step becoming his own person, finding a path for himself that was not only in the shadow of his twin.

"Here, I have something you'll find more interesting," Alezian said, breaking off his description of the famous paper-makers of Vezias when Damian showed distinct signs of boredom. "I thought of you when I was in Vezias—though not at the paper market!"

He laughed and reached into his sack for a small sheathed dagger. "I couldn't afford a sword for you—not *this* voyage, anyway—but here's a knife from the Starmakers, who trade there too. They're supposed to be the best metal-smiths in the south."

Damian snorted, but he accepted the dagger his brother held out to him, and Kasiar was pleased to see that Alezian was a little more patient, a little more *aware*, of Damian's ... character. "Thank you."

"You're very welcome. I bought myself a few books. I've decided to start a library for myself, for when I have my own house in the Crescent. It's going to be the new fashion, Barios says." He nodded. Kasiar felt a small tingle of pride that this son, at least, knew how to use his brain. "Mine will be the best."

Damian snorted again. He was balancing the knife in his hand, eyes alight, attention (Kasiar had thought) far away.

"What?" said Alezian. "There are better things in life than fighting."

"Excellence is always worth pursuing," Damian replied.

"That's practically high philosophy, coming from you," Alezian said, laughing. "What next? A seat at the university?"

Damian ignored this sally as if he hadn't heard it, saying merely, "I think this is a throwing knife."

Kasiar reminded herself that she had decided not to expect things of Damian that he was simply incapable of giving. She smiled at Alezian, who, as if on cue, showed her the new muscles in his arms.

"Not that I'll ever rival Damian in that regard, but then again, I need to spend time exercising my brain as well as my other muscles. Speaking of which, Ema, let me tell you my plans."

Alezian had come home with a respectable fortune, a whole host of new ideas, and muscles that even Damian was inclined to admire. His brother laughed when Damian mentioned his new silhouette.

"I won't be out-matching you any time soon, don't you worry!" But Alezian turned in a pirouette to show off his new outfit, long loose trousers and shirt in fine white cloth, a long sleeveless vest that went down to his knees in a slubby silk whose subtle colours teased at Damian's eye. Somewhere between mauve and violet, he thought, shading to blue and red.

Damian imagined putting on such an outfit, how soft the silk might feel, catching the least breeze. It would be foolish in the little glades in the reed plains, amongst the caravan guards, at the Inn of an evening. He would be able to move in it, but it would tear and soil almost immediately.

Jullanar might like it, but then again she wore practical clothing, pretty as far as it went but never something that she couldn't move in. It was one of the things Damian appreciated about her.

Alezian had come up as soon as they had finished unloading, he said, though Damian supposed he had to have taken the time to change his outfit, at least. "I brought you presents," he added, his deep pleasure in being able to audible. "And I want to hear all your news. Ema, you're still fighting the Alderman?"

"Always," she replied, her voice dry.

"And Damian, still at the Inn?"

He nodded, watching as his brother lifted his large trunk and set it on the table. It was very pleasing, he thought, to hear Alezian so happy, see him so fit as well as happily plump. That was the trunk Damian had carried down to the ship for him when he'd left; he recognized the purplish tint to its leather, the faintest hint of odour left from the dye.

"As talkative as ever," his brother commented, fussing with latches.

"Damian has been teaching a foreigner how to speak Calandran."

"Really? Good on you, Damian! Is he a great swordsman?"

Damian contemplated Jullanar. "No."

"What do you find to talk about, then?"

He shrugged. It was harder to find topics she did *not* want to talk about; he'd tried. Alezian laughed, his attention clearly on his treasures, and Damian relaxed slightly. His brother would laugh at Jullanar's shy concentration, Damian's own inarticulate guidance.

"These are figurines from Undrazh," Alezian said, lifting out small bundles and gently unwrapping them. He showed one to Damian, who nodded acknowledgement, uncertain of what he was supposed to appreciate. Jullanar would know what to look for, what to say, he thought unwontedly, imagining her there in the room with them. She would say ... what?

She would start asking questions about where Undrazh was, what the figurines were made of, who made them, why.

Perhaps his brother would like it if he asked questions.

"What are they made of?" Damian asked tentatively, that seeming to be the easiest.

Alezian turned in surprise. "Bronze. Surely you can tell? Brass is much brighter."

Damian looked down at the table, wishing he hadn't said anything. "Of course."

"Tell us about these," their mother said, reaching out towards something that swallowed the light. "They're beautiful."

"Those are called *torogoto* and they're made from the seed-pod of a tree that grows only at the very tip of the Cape Thuy. It's incredibly hard to carve, they have to use knives with diamond tips. The diamonds are from the beaches down below—the captain was trading for those."

Damian could hear the satisfaction in his brother's voice as he added, "The people down there say they bring good fortune. They've certainly been good fortune to me—I've already increased my fortune tenfold with them, and I still have a few to sell here. Not all of them, though. I thought you'd like one, Ema. As for you, Damian ..."

Damian could not see what was so special about the seed-pods, unless it was their depth of colour.

He wished he could, wished he could think of questions that were not stupid, wished he could enter into the whole world that everyone else knew.

But he could not: not even Jullanar, whom he had taught to look with new eyes at the quiet, subtle beauties of the reed plains, could teach him how to look at the city as other people did.

He looked at the treasures Alezian had brought to show them and could not see what made them better than any of the goods at any market-stall in Ixsaa.

Not that he went to the market-stalls very often. He felt stupid there, too, jostled by the crowds, harried by the sense that everyone else was chattering about ideas he simply could not understand.

Jullanar understood this inability of his, for she had asked one of the girls at the fountain to show her around the market and tell her the names of all the things that meant nothing to him.

He realized that Alezian was holding something out to him. He took it, muttering thanks, and felt in his hands the smooth cool weight of stone. He looked down, sliding his fingers around the object. The stone was dark grey, worn smooth like a river-rock, but with a hole in the middle. It had an attractive heft to it, pleasing to hold in one hand. He had no idea what it was, and ventured to ask.

"It's called a *wharolo* stone," Alezian said.

Damian relaxed slightly. Apparently this was not something he was supposed to be able to recognize immediately.

"Down at Cape Thuy—the same place where the *torogoto* comes from —the people split apart into different groups. Some are traders—they were the ones I was dealing with, obviously!—and some are warriors. They use spears and these *wharolo*. They put a short stick through the hole, like for an axe, and then use it as a war-hammer. I thought you could start a collection of weapons—I'll keep bringing them for you from all around the world. There was the dagger, and this."

"Thank you," Damian said, rolling the stone around on his knee.

"You're very welcome. Now, after Cape Thuy we came up the Narrows of Menay, which are just as amazing as everyone said ..."

Damian sat back, holding the stone—the *wharolo*, he thought, fixing the word in his mind—and watched as his brother punctuated his account of the voyage with various objects. He did not try to ask any more questions, knowing that having to stop to explain would disrupt the narrative.

He had forgotten how well his brother spoke, his words polished, never at a loss to account for anything. Their mother asked a few questions, ones that Damian would never have thought of if he had sat there all afternoon.

He did not have to, for finally Alezian came to the end of his voyage. "Well, Ema?" he said at the end. "What do you think?"

"What a splendid journey you've had, and what beautiful things you've brought back. Don't you think so, Damian? Which do you like best?"

Damian said, "The *wharolo* stone," for that was the one his brother had chosen for him, down there at the far end of the Etransel Gulf where Damian could be no use to him at all.

"Not the dagger?" Alezian said, laughing, but Damian did not know how to answer that. Of course the dagger was practical, a splendid tool, something Damian would certainly *use*. And yet—he ran his fingers along the smooth curve of the stone. And yet the stone *wasn't* useful.

"Are you off now to practice?"

Damian had been intending to stay home and torment himself with trying to read the next page of his book, but he would not be private with Alezian home, and he could not bear to have his brother watch him struggle even more than he had before. He nodded, therefore, and bid his adieus.

He paused in the anteroom to retie his sash so that his shirt did not billow out. He straightened his clothes absently, smiling to himself at the idea of Alezian climbing up and down the ship's rigging until he was sleek and lithe as a cat.

He heard, therefore, his brother sigh and say, "You'd think he'd be more interested."

"He is what he is," their mother replied quietly.

"I'd forgotten how hard it is to talk to him. It's like there's this blank wall where you expect ..."

Damian waited in agony for him to finish, to articulate that secret *thing* that Damian was missing that everybody else had, but he did not. Instead he heard their mother say, even more quietly, with resignation worse than any anger she'd ever shown him, "I know."

CHAPTER FIFTEEN

IN WHICH DAMIAN HEARS OF DISTANT LANDS

Damian ran.

He walked blankly through the Greenmarket first, sliding between the people drifting across in ones or twos after their siesta, barely noticing the sudden weight of heat reflecting off stone all around him. He exited the north gate, a bar of cool shadow, and veered west along the narrower trail because a party was coming along the other. Someone called out a hail, perhaps to him, from their group. Damian raised a hand in acknowledgement but kept to his course.

The sun was high overhead. Immediately north of the Flood Wall was an open grassy area, still green this time of year. In the winter it was grazed by sheep, but they were all up in the mountain pastures by now. Only a handful of wethers remained, being fattened for the spring festival.

After a couple of hundred yards the short grass ended at a ditch full of some sort of pale pink flower, and then there was a band of trees, tall narrow poplars whose leaves rustled in any least movement of air.

Damian leaped the ditch with ease and kept running once he landed. First along the line of poplars, then jigging north when he saw in the distance the dark shape of someone walking.

The open area—another grazing commons—was bordered on its far side by a stand of rushes, lower than the great reeds of the plains further north and hiding many runnels and sudden pools of water. He had gone too far west for the bridge and so turned again to run along the grass, following the edge of the marsh.

Usually it did not take long after he started to move for him to govern his thoughts. It was the heat, he thought at one point, beating down on him like a hammer, heavy, flat, featureless as a wall.

It made him gasp for air (he who could run the whole length of the Stair of Ten Thousand Steps), made the sweat pour down him, made him unable to sink into the physical, the moment of the movement, made those words beat round and round in his brain.

Well, he thought grimly, leaping another ditch, bypassing his little dinghy moored to its post, he would just keep running until they stopped.

He ran out of land first.

He nearly plunged over the levee bluff, only catching himself at the last moment and with a great wrenching of his muscles. He staggered back from the edge, grabbing hold of a smooth branch, lungs burning, face burning with heat and exertion. Down below him the Redwine ran, a deep plum this time of year, like the darker tints to Alezian's new clothes.

Damian sank down to the ground. His legs dangled over the edge of the bluff, his feet turning aimlessly in the air. He could feel the blood pounding in steady waves in his temples, his heartbeat itself sickeningly fast. He gasped, then made himself breathe slowly, in and out, while his body trembled and his muscles twitched.

Far out over the river, a white speck, the falcon hung on steady wings. Behind it the sky was the hammered grey of forming thunderclouds.

Damian stared at the plum-coloured river and the grey clouds and the white bird. Above him the sun rode high in its brassy haze. Everything around him was dead silent, disturbed by his clumsy passage or asleep in the heat.

It occurred to him that there was no tree along this part of the levees.

He turned to squint at the tree that had broken his plunge. It stood black against the sun and dazzled him so he had to turn away, but even as he did so the stumpy silhouette turned into a recognizable human form, and then it was Jullanar murmuring and lowering herself to sit next to Damian.

"You're too close," Damian said, his throat tight.

"Sorry," she replied, edging over a few inches. "Why are you upset?"

"I was running."

"You usually run like a fox."

Damn her *noticing*.

He stared out at the far horizon, his thoughts jumbled. Jullanar sat beside him, quiet and patient.

It's like there's this blank wall ...

He drew his legs up, wrapped his arms around them, rested his chin on his knees. His chest was still rising and falling too much. The falcon slanted upstream, then flapped its wings several times to gain height before hovering again.

"It's a very beautiful bird," Jullanar said. "I have been watching it. Do you know what kind it is?"

"A gyrfalcon," Damian said with an effort, remembering despite himself Rean saying he'd shoot it because it was there.

Jullanar ... Jullanar murmured the word over several times, anchoring it in her mind and mouth. Damian watched the falcon, wishing he did not have his mother's stories in his mind of what he ought to be, a poet-warrior, as beautiful and as fierce as the falcon.

He could try to maintain the standards of courtesy and polite behaviour, he could work to be the best swordsman in the city, the continent, the world ... and he would always be missing whatever it was that everyone else had.

He was seized with a sudden fury that Jullanar did not leave him in peace, fury so fierce that he had to bite his lip to keep from crying out. The distance blurred in his eyes. He lowered his head, tucking his chin in, blocking out the world and his own weakness as best he could.

Men did not cry.

Jullanar had gone out, hot afternoon though it was, to get away from the gossip from the fountain girls.

She usually did not mind gossip, as long it wasn't entirely mean-spirited, but she still only understood parts of what the young women of the Greenmarket were saying. They all spoke much more quickly than

Damian, their voices lilting and swift. If he were like one of the great grey herons of the marshes, slow, deliberate, majestic, they were like the little birds that flocked and chattered and sang all around.

Jullanar *liked* them: tiny Sasha who loved to sing, beautiful Petra who always wore red, Vera who had one dark eye and one blue one, and who said her odd eye gave her the Sight. They reminded her of more interesting versions of the girls she had known at Madame Clancette's. Instead of embroidery hoops they held drop spindles, and instead of soldiers they smiled at the caravan guards, but the talk was the same.

Sometimes Jullanar simply couldn't take it any more. The gossip of who liked whom, or what was coming into or out of style, or what ship was due in next, or what colours they were going to dye their next lot of roving, or what their parents said or thought, or what their elder siblings were doing ... Oh, sometimes she grew so homesick for a familiar face, a familiar voice, a familiar *tongue* that she had to get up and go.

Sometimes she spent time with her aunt, but she could not go to her every time she was homesick; she was embarrassed how often it was. Jullanar did not *want* to go back to Fiella-by-the-Sea, but that did not stop her from feeling the dislocation.

And she could hardly go to Damian every time, either. He had his own life to lead, and he surely got impatient with her questions and ignorance.

So she had put on her hat and gone for a walk, farther west than she usually went with Damian, following the edge of the Axhiniar all the way to where it fell into the great plum-coloured water she had learned was to be called the Redwine Arm of the river. She was standing there, not too near the edge of the cliff—she was not so foolish as that—when she heard heavy, thumping footsteps and harsh breathing.

She had turned warily and been considerably astonished to find it was Damian running flat-out towards her. She caught at his arm before he went headlong over the bluff, and reeled awkwardly with him in a parody of a country dance before he stopped.

Then he sank down, his face twisted with some deep heartache, so close to tears that Jullanar felt her own heart twist in sympathy.

He was such a private person, so reserved and so silent, that she knew he would not welcome her demanding of him what had caused such grief.

When he told her the name of the falcon she could hear how close he was to tears; when he hid his head she was sure of it.

She sat there for a while, the sun beating down overhead. Damian's hair shone nearly white in its fierce light; the river was darker than when she'd first seen it, almost maroon.

Jullanar wondered what to do, and then, because she was homesick and Damian was her friend and she didn't know what else to do, she began to speak.

"If you cross the river," she said quietly, slowly, fishing for the words, "there is a place on the other side where the boats can tie up. There are buildings there, white ones, and the end of a road."

Damian said nothing, but he shifted his head slightly, face still obscured but ear turned towards her.

"The road goes up out of the river valley for days. You pass the ruins of ancient villages, and in places the road is still paved with stones. The plants are fragrant, rosemary and thyme and lavender. There are many rabbits and fat brown birds that taste good when you eat them."

"*Gorala*," Damian muttered, his voice thick.

She was encouraged he was listening. She was sure she was making all sorts of mistakes with her words, her grammar, but he wouldn't correct her until he felt better or she made an egregious error. She assumed; usually he corrected her words as briskly and economically as he did her fencing form.

But he had run like—like an ordinary person, as if he had not spent all that time learning to be silent, as if he were ... just a young man, deeply upset.

Jullanar took a breath. "Then you start to climb more steeply, through trees. At the top of the ridge, if you turned and looked back, you would see the city like a white spot on the other side of the great river. But if you keep going the other way ..."

After a while he said, "Yes?"

She smiled, eyes on the hazy distance, where these details were invisible. "On the other side of the ridge there is a forest of cork oaks. There are old scars here and there, where people have cut the bark to make into bottle corks."

And hadn't she been pleased to have Aunt Maude explain that!

"The road turns a little north there, north and east, and slants down along the face of that long ridge. You would keep descending for several days, through oak forest and then, later, there are plains. After another day or two you come to cultivated fields, grains and cattle and horses, and then at last you come to Fovisse, where the great trading fair is held."

"And is that where you're from?"

She shook her head, though he still wasn't looking at her. "No. There is another road that heads west from Fovisse, towards the distant sea, I was told. If you follow it for a week or so, you come to a hilly area, full of rocks and trees and many streams, and many caves. There is a place where the road passes through a deep cut in the white stone, where there are trees with red bark that hangs off in long strips. There were many black and white birds there, with yellow beaks and long tails."

"Magpies," he offered.

"Probably," she agreed. "If you look carefully, on the north side of the road you will see a place where all the trees seem to line up to form a tunnel. There are two white *birches*—trees—making an arch to begin it. If you turn so you stand in the exact middle of the trees, and walk towards the end, you will find that it is a much longer journey than the road looks to be. It might take you two or three hours, even. There is a mist that rises when you are about halfway along, and I was told that if you lose the path and leave the tunnel, then you will find yourself lost indeed, in the Woods between Worlds."

Damian lifted his head then, not to look at her but to stare out at the distance, where the clouds were boiling ever higher and darker. The white falcon hung like a star against the blue-black masses.

"I looked to one side," she confessed, "and saw a valley that led to a castle with many towers and many flags all flying bravely, but no one else looked, or would say what they saw if they did."

"But you did not go that way," he said.

"No. I was coming here."

"And if you keep following the tunnel?"

She took a breath. "If you keep following the tunnel, eventually you come out into a different forest than you left. The mist clears, and the air is cool and moist, and all you can hear is the rustle of leaves from the ...

bamboo, it is somewhat like the reeds here but the stems are much larger, almost like trees."

"Grass the size of trees?"

"It is like wood, except that the trunks are hollow and so can be used as pipes," she explained.

"And that is where you are from?"

She shook her head again. "If you look around, you will see that there is a lantern carved of stone set in the bamboo forest. You must look through the opening in the lantern, and you will see a second lantern, and through that a third."

"And if you do?"

"If you do, you will see in the distance an open glade, all carpeted with ... *moss*. There is a track leading out, and if you follow it, you will find a road, and if you turn west on the road you will come down out of the bamboo forest in the mountains and into a river valley. If you keep following the course of the river downstream, west and a little north, you will find a place where another road meets the one you are on. There are *watchtowers* ... buildings there, but if you pass between them, you can follow the road that climbs up out of the valley to the north, and over the hills until you come to a great burned plain. And there you will see a great golden shimmer stretching like a wall across the sky and the land."

"What is it?"

"It is the edge of the Empire of Astandalas," she said, "and if you are permitted to pass by the magic and the soldiers at the Border crossing, you will find yourself only three week's further journey from where I am from."

Damian was not working at the Inn that night. After Jullanar told him her strange story, which he did not quite understand—but was that because he was so stupid, so much *a blank wall*, or because she still could only half-speak Calandran?—he went into the reed-plains, and fenced his shadow until he could not see for the sweat in his eyes.

He washed himself in the stream, wishing—wishing for nothing. Jullanar had left him to go home, of course, and he was ... he was himself.

He could not face going home, not yet. He caught a fish, lit a fire, ate the small meal alone.

Night fell, and the reeds were loud with all their choruses and companies of creatures. Damian put out his fire and, restless, belted on his sword, his daggers, ran eastward across the secret game trails until he came out to the places where the bloody games were held. Perhaps there would be a fight he could win tonight.

Alezian had missed his twin with an irregular ache at unexpected times. His new friend Barios was a delight, even a friend of the heart; by the end of the voyage Alezian was certain they would be friends for the rest of their lives. He could talk to Barios about philosophy, about ideas, about dreams, about plans, about business, about all the things that Damian could barely begin to comprehend.

But Barios was no challenge to make laugh. Alezian said a joke, or caught his eye, and Barios would laugh. There was none of the sense of triumph as when Alezian finally got Damian to smile.

Coming home he immediately recalled all the frustrations inherent in trying to do *anything* with his brother.

After an aborted attempt to interest Damian in his travels and trades, Alezian went to visit his friends. His mother had her own life, of course, and understood he wanted to catch up. Alezian was able to enjoy his friends' growing triumphs, what they had found with their new lives at the university, at the inns of court, at other merchant houses. Their conversations were easy, their interests understandable, their responses comprehensible. They did not sit on the other side of the room in silent disinterest, glowering when asked an opinion.

When they suggested the greyhound course Alezian agreed gladly. He was used to later nights and more exciting evenings, now. The intensity of the race was its usual drug, filling Alezian's mind with the rush and urgency of the bets and the competition. A few swigs of wine helped, no doubt, as did a few minor wins on the dogs. He was never going to bet much on them, but a little flutter was all part of the fun.

Sometime around midnight he and Barios agreed they'd had enough.

They left their larger group of friends and made their way towards the exit, arguing amiably about the merits of the two dogs in the last race as they went.

They were admittedly distracted, and slightly tipsy to boot, but Alezian did not think there was much they could have done to prevent what happened next.

They stepped behind the line of torches illuminating the edge of the grounds. Three men emerged out of the shadows in front of them.

He and Barios had met a few such thugs in distant ports. Alezian knew immediately what they wanted, and were—unfortunately—certain to take. He'd brought a knife with him, as had Barios, as was only prudent, but they didn't carry swords, which might not have been enough, anyway. These men were much older, harder, their eyes mean and flat. Alezian knew enough to know exactly how outmatched he and Barios were.

He glanced at Barios. His friend was still smiling foolishly, as if he hadn't realized their danger, but Alezian could see his mind whirring frantically with thought. Barios was lean and lithe, almost delicate of feature, not at all the sort to be able to overpower even one adversary.

"Evening, gentlemen," Alezian said genially, taking a step forward as if oblivious of the danger, too. "Enjoy the races?"

"Enjoy them more with a bit of money," the lead one said, drawing his sword with an unmistakable meaning.

Alezian's mouth was dry, his heart thumping. If only he'd brought a cutlass! If he wasn't slightly drunk and consequently could think of a way to talk his way out of this—

The lead footpad suddenly glanced behind Alezian. His eyes widened and the point of his sword dropped slightly.

Alezian tensed. He wasn't going to fall for *that* hoary old trick—

Then he realized the footpad was grinning and sheathing his sword and acting in every way as if it were totally accidental that his friends stood in a semi-circle around two others, blocking their exits.

"I, er, I'm sorry, I didn't realize they were friends of yours …. We'll leave you." And with a jerk of his head he gathered his friends and melted back into the shadows.

Warily, Alezian turned. Five steps away was his brother.

Damian stood there, hand on his sword hilt, expression stern, stance not menacing but completely unimpressed. He hadn't even drawn his sword.

Alezian had to admit he'd never been so glad to see his twin as in that moment.

Barios touched him on the arm. Alezian, glancing at him, recalled that his friend had never met his brother when he saw the confusion in Barios's eyes. "Barios, my brother, Damian. Dami, this is my friend Barios."

"Pleased to meet you," Barios said, only a touch quaveringly, sketching a bow.

Damian bowed back, as neatly and elegantly as he did everything of a physical nature, and said nothing.

"We're on our way home,"Alezian said, not sure if his brother would want to come with them or not. "We left our horses outside, in an olive grove on the way towards the Ochre Pits."

Damian nodded shortly and stalked off in that direction. He seemed to walk straight into the cliff, but when Alezian hastened to follow it became clear he was taking a narrow path Alezian would certainly never have found on his own in the dark, and probably not in daylight either. Barios gave him a mirthful glance, just visible in the half-moon light. "Talkative man, your brother."

Alezian huffed out a laugh. "Always." Damian strode on, as sure-footed and certain as in broad daylight. Alezian wondered how he did it; he and Barios were stumbling around the huge shadows of small objects and starting at odd noises.

Damian led them straight to the olive grove where they'd left their horses. *Had* being the key word.

Barios cursed softly. "Are they stolen?'

Damian glanced at him, then lifted the frayed end of a lead rope from where it hung slack against the tree. Then he stepped out of its shadow, looking not at the ground for tracks but at the middle distance where the open field met the edge of the swamp, obvious even in the dark by the thick clotted blackness of the reeds.

Alezian followed his example but could see nothing of use. Damian made a soft noise of satisfaction and set off at a loping run across the meadow. Alezian looked at Barios. "He does talk."

"I believe you, I assure you. I am embarrassed that we two sailors did not notice the state of the rope."

"At least it wasn't the knots."

"The mortification!"

They sat down on the ground beneath the tree, both tired now that the adrenalin had worn off. Alezian was nearly dozing when Barios said, "Do you think he's gotten lost? Or taken the horses and gone?"

"No, either count. They must have wandered farther off."

"Ugh, like my wits. Why didn't we bring our cutlasses with us? We knew things can get rough up here."

"Not as rough as some of the ports down south."

"We weren't stupid enough to go off without weapons down there."

"True."

"You sound half-asleep, Al. Come on, stand up."

Barios pulled him upright, making him laugh but at least ensuring that they were on their feet when the next lot of thugs surrounded them.

Alezian couldn't tell if they included the first three or not. This time there were five of them, swords drawn to glint evilly in the moonlight, and no pretence of civility. He and Barios were surrounded before they'd been the first emerge out of the shadows. Under the olive tree there was no room for manoeuvring. And no weapons.

The men in front of him wore dark clothes, faces concealed not in the half-masks of the Crescent Blade but in shapeless black cloth.

Presumably that meant that this was just a robbing, not anything worse?

Better to lose his purse and his pride than his life—or worse, his brother's. Alezian opened his arms, spread his hands, to show himself unarmed. Beside him Barios did the same.

Damian had other ideas. His return was announced by the whinny of one of the horses. Several of the robbers cursed, only to be told by their leader, in a rough growl, that it was only one man more, and not mounted.

Alezian was facing his brother's approach. Damian was indeed afoot, both sets of reins gathered in one hand. As he neared them he let them drop in what would have been a ground tie had the horses been their mother's and drew his sword.

Alezian said, "No, don't—"

But the robbers and his brother alike ignored him. Two stayed with Barios and Alezian and the other three turned to address the threat.

Damian took two steps forward to meet them. They raised their swords, moving to pincer him. He made a half-dozen leisurely strokes, sword a dreamlike flicker in the moonlight, and three bars of silver went arcing to the grass.

He turned to the remaining two. His sword was held so perfectly still it looked uncannily bright, the moon unwavering down its length. One of the two said, "Hey."

If he was going to say anything else he was too late, for Damian took three steps forward, his sword darted once-twice-three times, and the sword was out of the fourth robber's hand.

The fifth, perhaps a little smarter, grabbed Barios and set his sword to his throat. Damian made a kind of disappointed sound halfway to a sigh, and snaked his point around too quickly for sight, and with a twist like an oyster-shucker disarmed the man.

The robber cursed and reached to his waist for a dagger or another weapon, but Damian was again faster, his sword point dipping down to flick up again, the sword-belt falling behind it. With nearly the same motion he whirled around, lunged, and flicked his sword four times in succession. Four sword-belts joined the first. The nerve of the robbers broke.

Damian made no move to follow them. He loped back down the meadow to regather the horses, which had bolted away from the fight, and loped back again to present them to Barios and Alezian.

The whole thing couldn't have taken more than two minutes, including retrieving the horses for the second time.

Damian made a brief cast around the area, collecting swords and scabbards. After sheathing the swords he swung the belts over his shoulder and looked expectantly at them.

"Er, thank you," Alezian managed. "Back to town?"

Damian nodded, waited as they (very self-consciously) mounted, then ran easily beside them as they trotted to town.

Once they had clattered under the Flood Wall and into the familiar

Greenmarket Square Alezian relaxed. "They're Barios's father's horses," he explained. "We'll have to take them to the stables down in the Crescent."

Damian nodded, shifting the captured swords on his shoulder.

"What are you going to do with those?" Barios asked curiously.

Damian seemed to consider this for only a moment before he strode the remaining steps to the gallows-pole with the stocks at its base. No one had been hanged there in their lifetimes, but the pole continued to stand there as a grim reminder of the days when the Greenmarket had been its own village with the power of life and death over its inhabitants.

Damian leaped, caught the top of the gallows arm with one hand, swung there for a moment while he unslung the belts and draped them over the top, and as easily and lightly as a cat dropped down again to the ground.

He made another elegant bow to Barios and then turned and disappeared out of the circle of light cast by the torches outside the Inn.

Alezian realized his mouth was open again and closed it hastily. Barios uttered a soft, incredulous exclamation. "Are you *sure* you're related?"

CHAPTER SIXTEEN

IN WHICH JULLANAR IS FACED WITH A CONUNDRUM

Jullanar came back from her walk to the levee wondering greatly about what had bothered Damian so much. His brother had come home, she had gathered that much, and presumably said something to bother him.

Other than that, she had nothing like enough information to go on, and wouldn't have wanted to ask any of the girls at the fountain even if she thought they might know. Instead, she helped her aunt sort the deconstructed books that the university students paid to borrow and copy.

The whole *pecia* system was fascinating. Because they did not have anything like movable type here, all books of necessity had to be hand-written. While there were professional scribes and even scriptoria—Aunt Maude said there was a famous one run by monks to the north of the city, on the other side of the river—their products were precious and expensive.

The university students and anyone else who might want a text without paying exorbitant prices for it therefore had to copy their own. But even then it was too expensive to acquire an entire book at once, and so instead the students went to one of the Apothecaries' Guild members and paid a reasonable small sum to rent a single piece of the text to copy at a time.

She turned over the parchment. In the pecia system each text was divided into quires. A quire was a bundle of four sheets of parchment, folded to form eight pages. They were about the size she was accustomed to from novels back home, which her aunt said was likely enough as book construction wouldn't be particularly different in origin, and people made books of sizes that felt good in the hand unless for special purposes. Each quire was numbered, so that whoever was copying a book could keep track of where they were in it.

The strange knitted writing of Calandran was still entirely a mystery to her, alas. Damian had looked at her occasional recourse to note-taking with studied disinterest. But he never asked her *what* she was doing, or why.

She had learned the numbers, however, so at least she could sort the numbered quires into their proper order. She added one to the pile before her. Someone had drawn a sketch of a sword or a dagger in the corner of it, as if they'd been doodling when they should have been paying attention to their task.

"Do you think Damian knows how to read?"

She bit her lip. She hadn't meant to ask that so abruptly.

Her aunt put down the book she was examining, took off her spectacles, and contemplated her. "Now, that's an interesting question. Why do you ask?"

"It's not that he's stupid, precisely," Jullanar replied, trying to formulate her thoughts. "It's just that he seems, uh, ignorant, and I thought maybe it was because he doesn't read."

She felt a little disloyal, calling him *ignorant*, but what other word could she use for that strange blank bafflement at some of her questions?

"Come sit down, dear," her aunt said, patting the seat on the bench beside her. Jullanar obeyed, leaning against her aunt's comfortable bulk and thinking how different it was to her angular mother's insistence on 'upright carriage at *all times*, girls!' "First of all, you must know there are many forms of intelligence. Damian has extraordinary physical intelligence."

"The opposite of me," Jullanar replied, giggling despite herself. "I can understand that. Everyone seems in awe of him as a fencer."

"Damian is certainly functionally literate," her aunt went on.

"What does that mean?"

"He is able to look at a sequence of letters and understand what word they form." Aunt Maude gestured at the book she'd been reading, which was in Calandran. "It's not like you and Calandran, which is still a closed book to you."

"I've learned a few things," Jullanar said promptly. "That's the number *one*—"

"My point exactly. You remain illiterate in Calandran, though you are fluent in Shaian. Recognizing a few letters here and there is not literacy."

"You said he's functionally literate. So he is able to read the letters and understand the word ... Why is that different than reading?"

Aunt Maude sighed. "We come from a society where everyone is taught to read from earliest childhood. Those who cannot learn hide their ignorance as deeply as they can. It is not the same here. They do not *value* reading, Jullanar, especially the men who are not merchants. Merchants and clerks need to read fluently, of course, and among them you will find some who read—and write—for pleasure, but the rest are happy if they can scrawl their names. They leave the bookkeeping to women and clerks and priests."

"What a waste," Jullanar said fervently.

"Fortunately my store is only a cover for my studies," her aunt said. "Otherwise I should get discouraged indeed. I'm heartened to have a few people come seek out books—and some of the younger set among the merchant classes, the ones who *are* taught to read from childhood, are starting to realize there is more to be found in books than records of old transactions or the philosophy texts they need for the university. It's very early days for that, however, and there are more like your Damian than not. Indeed, he is something of an irregularity, for he *did* attend the law guild school, you see, along with his brother."

It was hard to imagine Damian thriving in a schoolroom. Jullanar said, "Perhaps he hasn't found the right thing?"

"A few years ago he broke his arm, and while it was healing his mother and I tried everything we could think of it to get him interested in reading. Nothing spoke to him. Jullanar ... you have to let it go. It's the same as any other interest or skill. You're not drawn to the physical arts, to dancing."

She was again disloyally silent, not speaking of the exercises Damian had taught her, how much she was coming to love the weight of the sword in her hand, the feel of her muscles extending as she lunged, the faintly growing hope that one day Damian would actually cross blades with her in practice.

Instead she said, "I know *how* to dance. We had to learn at Madame Clancette's."

"And Damian knows *how* to read. He's just not interested."

"Such a waste," Jullanar muttered, thinking of how Damian looked at the quiet, subtle beauties of the reed plains, and saw beauty where others saw only wasteland.

The next day she and her aunt were invited to meet Damian's brother over supper. To Jullanar's considerable relief Alezian was not another god incarnate.

At most a demigod, she thought, watching him smile charmingly at her aunt. He was much the same height as Damian, but dark to Damian's fair, and where Damian was all lean muscle and glowering intensity Alezian was comfortably proportioned, genial, and talkative.

Any one of Jullanar's sisters (except perhaps Clara) would have looked at Alezian's dark hair, his broad shoulders, his bright smile, and his clearly expensive clothing, and made a beeline to him.

Jullanar looked at Damian. He stood a little back, dressed as usual in worn leathers and plain linen, hair a little too shaggy, expression what Jullanar had named his 'town' face, a faint frown that emphasized the regularity of his features and the broodiness of his demeanour.

Not for town—not even his mother's house—was the fierce joy he showed out in the private country with a sword in his hand, nor the even rarer shy delight when Jullanar pointed out a small beauty in the wildlife of the river plains. Out there, out of sight of the city and all its inhabitants, Damian relaxed and sometimes even smiled and looked almost like an ordinary young man.

His town face was the face of the god of war. When he stalked through the Greenmarket people melted out of his way. Yearning and assessing gazes followed behind him; old stories were brought out and muttered over, though she was frustrated she could get no more than the merest gist of their meaning. Boys watched Damian and imitated his stride, his clothing, his gestures; the girls giggled and mocked them for not having the muscles to back up their pretensions.

With his brother home, his mother smiling with pleasure to have her second son there, Jullanar had expected to see at least a glimmer of the shy delight. Instead he stayed a step or two behind Alezian, faintly frowning, silent and intense. Alezian seemed to expect this, for he took it upon himself to foster conversation without ever turning to demand Damian participate.

Jullanar found herself frowning and had to keep smoothing her expression to a smile.

Over the first course of Kasiar's excellent cooking Alezian told them about his recent voyage to the southernmost tip of the Etransel Gulf, to Cape Thuy. Jullanar expressed a comment about not having seen that name on the charts in her aunt's store.

Alezian laughed hugely. "Of course not, pella. Few travel so far."

Pella meant 'miss'. It was not in the least derogatory.

(Damian had never once called her *pella*, though he always referred to her aunt as Pelan Maude, and the innkeeper as Pelan Cadia.)

She said, "I myself travelled a long way to get here."

"Certainly," he said, laughing again. "All the way across the Tyssian plain, I understand? A reasonable distance, a reasonable distance indeed, and one I can imagine you felt."

He gave her an assessing look, the second of the evening: the first had been to evaluate, and dismiss, her appearance; this was, Jullanar realized with dawning indignation, to do the same for her mind. She opened her mouth to defend herself, but it took a few moments to rally her Calandran and by then Alezian was back into fulsome narration of his own journey.

It wasn't that he was a bad storyteller, quite the opposite. He seemed to understand how to speak simply and yet eloquently. Jullanar could not deny that she was engaged by his account, that the descriptions of the places he had gone were fabulous, that he made her laugh with what she understood of his wit.

And yet ...

She had been learning, these past weeks when she could not understand more than a handful of words, to look to what the person's body language said. As her understanding of the language improved she discovered that her guesses and speculations from nonverbal cues had acted to open a new line of sight to her.

She had not hitherto realized how much there was to learn in watching *how* something was said; and by paying very close attention to the words she had started almost to hear a doubling-up of meaning. Damian spoke very little, but when he spoke he meant what he said: his whole body proclaimed it to be the truth as he saw it.

Alezian spoke beautifully. He told delightful stories. He was a pleasure to look at, his gestures elegant, his face eloquent. And yet ...

And yet he asked few questions of Damian or his mother or her aunt and none of Jullanar.

He barely glanced at his brother, and whenever he mentioned him, it was always in relation to Damian being the fighter and himself being the scholar.

Damian himself sat there with that faint frown, shrugging or nodding if his brother chanced to address him.

Jullanar made her face smooth again and smiled as prettily as she could at Alezian, who took it (handsome man that he was) as his due, and carried on.

At the end of the meal Alezian turned to his mother and told her was going to a party being held by some of his friends now at the university. Pelan Kasiar responded pleasantly enough to this statement, though Jullanar thought she might be slightly disappointed. Why she wasn't sure, until, as Alezian began explaining the details, it became clear that he had not included either Jullanar or Damian.

Jullanar had spent enough time in the Painted City by now to know that Damian was an oddity in this way as others, and not to expect a young man such as Alezian to do anything so strange as invite a (marginally, at least) respectable young woman anywhere. But his own brother?

"Shall you not go, Damian?" she dared to ask, turning from one brother to the next.

Damian was standing a few feet away, looking as lightly balanced on his feet as if he were about to turn a sudden somersault and leap through the window. His expression remained unchanged even as Alezian laughed. "Haven't you spent the last few months with him?"

Which meant what, exactly? Jullanar wondered. That she should have seen that Damian did not have friends at the university?

"He'll want to go practice, not spend hours talking about books and philosophy and art. Isn't that right, Damian?"

Damian shrugged.

"We play to our strengths," Alezian continued. "Best way, all round, I think. He's the strong and silent one, and I'm the smart and witty one." He grinned at his brother, who made no response, and winked at her.

Jullanar decided she did not like Alezian very much.

At least Damian, ignorant, narrow-minded, and obsessed with his fighting as he was, did not treat her as of no account because she was neither pretty nor wealthy nor very good at what he himself valued most.

He might scowl and be irritable when she failed to remember a word or a sword motion, but for three months he had devoted at least four hours of every day to teaching her.

~

Jullanar was often puzzled by Damian, but something about his brother's dismissal of him was deeply unsettling. She pondered the matter all that evening and well into the next day, when Damian was a particularly stern drill-sergeant over the exercises.

There was, she was growing certain, something she was missing.

Well, undoubtedly there were many things. Her vocabulary remained sadly lacking, apart from anything else. But there was something so very peculiar in the way Damian responded to some things but not others ...

"No," he said crossly, leaving off his own exercise on the other side of the clearing to come bounding over and re-arrange how she held her elbow. "That is incorrect. You will hurt your wrist if you practice like that. Like *this*."

She straightened her wrist in accordance with his brisk touch. He ran his hand lightly down her arm, as if checking the angles, brows furrowed and eyes narrowed as if in deep concentration—*why?*—and only then nodded.

"Good enough," he proclaimed. "Now lunge."

And so she lunged, wrist straight, back straight, head straight, and pondered why it was that he could see the nuances of her form so clearly from the other side of the clearing but not—

She tripped over her own feet as her mind slowed down to a screeching halt of realization. Even as she sprawled in the dirt, sword falling from her hand, Damian came leaping over to assist her.

"Are you hurt?" he demanded.

"No—no—I thought of something," she said weakly.

His expression suggested that this was a dire calamity, but he didn't say anything about the perils of *thinking* and instead said, "You need to learn to fall properly."

And so for the next hour, that was what they did. Jullanar was glad she'd taken to wearing a layer of short pantaloons made out of thin, airy linen under her skirt, for she sprawled far more often than she successfully tumbled at first.

But she did learn to tuck her shoulder in and roll back to her feet, once she'd mastered it a motion almost *easy*, and afterwards, as she sat in the shade sipping water from the clay bottle Damian had kept cooling in the stream, she was able to contemplate her moment of intuition and try to find corroborating evidence.

Point one: Damian was notoriously bad at anything involving details.

Point two: Damian was extremely finicky about every minutest element of swordsmanship.

Point three: Damian could name most birds and trees, but was wildly unreliable about plant names, and insects were a lost cause.

Jullanar considered that point and thoughtfully amended it to: *Insects were a lost cause unless they were big, brightly-coloured, or audible.* He had told her the words for bees, and butterflies, and dragonflies, and mosquitos, and flies in general. He did not distinguish between types of butterflies at any level more specific than *the red one* or *the blue one*.

She thought about the plants he could name. She had already noted he was best with things that were aromatic.

Birds he often described by their songs or their flight patterns. She had never really noticed, until he pointed it out, how some birds had undulating flights and others short periods of frantic flapping followed by short glides, and others steady, regular wingbeats, and so on.

Point four: Damian scowled unhappily almost the entire time he was inside buildings or in the city. He so rarely relaxed his expression, in fact, that no one ever commented on his scowl except to tease him when it was particularly fierce.

Jullanar's first thought on seeing it had been that he must have a ferocious headache to scowl like that.

What was the difference between town and here? She looked around the reeds, the birds singing, the insects humming, the frogs croaking and making that weird sound like gabbling ducks.

She watched Damian fence, fluidly and gracefully, face relaxed, eyes focused on the reeds across the clearing from him. It was a good twenty feet away, with nothing but the bare earth of his practice space to draw away his attention.

It was fairly rare for there to be twenty feet without anything one would normally expect to focus on, in the city. Certainly not inside buildings.

If he had some sort of vision problem that was exacerbated in town, he probably did have a near-constant headache.

Damian's predilection for standing at least six feet away from anyone was beginning to seem more like an attempt to see their faces—or at least their stance and deportment—than a dislike of close contact.

Her next thought was to wonder why he didn't wear eyeglasses, if his vision were so poor, but then she remembered the box she had conveyed all the way from Fiella-by-the-Sea for her aunt, and which had contained six pairs of eyeglasses of varying lenses precisely because her aunt could not get them in Ixsaa, which was a great trading city and one in which Jullanar had not seen a single person besides her aunt, now that she was thinking about it, who wore them.

She watched Damian switch into another of his routines, this one faster, choppier, and involving acrobatic leaps in the air.

It seemed unfathomable—surely she was wrong?—surely Damian had *realized* he couldn't see what everyone else did?

She thought of his brother, laughingly telling him to leave the thinking and reading to those who were better suited for them, and his own shy surprise when Jullanar had come for her usual lesson the next day, as if he'd expected her to follow his brother and dismiss him.

There were no physicians here to test his sight and suggest a remedy. He'd been told over and over again that the reason he struggled with reading and handicrafts and so on was because he was slow.

His mother encouraged him but it must have been obvious that Damian was not able to follow her example and become a lawyer or a scholar or anything of the sort, and if even Jullanar had sensed Pelan Kasiar's faint disappointment, how much more so would Damian?

Well. If she were his friend—and she rather thought she was—then she would have to see about remedying this. Surely amongst her aunt's collection of spare eyeglasses would be *one* pair that would help.

"Come," Damian said, landing beside her with a happy thump and a simultaneous sheathing of his swords. "We will return. I have work today and tomorrow will be hard."

"Oh?'

He smiled at her, one of those rare, beguiling smiles that lit his eyes and made his dimple appear. Jullanar could not help but melt a little at the sight. Even if she didn't have any interest in *courting* Damian she could still appreciate his beauty, couldn't she?

"Yes. Tomorrow we shall practice *together*."

CHAPTER SEVENTEEN

IN WHICH JULLANAR MAKES A DECISION

It was a few days later that Jullanar came up with a plan.

First she acquired a wood-and-wax practice tablet from her aunt, as they did not use slates here. She'd examined the wax and the wooden stylus that came with it, and thought privately that it was much more appealing than the screeching slates of her early education. The wax was a touch sticky but at least it smelled good, and you wouldn't end up with chalk dust everywhere.

Though perhaps that was just her.

The only snag in her plan was that she really couldn't take any of the spectacles without asking first, and asking only led to questions. Worst of all, Pelan Kasiar came in just as she was apologizing for disrupting her aunt, who was bookkeeping (wearing *her* own spectacles), and Aunt Maude insisted she explain all over again to Damian's mother.

"I was hoping I might have those spectacles you said were for those who ... had Xharos' eyes." She couldn't remember, if she had learned it, the Calandran word for *farsighted*.

Well, of course Damian wouldn't have taught it to her, not if she was right.

The two older women looked at each other. Aunt Maude seemed totally struck. "You think Damian—"

"I'm not *certain*," she stressed, though she was, nearly. "But if you think of how he always stands so many feet away ... and he always frowns indoors. If he cannot *see* close-to then of course he is always straining his eyes and would have a tremendous headache."

"So simple as that?" Aunt Maude murmured. "It's certainly worth trying." She turned and left the room, leaving Jullanar alone with Damian's mother.

"You really think this might be the case?" she asked in her beautiful voice, her tone faintly sad, not hopeful. "He's not the most *intellectually* gifted ..."

"He is not stupid," Jullanar replied fiercely. "He is kind and patient and thorough and doesn't care that I am—that I am—"

To her astonishment and embarrassment she realized she was starting to cry, more with indignation than anything. Damian's distress after his brother's arrival kept ringing in her mind, which Alezian's casual dismissiveness had only served to explain.

Kasiar regarded her with astonishment. "Jullanar ..."

"He's an excellent teacher," Jullanar said stoutly. "Excuse me, please."

A few minutes with the washbasin and a cloth helped her calm down and soothe her eyes, though she felt utterly mortified at her behaviour. Why could she never be calm and collected and competent? Passionate without starting to blubber like an infant?

Aunt Maude and Kasiar were speaking quietly when she came back. Aunt Maude was explaining the spectacles, Jullanar thought. She thanked her aunt for bringing them, and asked to be excused so she could meet Damian for their usual morning lesson. She couldn't quite meet Pelan Kasiar's eyes as she spoke, but she was sure Damian's mother must think her mad.

She tucked the felt-wrapped spectacles into the small bag that also contained the writing tablet and her contribution to a midmorning snack —small honey and almond cakes she and her aunt had baked the day before—and greeted the young women gossiping at the fountain in the Greenmarket Square while she waited for Damian.

The topic today was the apparently breathless anticipation of the rising of the river, which marked the change of seasons and the beginning of a prominent festival period. The festival itself took place some weeks after the river began to rise. Jullanar did not get to hear all of the features of this festival, most of which involved terminology she did not know, before Damian arrived with his usual scowl.

He nodded shortly at Vera and Petra and Sasha and the rest of the women, then tilted his head expectantly at her. "Have a good morning," Petra dared to say, batting her eyelashes at Damian.

Jullanar could have told her that he almost certainly didn't notice, but then again, he *had* stopped that six feet away, so perhaps he did. He gave no evidence of caring, however.

She had decided to wait until their break to broach the topic of the spectacles. When they were seated on their usual dead log, which Damian had moved so it would be in the shade at this time of day, she tried to come up with a good way of explaining what she'd surmised.

But every time she tried to formulate words to say, *I think you might have problems seeing*, all she could think was that Damian would quite logically retort that no, he didn't. For the whole problem was that he had no idea what it was he was missing.

In the end she went with a directness almost as blunt as Damian himself at his worst.

"Put these on," she ordered, thrusting the spectacles into his hand.

He regarded them blankly. "What? Why? What are they?"

"They help you see," she said, and turned them over in his hand so the earpieces faced him. "These hook over your ears—this bit sits on your nose —and you look through them. Here, I'll help you."

He flinched away and closed his eyes, but made no other move to resist as she set the wire-framed lenses lightly on his nose. "There," she said, and rummaged in her bag for the tablet. "Now, look at this—"

But he did not look down but out, and immediately put his hands up to tear the spectacles from his face. He sat there, face white as unbaked dough, and actually trembled.

She started to speak, but fell silent in the crashing disbelief of his reaction and her sense of her own stupidity—how was *that* at all the right way to go about this?

"That wasn't very nice, Jullanar. Did you—did you cast a *spell* on me? Everything went—different."

She could tell her was trying to sound calm, but his voice raised up into a panicked edge at the end.

Her heart clenched. "I'm sorry," she said. "I should have explained first."

She reached across the distance between them and took the spectacles from his hands.

"No," she said quietly, and replaced them on his nose. "It's no magic. Just glass lenses, made to have a certain kind of … curve to them, which helps people who have a certain … kind of … eyes … see clearly close-to. It has the opposite effect on things farther away. My aunt wears them for reading. This is … another type."

"How womanish," he said, but she could imagine that was fear speaking. He had still not opened his eyes, and the colour had not come back into his face.

"My father wears them for reading and for his … healing work," Jullanar went on. "It's very common for both women and men to have trouble—some can't see long distances, others can't see close to. I think you might find it easier to—to look at things close-by with them, that's all. If it doesn't work, it doesn't work."

She tried to keep her voice neutral.

But Damian opened his eyes to retort—and stopped, shocked, as he focused through the spectacles on her face, which was less than two feet away.

"Oh," he said softly, and even as Jullanar was congratulating herself on her perspicacity he had leaped up from the log and drawn his sword.

Damian was conscious of Jullanar's surprise at his sudden movement, but he disregarded her. His heart was beating painfully.

The glade around him swung dizzily in his vision, outside the ring of the glass lenses the usual gradual ascent from softly blurred shapes to clear outlines, inside their circle the complete opposite.

On first looking through he had been so certain she had somehow spelled him. When he looked at something close to hand, however, he was —it was—they were—

He clutched at his sword. He always felt better with his sword in hand. The world made more sense with his sword in hand.

It was his same sword, he knew that by the feel, but at the same time it was different. He had felt the etched lines in the upper part of the blade when he polished it and wondered what had happened to mar the metal; now he could see that they formed a pattern of curves to complement the straight facets of the blade itself.

He turned the sword in his hand, staring at it, *seeing* it for the first time. The wicked edge where he had been trying to sharpen away a discolouration in the steel that he had thought was rust. The smoothly worn areas in the banded hilt where his fingers fit so perfectly, the dark tarnish outlining discreet silver beading on pommel and hafts.

His hand itself, the peach-pink blurs resolved into strong sinews, long narrow fingers, faintly shiny oval nails. A thin white line—he ran his thumb over it, feeling the slight bump. That was the scar from when he had cut himself on a dagger left unwisely in a pile of clothes after he'd gone swimming.

He felt panicky in a way he did not understand. He re-sheathed the sword, his gaze lingering on the scabbard and belt. Now he could see the workmanship he had only felt, the tight stitches whose tautness he had been able to judge without knowing that they had been picked out in a light thread to make a pattern against the dark brown leather. The brown shape he was used to seeing had no such fineness of detail; he'd never even tried to look for it, as he did when he knew there was writing to be deciphered.

He circled warily back to the dead log they used for a seat. Jullanar was still sitting there, watching him. Her posture was always so straight and upright, no matter the surface she sat on.

This close the brown smudges on Jullanar's face he had vaguely attributed to either dirt or fashion were clearly patterns of spots—freckles? People spoke of freckles. He'd never really paid attention, setting them aside as part of the wide category of details he did not notice and did not care to look for.

He had never realized how literally it was that he hadn't *seen*. Was this what Alezian saw when he looked at his ledgers and his trinkets? Did he see all these—*details*?

Was this why he had struggled, when no one else seemed to? Why he had felt stupider and stupider in the guild school as everyone surpassed him, furious at himself for being unable to resolve those smudges and squiggles into meaning?

Were they simply smudges and squiggles? Were those invisible dots at the top or bottom of letters not truly invisible? Was that why Alezian could write so neatly and swiftly, and Damian couldn't?

And did this mean *he* would be able to?

He looked helplessly at Jullanar.

"It's going to be all right," she said, smiling, but she was weeping, and he could see each tear as it rolled down her cheek, briefly magnifying each spot (freckle?) as it slid down, and he found his own control wobbling and he gripped his hands tighter still, for was he not a grown man who should not cry for such a womanish thing as suddenly being able to read—

A crow called somewhere deeper in the reeds, and he jumped as if stung, as all his emotions crashed over him like a wave from a broken dam.

He tore off the spectacles and fled for the welcome familiarity of physical exertion in the deep plains, where nothing else could read, either, and never expected him to.

Somewhere deep in the green-blue pools of the nameless stream to the north of the Amberwells, Damian ran out of dry land.

After staring at the water, the birds thronged amidst the bulrushes, for a while, he turned east. He followed a narrow game-trail as it twisted through the reeds, noting idly that the ground was rising gently as he went. He passed through an outcropping of sandstone, not really high enough to be easily noticeable at a distance, though they were crowned with tufts of aromatic shrubs. He passed his hand along the needle-like leaves of rosemary, the resinous scent clinging to him after he'd passed.

On the other side of the outcroppings the land fell away again, but not so low as the reed-plains proper. This was the beginning of the region where other people went; long ago, in the times of the Calandran empire, there had been some sort of village here. Damian walked through the ancient ruins, blocks of pale limestone brought down from the mountains. There were rabbits here, and the little deer.

He came to the ruined temple of Arkhos from the back. There was another gate here, unmarked by anything but the festoons of wild grapes that draped over everything. Damian ducked through the back gate. He found himself in a narrow passage between two walls, still higher than his head. Ahead it was brighter, and in the surcease from the constant wind in the reed-plains he could plainly hear the sound of water splashing.

Damian had never explored in here; his interests had always been with the wild things, not the ancient ruins. He had wanted the forecourt of the temple complex, where the duels were held, and had felt, somewhat obscurely, that it was incorrect of him to enter anywhere before he could enter there.

But he had been welcomed to the duels, and spilled blood in honour of the god of war. Damian hesitated, then followed the sound of water.

At the other end of the passage was a walled courtyard. It was paved in great flagstones. A few of them had cracked, and there were small creeping and tufted plants in the crevices. Damian stepped on some and smelled thyme, more rosemary, something a little more pungent—rue? Or perhaps it was hyssop. He'd never quite worked out which of those were which.

Because, the thought came, he hadn't been able to *see* them to know the difference.

The court was small. Around the four sides was a sort of covered walkway with columns, all heavily overgrown with grapes. The musky scent of the grape-flowers mingled with the herbs; Damian breathed deeply, feeling his shoulders relax.

The centre of the courtyard seemed very bright, all pale stone gleaming in the sunlight. Damian walked around the covered way instead, squinting against the light to see where the water was. It was not in the centre, as he'd expected. Or rather, there was a pool there, but it was filled by a channel running from a fountain on the wall opposite the entry.

There were stone blocks on either side of the fountain, like benches. Damian sat down on one, dipping his hand into the water. It was cool and smelled delicious, and he washed his face, first, before deciding to risk it and drink from the basin. The ancient Calandrans had been amazing engineers with water, he knew. The great aqueduct feeding the city's fountains was their work, still working after who knew how many hundreds of years.

He might know, if he could read.

Damian leaned back against the cool stone wall. He held the spectacles in his right hand. He'd been clutching them the whole time he ran. He ran his fingers over the thin metal, the smooth glass, unable to see more than a blur of white reflection and brass.

He closed his eyes for a long time before he was able to bring himself to put them on.

This time he did not panic when he opened his eyes to see the world in stark clarity. He did catch his breath again, eyes darting from one thing to the next. The texture of the stone—not simply rough or smooth or gritty under his fingers, but *visible*. He reached down to his feet, where a dried branch of something had blown up against the block. He examined the leaves, the stem, the ... details.

There were so many details.

And the water, and his own hands, and the cloth of his tunic, which was different from the cloth of his coat, which was different from his breeches, which was different from his sash, which were all different from his boots ... He stroked the leather. He had *felt* the differences. This was not so different from that.

It was entirely different from that.

He watched the water for a long time, the play of ripples and the odd flash of reflected light. It poured out of a spout in the wall in a smooth arc, before breaking and flaking apart to drop into the basin at the foot of the wall. Then it ran in the channel to the pool in the centre of the courtyard, and after that he could not quite see where it went, either with our without the spectacles.

The spout was green metal, set into the stone. Above the spout was a marble plaque on the wall, and that was carved with words.

It took him a while to work out the letters. It was in ancient Calandran, of course, which was not wholly different from the modern language, but the spelling conventions were somewhat different. So was the manner of writing, but as Damian had never really been able to grasp a written word as a single object, the fact that he had to sound out the letters and decide where the words were split himself was not entirely bizarre.

He ran his fingers over the inscription, marvelling at the fine incisions, the even shapes of the letters.

Here is the water of Hiphania, it said, *the healer of all cares.*

Damian dipped his hand in the water again and wondered whether it was so wrong to give thanks to a divinity not the Lord Phoenix of his mother's altar.

CHAPTER EIGHTEEN

IN WHICH DAMIAN WISHES TO RECIPROCATE

The day after Jullanar had taken the *spectacles* to give to Damian, Kasiar woke early.

She had not, in truth, slept much at all, her mind roiling with questions for which she had no answers and hopes for which she had no names. Jullanar had come back early, somber and a little bewildered, and said only that Damian had wished to be by himself for a time.

The young woman had spent the rest of the day spinning with the girls at the fountain, amassing a respectable skein and a goodly amount of gossip by the end of the day. But Kasiar had seen how she looked often at the gate to see if Damian would come back; but he had not, before sunset sent them all home.

Kasiar lay in her narrow bed, wishing passionately for her gentle, beautiful, brilliant husband to be there at her side, to talk through her fears and questions, to help her keep her feet firmly planted and her thoughts firmly grounded. Sixteen years and more he had been dead, the whole of the lifetimes of his sons. She had been bitterly happy at times that he had not lived to see the mess she had made of raising them.

She dressed and made her way to the kitchen to make a morning pot of coffee. It was not yet dawn, so Damian would not have returned from his practice.

He was sitting at the table.

She stopped in the doorway, watching him. He was sitting in the gloom, profile to her, staring at the wire and glass spectacles in his hands. He flipped them up and down, up and down, but otherwise sat completely still. He was not wearing his practice clothing, was wearing the clothes he had worn the day before, though they were dusty and she could smell the cooled sweat on them. Had he run through the whole day and night?

If he had, what had he run from?

Or towards?

"Damian," she said softly.

He didn't move at first, except for the steady slow flick of the spectacles in his hands. She waited, hearing her pulse loud in her ears. His face was pale, grim, and he looked to her like her husband had looked on the eve of the battle in which he had died.

Then he said, his voice toneless and dull, "If it pleases you, would you light the candle?"

She caught her breath, her tiny gasp sounding very loud. When was the last time one of her sons had initiated a conversation in Tanteyr? Had they ever once they were old enough to understand it was not a language spoken in public?

Or for that matter, acknowledged her small gift at magic?

She seated herself across the table from him. He was still flicking the spectacles up and down, up and down. She reached forward, pinching the candlewick with her thumb and forefingers to assist with the magic. It was not a very elegant work of magic, but she was out of practice. The Ixsaan attitude to female magic-users tended towards the stocks at best and the bonfire at worst.

The lenses flared gold in the light. He looked up at her, her son, his eyes anguished and bewildered. She did not understand the anguish.

She waited. She had eventually learned patience, just as she had eventually learned the cost of too narrow a focus. She hoped with every beat of her heart that her son's learning would not be so painful as her own.

He lifted the spectacles and placed them the way she had seen Maude wearing them, the hooked bars over his ears, the crooked join settled on his nose. He looked at her through them without speaking. His eyes seemed magnified from this side, or perhaps that was a trick of the candlelight, catching them to a luminous grey.

She waited, regarding him as steadily as he regarded her, trying to adjust to this view of him with the strange wires and lenses across his eyes, wondering what he saw—and what he had seen.

After a long while he shuddered and slid his hands up as if to cover his face from her seeing him, fingers sliding under the lenses to cover his eyes. She waited, wondering if now was the time to speak, sensing that it was not, that it was time to wait, to let him come to her with his words.

As simple as that? Maude had said in disbelief when Jullanar had voiced her idea.

As simple as this, Kasiar thought: a mother and her child sitting across from each other in the dark, a single candle illuminating the space between them.

"I had no idea," Damian said, in Calandran, his voice muffled. Kasiar suppressed any disappointment that he had reverted to what she had to admit was his primary language.

Then he said it again, in Tanteyr, slowly and formally, still hiding his face. "I had no idea I could not see."

She hesitated, and then slid from her seat to the one next to it, from which position she could take him in her arms. He let her embrace him, leaning against her breast, as he had not since he was quite a little boy. She could feel him shuddering, and then a dampness that suggested he was weeping, her son who had learned so young the Ixsaan way to hide emotions.

She held him there for a long time, while the room slowly lightened with the dawn.

He said only one thing more, so softly that she was not entirely sure he had in fact spoken it, or if it was her own longings that had made her hear it: "I thought I was so stupid."

She rested her chin on his bent head and ached with hope.

Fortunately or unfortunately, Alezian was still in Ixsaa, and was home that morning.

He was unutterably fascinated by the spectacles. Not so much for his brother's sake, Kasiar thought, as for the possibilities the devices had for trade. Something so simple that could improve vision?

(Except that it was not simple. Maude had spoken of the need to grind the lenses to very particular standards, and Kasiar had never seen such quality of glass in Ixsaa. But the trade-goods were coming from the west in ever-increasing numbers, and she knew that much as Alezian loved the sea, he loved his ambition to be a great merchant prince more. To be the one to introduce *spectacles* to Ixsaa?—oh, he would give much for that privilege.)

Alezian reached out towards Damian's face. Damian flinched back, eyes huge as he stared at his brother. Alezian chuckled wryly, casting a sidelong glance at Kasiar, who smiled reluctantly at his silent amusement.

Damian looked from one to the other, his brows furrowed in his familiar confusion. Alezian had his father's smile, that crooked little smirk at the corner of his mouth.

It did not mean, as Kasiar had thought when she first met the man who would be her husband, that he meant to mock; but she was not surprised that Damian found the expression infuriating. Her own smile grew despite herself as she watched her two sons, so different and yet so occasionally alike.

Then Damian thrust himself back from the table, tearing the delicate eyeglasses from his face and coming around, like a stag at bay, at his usual place across the room. Kasiar and Alezian stared at him in surprise.

"I don't understand what your faces mean!" Damian cried.

His face was working, colour high and eyes brilliant, breath coming hard and fast.

Alezian took a few steps towards him. Damian retreated to keep his distance. "Damian ... It's ... Calm down, will you?"

Damian stared at him distrustfully, almost fearfully. Kasiar's throat felt thick. What had Maude said? That the eyeglasses gave Damian a way to see clearly things that were close to him. Which meant, by necessary corollary, that he was otherwise unable to.

"Damian," she said softly. Her son turned his head, his eyes wild, his hand gripping the glass and wire contraptions, his body poised as if to flee.

She patted the chair he'd left. "Come sit down again, please, and we can talk this out."

Damian was no great talker, and he hesitated, before nodding sharply and returning to his seat. After a moment of scowling intently at them he put the spectacles back on.

"Now," Alezian said, watching Damian as if concerned he might jump up again. "This ... contraption ... is to help you see better?"

Damian nodded tensely. His eyes were wide; almost hungry, Kasiar thought.

Alezian said, "One of the sailors on my ship was amazingly farsighted. He was the best look-out, but he was nearly blind about anything close to him. If you moved things from their spots he'd trip ..."

"I'm not *blind*," Damian snapped.

Alezian smiled. "Since we never thought you had problems seeing, obviously."

Damian settled again, like a bird ruffling its feathers. His hands were folded together, gripping each other tightly. Alezian watched him with obvious curiosity. "So ... when you look at something close to hand, like this ..." he said slowly, pulling a small enamelled dish out of his pocket. "What do you see? Without the spectacles? If you were to describe it?"

Damian took off his spectacles and glowered at the dish. "It's blue," he said reluctantly, then reached hesitantly to take it. "Is it enamelled?"

Kasiar realized then that she had never noticed how much Damian used his hands to understand small objects. Now that she was aware of it, she knew she had seen him do this time and time again: picking up a dagger, or a stone, or one of Alezian's small treasures, running his fingers gently across the surface. She had always assumed he just enjoyed the textures.

"And with the spectacles?" Alezian pursued.

Damian put them on. He looked down at the dish in his hand, and Kasiar, who was watching his face intently, saw the flash of surprise and delight that washed over it. "It's ... pretty," Damian said, still trailing his fingers over the bumps of the enamelled flowers and vines. "These are ... plants. That one is ivy." He traced out the distinctive birds-foot shape.

Kasiar wasn't entirely certain that she had ever seen that smile on her son's face before, though she knew it—oh, how well she knew it!—from her husband's. She turned her head to hide the lump in her throat, the stinging in her eyes.

"And here I thought you just didn't care," Alezian said.

He probably did not intend for his voice to come out as snidely as it did; but it did, and Damian, unsurprisingly, took offence at it. He set the dish down with a soft clink and leaned forward.

"You are not always right," he said.

Alezian leaned back, affronted. "I know that!"

"Not everything is about money or power," Damian went on, gripping the table with his hands in emphasis and, perhaps, Kasiar thought, while Alezian stared in astonishment and Damian looked fiercer and more defiant by the second, because he had never disagreed so openly with his twin before.

"I know that too," Alezian muttered truculently.

"You do not *live* it," Damian retorted. "You say: friends are good for what they can do for you, things are good for what money they can sell for, all is *valued* only for their *usefulness*. But that is not true. Some things are good to do just because they are good to do, because it is pleasing and satisfying. And some *people* are good to be friends with because their company is pleasant and they help you to become a better person."

Alezian opened his mouth, then stopped. "Is this about—what was his name?—Rean?"

"Rean!" Damian said dismissively. "No. He was no good friend. I tried to follow your rules, but they were stupid. It is not good to be always looking for the *transaction*."

Kasiar caught her breath. Had *that* been the cause of their quarrel?

(And Damian, poor Damian, wanting a friend who might understand him ...)

Alezian cast around. "Pelan Maude's niece, then? You know, if you fancy her ..."

Damian spoke flatly. "Jullanar is to be a Maiden Oracle."

This appeared to flummox Alezian. "Well, then, Damian, I don't know what you mean? I do think that it's good to make friends who are useful—why wouldn't it be? But you have to find people you *like*, too."

Kasiar admitted she was glad to hear Alezian say that. Why exactly this had all been prompted by the spectacles she didn't know, but it was the most she had ever heard Damian say at once and she hoped more would be forthcoming.

She felt as if her entire understanding of her son was shifting—

"Excellence is its own reward," Damian said.

"Yes, that's from Dimarius' *Sentences*. We read it in school ... Did you get that far, in the end?"

Damian gave him one of the frowns that scared half the Greenmarket Inn's patrons into sobriety and good behaviour when he turned it on them. "I did," he said stoutly. "And it's *true*. You didn't think so, you argued it was wrong, but it *is*."

Alezian laughed. "Oh, Damian, those were just debates, you know that!"

But Damian *hadn't* known that, Kasiar thought. And yet he had listened while he tried so valiantly to read the ancient Calandran text, unable to see much more than blurs and colours, squinting desperately to force some sort of coherency and significance from the page before him.

He hadn't been able to see the designs in the enamelled dish. How had he been able to read *anything*?

And yet he had tried: he had not wanted to, had asked more than once if he could stop going, but when Kasiar refused to let him, he had continued to try, no matter the mockery and ... pain. She bit her lip as her eyes prickled. How much had *she* compounded that pain? She had not listened to him—had thought it unwillingness, not inability—

Damian was not done with what he wanted to get off his chest. "It is not necessary that we pretend we are only Ixsaans," he said, biting off the words. Kasiar shook her head, unable to believe what she was hearing.

"We can be Tanteyr as well," Damian said forcefully. "We do not need to avoid our language and our history, it is *ours* and I don't care what you think, I want to know about it. You said we should not, we should be Ixsaan, but what good is that? We *are* not only Ixsaan, and we should be who we are."

That silenced Alezian. He met her eyes and then looked down in shame, a dull flush suffusing his face. He had been the one to say no to the bedtime stories, to stop speaking in Tanteyr, to refuse to read or write it when she gave them passages to practice. Damian had followed along, as he always did—or as he always had.

We should be who we are. What a thing for her son, her silent brainless brawny swordsman of a son, to throw down as a gauntlet.

"And I," Damian said finally, his breath coming fast with his emotions, his eyes brilliant and fierce and so, so alive, for the first time *focused.* "I, I am *not* a blank wall! I'm *not*! Just because I don't understand everything doesn't mean I am—entirely *stupid*. I'm not!"

And that made both of them startle in shock and embarrassment, for Kasiar remembered well the moment Alezian had said that about his brother, and that she had agreed. "Dami," she said softly, but Alezian spoke over her. "I didn't know you heard that."

Damian gave him an impressively scornful glance. "And so it is all fine if you say it behind my back? I wasn't eavesdropping, I just hadn't left yet. But it isn't *true*."

And Alezian looked at him with shame and mortification warring, and then he suddenly smiled, the expression again one of their father's, and he leaned forward and grabbed Damian's hands with his and said, "No. It's not. You're not."

"I'm not," Damian insisted again, more quietly.

And Kasiar said, helpless in the face of her own failures, "I'm so sorry, Damian."

CHAPTER NINETEEN

IN WHICH DAMIAN OFFERS A GIFT

It was an impossible gift Jullanar had given him. When Damian looked at one of his schoolbooks through the spectacles, in the clear light of day, the impossible letters were ...

He traced out a few letters, stylus running under the lines as usual, but ... but the invisible dots were there, pinned in place, unmoving, *legible*. Words. A sentence. Two sentences. A paragraph.

He set the book down and took off the spectacles, shivering as his room returned to its usual blur of colours and shapes. Alezian's trunkful of clothes and trade goods was a great splash against Damian's spare, undecorated half of the room.

He had never understood the point of *any* of that before.

He had never been able to read a paragraph in a breath or two before.

He swallowed, and put away the spectacles into their felt case, and then he slipped through the house and out into the square, out of the city, into the reed plains, so he could think.

He could never reciprocate in kind. This would be a debt that lingered ... except he knew this was not a debt, not to Jullanar. It was a gift, freely given.

She loved the wild things, Jullanar did, and the small beauties Damian had shown her. She had spoken to him of her faraway home, of magic and wonder, and, moreover, told him carefully how *he* could go there, if he wanted, one day.

He ran, the wind in his face, the sun on his head, the falcon flying above him, its shadow always a few steps ahead.

Damian had a few beautiful places he had not yet shown Jullanar. He could show her more patience and teach her more with the sword. And—perhaps—perhaps one day he could tell her a secret or two, such as he had never been able to tell anyone before.

He had not had to *tell* her anything, had he? She had seen for herself that he was different, and far from minding, seemed to prefer his company to Alezian's, which no one had ever done. And then she had realized for herself one piece of the puzzle, and given him that unfathomable, impossible gift of being able to read.

He had poor thanks to offer her, it was true. But somehow he didn't think she would mind.

~

The dawn light was rich and deep-toned, kindling the tops of the reeds, the dust-motes, the very air into a luminous golden-orange.

Jullanar was minded of the arc of the Empire's magic as she'd left it behind. But this magic was in her eyes and heart, in this land and this light. It tasted like sweet hay and the salty tang of the water, the thin cool air sending tendrils down from the distant mountains, the even more distant sea.

All around them the midges rose up. By now she was mostly used to them—her aunt had given her a cream that was a great help—and she was able to mostly ignore them. The noise of the waterfowl chuckling and chortling was all around them. The sky above them was washed with apricot.

This morning excursion was some sort of oblique return for the gift of the eyeglasses several days before, she understood. Damian had been serious and earnest as always when he had invited her, coming to her aunt to ask permission to take her to a village some distance away from the city. Her aunt hadn't objected, of course, though she'd clearly found it amusing that Damian was so punctilious in this after all the time Jullanar had spent alone in his company in the reed-plains.

So it was that Jullanar sat in the little dory as Damian rowed.

She admired his motion, the soft splashing of the oars, the faint breeze on her face, the strange milky pink water. On her left were the tall reeds, on the right tangled shrubs and vines between the stream and the pastures. On these small, simple rivers and streams she did not grow queasy as she had coming across the great expanse of the Redwine.

Damian rowed, apparently inexhaustibly, up the pink river to a place where it suddenly bent into the marshes. There was a small beaten-earth ramp here leading through the tangled growth, upon which he grounded the boat.

He handed her out, but instead of tying the rowboat up to a mooring post, he indicated she should step back, fastened the oars to the seats with some rope ties she hadn't noticed before, and, with a sidelong glance, handed her a small canvas sack to hold. She assumed that was so she didn't feel useless, something she was just becoming able to articulate. The weeks of immersion and Damian's language lessons were at last starting to come together to the point where she could hold something of a conversation.

Damian then squatted down and grasped the two cross-bars before heaving the boat out of the water and over his shoulders in a fountain of water droplets.

Jullanar opened her mouth and stared at him.

"Come," he said, ignoring her reaction. "We shall cross the meadows to the Tuparné. It is shorter than going up to the Goldtree and across that way. Also you will like to see the *Veizanoi*."

Jullanar had not found any maps of Ixsaa that showed the many water-courses around it. She had finally begun to realize that most of the streams had names that described their colours, which according to her aunt were due to the various sediments they carried. When she had asked Damian for further clarification, he had given her a somewhat incredulous look and the unsatisfactory explanation that the stones were coloured and therefore so too was the river.

She thought her aunt's story of the River that Ran Away to Paradise was much more interesting, but Damian said he'd never heard of it.

Tuparné—she'd been starting to disentangle how Calandran place-names worked. So *tupé* was the feminine form of *tupé, tupu,* and it was a metal word ... not one of the ones used for weaponry, so not steel or iron, but there had been something decorative ... Copper, that was it. Like her aunt's copper pans.

And *arné* was a noun, and it meant ... line, that was it. The *Tuparné* was the Copperline. Jullanar felt very proud of herself for working that out.

"Come on," Damian said, voice echoing a bit inside the curve of the boat.

"I'm coming!" she replied, scrambling up the bank much less easily than he had, and she was only carrying a sack. Damian, naturally, was striding as quickly and effortlessly as he ever did when *not* holding a two-person wooden rowboat on his back.

Really, how did you even *get* muscles like that?

Their portage took them past a small herd of short, stocky horses, which Damian told her were called *hiphae*, though he also sounded quite disdainful and went off onto a discourse she didn't fully understand about different kinds of horses and how these weren't particularly good ones.

Jullanar tried to describe the horses she'd seen in Fiellan, which seemed to interest him as much as anything she'd mentioned had—she'd exhausted her knowledge of Alinorel swordsmanship very quickly—but she didn't have the vocabulary to say more than that they were *big* and *strong* and *fast.*

Damian was not big, but he was certainly strong and fast. He was like one of the aristocratic racehorses she'd seen grazing along the road near Tara. They had looked like equine royalty, coats blood bay and black and a shining, shimmering gold like Damian's hair.

It might be true that Jullanar had developed something of an appreciation for Damian's beauty.

It might also be true that she still couldn't quite believe his interests could *all* be drawn back to the one topic of the art of defence.

Although—perhaps that was the only thing he liked to *talk* about. She could understand how moving quietly in the marshes was helpful, in its way, for someone training to be a warrior. But there was that shy smile that he so rarely gave when presented with something purely beautiful which could not be rendered down to that simple explanation. And his reaction to the spectacles ... No. That was not *all* he was, by any means.

She was sweating heavily by the time they reached the next river, the sack unpleasantly heavy. Damian set down the boat into the little curving bay without any apparent strain. Jullanar felt, obscurely, that this was one of the most exquisite feats of strength she'd ever witnessed, far more impressive than breaking anvils or whatever at the harvest fair.

This river was larger than the Pink, and a rich orangey-red almost the colour of copper. The Copperline, then. The boat looked quite splendidly blue against its water. Damian handed her in, and she settled herself into her seat in the prow, grateful that the months of practice had made this part much smoother. Damian nodded approvingly, untied the oars, and set off downriver.

"We shall come to the Veizanoi soon," he said after a few minutes of silence. "It is around the curve, before the confluence."

It was a measure of Damian's priorities that Jullanar had learned the word for a meeting of waters well before she had found out that *Kistaron*, Greenmarket, was the name of both the square in front of the Inn and also the neighbourhood in which they lived. Aunt Maude despaired sometimes of her ever being able to have a regular conversation, and kept telling her useful domestic words so she could talk with the young women at the fountain. Jullanar wondered, privately, whether Damian himself knew some of those kitchen utensils.

The current sped up slightly. Damian angled them towards the south, though the river was bending more and more north as they continued. "Look," he said, gesturing with his chin to the northern bank.

Jullanar looked, and caught her breath at the way the bank caught the dawn light. The last time she'd looked she'd seen a low bluff, remarkable only in how exactly the colour of the water matched that of the visible stone. Most of it was overgrown with sheets of vines, which seemed to be flowering (though she couldn't see any visible blossoms) given the scent of honey and musk that rose from them.

Now the bank was rising higher, pushing the river to curve around a taller mound. There was some sort of harder stone on top, she assumed, forming a whitish-grey cap. Under it the river had swirled away the outer layers of stone and earth to form sinuous curving cliffs, their shapes somehow alien and beautiful at the same time.

Yet what caught Jullanar's eyes were the colours. Damian did something with the oars that swung them out of the current and into an eddy on the far bank, so she could look her fill across the copper water to the cliff, which rose up in fantastic streaks and stripes and bands of colour: orange, copper, red, yellow, white, pink, even one narrow band of green-blue, all of it saturated by the rich early-morning light.

One glance at Damian's small, proud smile and Jullanar realized he'd timed their journey specifically to show her this.

After a few minutes Damian let the current take them. Jullanar paid him little attention, her eyes on the stone—what was the hat called? Why did that layer not erode as the rest had? Why here, but nowhere else, were the colours exposed?—except that wasn't true, was it? She'd seen that copper-orange layer all along the river, and the layers above it were only a shade or two darker, and perhaps she hadn't seen them under the shadows of the overhanging vines.

The fantastically eroded and coloured rock formation continued for maybe half a mile. Jullanar couldn't believe that no one else was there on the river admiring it. No ramblers picnicked anywhere she could see; no painters sat there with their easels to record its changing colours (even she, no watercolourist like her sister Lavinia, knew how much the time of day would change the effect of the light); no fishermen had chosen to pursue their prey with that to occupy their minds and eyes while they waited.

No one but them there in the early morning, half-drowning in beauty. The birds were singing lustily all around, undisturbed.

"Why is no one here?" she asked finally, when Damian had stopped idly steering by way of one oar and had gone back to rowing. "Does no one know about it?"

Her aunt had never mentioned a rock formation such as this, and Jullanar knew Aunt Maude appreciated them. Each of her few visits to Fiella-by-the-Sea had involved a family pilgrimage to the Sea Caves up the coast to admire the formations there.

"They know," Damian replied. "It is like the marshes. People go when they need things."

Jullanar didn't have the right words for this. She tried anyway. "Why don't they care?"

This was not the sort of question Damian did well with, though he always did try. He considered, brow furrowing into the familiar glower. "They do not see," he said eventually. "They do not *look*."

"But you look," Jullanar said. He'd seen this, known this was here, brought her here on purpose.

Damian shifted uncomfortably, glancing behind him for nearly the first time to see where they were. (Another item of astonishment: he knew all the waterways *backwards*.) They were sweeping around lower bluffs, these ones striped orange and yellow, with a wide purple band like a cummerbund across the middle. She could make out a wide green space ahead of them, perhaps their destination.

She pressed on. "*You* look."

Damian shook his head, tight-lipped, face set into his city expression, closed and fierce. He was also rowing harder, straight down the middle of the current. When she leaned forward to say something else, he snapped, "Hold *on*!"

Startled, she grabbed the cross-bar in front of her. Damian nodded once, and then they were suddenly in a mess of whirlpools and back eddies and cross-currents and were those *waves* and—

And, oh, the wide green space was not a field, not a marsh, not a bog, but the Greenwater Arm of the river Oonar.

Jullanar did not like this.

She clutched at the gunwale, if that was the right word for it, as Damian rowed out into the middle of the stream. Current. Ridiculously giant river. Where was this even hiding? It was as big as the plum-coloured Redwine on the other side of the city, but she'd seen no evidence of it at all.

It hardly seemed possible that this was something one could simply *miss*.

Damian was humming tunelessly, gaze focused over her shoulder as per usual, rowing with the same easy, regular motion as on any of the smaller streams. She reflected that he'd just carried the boat for fifteen minutes and wondered, again, just how he was that strong.

She swallowed against what was *not* sea-sickness or rising terror of this giant river. She looked carefully over the side, but the river had *waves*, she was sure of it, and she couldn't—

No, she had best focus on something inside the boat and other than her queasy stomach. What had she been wondering about most recently?

"What do you *do*, the rest of the day, Damian?"

He furrowed his brow slightly. Jullanar waited, knowing it sometimes took him a while to think through a question. The weeks of forced patience while she tried to work through her minuscule vocabulary to ask questions and follow up comments had led her to the realization that if she waited long enough Damian *would*, in fact, have something to say.

You had to wait for quite a long time, however. Jullanar had received the distinct impression that not very many people had ever bothered.

"I practice," he said eventually. "Work at the Inn, some nights."

Somehow that had not yet come up. "Really? What do you do?"

It was so *amazing* to be able to talk, even if in short, broken sentences and on limited topics. Aunt Maude had given her a few more words and help with some linking phrases, and now she felt as if she were starting to get somewhere.

Of course, Damian then said something she did not understand in the least. Still, he was quite good at giving her several ways of saying the same thing until something stuck. The frown deepened as he thought through the words.

"There are those who drink too much wine, and fight," he said at last. She was pretty sure that *graniom* meant wine, anyway. There were all those wild grapes growing along the banks of some of the rivers, and from context it had to be some sort of liquor.

"Yes," she said, to show she'd understood.

"I stop them."

Jullanar regarded him in perplexed admiration. While it was no surprise that he would do something that involved physical strength and fighting skill, he was so ill at ease inside the city that it seemed incredible.

"Why?"

That was always a hard question. He pondered for a while, turning around once to check their location. Jullanar glanced up, over his head, to find that they were well away from where they had entered the river and were now somewhere in the midst of a great swath of glittering green water, with yellow and white in front of them. The mountains looked much closer here, though the eastern bank of the river below them was still shrouded in a bluish haze.

"Money," he said eventually, which was actually fair enough. She couldn't think of a good follow-up question—*Do you enjoy that?* was the sort of thing that would cause Damian to stare blankly, which she at least found distressing—but her long silence ended up being rewarded with a further detail: "It's good to be useful."

Jullanar gaped at him, grateful for once that Damian so rarely looked at her face. In the rowboat they were too close in proximity for him to be able to read her expression, anyway.

It had been such a relief to discover that half of his scowls were due to being extremely farsighted and not knowing it.

But having uncovered that characteristic did not mean that Damian's eccentricities and idiosyncrasies had all disappeared.

That—what *was* that? It seemed like such a simple statement, but then again ... there was a strange look in his eyes, nearly defiant, but that made no sense. Why would he feel defiant about working as security (as that's what that sounded like) at the Inn, which even Jullanar knew was owned and run by his mother's close friend?

She didn't have any of the words to ask these questions. She sat there instead, focusing on her own hands gripping the gunwale, and tried to think over what she knew of Damian and his mother.

His mother was beautiful, daunting, and learned, working as a lawyer. Even in Fiellan that would have been unusual for any woman, let alone a lady, but here it was nearly unheard-of. Aunt Maude had told her that it was only in the Greenmarket, technically outside of the original city walls, that women were allowed to own businesses or follow certain professions.

She considered Damian again. There were many words she could use to describe him, but *learned* was not one of them. Not in the way that a lawyer or a scholar was learned, anyway, or even a merchant of this city, like the one his twin brother was learning to be. Not *all* of that was due to his difficulties in reading.

Perhaps it *was* a form of defiance for him to break up fights in an Inn.

Damian was a little worried he had broken Jullanar by telling her that he worked at the Inn because it felt good to be useful. He was cursing himself a little.

He should have stayed with money. That was the sort of reason anyone understood. Alezian always said that everything boiled down to money in the end, although Damian had considered that carefully and *still* couldn't see how it could possibly be true. He feared it was one of the things that everyone else understood and he just ... didn't.

He decided a diversion was in order, and therefore began to rally his thoughts together to explain his errand, which involved several new words that would be a lot easier to explain when he had things to point to and Jullanar stopped holding herself as if she were terrified the boat was going to come apart around her. He had just decided to begin with the upcoming festival when there was a strange whistling noise and a shadow passed between them and the sun.

Jullanar had heard it too, and peered upwards. "What *is* that?"

Damian looked up, expecting a large bird, and was deeply, utterly, completely flabbergasted when a person fell out of the sky and landed on them.

CHAPTER TWENTY

IN WHICH DAMIAN AND JULLANAR MAKE A NEW ACQUAINTANCE

"What," said Damian flatly.

Jullanar didn't look at her friend. She couldn't. All she could do was stare, conscious of a slight astonishment that she had actually managed to draw her feet out of the way of *sudden plummeting people* so that said sudden plummeting person didn't land on them or tip them over or sink the boat.

The boat itself tipped wildly and splashed up a huge mass of water as the person landed. Damian rowed furiously and got them back into some sort of equilibrium long before Jullanar had quite caught her breath.

Right there in the middle of the boat between her feet and Damian's, wedged between the two horizontal gunwales, was a prodigious quantity of royal-blue velvet enveloping someone—*dear Lady let it be a* someone—who was making strange noises as he, she, or it tried to work free.

It took some doing before Jullanar was able to pry her fingers from the gunwale in front of her. She reached out to grab the edge of the velvet and emitted a startled "Meep!" when strong grasping fingers clutched at hers.

Her *meep* was echoed half a second later by a deeper, masculine, and very surprised, "*Oh!*"

Long-conditioned reflex meant it was she who said, "Oh, sorry!" in

Shaian. Whoever it was let go of her fingers and let her pull the fabric away. Sprawled in the bottom of the little boat was a very strange young man.

Jullanar blinked, and blinked again, and looked at Damian, and back down at the suddenly arrived young man. No, he still seemed very strange indeed, though it was hard to say why, exactly.

He was very dark-skinned, but Jullanar had met, or at least seen, people of nearly such colouring. The King of Rondé had come to Fiella-by-the-Sea once to see their duchess, and he was very strongly aristocratic in the Shaian mode, with deep brown skin. One of the proctors at the Entrance Examinations had been a Scholar with skin nearly the colour of jet.

Jullanar had been conditioned from an early age to associate such colouring, if at all supported by other points, as indicators of very high rank within the Empire.

There was the prodigious quantity of blue velvet, which she had no idea what to do with.

The young man was wearing what she would consider a scandalously short white linen tunic—indeed she had to lift her gaze immediately when she realized just how short that tunic was and the fact that he was sprawled in the bottom of the boat, legs and arms equally akimbo, without apparently realizing that he was therefore revealing more of the male person's anatomy than Jullanar had ever seen before. She could only be glad that the folds of his tunic hid most of—

Dear Lady, her aunt was going to *thrash* her.

She forced her gaze up to his face. He was looking brightly at her with a wide, delighted smile.

He couldn't be far off her own age, really.

He had extraordinarily white teeth, she thought absently, and strange light-brown eyes almost exactly the colour of the Amberwells stream with its dark brown water and golden bubbles. The more she looked the more convinced she was that his eyes were *deeper* than normal eyes, and the golden flecks of light were coming up from some unfathomable—

He blinked and turned his head, and Jullanar sank back on her seat with a solid thunk and a sudden splitting headache and the immediate incontrovertible realization that this young man who fell out of the sky was magical in a way utterly foreign to the Schooled Magic of the Empire.

Dear *Lady*.

It took her a few moments to recover her breath. She forced her hands to relax on the gunwale and looked up in time for the young man to sit up slightly and turn his head to regard Damian, which gave her a glimpse of his profile and a feeling as if she had just been stabbed in the stomach.

"Who in all the Nine Worlds and the lands Beyond are *you*?" she whispered.

She had *no idea* why that profile should shake her so. She didn't know him—he didn't look like anybody she *could* know!

The stranger lifted his eyebrows conspiratorially, and apparently happily followed the lead in linguistic register. "Would you perchance believe me if I were to say I were the Prince of the White Forest, come down from the high places to test hospitality and good humour?"

What?

"Is that a god?" Jullanar asked; she was hazy on any beliefs other than her own in the Lady of the Green and White. "I doubt that you would say, if you were."

The stranger laughed gleefully. "Perchance a scion of the Sun-in-Glory—no?"

Jullanar had no idea what that even meant, but she was pretty sure it was not a title anyone could actually lay claim to. "No?"

"Peradventure a lover of the Moon ..."

She blushed, but she *did* want to be the sort of person who had adventures. She was trying so *hard* to be that kind of person. She cleared her throat. "Per-peradventure drunk."

"Only on life, fair lady, only on life. You may call me Fitzroy."

Jullanar waited but there was no surname, patronymic, house, location, title, or occupation to follow this. She did not reflect on her ignorance of central Astandalan culture; she merely thought it strange.

She also added it to the tally of things suggesting that the stranger was drunk on something fearsomely effective and probably magical, before midmorning as it was.

But then it could have been any time at all wherever this visitor was from.

"Jullanar," said Damian crossly, "what are you *saying*?"

Jullanar looked across the stranger, still sprawled in the bottom of the boat, still apparently unconscious of his lewd display, still grinning happily at them. Damian was wearing his most ferocious scowl.

"I'm not saying much," she pointed out. "I don't know what he is, either."

"*Who*," he corrected her, then glanced over his shoulder and with a bitten-off expletive began hastily to row, having stopped doing so for the past several minutes.

"Two languages," the stranger said, as if this were a gift the universe had presented for his delectation.

He spoke the one Jullanar understood best, at least. She fixed him with as stern a glare as she could muster. "Who *are* you, sir? Your arrival on our boat is most unexpected."

"Oh, is this a boat?" He sat up finally and casually flicked his tunic down, much to Jullanar's relief. He was still showing a scandalous amount of thigh, but at least it wasn't ... that. The dinghy rocked with his motion and Jullanar hastily grabbed the gunwale again for reassurance. She trusted Damian, she really did, but—

"You just fell out of the sky on top of us!"

The stranger stared at her. "Yes?" He paused, then continued. "Doesn't that sort of thing happen here?"

All her thoughts felt like a repeating chorus of *what*.

"No!" Then, because she had never been very good at decorum and polite discourse, she went on: "Where did you *come* from?"

"Oh ... a tower at the end of the world. I've come in search of my fortune."

So she wasn't the only one who wanted ... more.

Except ... except that this person, whoever he was, had *fallen out of the sky* on top of them.

He seemed abruptly to realize something. "Will you require a wish or a dream or the colour of my hair in exchange for passage?"

Jullanar was wrong-footed by this question, which sounded even more out of a book than her own initial one. Not to mention that the stranger, now that she looked at him again, was completely shaven bald, in the way of high (very high) male Astandalan nobility. She looked again at

Damian for help, but he was fiddling irritably with the oars and was of no assistance at all.

Rather hesitantly, she said, "No?"

The stranger looked around in puzzlement, which made Jullanar, even more hesitantly (and with a good grip on the gunwale) do the same.

The Greenwater Arm, over half a mile in width at this point, was a rich milky green in colour, which hid the abundant aquatic life and much of the surface greenery, though mats of white waterlilies were in evidence closer to the bank.

Damian and Jullanar had been not quite halfway across when the stranger fell out of the sky, and the period of drifting had taken them some five or six hundred yards further downstream, into a portion covered with yellow water kingsfoil. At least that's what she thought it would be called at home.

The sky above was uniformly covered with clouds, but they were high and bright grey, nearly silvery in places, fading to a rich blue haze in the distances as the land piled up into low hills on its way to the mountains. A freshening wind bustled around them as the boat rocked gently across the current. A few gulls wheeled over another boat off to the south, and a low-flying bird shot across their bow in a flash of black and white and orange.

Hoopoe, Jullanar remembered. Damian had pointed it out when he showed her what moving silently through the reed plains actually *meant*.

The stranger frowned. "Is this not the Lands Beyond, as you so beautifully put it?"

"No!" Jullanar hesitated. Though he wasn't dressed like anything she'd seen, even in *The Atlas of Imperial Peoples*, and his accent was entirely unfamiliar, he spoke Shaian fluently and that suggested he was from somewhere in the Empire. Thus—"Well, yes, to a certain degree, this *is*, if you're from the Empire that is?"

"I suppose that depends on which Empire you mean."

"Astandalas?"

His cheer dimmed slightly. Very slightly. "I had hoped to leave all thoughts of Astandalas behind. But yet, even here, in the Lands Beyond, where a fairy prince and his fair lady are engaged on a no-doubt glorious quest of magic and daring and chivalry—"

Jullanar's doubts as to this strange young man's nature evaporated with a sudden fit of the giggles.

He seemed to find them contagious, for he began to laugh as well, though his version was a deep, unexpected whoop that echoed across the still river. Damian heaved a great sigh of discontent and kept rowing.

Jullanar did not have any of the words to explain what was so funny, and to be honest, she had yet to discover whether Damian had any conception of humour at all. She decided to try and get the key information first and then try to summarize as best she could for him.

"I do beg your pardon," she said when they had both more or less calmed down. "This is not Fairyland, and our journey is no quest so noble."

Sadly. But true.

The stranger appeared entirely unconvinced. He glanced around meaningfully. "Here you are crossing a river the colour of jade under a sky like mother-of-pearl on a boat the colour of sunlight and sky. Yon knight wears no armour, that is plain, but his sword is at his side and his eyes are keen as a falcon's on its prey, and his is a beauty of which the poets must sing. Your face, my lady, is full of nobility and charm as any I have ever heard tell."

That was perhaps the nicest compliment anyone had ever paid her, but Jullanar had barely stopped blushing since he'd arrived and this new wave wasn't anywhere near what had resulted from indecent exposure.

"Thank you," she said briskly, having observed from her sister Clara that this was usually the best response to overly fulsome compliments from strange young men. "My name is Jullanar."

"A name fit for a fairy queen," he interjected. "I fear I cannot bow as would be appropriate, my lady, and can only offer you my wits and my magic and my harp as poor assistance on this quest of yours. My name is Fitzroy, and I am a bard like the bards of old."

Jullanar stared at him a little more, but he seemed—well, hardly *serious*, but certainly sincere.

She glanced at Damian, whose face was set into its forbidding glower. She pulled up the Calandran words. "Damian, this is Fitzroy, a ... person who writes songs."

Of *course* Damian had never told her the word for poet.

She switched her attention to Fitzroy. "Er, Fitzroy, this is Damian, a great swordsman."

That was self-evidently true, even to her.

"Enchanted," said Fitzroy the bard, grinning at them.

CHAPTER TWENTY-ONE

IN WHICH DAMIAN STRUGGLES SEVERAL WAYS

Damian was a little annoyed that Jullanar spoke the language of the stranger, but then again she was training to be a Maiden Oracle. Learning the ways of the gods was part of her trade.

(If this person was a god. But who else *could* fall out of the sky like that?)

She blushed enough to show that she was no worldly woman, that was certain. Even Damian knew what that deep pink flush meant.

"Who is he?" he asked once she seemed to have stopped laughing.

"This is Fitzroy, a writer of songs," she said, then turned and said his name to the stranger, who looked up at him with an expression that Damian had no idea how interpret at all.

"He says ... I don't know the word," Jullanar said in mild distress. "It means ... magical? It's a way of saying he is pleased to meet you."

"He says it's *magical* to meet me?"

"Er, yes, I think you could say that. He thought we were in—the kingdom of magic?"

Damian dropped one of his oars in an unexpected great burst of laughter. If there was anything you could say about Ixsaa, it was not *that*. It was a city of commerce and merchants, of lawyers and clerks, of people drawn from all the land round-about to try their hand at pigments or shopkeeping or all the small jobs in the city,

Jullanar was staring wide-eyed at him. Damian realized he had never laughed like that in front of her; he rarely found something that struck him as funny. Usually everyone else was laughing at things he did not understand at all. But this—oh, this, he did understand!

The stranger, Fitzroy, returned his laughter out loud, looking utterly delighted not to be in the 'kingdom of magic', whatever he thought that meant out of an ancient story. He said something, which Jullanar interpreted as, "Where are we, then?"

Damian twisted to check on their progress. They were far downstream of the Umberwells docks, nearly at the mouth of one of the many side branches to the Greenwater Arm. He said, "We are nearly at the South—*Phoenix!*"

"That is an interesting name," Jullanar began with her usual curiosity, only to stop when Damian kicked off his shoes, pulled his surcoat, shirt, and swordbelt over his head, and dove headfirst into the river.

Jullanar gripped the boat as it rocked in the wake of Damian's abrupt departure, utterly uncertain what she should do. Fitzroy the Poet was watching avidly, seemingly unaware that there might be any cause for concern.

She realized that Damian was swimming towards a piece of wood that was floating merrily downstream, and deduced from its yellow and blue colouring that it was one of the oars. Fitzroy seemed to make the same deduction, for he picked up the one that was still in the boat.

"Please—please don't drop that," Jullanar said. She regretted how utterly *wet* she sounded. Damian was swimming away from them.

"Isn't he beautiful," Fitzroy said.

"Well—yes, he is, but—"

"And so strong."

"Er, yes, but—"

"Competent, too."

She opened her mouth, closed it, and smiled weakly at him. "True."

"And look at those butterflies!"

It was true that there was suddenly a cloud of bright green and orange butterflies in the space between them and where Damian was even now catching up with the oar.

"Fairyland couldn't be *any* more marvellous," Fitzroy said blissfully.

Jullanar stared at him.

In the water, Damian caught up with his oar, turned, and started back towards the boat, which had been caught in a faster current. It was now shooting past him towards the still-distant bend where the river narrowed before going under the aqueduct footings.

That was a treacherous bit of water, one where someone had drowned the year before, and he swam hastily to catch the boat. He wasn't sure what Jullanar could do with one oar, and at any rate it was obvious that neither Jullanar (staring at Fitzroy) nor their sudden visitor Fitzroy (laughing at the butterflies) was thinking about trying to do anything but hold on to the boat.

One butterfly diverged to investigate the sun glittering on Damian's wet hair. He had to slow down to a dogpaddle to bat it away from his face.

The boat was now caught in a back eddy and heading towards the bank. Fitzroy was waving the oar vaguely in the air. Jullanar was gripping the boat with one hand and reaching out to stop the oar from hitting her in the head with the other. Reoriented, Damian looked into the foreground again in time to see the butterfly dip towards the water and disappear.

There was an arc of iridescence, and ripples in the water.

Damian was not a river person, but he knew what that meant. Every Ixsaan child had heard stories of the venomous rainbow snakes of the river.

He reached automatically for his sword and got a face-full of water as he reached for his hip as if he were upright on land instead of procumbent in water. Well, semi-vertical now, his feet sinking.

He hadn't brought his sword. He'd been diving after the oar, not expecting a water snake in this branch of the river. He didn't even have a dagger anywhere handy, which was a mistake he would not make again. His sword was back in the boat, useless, on the far side of the snake—he looked up and realized that Jullanar was there—called out— "My knife! My knife! Throw me my knife!"

On the boat, Jullanar looked blankly down at Damian's discarded belongings. It took her two tries to get Fitzroy to move out of the way of the scabbard and tangle of straps, what with the blue velvet absolutely everywhere and his feet and his too-short tunic riding up and dear Lady, she was going to *hell* for this—and then she was faced with throwing the weapon.

This was not something Damian had taught her yet. "Are you sure you want your *sword*?" She called out. Surely there was a dagger here some-where?—Had he called *horkha* or *horkhela*?—

Fitzroy had seen something in the water. He was not of a culture where much emphasis was given to physical strength or skill; he had not thrown anything heavier than a piece of bread in years. However, he could see that Jullanar was trying to find one of his new friend's weapons. He grabbed the sword awkwardly by the twisted metal prongs on the hilt, and then with a prayer and an effort at practical magic that both education and experience had entirely unprepared him for, heaved it off at his new acquaintance.

Damian realized how stupid an idea that had been when he saw Fitzroy stand up in the boat with his sword. Jullanar dropped any attempt to hold sword or scabbard in favour of clutching at the gunwales again. Damian reflected briefly that he really needed to make sure that she knew how to swim, and then his attention was focused on not losing his sword.

He had to lunge right towards the serpent to catch it, and the momentum of its weight coming down made the point sink straight down into the water. He held the hilt with both hands, fingers slipping around the quillons and knuckle guards, until he managed to get a firm grip on it with his strong right hand. Even as he lifted the blade out of the water it caught on something hard, heavy, and writhing.

From Damian's perspective what followed was ten minutes of splash-ing, kicking, submersion, near-strangulation, and a nightmare sense of being unable to move.

Fitzroy and Jullanar, watching Damian's progress open-mouthed from the boat, saw the black s-line of the snake in the river. Before their shouts of warning had risen to their lips Damian had demanded the sword, caught it, and plunged it down into the jade-green water with one smooth motion.

Then, six movements that to Jullanar were as perfectly executed as any of the exercises Damian had shown her. When Damian raised his sword it bore something long, black, and spitting that coiled viciously around its length, sending water in rainbow droplets all about them. Jullanar gasped in fear and amazement. Fitzroy cried, "Yes!" exultantly.

Damian ducked briefly under water, rising up again in a great spume of water with his legs gripping the snake's body, feet pushing down against its hard muscles, slipping down the scales.

Three they went under again, right under the boat—Fitzroy hastily tried to turn to follow, getting the oar fouled in the folds of his cloak. Jullanar instinctively leaned away from the flailing oar and the alarming dip in the boat. Their combined movements rocked the boat considerably, inadvertently—albeit fortunately—preventing it from whacking Damian on the head as he emerged, but doing nothing to go any direction but down over a standing wave into the next eddy.

Four Damian spouted upwards a good foot out of the water, kicking out with both his legs so the serpent slid between them and straightened until, *five*, he got his left hand under its jaw.

And *six*, arching his back and kicking out again so that the snake suddenly sailed free, the reaction pulling Damian up out of the water again, he brought his sword arm around in a forceful curve and sliced the snake right in half.

It sprang apart like a compressed spring. The head landed in the boat. Jullanar jumped half-upright out of its path, and a moment later the second bit landed on her.

She cried, "Eurgh!" at the gouting blood and gore and threw herself back with instinctive recoil. Her foot caught on one of the benches before she could go overboard, but Fitzroy, reaching out belatedly to catch her, overbalanced and went headfirst into the water on top of Damian.

Damian saw him coming with sheer disbelief that anyone could be so stupid.

This did not prevent him from plunging under the dead weight of the poet. Damian had to wallop him on the shoulder to get his attention, then pulled his head up out of the water so he could sputter and breathe and stop flailing. Fitzroy's eyes were very wide and frightened.

Holding Fitzroy more or less above the surface while he treaded water, Damian saw that the boat had snagged in one of the mats of waterlilies closer to the shore. They'd somehow managed to get within a few hundred yards of the bank, in a quieter stretch between a rocky outcrop and the beginning of the narrows proper.

He was hampered by his sword and by Fitzroy's efforts to be useful. Jullanar was calling something from the direction of the boat that Damian didn't understand, but which the stranger seemed to, or at least he started kicking his feet and let Damian direct their movement.

Damian had never actually had to rescue someone from drowning before, and wasn't sure how to get Fitzroy to shore except by bodily pulling him.

It was appallingly slow through the waterlilies, whose long sinuous stems were covered in slime and some sort of snail whose shells came to a sharp point. Both of them got badly scratched despite Damian using his sword to push the stems aside as best he could. He was relieved when he finally got his feet under him.

"Can you walk from here?" he asked, casting around for Jullanar, who was, thank the gods, still in the boat. She was gripping one of the waterlilies by its stem to keep from drifting but it looked as if the ripples from their motion were starting to detach it from its place.

He watched Fitzroy take a few tentative steps forward, long enough to see that he appeared entirely likely to fall over once left to his own devices. Deciding that his sword had been abused enough already for another indignity not to matter too much—though he also begged silent forgiveness—he passed it to Fitzroy to use as a staff.

Jullanar seemed to have grabbed hold of another plant and although she was leaning precariously with the way the boat was spinning around, she hadn't quite been drawn back into the current. Damian took a breath and shoved at the stranger so that he could grab hold of the bank.

Thus disencumbered, he was able to swim to the boat and tow it to a makeshift anchor in the form of a bankside willow in the same time it took Fitzroy to get to the shore and stop, bemused, at the two-foot clamber facing him.

Damian helped Jullanar out first, whereupon she promptly sat down on the grass to breathe deeply and look unhappy, then trotted back along the shore to their unexpected companion. Fitzroy passed him the sword first, which Damian took gratefully, then required several attempts and Damian's full assistance before he could get his foot high enough to get onto dry land. Once he finally got there he stood panting, tired, scratched, and rather confused; but he grinned at Damian in exhilaration.

"That was amazing!"

From behind him, Jullanar murmured an exhausted translation.

Damian stared at him. Fitzroy was wearing a soaking wet thigh-length tunic and had lost whatever footwear he'd been wearing, and being now half-naked seemed—perhaps because of his unconsciousness of that fact —even more foreign than he had initially.

At length Damian shook his head and turned to Jullanar, who seemed the very epitome of sense and reason in comparison. "Do you know how to swim? Move, in the water?"

She was shivering, he saw, though the air was warm, nearly hot with approaching summer. "N-no."

Damian had no idea what to do next. He left Fitzroy to his own devices and went over to his student, who was his first concern. He tried to think what his mother might say. "Is there anything you need?"

Jullanar smiled up at him. "I ... I think I'll be well, thank you. What— that was amazing, Damian, how you fought that ... what was it?"

"A rainbow serpent," he said. "A snake. Very poisonous."

He stared gloomily at the boat, which was liberally splashed with the snake's blood. At least it was *his* boat, a gift from his mother and her friends for his last birthday-but-one. He still didn't look forward to cleaning it.

Nestled amongst the folds of blue velvet cloth was a small brown leather bag. It didn't seem like anything much, really, but it wasn't his and Jullanar hadn't had it earlier, so it must have come with their ... visitor. He knelt at the bank and pulled both it and the clay bottle of water out. Jullanar would calm down with something cool to hold onto, he thought vaguely, passing it to her.

"Thank you," she said in her careful Calandran. "That must be his?"

"Will you ask him?"

"Er—yes." She turned to the stranger, who was standing on the bank smiling around at them and their surroundings without any apparent care, and spoke to him for a few minutes. Approximately three sentences in she was blushing, and Damian felt a protective urge rise.

"No—Damian, don't look like that," she said. "He's ... he just said he had not been in, uh—clothes that have water?"

"Wet?"

"Yes, that's the word. Wet clothes. He hasn't been in *wet* clothes before."

How was that even possible?

If he was a god—no. Damian found that hard to believe. *No one* actually believed in the ancient Calandran gods.

No, it must be that the world was far stranger even than Damian had ever thought.

Jullanar had told him of crossing a misty wood between her country and this, and she had, he thought, almost suggested it was a different *world*, inaccessible except by that one passage. And if she had come by such mysterious ways, what did that mean for what other people might do?

(Or be?)

Damian weighed the bag in his hand before tossing it at Fitzroy. It did not feel heavy enough to hold more than a loaf of bread or two and a coin pouch, if that, but Fitzroy made a little mewling sound of exasperation when he failed to catch it and it landed with a *thunk* on the ground.

"What on earth do you have in it?" Damian asked, then had to wait while Jullanar, once more curious, translated both question and response.

"Oh ... books and clothes and things."

"He has an extra change of clothes?" Damian paused in pulling on his own shirt to look over. Fitzroy had pulled out a billowing piece of some lightweight material in a vivid pattern of orange and blue.

While Damian slowly continued to dress himself in the clothes he'd so easily shucked (not thinking, at that moment, of the righteous embarrassment his Maiden Oracle-in-training would feel as a result), Fitzroy fought with the billows. It didn't seem to occur to him to turn so that his body blocked the wind. Damian considered suggesting this, but decided against it, as evidently also did Jullanar. Fitzroy finally compressed the orange cloth into a bundle under his arm so he could keep digging inside the bag.

He pulled out swatch after swatch of bright fabric—pink and yellow and green, vermilion and purple and white, all sorts of designs and fabrics. Damian had never seen such riotous colours for clothing, even amongst the richest and most daring of the merchants; they looked like the city walls, but even brighter.

Fitzroy eventually found what he was looking for, a white tunic similar to the wet one, and stuffed the rest of the clothing back into his bag. At this point Damian realized how extraordinarily full the bag was, but he was distracted from asking about its unusual capacities by Fitzroy stripping himself naked and then just ... standing there.

Damian hastily turned away. Taking off a shirt in front of other men was one thing—and in the city proper it was rather frowned upon—but to stand in the nude with complete nonchalance was something else altogether. What it was exactly he could not say, but he could look at Jullanar, flushing red as the Ochre Pits soil, and know that she, too, felt it keenly.

He felt a sudden stab of gratitude that he had met her, this young woman who was his opposite in almost every way but for the fact that she, too, was that little bit *counter* to everyone else. He had known her long enough now that he didn't think that she was ever easily in the centre of things. Perhaps that was she had decided to enter the cloister.

Jullanar kept her eyes well down as she said something pleadingly to their—visitor. Her voice came out a little strangled, but Damian couldn't blame her for that, not when even he felt the same. It was one thing in the baths, another in public, in the presence of a woman—a Maiden Oracle, no less!

Damian pulled out the end of his sash and began vigorously wiping off his sword, grateful that Fitzroy shrugged and did as he was bid, putting on the white tunic and then a particoloured length of cloth banded in purple, white, and green which he draped over himself so he looked even more like one of the statues of the gods.

There were stories, Damian thought uncertainly, of Orophon, god of crossroads and liars and merchants and thieves and certain types of poetry.

Once upon a time Calandran had been under the dual protection of Orophon and Arkhos, the god of war.

Fitzroy then said something cheerfully to Jullanar, who stared at him, once more with an open mouth.

"What did he say?" Damian asked in some trepidation.

Jullanar was pink again. "He asked what we were doing and if he could come with us."

Damian considered his errand and the fact that he already had Jullanar along with him, and the fact that every possible story his mother had ever told involved the solemn and sacred duty of hospitality.

Was this how an adventure began?

In ancient Calandran myth, which sometimes the guild school teacher would read to them as a reward at the end of the day, if not even Damian had messed up the lessons, the gods would sometimes come down to the ordinary world and challenge human beings to quests of courtesy and kindness and—

He didn't *believe* in the Calandran gods. *No one* believed in them.

But—

Always treat a stranger well, his mother said, *for you never know who they might be.*

This *could* be the Lord Phoenix come down to see if he was worthy.

He wasn't worthy, but—Damian wasn't sure how to say it, even to himself, except—he *wanted* to be worthy. He couldn't be the great poet, the prince, the eloquent and learned warrior, but he could be courteous, and chivalrous, and *try*.

"Very well," he said brusquely. "If you have no objections."

Jullanar had flung herself on her aunt's hospitality with no warning whatsoever barely more than a month before. She said wryly, "I can't well complain about someone else showing up unexpectedly, can I?"

CHAPTER TWENTY-TWO

IN WHICH JULLANAR TRIES TO TRANSLATE THE UNTRANSLATABLE

Jullanar watched out of the corner of her eye as Damian tied up the boat more securely. Fitzroy the Bard stuffed all of his multitudes of fabric swaths back into his much-too-small-to-hold-them bag and grinned happily at her, Damian, and the surroundings. Jullanar was not much given to assuming people were drunk, but truly, in this case, she *did* wonder.

It was easier than thinking about the gruesome remains of the serpent in the boat, or how Damian had just picked them up and flung them out into the river with barely any change of expression at all.

"Where did you come from, Fitzroy?" she tried again.

"Does it matter?—Oh, look at that white bird! Is it an egret, do you think? Those plumes look like hats."

Jullanar looked where he was pointing. She was fully prepared to deny any resemblance, but the bird *was*, in fact, spectacularly plumaged, with a bright green patch above its beak and great sweeping plumes like a cape or a veil or, yes, an extravagant hat.

"Damian," she asked cautiously, "do you know what that bird is called?"

He glanced incuriously at it. "*Velida.*"

She frowned, trying to recall her notes. "Isn't that the same name as the grey bird we saw in the marshes yesterday?"

His scowl, usually lighter away from the city, was approaching Green-market-on-market-day levels of intensity. "*Naré velida*, then."

"What is he saying?" Fitzroy broke in eagerly.

"I was asking for the name of that bird here."

"And is it an egret?"

Jullanar took her eyes off the bird, which was regarding them with what she swore was nearly amusement, in order to glance incredulously at Fitzroy the Poet. Surely he knew the word would be different in a different language? And also, that if she were asking the name for it then she didn't already know it herself? "Er, it's a white heron, if I understood him correctly."

"What was the word? *Naraveld*?"

"*Naré velida*. *Naré* means 'white'. *Nar, naré, naru*." Calandran had three genders of nouns, masculine, feminine, and neuter, and hadn't she been glad to have Aunt Maude's preliminary grammar to hand to help her work through their declensions. She wished, not for the first time, that she'd paid slightly more attention at school.

"Tell me more!"

"I beg your pardon?"

"Will you teach me this language?"

"What is he saying?" Damian interjected.

Jullanar was beginning to feel a little dizzy, turning back and forth. She focused her thoughts on Calandran first, which still took quite a bit of effort to make sentences in. "He was asking after the name of the bird also, and then wants to know if I am teach him Calandran."

"*Will* teach him," Damian corrected, and sighed reluctantly. "I suppose there's no harm, as we said he could come with us."

"Thank you," Jullanar replied, and turned to Fitzroy, who was still watching the egret preen itself. She was struck, looking again at him, by how utterly foreign he looked standing there on the bank. There was an almost stormy feel to the air around him, as if he—

She shook her head. He was obviously a wizard of some degree, even if he hadn't chosen to say what. The fact that she'd never personally met anyone with sufficient power for those as unmagical as herself to feel it didn't mean it wasn't a known, and explicable, phenomenon. It didn't *mean* that he was ... *other*.

He'd asked *them* if this were the Lands Beyond, the kingdom of Faerie, for the Lady's sake!

She repressed the small inward voice that murmured that he *would* say that, wouldn't he, if he were hiding something ...

Damian gave her a long-suffering sigh and set off inland. There was no clear path, but the grass was quite short and easy to walk on, even for Fitzroy who had—now it was Jullanar's turn to sigh. Who had no shoes on.

Fitzroy wriggled his toes in the grass, then trotted along to catch up with her. "Look at the flowers!"

Jullanar looked around, trying to orient herself. The great jade-green river was at her back, the bright orange-red-peach mass of the city visible on its other side. The green banks were much more meadow-like than anything but the grazing commons in front of the city, but like most of those, empty of grazing animals. She lifted her gaze to where Damian was halfway across the field ahead of them, striding purposefully towards a cluster of yellow and white buildings with red roofs some five hundred feet away.

"Come along," she said belatedly to Fitzroy, who pattered along beside her, murmuring words to himself and occasionally loudly enough to make her think they were for her.

A long list, presumably of flowers, whose names she was intrigued to hear—she didn't know more than one or two of them, though she was fairly sure Fitzroy was still speaking Shaian—but possibly not for soon Jullanar heard, "Oh! There's the Sun come out of hiding!—No, there he goes back again behind the clouds."

She glanced up, at where the haze was thinning a little, then back down to where Damian was now waiting for them at a break in the wattle fence that surrounded the village. Jullanar was much struck by the fence, and would have liked to examine it—it seemed to be made of bundles of reeds woven together—but one glance at Damian's thunderstorm of an expression had her smiling apologetically instead.

Damian nodded stiffly, then seemed to reconsider and gestured at the fence before naming it, the gate, something that she was fairly sure was intended to be a name for the reed bundles and decided inwardly to translate as 'wattle' until she heard otherwise, and the village itself, which appeared to be called Arkhalops.

Arkhos was the name of the ancient Calandran god of war, not to be confused with the similar *arxhos,* the word for the colour amber. *Lops* or *alops* or some related word she did not know. Looking at Damian's expression, she decided not to ask him just this moment.

"We are here," Damian announced when Fitzroy had eventually ambled up to join them, "to pick up *piriki* and *dolamaves* for the Innkeeper." He eyed Jullanar with a quelling gaze. "They are specialties of this village. Come."

She translated as best she could. Fitzroy did not seem at all perturbed that she had no idea, as of yet, what *piriki* or *dolamaves* were. He asked her for colour words, and plant names, and architectural elements she could barely name in Shaian, and took them all in with a beaming smile.

The village appeared deserted in the midmorning heat, though Jullanar guessed that there were people indoors, doing whatever they did here besides make the mysterious objects of their journey. The houses were simpler versions of the ones she'd seen in the Greenmarket, square, squat, with arched doorways and windows with slatted wooden shutters. Some of the roofs were sloped and tiled, with eavestroughs running along to channel water into great pots at the corners. Others seemed to be flat behind low parapets.

Damian led them to one particular house, pink with a door almost as green as the patch on the egret's face. He knocked vigorously on the door, bouncing it open.

"Coo," said Fitzroy, evidently thinking this was on purpose.

Jullanar bit her lip as Damian, already a little pink from the sun, flushed a deeper colour. Fitzroy ignored them in favour of peering curiously and a bit nearsightedly at the pot of herbs on the stoop. "Look," said he said, "a bee!"

Jullanar told him the Calandran name for the insect, and also the herb —spicy-scented basil, a herb she'd been unfamiliar with before arriving here.

Fitzroy said, "Oh, really? Do you think it has a person's skull buried in the pot?"

There were heavy footsteps coming from inside the house. Jullanar, however, was staring in horror at Fitzroy. "I beg your pardon?"

"You know," he said, rubbing a leaf between his fingers to release its spicy, warm scent into the air. "Like in the poem about Isabella and her murdered lover—It's called *Isabella and the Pot of Basil*. By, hmm, Threnody Orne, I believe."

Damian put his hand on the hilt of his sword and swung it out of the way as Fitzroy backed away from the bee, knocking against the half-open door as he did so. A heavy voice matching the footsteps grumbled, "I'm coming, I'm coming, hold your horses—Oivay! It's Cadia's young swordsman. Damian, isn't it?"

"Yes. I am here for the Innkeeper's—"

Fitzroy started declaiming a poem even while turning so he could stare fixedly at the man in the doorway. Jullanar's knowledge of Calandran was just good enough for her to catch fragments of the argument Damian and the villager started to have, but she also missed most of the context by virtue of Fitzroy's surprisingly resonant voice and the gruesome tale of the poem.

The villager was a plump middle-aged man, much shorter than Damian, with gingery hair quickly disappearing. He scratched a dirty apron, the movement revealing markings in red and blue running up his arm. "You're not—"

"*And her father said she would wed Lorenzo of the olive tree ...*"

Jullanar edged a step closer to Damian, who said, "He's a stranger."

"*No matter what her father said, Isabella vowed she'd never wed ...*"

"I can see that. Wherever did you acquire him?"

"*So her brothers came in the night and slew him dead ...*"

Damian gave him a truly impressively unimpressed stare. "On the river. Now, about the *piriki*?"

"*All so fair Isabella would wed Lorenzo of the olive tree ...*"

The fishmonger gave a leering sort of lopsided smile at him, then hastily added, "I'll get the parcels," and stumped off back into the gloomy depths of his house.

Damian took a deep breath and turned to Jullanar, who had no idea what to say. She had not interacted with very many people in Ixsaa yet, outside of her aunt and Damian and a few shy conversations with Damian's mother and the young women at the fountain in the Greenmarket square, but even considering Alezian, never had she been so resolutely *ignored* before.

It was one thing to know no one was particularly interested, and to be perfectly well aware that Fitzroy was in all ways far more intriguing than she herself, but ...

Jullanar hugged her arms around herself for a moment, turning away from Damian and the still-declaiming Fitzroy to look at the rest of the village.

There really wasn't much to it. Perhaps a dozen houses, no signs indicating any sort of mercantile operation, and an orange cat laying flat in the middle of what passed for the main street. From here Jullanar could see behind a couple of the houses, where there were lines with washing pegged out—mostly white sheets and a few coloured smocks and things—and more of the ubiquitous terracotta pots of plants.

Fitzroy had finished reciting his poem. "Thank you," she thought to say, turning to smile at him.

He looked genuinely surprised that she had done so, and faltered a moment before giving her an enthusiastic, "You're most welcome! What are you looking at? Have you found a mystery?"

Jullanar laughed ruefully. "No, I've never been here before. I was just ... observing the village."

"It is a most curious place," Fitzroy said solemnly, pattering over to join her. He didn't seem bothered by his bare feet at all, which now struck Jullanar as perhaps the strangest thing about him.

Well, besides the whole falling-out-of-the-sky part.

"What is that, over there? The rows are very tidy, aren't they?"

Jullanar followed him to a gap between two houses facing not the river but the land between them and the still-distant mountains. Jullanar said, "They're grape vines, I think," absently in response to his question, her eyes on the white peaks rising out of the blue haze and her heart rising into her throat.

They looked so much closer than they had from the city.

"Look at the *mountains*," she said, longing making her voice tremble.

She'd been impressed by the mountains between Rondé and Lind, the steep hills of East Oriole. But they were not these mountains, rising up into untold heights, their peaks brilliant white with snow even as their laps were a dim bluebell-colour.

The wind was blowing from behind them, from the west, but Jullanar could imagine that she might smell their clean cold air.

What strange and wonderful creatures might there be in such mountains, a world away from the Empire and all its armies and magic?

"They are magnificent," replied Fitzroy. "Do you think there might be dragons there?"

She glanced at him, startled to hear her thoughts echoed so clearly, and he gave her a guileless, curious grin back. "I don't know," she admitted, knowing that she had no idea what the word for *dragon* might be in Calandran.

"When this adventure becomes boring," Fitzroy said, "we can seek our fortunes *there*."

Jullanar opened her mouth automatically to protest this proposal—she had no skills or knowledge for living in the wilderness; she was a respectable young woman of Alinor, thank you very much; she was not here to hare off into the Wild Blue Yonder with a very strange and suspiciously magical young man she'd met all of an hour before—but something within her revolted at being sensible and proper and respectable.

"Absolutely," she said, smiling at him.

Fitzroy did not laugh at the joke but instead made her a solemn, not-exactly-theatrical bow.

It was at that moment that Damian rejoined them. He looked at Jullanar flatly. "What is he doing?"

Jullanar blushed, but wasn't sure how to explain what had just happened. "He is being foolish," she said instead, trying to emulate Aunt Maude's briskness. "Did you get your *piriki* and, er, *dolmas*?"

"*Dolamaves*," Damian corrected, "And yes." He indicated the baskets he was carrying, one containing several clay jars stoppered with cork and the other a covered wicker basket that smelled somewhat of cheese. Jullanar thought it was quite a small thing to send someone to get, but then perhaps there was something more valuable in the jars.

"Is that everything you need to do here?"

Damian turned his scowl away from Fitzroy, who was edging down the gap between the houses towards the vineyard. "For that errand, yes, but I thought you would like to see the horses. My mother keeps some of hers here."

Jullanar smiled at him. "I'd love to. Thank you, Damian."

Damian merely grunted, but she could see he was quite pleased. After ascertaining their direction she turned to tell Fitzroy where they were going, just in case he was distracted and dallied behind them.

It was a very small village, and it was hardly as if he could get lost between the vineyard on one side of the village and the pasture on the other.

It took them, the stablehand, and half the village of Arkhalops a full hour to find Fitzroy.

Jullanar could see that Damian was briefly tempted to abandon their visitor to his fate, but curiosity, responsibility, and a certain resignation to the inevitability of things won out over those unworthy impulses. It was unfortunately already more than obvious that Fitzroy had the common sense of a gnat.

"And my family thinks *me* prone to daydreaming," Jullanar muttered as she stopped to ask a woman checking her washing whether she'd seen a stranger. The woman, who had an accent nearly impenetrable to Jullanar, had not seen him, but did suggest that 'your lovely young man' could go ask at the tavern.

Obviously nice young women did not go to the tavern. Jullanar duly reported the suggestion to Damian, with a tentative question as to how they would know which building was the tavern. Damian sighed mightily and reluctantly sent the stablehand back to the horses.

The horses were a decided puzzle. They were far more beautiful than the shaggy beasts the merchants had boasted, obvious riding horses of a quality Jullanar very much wondered at, given Pelan Kasiar's status as a not-especially-wealthy notary. Damian had spoken to the stablehand who had met them at the building, relaxing slightly from his earlier tension. Jullanar had been so delighted in getting to see the horses that it had taken them both far longer than it should have to realize they'd lost Fitzroy.

The tavern, it appeared, was marked by virtue of having a grapevine in a terracotta pot growing up the *front* of the building, not just the rear. This immediately made Jullanar wonder about things like succession and ownership—were *all* buildings with a grapevine up their frontages taverns? What if the new owners didn't want to be tavern owners? They could cut down the vine, of course, but then they might lose a great deal of fruit.

Jullanar decided not to strain Damian's temper any more than it already was, and kept these questions to herself as she trailed along behind him to the tavern. There she had a bit of a surprise, for there were several old women sitting under the grapevine on an old wooden bench.

While Damian went inside (having suffered through a series of comments whose obscene innuendoes were obvious even to Jullanar, who didn't understand more than a quarter of the words), Jullanar found herself the focus of an interrogation. None of the old women seemed particularly bothered by the fact that Jullanar couldn't answer their questions even when she thought she'd understood them.

Damian came back out, took one look at her, and proceeded to scold the old women. Jullanar felt horribly embarrassed. She was hot and sweaty and wanted nothing more than to sit down in the shade of her aunt's back courtyard with a cool drink of water and a nice, simple, book, and she must look horribly overset for Damian to be so vehement in her defence.

The old women kept laughing and making the comments until Damian snapped out, "She is to be *haré nyria*, do you understand?"

That shut the old women up. They gave Jullanar apparently sincere apologies, and one woman said, "Bless you, child, for your *erianu dar*. Forgive us for our comments."

Jullanar gave Damian a confused glance, but he was still glowering at the old women. "Thank you," she said finally, giving them the polite curtsy Madame Clancette had always insisted on. "I take no offence."

"Thank you, child," the one who'd blessed her said. "Now go, and let your friend here take care of you."

"I will," Jullanar replied. Damian gave the old women a final sharp nod and stalked off down the street beside her, expression so thunderous she didn't dare ask him what he'd meant.

They eventually found the poet by following a trail of astonished people and aggravated livestock. Fitzroy was sitting on someone's front porch being menaced by a rooster. He looked deeply relieved when he saw them.

"Jullanar," he said plaintively, "this bird is very angry with me."

Jullanar bit her lip to keep from laughing. "What on earth were you doing?"

"I was just looking at it! It got mad at me and starting kicking. Look!"

He held out the end of his purple and orange mantle to show her the tear on it. The cock immediately made an indignant noise and flung itself up, feet thrust forward, spurs sharp and extended. Fitzroy jumped back again with a yelp. The cock let out a satisfied crow and proceeded to strut along the top step.

When everyone had stopped laughing, and the owner had captured his rooster, Fitzroy clambered down from the stoop after many assurances from Damian (via Jullanar, who did not fully translate either's comments) that he would protect him, if necessary, from the other chickens.

"Finally," said Damian as the various villagers dispersed, scattered laughter and sly glances making it very clear that they were still talking about the three of them. "We are going to the city now."

Fitzroy gawped at them once Jullanar had translated this. "This isn't the city?"

Jullanar felt there was an excessive amount of staring at each other in surprise. "This is a village," she said.

"There are a lot of people here."

All she could think of to say was, "There are more in the city," but before Fitzroy could comment further on this they came out of the shadows cast by the buildings to discover the sun had finished burning through the high clouds and was now brilliant in the sky.

"Augh!" Fitzroy cried, and leaped sideways into Damian.

Damian picked himself and the baskets up and stared at where Fitzroy lay sprawled in the dirt. "What is *wrong* with him?"

"I don't see any more roosters, do you?" Jullanar said, unable to keep herself from giggling.

Fitzroy pointed shakily at the ground. She and Damian followed the line of his finger. After a moment Jullanar said, "It's your shadow." She was proud of how even her tone was.

Fitzroy sat up, looking at the underside of his arms where the shadows lay across the ground. "It's attached to me! What is it? Where did it come from?"

"It's your *shadow*."

"You have one too," Fitzroy said.

To Jullanar's amazement he seemed close to tears. She kept herself from scowling like Damian, or laughing as she rather wanted to do. Fitzroy seemed genuinely upset. "Of course I do. The clouds have burned off, the sun has come out, and, and so have our shadows."

"They're not bad?"

"They're *shadows*."

"I've never had one before," Fitzroy said. Which—no. She truly had no idea what to do with that comment. He squatted down, winced, contorted himself awkwardly until he got his knee on the ground. He traced the line of his shadow, touching his feet cautiously. "It doesn't feel like anything."

Jullanar stared at him. "It's a shadow."

Fitzroy poked at it a few more times. Their shadows puddled darkly about their feet in the late morning sunlight. Jullanar looked at Damian, standing a few feet away, who said, "It's the ground that's bothering him, then, is it?"

"He's confused about his shadow," Jullanar explained slowly, completely at a loss for how to account for this. She was surprised when Damian frowned in obvious consternation. "Do you know something about that, Damian?"

"There are stories," he said vaguely. Then, more certainly: "Invite him to come with us."

Jullanar thought better of questioning him when she saw his deeply troubled expression. She turned instead to the poet with what she hoped was a suitably welcoming smile. "Look, Fitzroy, I promise you your shadow will follow you to Ixsaa. You're welcome to accompany us, but we should get going, as I believe Damian has things to do this afternoon."

"What sort of things?"

Jullanar still hadn't figured out what exactly Damian did in the afternoons when he wasn't at the Inn or visiting her. Surely it wasn't *more* practice? "Chores. Tasks. Duties."

"Obligations? Oh, I must not keep you from your rituals." He scrambled up, though not without tracing out the edge of her shadow with his fingers. "Yours doesn't feel any different than mine."

"Why would it?"

"I suppose you're right," Fitzroy agreed solemnly. "We are both young people. Perhaps shadows come at a certain age? Do children have shadows? Elders?"

"Everyone has shadows," Jullanar said, finding herself rather regretting that she was even entertaining this conversation. "It comes with being material."

"Are they different from each other quantitatively? Qualitatively?" Fitzroy picked up his feet excessively, frowning down at the shadow moving under him. "How curious that it doesn't weigh anything."

Jullanar had never thought so long about shadows in her entire life. Damian was stalking ahead of them again, striding out of the village and across the field in the direction of the river. She and Fitzroy followed along, Fitzroy silent for a few minutes before suddenly coming out with:

"Birds have a different kind of shadow."

"I beg your pardon?"

"Their shadows aren't attached to their bodies."

She glanced at him. If he were joking, he was an extraordinarily accomplished actor. "You don't have a lot of experience with the real world, do you?"

"Do you think that's what happened with mine? Do you think it was far away, and when I crossed through the Border between the worlds, it found me?"

"That would be one possibility."

"Perhaps it was kept away from me by a wicked enchanter!"

"That's another one."

"In the *Tale of the Seven Hungry Brothers* the Sorceress steals the shadows of her enemies, and enslaves them, torments them, forces them to spy for her. It's only when their sister drinks the blood of the dragon and finds the golden rooster of the Sun that—oh!" he said, and laughed merrily. Jullanar had brief hopes that he would reveal the joke, but no: "Now I know what a rooster is! I can see why it was hard for her to steal it."

"Mm."

"I say, Jullanar, do you think that's what happened to my shadow? The blood from that serpent spattered all over me—and then I found the rooster—and here's my shadow!"

Jullanar said, with relief, "And here's the boat."

It took them a few tries to arrange themselves, the baskets, Fitzroy's leather bag, and the extravagant blue velvet (still puddled in the bottom of the rowboat) in a manner that Damian agreed was acceptably balanced and which seemed unlikely to permit Fitzroy to fall out again. Jullanar settled onto her seat in the prow with a tight grip on the gunwale, grateful the blood had spattered more at the other end, as Damian didn't seem to mind sitting on it.

Damian undid the ropes and pushed off with one yellow and blue oar before setting himself to the task of rowing back to the city.

"Poor little shadow," said Fitzroy, patting the shady side of the boat. "What horrors you must have faced finding me."

CHAPTER TWENTY-THREE

IN WHICH DAMIAN OFFERS HOSPITALITY

Fitzroy the Poet was entirely unconcerned about getting back on the river.

Jullanar herself clutched the gunwale with a painful grip and tried very hard not to look at anything besides the orange blur on the horizon that was the city.

"Is water always green?" Fitzroy asked.

She looked down at him despite herself. He had been sitting facing Damian, but at Damian's glowering silence twisted around to look up at her.

"No," she said after a bit. "It changes according to the sediments in the water."

"Sediment," he murmured, tasting the word.

"Silt and soil," she explained. She'd finished all of her aunt's Shaian books by this point, and had moved on to the hydrology books from Marianne. The way rivers worked was surprisingly interesting ... though not maybe interesting *enough* to do an actual degree of study in. "The stone around here is in many layers, with many colours, and so the water is too. This is the Greenwater Arm of the River Oonar. The Whitefeather, that means."

Fitzroy looked around with keen interest. "How splendid! Is there another arm, then?"

"On the other side of the city. That one's called the Redwine. It's even bigger than this."

"A prodigious river indeed." He nodded in satisfaction, then turned around to face Damian with a dreamy expression and a quiet hum.

He apparently *was* enough of a musician that it was a tuneful hum, at least.

Damian rowed them to the Goldree, which was quicker than back to the Copperline. He would, he decided, come back tomorrow to fetch his boat from the public docks near the ferry across the Goldree. He wanted to get the cheese and liqueur to the Innkeeper as soon as possible, and of course he needed to speak to his mother about hospitality.

He tied up the boat and helped first Fitzroy and then Jullanar out. It would never have occurred to him, he thought to himself, that there would come a time when *Jullanar* would be the one to be skilled and steady. Damian was very proud of his student, and in awe at her ability to switch between her language and his.

He had been learning words in hers, but could not catch more than a few hints of what she and the stranger were speaking about. Damian gave Jullanar the packages to hold while he collected his sword belt and examined his poor sword. He would have to spend tonight polishing it and oiling the leather.

He could wear the new spectacles, and—and *see* what he was doing.

This afternoon, perhaps, he corrected himself. He was back to working at the inn tonight.

He squinted back at the boat to see if he'd missed anything. It was still bloody—there were great patches of red where the snake had fallen—so highly unlikely anyone would take it.

"Very well," he said, taking the parcels back from Jullanar. "Come."

Fitzroy managed to trip on practically every irregularity of ground between the river and the city, and was only saved from going headlong into one of the ditches by Damian grabbing his arm. Jullanar kept trying to come up with polite commonplaces to say and simply couldn't.

"How did you come to fall out of the sky?" she managed finally, bluntly.

The poet gave her another sunny smile. "I tripped!"

Of course.

She really didn't have anything else she *could* say, to that, did she?

Just inside the gates were a gaggle of children. *Urchins*, some part of Jullanar supplied. She considered them discreetly. They were dusty, to be sure, but not really *raggedy*. Mostly they looked like any group of boys sent off to play, who had decided the best game would be irritating the adults by hanging around the gate to see if anything interesting happened.

It appeared that today's interesting activity was their arrival.

"Scat!" Damian cried, with a scowl at the urchins.

The children giggled and moved away, several of the older boys trying to swagger the way Damian himself did. Jullanar fought to keep from laughing. Damian was unlikely to notice but it was still a trifle unkind, and of course she knew she shouldn't encourage them.

"I didn't know there were pygmies here!"

"I beg your pardon?" Jullanar replied, stepping around a pile of wood that seemed to be left over from the children's game.

"Little people. In 'The Siege of Mon'—"

"I have no idea what you're talking about, Fitzroy."

"In 'The Siege of Mon' they meet the pygmies. Half-sized people." Jullanar regarded him in puzzlement; Fitzroy waved vaguely at the children.

"I've heard of pygmies," she said slowly, "but these are children."

"Children?"

No one could be that ignorant, surely?

No one *human*, whispered part of her. She disregarded it as being utterly ridiculous. He *might* be from Fairyland, but then again—

No. He was surely playing a joke, that was all.

"Good one," she said therefore. "Come along, Fitzroy, I think Damian needs to deliver his parcels."

Damian had, indeed, already passed through the gate and into the Greenmarket square proper. He had been accosted by someone carrying a large box, and was answering questions impatiently. Jullanar decided to follow him, as she did not know what to do with Fitzroy—what *was* her aunt going to say? It was bad enough to be friends with Damian, let along bring yet another strange young man into her acquaintance—and angled across to rejoin him.

Fitzroy made a small noise and pressed tightly up against her back.

Jullanar stopped hard. He bounced off her and she turned to look at him, face flaming with embarrassment. "What are you doing?" she hissed. "That is no way to behave!"

Fitzroy said, "This is very busy," in a plaintive tone.

Jullanar took stock of the Greenmarket square. There was the usual handful of young women hand-spinning by the fountain. Otherwise there were only a few people wandering past on their own errands. Most were staring at them, knowing Damian and Jullanar but not, of course, their exotic companion.

"There are so *many* people," Fitzroy said.

"Twenty, at most."

"I've never seen so many strangers at once," Fitzroy said, in a tone somewhere between panic and delight.

Jullanar wanted to scoff at first, but then second thoughts took hold. What if he *had* never seen so many strangers at once? He'd thought the village Arkhalops a city, and to move from that to this—well! Even Jullanar had found Ixsaa crowded and confusing after Fiella-by-the-Sea, and her hometown was hardly a tiny hamlet in the middle of nowhere.

She glanced at Damian, who was frowning mightily as he argued with the man about whatever it was. He was paying no attention to them, but probably—yes, probably he would guess she'd taken Fitzroy to see her aunt.

"Come with me," she said gently, touching the poet on the elbow. Fitzroy startled, then grinned at her, his eyes sparkling.

"Where are we going?"

"We will go see my aunt," she declared. "This way."

She led him around the fountain and slightly away from the open door of the inn. It wasn't yet noon, somehow, so while the door was propped open there wasn't any great number of people approaching it. Her aunt's store was likewise empty as she opened its door and set the shop bell tinkling.

The interior was dim, the stationery and books neatly arranged. Her aunt must be in the back, Jullanar decided.

"It's a bookstore," she replied. "Well, also a stationery store. They don't have printing here, so it's a place where people can pay to copy them."

"Oh," he said, blinking around.

"No one else in the city reads Shaian," Jullanar said, going to the shelf in the back alcove where her aunt kept the handful of books in their own language. "Here, if you'd like to have a look ..."

Fitzroy came over eagerly, attention immediately focused on the paltry offerings.

"I'll ... be right back," she muttered, and hastened to find her aunt.

At the door to the courtyard she glanced back uncertainly. Fitzroy was already deep in a book. He was standing in a shaft of sunlight, which striped his torso and hid the mud nicely, instead picking out the gleam of his bald crown and the glint in his eyes.

He looked, Jullanar thought, the very image of a studious lord. She felt another pang of unease, and something like wonder, at his innocence, his inexplicable arrival, his solitude.

Where were the trains of servants even a Fiellanese nobleman would have, let alone one of the fabled princes of the upper houses of the Empire? Who would be searching for him?

Who *wouldn't* be searching for him?

Kasiar was tidying up their main room when Damian came in. She had not expected her son back so soon, and startled badly when she saw him. The fact that his clothes were liberally speckled with blood and his face was decidedly grim did not help.

"Damian!" she cried. "Whatever has happened?"

He stopped his usual six feet away, sticking his hands into the sash at his waist. With the sword belt slung over his shoulder and his general state of dishevelment he looked incredibly like his father had any time during that interminable civil war.

His expression shifted into something strangely uncertain. "You would agree, Ema," he said obliquely, "that it is obligatory to give hospitality to the needful stranger?"

Kasiar stared at him. And *that* was in Tanteyr. Damian never initiated conversations in Tanteyr.

And then she remembered that unexpected eruption after receiving the spectacles, when he'd declared he would no longer follow Alezian's lead in pretending not to be Tantey. And his fierce cry that just because he wasn't good at speaking that didn't mean he had no thoughts or ideas—

She recalled, too, Jullanar's tearful defence of him as a tutor, as a friend, as a fine young man.

Kasiar swallowed. Damian hardly ever asked questions. Let alone about first principles. But somehow, since Jullanar had come, that secret, mystifyingly unspoken heart of him was coming to the surface.

"Yes," she said. "Damian, why ..."

He ignored the question, rocking back on his heels instead. She bit back her words and waited while he formulated his next question.

"And you have also said that it is obligatory to be courteous and give assistance to those who ask."

Still in Tanteyr.

Kasiar was growing curious now, her doubt fading in the face of this apparent introduction to—what?

Well, obviously Damian had met someone he thought she might disapprove of but whom he felt they should offer hospitality to.

How *extraordinary*, she thought, and just barely kept herself from smiling. Who on earth had he managed to find?

"Yes," she agreed gravely.

He hesitated again. She waited more patiently than she felt.

"For it is always uncertain what is the will of ... the One Above, save that we are tested on what we do with the gifts and opportunities we are given."

Kasiar felt for a moment as if the world had turned on its head about her, and for a moment she saw his father in him so clearly her heart nearly broke again. "Yes," she breathed. "Dami ..."

But he simply nodded sharply, her serious son, and stood there, light on the balls of his feet, and said nothing more.

Eventually Kasiar said, "Did you offer our hospitality to someone, Damian?"

He nodded, glower deepening.

"Who is it?" she prompted.

"Jullanar says his name is Fitzroy the Poet."

Kasiar blinked. "Jullanar says?"

Her son's burgeoning friendship with Maude's niece was inexplicable, if welcome, but it had not hitherto taken on the less-pleasing qualities of Damian's friendship with Rean. Kasiar had hoped it was because Damian considered Jullanar his equal, knowing it was much more likely that he didn't respect women enough to follow one in that manner; but perhaps it was that Jullanar's grasp of Calandran hadn't been sufficient for Damian to learn her opinions before?

Or not, for Damian said, "She speaks his language. He is very strange." He glared suddenly at his mother, brows furrowed, eyes flashing, as if she'd started to protest or argue. "It is not correct for him to stay with Jullanar and Pelan Maude."

Kasiar shouldn't laugh at her son's—either of her sons'—earnestness, but although she managed to keep her countenance, inwardly she was fighting off giggles. "No doubt," she managed, her gravity undoubtedly false, but Damian was never one for such nuances. He'd—of course. He'd never learned to *see* them.

He nodded again, apparently satisfied, and turned as if to go fetch this … Fitzroy the Poet.

"Damian—"

He turned from the door, his expression impatient if still-polite (though not, ever, curious).

"Where did you encounter our guest?"

He considered. "He fell out of the sky when we were crossing the river."

Well. That … changed things.

～

Unlike Jullanar, whose only exposure to the high aristocrats of Astandalas past and present were the images of emperors on coins and the not-particularly-good engravings of various dignitaries at Madame Clancette's Finishing School for Girls, Maude had met several scions thereof and seen many splendid oil paintings housed in the picture gallery at Morrowlea.

When Jullanar introduced her aunt to Fitzroy the Poet, Maude's first thought was that she had seen that nose before.

"How do you do," she said faintly, racking her memory.

The strange young man beamed at her. "I do excellently well, thank you!"

No aristocrat—hardly anyone at all, but for the village simpleton—had ever given her a smile of that guileless radiance. Maude looked at her niece, who shrugged helplessly. "He fell out of the sky and landed on us."

Maude turned to the young man. "And where were you before that?" she asked slowly.

He smiled on, unmoved. "I don't know."

"Will anyone be missing you?"

Something flashed through his eyes, which Maude read as combined anger and mischief. "I shouldn't think so."

His accent was refined, if not exactly the Astandalan Court Maude had heard from a few of her fellow students at Morrowlea, which was one of the Three Sisters and therefore attracted students from the highest families. His features—that nose!—and colouring both suggested he was from one of the very highest families indeed, and though his clothes were particoloured with the mud of many of Ixsaa's surrounding streams they appeared to be of excellent quality.

"Did you run away from home?" Maude asked.

He raised his eyebrows at her. The mischief was stronger now, lightening further his oddly light eyes. "No, I was already in exile," he said. "That's why I don't think anyone will miss me."

Jullanar gasped. "What did you *do*? Why were you in exile?"

He gave her a puzzled, puzzlingly innocent look. "I didn't do anything; I've always been in exile."

"Do you have another name?" Maude persisted.

He turned that bright smile back on her. "Not yet! Just Fitzroy."

"The Poet," put in Jullanar, with an odd expression on her face.

"Yes, that's right," he said complacently. "One day it will be renowned the Nine Worlds over."

Maude was fairly glad that Damian came loping into the house then, the store-bell jangling as he shut the door behind him and pushed through the beaded curtain between store and private quarters. He nodded with his usual impatient courtesy to Maude before directing his attention to Jullanar. Fitzroy the Poet gave him a bright, happy smile. "You came back!"

Damian spoke only the handful of Shaian words Jullanar had taught him, mostly numbers from what Maude had gathered. He gave the stranger a short, reluctant nod. "My mother has agreed it is proper he stay with us," he announced in Calandran. "Tell him we offer him guest-right of hearth and home and hand for so long as he has need, asking only that he repay us with courtesy."

Maude felt her own eyebrows raise even as Jullanar (asking clarification for the Calandran word for 'guest-right') repeated these words to Fitzroy in Shaian. Damian's words had overtones of ancient customary practice from their own culture, for that was not the Ixsaan way at all. People would offer some support—a meal and a bed for the night, perhaps —to a chance-met stranger, but hardly that all-encompassing hospitality.

Fitzroy's response was equally interesting. After Jullanar had conveyed Damian's words, he turned to face the young swordsman, face serious. He bowed deeply, in a style that seemed straight out of one of the high-court manuals of etiquette she had read at university, and replied: "I thank you for your hospitality, and swear that so long as I am a guest under your roof your family will be as my family, your foes as my foes, your friends as my friends."

Someone has been reading too many ancient epics, Maude thought in amusement, but Damian accepted the translated words with due solemnity.

～

The strange ritual of hospitality completed satisfactorily—Jullanar was *full* of questions she did not yet have the words to ask Damian—Fitzroy edged over to Jullanar and asked plaintively if he could have a bath.

Jullanar had to laugh at the comment, but when she looked the poet over she realized he truly did seem distressed. His once bright linen—was that only from this morning?—had dried from its various wettings, but the muds of the North Road and the Greenwater Arm were now joined by that of Umberwells, Whitebank, and the Goldree. "What is he saying?" Damian asked.

"He'd like to clean up," Jullanar replied, daring a glance at Aunt Maude, who was about to speak when Damian snorted.

"Very well," he declared. "I can show him the horse trough on our way home. What's wrong?"

Jullanar had never discussed such an intimate thing as bathing with Damian. She blushed, and couldn't look at her aunt, but managed to say, "Damian, he's ... I don't think he would be used to a horse trough."

She'd been appalled at the disregard for hygiene when she'd arrived in Ixsaa. Her aunt had that tiled room with a large wash-tub in it, but that was unusual for Ixsaa, apparently. Ixsaans didn't like to discuss hygiene. They hid their facilities away from sight, smell, or hearing, though Jullanar could understand why that was necessary, when there wasn't running water except in parts of the Curve, where the richest merchants, guildmasters, and nobility lived, and the toilet was a well-concealed outhouse, and the bath a basin.

There was one public bath in the city, down by the wharves. It was not Astandalan style but simply a place for ships' captains to forcibly clean their sailors, next to where they cleaned the bilges.

She could almost see Damian's thoughts turning towards it and felt a minor panic at the thought of what the Astandalan poet would think of them. Fitzroy was certainly of the class whose baths were the object of praise poems, if not of the level where they were the location where imperial policies were made (and nameless orgies were held, according to the sorts of romances Marianne Faraday loved). He had almost certainly never been to a public bathhouse in his life.

"Very well, he can use the basin in the house. He'll have to carry his own water, mind," Damian said. From his expression she could tell he felt that this would be a bracing learning experience for their new friend.

"He can use ours," Aunt Maude put in. "We'll come by with him for lunch, will that be acceptable, Damian?"

"I shall tell my mother," he declared, and with another short, jerking nod, swept back out.

"Go on, then," Aunt Maude said placidly to Jullanar, just as if this were a perfectly ordinary, perfectly *respectable*, thing to do. "Show him the facilities."

~

"You don't immerse yourself fully?" Fitzroy asked, staring at it in fascination.

"No."

"Hmm."

He walked around the wooden tub, which was about four feet across but only a foot or so high around the rim, just high enough to catch the water. Jullanar went to the cupboard and pulled out a fresh sponge for him. Apparently the sponges were used for some part of the house-painting process—whether cleaning or actual painting Jullanar hadn't quite understood—and so they were quite readily available.

Jullanar had never thought about where they came from before, until Damian had told her that his brother the merchant had told him that they were some sort of sea plant that was harvested, cleaned, and dried.

"And the water?" Fitzroy said finally.

Jullanar showed him the pipe that came down from the cistern on the roof. "Don't use too much of it," she explained. "My aunt says that there is not much rain here in the summer, and she needs to keep the cistern full. It'll be lukewarm from the sun's heat ... unless you want to heat it up yourself, but—"

She stopped, for the young man was clearly not attending to her, and had in fact put his hand to his garments with the obvious intention of stripping off.

She blushed and hurried back out to where her aunt was preparing a light evening meal. Her aunt frowned at her flustered appearance. "He didn't say or do anything untoward, did he?"

Jullanar stammered out a disclaimer, but her aunt only laughed when she understood the situation. "Not quite so fine a sight as Damian at the horse trough," she said, "but worth appreciating even so, eh?"

Her mother would certainly never have been so blunt. "Can I—is there anything I can—help you with, Aunt Maude?"

"Come out," her aunt said, gesturing her through to table in the courtyard, where she resumed her interrupted task of shelling broad beans for lunch. Jullanar sat down beside her and pulled a handful of the large pods towards her. "Tell me again how you came across him?"

She listened to Jullanar's account with a frown, nails digging into the woolly interior of the bean-pods as she considered.

"If he did fall randomly through a passage in the worlds—which is what it sounds like—then I don't imagine that anyone who was looking would have a hope of finding him. Those untended and unintended passages often have strange requirements to pass through, and if it was a certain time of day or year or phase of the Moon or the like, it could be a hundred years before anyone else stumbled on the same way through."

"So we don't need to worry, then."

Maude looked at her. "We?"

Jullanar knew she was blushing again. "He was so *happy* to meet us, Auntie. And ... he'd never seen a city before. Or more than a dozen people at once. Or a bookstore. Or anyone as pale-skinned as Damian or even me."

"The only thing I can think of," Aunt Maude said, sighing, "is that he's someone very important's illegitimate son."

Jullanar could not prevent herself from gasping in shock.

Aunt Maude nodded decisively. "So long as he stays away from the Empire and anyone who might recognize him, he should be fine," she decided. "It's not as if anyone *here* is going to think him important."

CHAPTER TWENTY-FOUR

IN WHICH JULLANAR ENTERS A TAVERN FOR THE FIRST TIME

Fitzroy came out of his bath clean and dressed in a new outfit, this time a kind of loose trousers and tunic of some sort of silky cloth, the colour a vivid green. Over top he had a kind of sleeveless over-robe down to his knees that was dyed an eye-smarting magenta, a colour Jullanar had only otherwise seen in flowers. After a disbelieving moment while her eyesight recovered she saw that the over-robe was figured with paler pink blossoms near the hems.

Aunt Maude smiled as he hesitated in the doorway. "Ah, there you are, Fitzroy. We're going to Damian and Pelan Kasiar's house for a noon meal, and then you can get settled there. Rest, if you wish, after your ... adventures this morning. And then if you wish you can go play for the inn's customers tonight—"

Fitzroy startled, his light eyes wide with sudden, astonished, amazement. "You mean—" he gasped, apparently sincerely. "I could *perform* for them? Oh, happy, happy day!"

After asking Jullanar to fetch another pitcher of water, which the young woman went to do gladly, Kasiar looked at the young man her son had found, and struggled once more with containing laughter.

It wasn't that the young man—Fitzroy the Poet—was risible in himself, but he was so very much the opposite of Damian that it was hard not to find the contrast delightful. They were nearly the same height, the stranger perhaps an inch taller, but there the similarities stopped.

Where Damian was pale-skinned and blond, this young man was near-black and bald. Where Damian was serious and intense and glowering, Fitzroy was wreathed in brilliant smiles and alert curiosity. Where Damian was broad-shouldered and lean-waisted, each muscle perfectly defined, their new guest was just on the edge of plump and noticeably soft.

On seeing Kasiar he bowed and gave her a long, flowing greeting in his own speech.

Damian said, "Jullanar says she told him that we didn't speak his language. I *thought* Pelan Maude was coming too."

"I expect she'll be here in a minute," Kasiar said, and curtsied gravely to the young man, who beamed at her. "Damian, I've sorted out the spare room for him, if you'll show him the way. Alezian's, ah, speaking with his merchant-master, and won't be back till ... later."

The next morning, probably. Hopefully. Alezian was not dealing well with discovering that Damian had thoughts and dreams he had never shared.

"Thank you, Ema," Damian said, and then turned his glower onto his new friend, who appeared to disregard his expression entirely. "Come."

Fitzroy the Poet pattered along behind him, still talking incomprehensibly and gesturing happily at things he was noticing. Kasiar watched them go, utterly bemused. Damian's voice punctuated the foreign prattle with his usual brisk, economical use of words. Neither young man seemed to give any heed to the fact that the other could not understand a word he was saying.

Dear Lady, but Fitzroy could *talk*.

Jullanar sat beside her aunt, feet crossed primly and back straight, as she watched Damian and Fitzroy across from her. Damian was eating in his usual slow, methodical fashion, cautious with his cutlery: now that Jullanar knew it was because of his vision, this caution made a great deal more sense.

Fitzroy, on the other hand, was enthusiastically talking about everything that came into his sight and seemingly his mind.

He had begun with requesting Jullanar pass on his gratitude to 'Lady Kasiar', which she did gladly.

"The bed is a marvel," he informed Jullanar next. "The mattress is on *ropes*, can you imagine? Ropes! It's deliciously springy."

She regarded him as he continued to speak about the bed for a good few minutes. He compared it to the other two beds he'd ever slept in, both of which sounded frankly grand, with digressions onto beds mentioned in poems he knew.

He knew a lot of poems.

More of them had beds in them than she'd ever thought about.

She supposed it came of being a bard. Whatever exactly that meant.

"And then," Fitzroy said, "there are *chairs*! And you *sit* on them!"

Jullanar glanced at her aunt, whose lips were twitching but who was resolutely focused on Pelan Kasiar. They seemed to be talking about why the innkeeper wasn't there for lunch with them.

"Where is Cadia, do you know, Damian?" Pelan Kasiar asked her son.

Damian shrugged. "I didn't see her. I gave the cook the cheese."

Fitzroy cocked his head, then caught Jullanar's eye. "What a mellifluous language! You are very quiet?"

Jullanar blushed for him. "I was listening to you," she replied.

He stared at her. "Truly? No one ever has before! Shall we be friends until the end of time, Jullanar?"

"Oh, and beyond, most certainly," Jullanar replied, giggling, before she caught her aunt's knowing eye and blushed again, more genuinely. "Tell me, why are the chairs so interesting to you?"

He picked up his fork and twirled it. "This is a fork, is it not? And you sit a high table." He considered his plate and carefully used his fork to corral some of his stuffed vine leaves.

"What do you mean? Wouldn't you eat at a table?"

He gestured vaguely downwards. "At a low table, with reclining couches, not these chairs. My tutor told me in Alinor they do not recline as we do, and that some elsewhere take that custom. He had chairs and a table made so that I could learn the proper etiquette, and he had brought forks too. But I thought no one really did it, except perhaps on the outworlds." He paused. "I suppose this is one of the outworlds."

It *was*, but after a month Jullanar had come to the conclusion it wasn't *as* different as one would have expected. Fitzroy was the most curious thing she'd seen so far. "How can you eat lying down? Isn't it uncomfortable?"

None of her books had ever mentioned such vital details as to whether the characters were sitting in chairs at table or reclining on couches. And some of them—many of them—were set at what purported to be the Astandalan court.

If Fitzroy were from the Astandalan court. But where else *could* he be from?

She took a breath, but she *was* curious, and it was hardly as if he seemed the sort to be offended by her reciprocal questions. "What sort of furniture do you have?"

"I beg your pardon?"

"What kind—I mean, if you don't have chairs and tables, what do you have?"

"I've not thought about it. We have tables, just not so high. Couches. Boxes, I imagine, for storing things. Wardrobes." Fitzroy appeared to ponder the question gravely, falling silent while he ate his meal. Jullanar watched him—he had beautiful manners when he wasn't talking—before turning to Damian and asking him what his plans were for the rest of the day.

"I am working tonight," Damian said.

His mother turned to him. "Dami, are you busy this afternoon? Were you going to practice?"

Damian considered this seriously. Beside him, Fitzroy appeared to be counting on his fingers, but quietly enough Jullanar couldn't decipher what precisely he was saying. "No," Damian said eventually, edging away from the poet slightly. "I must fetch my boat and clean it. And my sword."

Jullanar shuddered at the memory of the snake, and then realized this was a way she could repay Damian for the visit to the Vez-Vez—whatever those colourful cliffs had been called. (That was how friendship worked, wasn't it? A gift, a reciprocal gift, a shared story ...?) "Damian fought a—what did you call it, Damian? A snake? In the river?"

Pelan Kasiar turned to stare at her son. "A river snake? A rainbow serpent?"

"Yes," he said briefly.

"We were crossing over the—the Greenwater," Jullanar supplied, fighting for the words. "When—when Fitzroy down falls—"

"Fell down," Damian corrected.

"When Fitzroy *fell down*, Damian dives—dove—into the river," Jullanar amended, and when he nodded almost encouragingly, she told the story as best she could. It was hesitatingly, simply, straightforwardly. But she managed to find the Calandran words, corrected occasionally by Damian in his usual brisk manner, and she could see the pride in Aunt Maude's eyes for her being able to tell a story even so hesitatingly, so simply; and she could see the pride in Pelan Kasiar's, and could guess it was only partly for the magnificent feat slaying the snake while *in* the Greenwater, for she smiled at her son whenever he spoke.

At the end of her tale, Damian stirred uncomfortably. "So you see, the boat needs to be cleaned. And my sword."

"Yes, I can see that," Pelan Kasiar murmured. "If you don't wish to rest?"

Damian scoffed, but Jullanar was quite glad that he said, "No, but Jullanar might."

"And—our guest?"

Jullanar turned to ask Fitzroy, who set down his fork so he could lean around the water jug to peer earnestly at her. "There were twenty-three pieces of furniture in my old place," he announced. "That's if you count the bath, of course."

After lunch and cleaning up—which was a task Fitzroy had clearly never done, or even thought about doing, before, but to which he set his inexpert hand cheerfully, only breaking two plates—the poet went to rest in the spare room.

Jullanar finished most of the tidying up, and then she and her aunt returned to their house while Damian went off to his boat.

"That was quite the story," Aunt Maude said once they had returned to her house and were collecting their handicrafts and a pitcher of cool water.

"It was quite the sight," Jullanar responded, smiling wryly as she set the water and squat glasses on the table. "It's good to be able to speak, at least a little!"

"You're doing very well," her aunt assured her. "Damian seems to be a good teacher."

"He is."

Her aunt surprised her with a sudden embrace. "I'm proud of you," she said, and then, almost embarrassed, fussed with the shade umbrella while Jullanar flushed with pleasure at the compliment.

∾

They ate a light meal around sunset, and then Jullanar went to Pelan Kasiar's house to see if there was any translating necessary. Pelan Kasiar told her that Damian had gone to the Inn and taken Fitzroy and his harp with them there to perform, and that all seemed well.

Jullanar wondered where the harp had come from, but remembered that Fitzroy was a wizard, and thus ... well, thus *magic* was probably the answer. She returned home in good spirits, with only a shy, regretful glance at the noise spilling out of the Inn. It was not, *really*, a place for her; even her aunt had said so.

She could still be curious—of course she could.

She sat down next to her aunt with an oil lantern and one of the denser tomes from Marianne, trying to make sense of the description of how dykes and their sluice gates worked, and was enormously, ridiculously glad when not even a quarter-hour later they sent for her.

It was not Damian or Fitzroy, but rather one of the other staff: the shy, androgynous Luce from the stables.

"Please, Pelan Maude," the ostler said, "Damian asks if Jullanar might come translate. 'E says there won't be no mischief offered."

Aunt Maude frowned. Luce, thin face earnest, hastily added: "There hain't been no problems since he came on, not for me, not for the girls on the bar, not for no one. Not that Pelan Cadia holds with that, but she can't be everywhere."

"And Damian can?" Aunt Maude said slowly, but with a faint smile in her eyes.

"'E hain't one to listen to excuses," Luce said simply.

Jullanar had to listen very carefully to understand Luce's accent. But she could agree with that: Damian did not actually *see* most of the details that other people took for granted, including how people were reacting to his thunderous scowls.

Of course, he had a near-permanent headache from trying to focus on near distances in town.

"Is Pelan Cadia there?" Aunt Maude said.

Luce shrugged. "She got the headache, Pelan Maude. Zurannah's in the kitchen tonight."

Aunt Maude smiled apologetically at Luce and switched to Shaian. "Are you comfortable going over to translate, Jullanar? It may be a bit rough—I love Cadia dearly, but the inn after sunset really isn't a place for a young lady. I'll not be far, I know Cadia's headaches and I'll take her some herbal tisane, but it'll still be you."

"And Damian," Jullanar pointed out stoutly.

Everything she'd been taught growing up should have made her resolutely avoid the place and all it represented. Drinking! Gambling! Fighting! And for all that Pelan Cadia was a woman, and bar Damian and the cook so too were her staff, it was certainly not a *respectable* place for a young woman to go.

She had to admit she was deeply, deeply curious.

"I'd like to assist, Aunt Maude," she said as demurely and candidly as possible. "I promise I will be safe."

"Stay in Damian's sight," her aunt said sternly. "And do *not* go off with any strange young man."

"Of course, Aunt Maude," she promised, though even as the words left her mouth she wondered just what Fitzroy would lead her into that evening.

～

Jullanar looked curiously around as Luce led her through the crowd. The room was quite large, low-ceilinged and redolent with drink and dirt and musk and something strongly garlicky. It was warm and crowded, with a buzzing sort of atmosphere, half-audible and half-simply felt. Jullanar grasped her skirt with sweaty fingers, hoping she did not look anywhere near so awkward as she felt.

This was very much not a place for the likes of *her*. And yet—she'd been asked, and her aunt had given her permission ... Why?

Not that it was entirely populated by men: a few women were scattered through the crowd, though most of them seemed to be ... Jullanar blushed, not quite sure what she was looking at but knowing it had to do with what the girls at Madame Clancette's whispered about after curfew. The woman were lush or slim, their garments tighter than Jullanar's own Ixsaan-style gown; their hair was more elaborately styled, and they wore colour on their faces, rouge on their lips and something shimmery around their eyes.

She knew she was probably supposed to disdain them, these ... loose women ... but something in her was more curious and intrigued and, well, excited. The room seemed to be full of secrets, and Jullanar yearned to understand them.

Damian was standing next to a long and sturdy-looking counter set towards the back of the room, his face at its most forbidding. He glanced up at the door when Luce opened it, and his face briefly softened as he nodded at Jullanar. A slight motion from somewhere in the crowd had his glower sharpen even as his head snapped in that direction. Someone exclaimed something and a wave of laughter rose up as someone else made a sort of apologetic rant. Damian's face did not soften again, but he did look away from the group.

In the corner between the bar and the large fireplace that must warm the room in the winter—unlit this hot evening—was a small stage wedged between the chimney-breast and a partial wall. Standing there and regarding the crowd with absorbed wonder was Fitzroy the poet in all his eye-blinding magenta-and-green glory.

Luce tapped her on the shoulder. Jullanar leaned over for the ostler to say in her ear, "Zurannah said to tell Damian to serve the bar."

With that the ostler disappeared into the crowd, like a rabbit going into its cover, and left Jullanar standing there alone and self-conscious in a small circle of empty space. A few men were looking at her and muttering to their companions, but nothing she could hear.

Face burning, she lifted her chin and walked as steadily as she could manage to the bar. Damian grunted when he saw her, then at her sharp glance—for she could not help her reaction—he nodded shortly and said, "Thank you for coming," which was quite a concession from him, really.

"What's the problem?" she asked, even as she watched the room.

"He won't do anything," Damian said, gesturing at Fitzroy, who was still in front of a chair with an instrument case in his arms and his face in an unfortunately asinine grin. "It's embarrassing."

Jullanar considered this. *She* was embarrassed for Fitzroy, and she'd only been in the room a couple of minutes. She nodded slowly. "Luce says you're to serve for now," she said, recalling the instructions.

"Luce doesn't give orders," Damian grumbled, but after uttering one of his sighs he casually vaulted over the counter.

A mild cheer went up, partly for the feat and partly because he snapped out, "Anyone wanting a drink should come up. No table service."

That caused a murmur, and also a general shifting of position as the patrons conferred briefly—amazingly briefly, really—and sent emissaries from their tables up to get drinks. Jullanar pushed her way uncomfortably through the crowd, but she was given just enough space to pass through without having to brush up against anyone.

"Hullo," she said to Fitzroy when she made it to the stage. There was no room to stand before it, so she stepped up to join him.

It was only half a foot or so above the ground, but that was enough to give her a sense of view, even of superiority, as she surveyed the room. No wonder Fitzroy was so captivated by all these men (and those few women) scattered around, half-paying him attention. He'd already made it clear he found men attractive, and there were some fine examples in the room even excluding the scowling Damian.

"Oh," he said, starting. "Jullanar! You're here!"

"I am," she agreed. "Damian sent for me to translate. What seems to be the problem? Do you need something before you can play?"

He turned his amber eyes on her; they caught the torchlight like her mother's tiger's-eye agate brooch. "I have never played in public before," he whispered. "I don't know what I'm supposed to *do*. All the stories make it sound easy."

"You have your harp there, I take it," she said, gesturing at the case. "Is it ... tuned up?"

"I tuned it in the back room, yes," he agreed, wrenching his attention away from a man who was picking his nose.

(Not everyone in the room had the standards of hygiene to which Jullanar was accustomed, she had to admit. Her nose seemed to have shut down as she crossed the room, so the pong no longer seemed quite so invidious.)

"No one can understand you anyway, besides me," she said pragmatically. "So I would just take it as an excellent practice run for future adventures, and play whatever you like. When you're tired ..." She glanced around, but it *was* a tavern, and inspiration quickly struck. "Damian will give you a drink then, as ... payment."

There might be actual pay involved if he were any good, but Jullanar felt she should not promise anything. It wasn't as if *she* had any Ixsaan money besides the handful of coin her aunt gave her to spend.

Fitzroy swallowed, his throat flexing. "My stomach feels odd," he admitted.

"Just a small case of nerves, they'll go away when you start," Jullanar declared blithely. It was what her father had told her, and what she herself had never personally experienced—in her experience the nerves were present all the way through any given activity, such as writing a major exam for instance—but Fitzroy appeared to believe her, for he nodded resolutely.

"I shall begin," he said, "with 'The Siege of Mon', in honour of the pygmies we saw earlier."

"They were *children*," Jullanar said, then had to jump off the stage as Fitzroy suddenly swung around, set down his case, and sat down in the chair.

"I begin," he said solemnly, and began to play.

Jullanar had to admit, from where she stood in the press of doubting, drinking listeners, he wasn't actually all that bad. At the end of the song, several people even clapped.

Fitzroy gave them such a glowing smile that Jullanar was not surprised to hear a few whispered oaths, but he merely announced, "'Oraphu'," and launched straight into another song.

Jullanar found herself edging through the crowd to stand in Damian's previous spot. He was busy acting as the bartender, but still obviously keeping a sharp eye on the room, for he nodded at her and then briskly informed the next hopeful drinker that he would see his money first or there would *be* no more drinks.

The response was slurred and incomprehensible to Jullanar, so she leaned back agains the counter and listened to Fitzroy. For someone who claimed to have never performed before, he was surprisingly adept.

Mind you, he'd expressed surprise over the fork and clearly known how to use that, too.

What a strange person, was her final thought before she gave herself over to enjoying the sound of her own language. The songs were unfamiliar and Fitzroy's accent odd, but still ... it was a *little* exciting, she decided.

Just a little.

CHAPTER TWENTY-FIVE
IN WHICH SEVERAL THINGS HAPPEN

After three-quarters of an hour or so Fitzroy stopped playing. He bobbed his head in surprised acknowledgement of the smattering of applause he received, and permitted one of the more enthusiastic listeners to draw him across the room to the counter.

Once there, Fitzroy turned to Jullanar, beaming with an almost frightening level of intensity. "That was fantastic!"

"You sing nicely," she replied honestly.

"All these people! Listening! To *me*! This truly is the best day of my life."

"I will buy him a drink," his enthusiastic listener said to Damian in Calandran. "That was the funniest thing I've seen in years. And he wasn't so bad at the music, neither. What'll ye have, lad?"

Jullanar translated the last sentence. Fitzroy gave her a wide-eyed smile. "What does he want to give me?"

Jullanar was beginning to realize why people skipped over the necessities of translation in books set outside the Empire, or in those remote parts of it where Shaian was not yet well known. She sighed and translated this, too.

"*I* recommend the red Linnet," a new voice said, pushing up between Jullanar and Fitzroy's new patron. It was the dashing young man from the storeroom, looking even more dashing even if somewhat older in the inn's fitful light. He had dark curly hair, like most Ixsaans, and tanned skin with a smattering of freckles across his nose. He ignored Jullanar in favour of leaning on the bar so he could regard Damian intently. "Hullo, Damian."

"Rean," Damian replied stiffly. "You're back from across the River, then?"

"Just got in today," Rean replied, tossing his hair back. He wore a golden earring with a red jewel in it, and his teeth were very white as he laughed. "I've missed you."

Damian nodded jerkily. Fitzroy said, "I am rather thirsty, if there are drinks to be had, now that you've mentioned it, Jullanar ..."

Jullanar thought she saw Rean's his eyes turn calculating an instant before she began to speak, but he was only leaning even further across the counter to whisper something in Damian's ear. Damian's visible discomfort was a surprise, even more so when Rean settled back with a self-satisfied, smug sort of smile. "A bottle of the red, then, Damian, if you'd be so good. I'll share with your new ... friend."

Damian met Jullanar's querying gaze with a fierce scowl. He couldn't *see* her expression, she reminded herself. Rean shouldered her and the other man out of the way with an easy, inoffensive motion. He then slung his arm over the poet's shoulder. "Shall we be friends?" he said, barely waiting for Jullanar's translation. "This wine is the best in the Inn. Make it two bottles, Dami. Your friend here looks like he can hold his own."

Fitzroy looked nothing of the sort, as even Jullanar could tell. She frowned from Rean to Damian, but could make nothing out of the situation. Damian had not mentioned anyone named Rean to her, had he?

"What does he want?" Fitzroy asked, regarding Rean's arm with mild puzzlement. "Why is he touching me?"

"I think he wants to be your friend," Jullanar said, a little doubtfully. "He's asking you to sit and drink with him."

"What custom is this?"

This flummoxed her. She knew men went to taverns to drink, and seemingly enjoyed it by the number of drinking holes in existence. Why precisely they did so was something of a mystery. "I think it makes you feel nice to drink," she hazarded.

Certainly the angrier tracts *against* drinking made it sound enjoyable.

Preferable to yet another evening spent embroidering with her sisters while her mother read from *Sermons for the Moral Improvement of Young Ladies*, at any rate.

"And so he gets the bottle," Fitzroy said, regarding Rean who was now jollying the first man along, and in fact appeared to have managed to inveigle him into paying for the wine, as the man produced coins and Rean clapped him on the back with a crow of triumph. "And then ... we drink it?"

"Yes."

"Is it a competition?"

Jullanar hesitated again. "I think some people try ... to drink more ... than the other ..."

Madame Clancette had given her girls Warnings about the Great Dangers awaiting them at university if they weren't sufficiently cautious. Even before she'd so nearly failed the Entrance Examination and thus shamed her family Jullanar had started to wonder why all the forbidden Great Dangers sounded so much more appealing than the expected *appropriate* behaviour.

"Like a tournament to win the ribbon of a fair lady," Fitzroy said, nodding. "I shall not fail you, my lady!"

"Well—"

But he was already beaming eagerly at Rean and spouting some sort of nonsense about jousting and drinking and tournaments of strength as he reached for the clay goblets Damian had set on the counter.

"You'd better take it over to a table so others can get to the bar," Damian interjected.

Rean laughed. "We won't *lose* you custom tonight, Damian, never fear," he said, winking before leading both Fitzroy and the original man to a table near the centre of the room. It had been occupied, but emptied at the word of a drinking competition—or perhaps it was just Rean's reputation? People seemed to know him, by the laughs and the glad slaps on his back and the eager expressions.

Jullanar glanced at Damian, bit her lip, then made her way to stand next to the poet. "Fitzroy, do you know what you're doing? Are you a great drinker? You might find ... Daven liquor different than what you're used to."

"I'm not used to anything, I've never drunk wine before."

Her expression must have faltered, for Rean gave her an intrigued, bright-eyed glance. "You're translating, then?" he murmured. "Tell him the loser ... hmm. What *shall* we wager?"

Jullanar did not have the least clue what sort of things men wagered on drinking competitions, and feared her face said exactly that.

"Such an innocent young lamb," Rean murmured, giving her a slow, deliberate look that made a shudder run through her. He grinned, more coolly than Fitzroy (who was examining the goblet with interest). "Let's make this interesting. I'll wager my sword against his harp."

There was a widening pool of silence. Jullanar glanced at Damian, who was frowning very sternly at Rean, but no one said anything.

She turned back to Fitzroy. "He, he has suggested you bet your harp against his sword."

Unsurprisingly, the poet frowned. But then he said: "He has seen my harp, but I have not seen his sword."

Jullanar swallowed a nervous titter and repeated this. Rean nodded, as if impressed, but there was an impatience to his bearing and a certain disdain in his eyes. Nevertheless, he reached to his side and withdrew a steel rapier with a quiet, satisfying hiss.

Having spent all those months learning Calandran from Damian Raskae, Jullanar now could tell that this was quite a good weapon. Fitzroy examined it carefully, though he didn't focus on any of the features Damian had taught Jullanar to look for.

"That is a worthy wager," he declared eventually. "I accept."

There was no way, Jullanar thought even as she translated this for Rean, that this was going to end happily.

Fitzroy grinned at Rean and sat down with a little flourish of his magenta robes. Jullanar wondered how he knew how to do that if he wasn't used to chairs, and hesitated in contemplation, wondering if he was quite—well, what? she asked herself.

Real?

What did that mean, in the context?

Her aunt's comment that he was like a parody of an Astandalan lord came to mind. But—could *anyone* pretend that successfully to be that innocent of ordinary life?

By the time she'd found a chair to sit next to the two bettors, close by to translate (and not at all because she was curious, no, *not at all*), a crowd of people had gathered at the bar. From their conversation she gathered they'd figured out that a drinking game was on, and were now buying drinks and laying bets on the outcome. Someone asked for food, only to be told it was delayed.

Rean opened the bottle of red Linnet and smiled at Fitzroy as he poured full goblets. "To your health," he said, lifting his.

Fitzroy lifted his. "*Agyurkin.*"

Rean drank down his goblet in one pour; Fitzroy made a good effort but took three swallows to finish it off. They both set their goblets down together.

"Your turn," Rean challenged.

"You should pour the wine this time," Jullanar supplied. "What did your toast mean?"

"Toast? Oh—'To the last drop', it's from *Ezuridon*, there is a drinking competition there. The god of wine challenges the god of beer to see which of them can drink more. This is wine, isn't it? Not beer?"

"Definitely wine," Jullanar managed as he drank down his second cup.

Fitzroy peered at the remains in the goblet. "That second time tastes better. Is there going to be food, do you think?"

"I ... can see," Jullanar said. "Unless you need me to translate?"

"Not if all we're doing is this," Fitzroy replied.

Damian was leaning pensively on the bar. His shoulders really were magnificent, Jullanar decided even as she pushed her way towards him. The crowd once more parted, for whatever reasons seeming to accept that she had the right to be there.

"Is there any food?"

Damian heaved one of his great sighs. "The cook's gone off. Zurannah's there, but ..."

Aunt Maude had muttered, once or twice this past month, that the Inn's cooking wasn't very good.

"It's busy," Damian said, knitting his brow together. Jullanar wondered just how bad his headache was, in the busy Inn. Possibly even with no supper! "People are itching for something to happen," he went on unexpectedly. "That better not get out of hand."

Jullanar and he both looked across the room. Fitzroy's magenta and viridian were easy to spot through the duller crowd. "If it's his first time he won't last long," she said comfortingly. "I hope he understood he was betting his harp, though."

"Yes."

Damian looked even more disgruntled than usual. Hungry, Jullanar reminded herself. "We had some spinach pies left from supper. I'll run and grab you one. Stay there."

"Where else would I go?" he retorted, pulling out a cloth. She left as he began wiping the counter moodily.

Outside it had gotten very dark. Jullanar went quickly to her aunt's house, fetching a plate of pastries from the kitchen and then hurrying back to the Inn. Its doorway was marked by torches, and the sounds pouring out the open door seemed merry and inviting.

All those tracts, Jullanar thought, and *none* of them mentioned the smell. And yet that was really the main problem with the tavern.

When she came in, Damian was leaning on the bar, forearms crossed. The pose showed off his musculature beautifully. ("All that work he puts in," Aunt Maude had said more than once to Jullanar, "it'd be a shame if no one appreciated it.") He was frowning at the thick crowd cheering Rean and Fitzroy the poet, but brightened when she slid the plate before him.

"Should I go help in the kitchens, or stay here?" She asked. He looked at her. Even though she knew the scowl was not really aimed at her, it was still disconcerting, and she nearly capitulated to his unspoken disapproval when a sudden roar erupted and stole Damian's attention. Someone cried, "Ahoy there bartender! Another bottle!"

Damian hastily swallowed the second half of his pastry and turned to his supplies even as Fitzroy called out to Jullanar to translate some ripe joke Rean had just told, to much laughter from his audience.

Damian was extremely grateful for Jullanar's kindness in bringing him food—the herbs were in a different combination than he was used to, which suggested the pastry had come from her house—though he wished she would go home. And stay there.

He was still in control of the room. He would have been gladder if Zurannah could come out the front, and gladder still if Pelan Cadia were here as usual—but still, nothing serious had happened. Yet.

He glowered at Rean, confused by the man's behaviour. It was even harder to understand from his position at the bar, what with people shouting at him for food and drink, and shouting at Rean and Fitzroy for the sheer glee of it, and the smoke from the torches and the smell of all the wine and bodies, and—and all the close quarters, without his spectacles— not that he would wear them *here*.

Damian took a breath and centred himself. He still had his job to do. He could watch people's demeanour from behind the bar.

Word had somehow gotten out that a serious drinking match was under way, and since Rean was well known, and Fitzroy entirely *un*known, it was proving far more intriguing than Damian would have suspected.

He half-heard someone say something about the greyhounds being off that night because of a problem with flooding. That would explain the eager interest in the Inn, for on greyhound race nights there tended not to be much else going on in the floodplains.

But it worried him. The Whitefeather was beginning its summer rise, but it shouldn't have broken the levees this early.

The balance of people shifted from those he knew to strangers. Some of them he recognized from his nights prowling the crowds at the races, and he kept careful watch on those he'd long since marked as predators. He kept particular watch on the ones closest to Jullanar. She had some protection because of her status as a prospective Maiden Oracle, but she was also young and foreign and despite Damian's efforts over the past few months, still far too easy prey.

Rean called for a fourth bottle. Fitzroy watched wide-eyed as someone else fell over with a crash onto the floor beside him. Drunk on his own bottle of fortified wine, Damian identified. Jullanar was whispering something to the poet, who looked intrigued.

Damian winced. He might have only known Fitzroy for half a day, but he was already fairly certain him looking intrigued was a dangerous sign.

The drunk man's cronies hauled their friend out of the way. One of the watchers supplied the bottle and Rean poured it, his hands not quite steady. Damian narrowed his eyes at him. He'd spent enough time around the older man to know that another goblet would see him cross the line from drunk to catatonic.

Fitzroy himself showed no sign of inebriation. Mind you, he'd been so odd all day Damian was not entirely convinced he wasn't already under the effects of something.

Someone bought another round for one half the room, Damian tensed his muscles to leap over the counter when he saw someone starting to prod another, prelude to a fight—but the man's neighbours saw Damian's reaction and quickly shoved them both away, out the door. Damian nodded grimly to himself and calculated how much was currently in the small chest he was using as the till.

Usually it was his job to carry the strongbox to Pelan Cadia's strongroom. As she'd taken the key with her, he'd have to hide it in the kitchen cellar. But that meant he would have to leave the taproom. Which seemed a poor idea.

Rean and Fitzroy moved on to the fifth bottle. The Linnet was strong stuff, and Damian could see that Rean was feeling its effects. His motions were slower than usual, and more exaggerated, and his Tholarri accent was growing thicker.

One goblet down. Two. The third from a bottle (or rather the fifth and sixth) was always smaller, but—

Yes. That was Rean's limit. He managed to swallow half of it, gagged slightly, hesitated, and drank another small mouthful before his entire body declared revulsion to the idea of any more alcohol that night.

He set the goblet down with a loud clunk, splashing out a bright puddle. He tipped over the goblet for good measure, the remaining wine spreading across the table. "'Zat'z it," he said, slurring. "No more. You win."

Jullanar translated that with a confused but somewhat proud expression. Damian thought she was proud of Fitzroy for his stamina, and probably just as curious as to just what and why the poet was capable of it.

Fitzroy gave the room a bright, alert smile, and said something that was so obviously a challenge no one needed Jullanar's reticent translation of, "Anyone else?"

One of the many consternations of Alderman Coster—the member of the city government most opposed to the general persistence of the Greenmarket as its own small community—was that there was no law to enforce closing times in the Greenmarket. Cadia generally stopped the kitchen well before midnight, though she kept serving drinks until she herself wished to go to bed.

Damian, beside himself with frustration, did not think of closing. His demeanour was both terrifying and efficient, and more than one person who'd in the past speculated he was all muscles and no brain had to admit that he was, at the very least, quite competent when it came to ensuring anyone who wanted a drink paid for it. Only one person even hinted at credit, and he was given such a fierce glare that he shrank back into the crowd and refused to go back up again.

Rean was followed by Tarka, a big man in his late twenties. He was the son of the head of the Farmers' Guild, and was rumoured to wrestle bulls for fun. He did not run with the caravan guards—quite the opposite, in fact. He and Rean had a strange way of circling about each other, never quite sparring, never quite comfortable.

He'd been drinking, but nowhere near so much as Fitzroy, and came with all deliberate majesty from his seat in the corner, casting many a wink and a grin to the crowd.

Damian had heard a snippet of conversation from two of the Guilders, up at the bar to collect more wine, that Tarka would challenge Rean after the bout was won. Drinking contests usually ended up with one or the other of them winning the pot, though Pelan Cadia tried not to let them both compete in the same evening.

Tarka didn't seem to mind that instead of the famous guard it was the unknown Fitzroy who greeted him amiably. He grinned complacently. "I'll take Rean's sword off you when I win." At someone's scoff, he added, "And if I lose, my good black horse. Damian, new bottles! None of that Linnet schlock now, bring us something real. The sinners' casks."

Tarka's black horse was an excellent prize, Damian acknowledged even as he grimaced at Tarka's rudeness. Jullanar tried to catch his attention, but he shook his head severely at her—he had to work, not chat. He took the money-chest on the excuse of leaving for the cellars, where he brought up a fresh cask. At least Fitzroy was safe from losing his harp, now. Even if Rean would be *furious* that Tarka had won his sword—

Well. Rean had made it clear he wasn't going to resume Damian's friendship after Damian had spurned his offer to go west with him. Damian had *known* the friendship was all for the future use he could be to the older man, but it still hurt.

The sinners' casks contained the rough red wine made to the east of Ixsaa. It was preferred by that subset of the Inn's customers who didn't like the fashions set by the Curvers or the university students (or, the unkind said, their tastebuds either).

Damian reluctantly shouldered a fresh cask of the stuff. He plunked it down on the table along with two of the glass tankards used to drink it. As he forced open the bunghole Fitzroy grinned at him, seeming as mad as ever that afternoon, perfectly at ease, and not at all drunk, though how that could be the case after his share of five bottles of the Linnet Damian couldn't fathom.

Before returning to the bar he made a circuit of the room. He forced a few caravan guards he knew were Rean's usual hangers-on to pay his bill. They had all met him on the practice grounds, and despite grumbling about the injustice of it all made no strong protest.

The couple of pickpockets and belligerent drunks he escorted out were not so belligerent, yet, to require him to draw his own sword. He only had to pick up one by the back of his shirt to ensure he actually left the premises.

He gathered a tub full of emptied goblets and bore them to the kitchen, where Luce appeared to have been commandeered into dish-washing duty. He nodded at Zurannah, who was deeply unhappy and making sure everyone knew it from the quality of the food she was preparing, and collected an empty chest from a stack next to Pelan Cadia's storeroom. It smelled of salt fish but that couldn't be helped, Damian decided.

At least there'd be good takings tonight.

At midnight or so Fitzroy had just set down the dregs of the second of the sinner's casks. Tarka still had half his last tankard in hand. In an expectant pause he raised his arm—which trembled—lowered it—raised it again—and couldn't bear to tip the glass back. He crashed the tankard into the fireplace with an oath of disgust.

His supporters groaned. Tarka shook his head with drunken ponderousness, offering his hand to Fitzroy to shake. The poet required instructions in the custom from Damian via Jullanar, who'd come round to make sure all the glass was in the hearth, then shook the farmer's hand with a pleased smile.

"I must use the privy," he added under cover of the excited buzz that began when Tarka stood up, shook off a friend's hand, took three steps, and fell over like one of his own stunned bulls. "Then if there is another challenger?"

Jullanar murmured a translation, biting her lip as she finished the second sentence.

"I need to close the Inn soon," Damian replied. Unfortunately his words arrived in a lull, so that everyone nearby heard.

These raised a clamour of "No! Don't say that! It's barely midnight! I'll stand another round—"

One man called out, "He'll take on someone else. Who'll stand up for the city? Ixsaa's honour is at stake! Not to mention Tarka's black horse and Rean's sword *and* a fine new harp."

Damian tried to see who the person was, but the crush was too thick. He pushed back to the bar, looking longingly at the door. He saw a swirl of bright pink as some of the caravan guards escorted Fitzroy out to the privy, along with several members of the audience who hadn't heard what the excursion was for and wanted to make sure the stranger didn't disappear on them.

Luce entered the bar with a tray of clean glasses and a desperate attempt to keep from yawning. "Will this be enough?"

Damian looked at the latest box of earnings, and thought about how grateful he'd been to Cadia to keep him on even though there had barely been any problems since he started.

She'd like it if he made more money, surely?

Perhaps there would be enough to pay Fitzroy to play again.

If they wanted to encourage that. Still, music was music and there hadn't been any new minstrels through for ages.

While he was still dithering the noise ratcheted up. Damian relented and began serving another round, more to give himself space to think than anything.

He collected payment for the two casks from Tarka's brothers, who'd appeared from the back of the crowd. He was rather worried about Fitzroy. And Jullanar, who was blushing fiercely and had refused to accompany the men outside to the alley.

The next challenger was the Delta man, Ghanau mir Aviroth, who had given Damian his first duel.

"Friend of yours, I take it?" he growled as he came to sit in the empty seat with Rean's sword and Tarka's Guild badge in front of it. "Good wagers. Against the harp?"

He had been nursing one goblet of wine all evening. Damian hesitated, but Fitzroy surely knew his business best. He nodded shortly.

Ghanau considered. "I'll wager my smaller boat," he said after a pause, and placed a Delta trading medallion on the table.

Fitzroy came back in, asking Jullanar questions that made her blush like a sunset. Damian saw a few of the patrons look at her and nod. She was so clearly respectable that Damian was surprised she was willing to stay translating at the drinkers got rowdier.

"Bring out the brandy, Damian," Ghanau said, and introduced himself to Fitzroy.

"I am Fitzroy the Poet," said Fitzroy, in a horrendous accent but recognizably in Calandran. Jullanar shifted position but said nothing.

Damian thought again that Fitzroy needed a proper surname.

He brought over two bottles of the brandy. "Take those pansy glasses away," Ghanau said, regarding Fitzroy about as intently as he'd regarded Damian before their duel. "The foreigner and I are real drinkers. I've not met one with such a gullet for many a year, not since I drank with Nebbor the Sot of a week's end. We were young things on the Tschalorian border then, drinking that vodka they make up there. He outdrank two Tschalorian monks once on their own tipple, but he could never drink me under the table. Still interested, Fitzroy the poet?"

Damian reluctantly left the sinner's tankards and took away the brandy snifters. Neither Jullanar nor Fitzroy the poet could ever have heard of Nebbor the Sot, whom Damian knew as a master swordsman some said was the greatest at knife-and-bladework in all the world, but he did not think he had ever told Jullanar about him.

Fitzroy grinned at Ghanau and, with Jullanar's assistance, declared, "This is still most enjoyable. I thank you."

He'd developed a coterie of admirers by this point, not simply the ones who enjoyed seeing either Rean or Tarka brought low. They cheered this declaration, and cheered him again at every drink through that bottle, and the second, and halfway through the third, when Ghanau mir Aviroth put his head down on the table in defeat and people started muttering about witchcraft.

"It's time to close," Damian said firmly when he heard that rumour. "Last call, everyone."

In the rush of final orders, Fitzroy got up from his chair and staggered a little stiffly over to the counter. He was joined there by the adoring girls who usually hung around on nights Damian was working, as well as the remaining guardsmen and a few other locals and strangers staying the night. Damian sent a much-relieved Luce off to send the kitchen workers to bed, served orders and collected money, and was unable to find a moment to speak to Fitzroy or Jullanar. Jullanar brought over the harp, sword, and tokens before taking the tub of dishes to the kitchen.

The poet didn't seem to mind: he was smiling glassily (about time! thought Damian, putting the harp and other items next to the strong-box for safe-keeping) at the decorative carving along the ceiling beams.

There was a man along the bar that Damian whom was trying to keep an eye on. He thought it was the person who'd been egging on the drinking competition, and who was watching the crowd with an air of raffish superiority Damian didn't much like.

He had curly black hair and a disdainful smile; he came in every few months, and people said he was some sort of dilettante painter or university student. He liked to make sure people saw his increasingly glamorous clothing and fancy sword, and encouraged the young women of the Greenmarket to fawn over him.

Damian was just itching to try out his reputation but the other man had not so far come to any of the dawn duels.

This man said, "Is he using witchcraft?" with a challenging, direct glare and a too-loud voice for such an accusation. Jullanar had come back in time to hear this and translate; Fitzroy looked mildly offended. Others looked alert and concerned, and one of the admirers cried, "No! How dare you suggest that?"

"No witchcraft," Fitzroy said firmly. Then he waved vaguely with his hand at the carvings on the beam overhead and said something else.

Jullanar stared wide-eyed at him and say anything. But her gaze followed Fitzroy's gestures, and Damian realized he did not need a direct translation at all.

He had never paid much attention to the beams. They were far enough overhead that he could see that they were carved, but it was always too dim and dirty for him to decipher any details.

Now he could see that they were ... leaves. Were they carved to be the branches of trees? He looked around. The pillars on the other side of the room were definitely looking more like trunks. And there was motion up there, and a soft sound just like leaves rustling.

Not only rustling, but colouring, as if painted newly green and ruddy, with flowers opening from hidden buds with soft pops.

Within a few seconds, the entire room was festooned with a colourful mass of delicate wooden greenery spotted with flowers. It was rather pretty, Damian had time to think, before "Witchcraft!" was cried and the situation devolved rapidly.

Fitzroy himself looked around in bewilderment. Someone—and this time Damian was almost certain it was the odious ringleader, but someone else's head got in the way of him seeing for certain—said: "Get him! He's a witch!"

Damian vaulted the counter to throw the man out. Unfortunately, he knocked into someone along the way, who knocked into someone else, and within four seconds—the time it took for him to get to the table where the man had been sitting—a full-scale brawl had erupted.

There were too many people with weapons. Damian couldn't draw his sword in the throng. He jumped up onto the nearest table to get elbow room, only to see the curly-haired man slip sideways out of his sight.

He took a few seconds to orient himself. Fitzroy was over by the bar, the centre of a vigorous debate conducted with fisticuffs and some fierce scratches. He wasn't moving, was simply staring, Rean's sword, his harp, and the two tokens from Tarka and Ghanau clutched in his arms, as people fought and clamoured around him.

Damian decided Fitzroy would have to look after himself for a few minutes while he did his job, and with a great feeling of relief gave over his attention to clearing the tap room.

"Closing time!" he bawled, and leaped down from the table flourishing his sword.

He used the sword mostly as shield and bludgeon—Pelan Cadia would want most of these back as customers tomorrow night—and his left hand to grip people by collar or arm and haul them out the door.

The congestion eased considerably when a loud crash and a flash of light was followed by a billow of cool air and some howling. He assumed Fitzroy had done something magical and concentrated on evicting those stragglers who were still movable.

It was so good, he kept thinking, to be *moving*.

At last he could stand up to review the scene.

There were a dozen or so men lying on the ground. Most were under tables and several were smiling, and a couple more he'd noticed earlier; these he assumed were safely inebriated. One of the caravan guards was more seriously hurt, with a bruise on his cheek suggesting a blow. Damian turned him on his side and checked for other injuries. During the course of this the guard awoke and cursed him feebly. Damian finished his examination, helped him to a sitting position when it became clear nothing major was wrong, and kept looking.

He was still looking through the broken front window out at the empty square, wondering what had happened to Fitzroy and the other fifty or so people who'd been in the room, when Jullanar's aunt Maude appeared in the gap. She was in her dressing gown and frowning mightily whilst simultaneously yawning, which made her look like a sleepy hawk.

"Damian, whatever is going on? Did a riot just erupt? What on earth were you doing?"

"Trying to close," he said glumly, thinking *erupt* was the right word for what had just happened.

Maude quirked her lips as if trying to spare his feelings. Damian didn't know what to say further; he scuffled despondently over to the bar counter. The picture window was—had been—Pelan Cadia's pride and joy. It was the only large window in all the Greenmarket, said to have been magically created by the great wizard Mirshave the Silver on the occasion that the inn had been named the Rose and Phoenix.

Someone had taken the opportunity to abscond with the remaining bottles, though no one had gone near Fitzroy's harp or the fishy chest containing the last hour's takings.

Above the counter, one of the new vines produced an egg. Damian looked up at the faint pop as it hatched into a butterfly, its colouring scarlet and sky-blue. It opened its wings—another 'pop'—closed them—'pop'—'pop, pop, pop'.

PART FOUR
THE OUTSKIRTS

CHAPTER TWENTY-SIX

IN WHICH JULLANAR AND DAMIAN SEEK A POET

Things looked no better in the morning. In fact, they looked abundantly worse. Damian woke up with aching muscles from the bits of things on the floor; he'd slept in front of a table pushed up to block the broken window. Pelan Maude had come down from Pelan Cadia's room to help him carry the injured caravan guard upstairs before returning home with Jullanar. The drunks were still sleeping things off in the plaza.

The tap room was full of broken glass and pottery along with food, spilled wine, a bit of vomit and blood, and broken furniture. The food and wine was reasonably normal mess, but Damian had never seen it look so bad, not even after the free-for-all that had happened on Pelan Cadia's grand re-opening last summer.

The wood carving was still in motion and still colourful, with the butterflies still fluttering about it. Damian's mouth was stale; the room was stale. He staggered out through the unlocked front door to the horse trough, head pounding as if he'd drunk all the wine himself. He thought the morning sunlight was far too bright.

The square was full of people about their morning business. Several called out to him—"What a party at the Inn last night!" or "Cadia'll be glad she left you in charge, eh?" and other stupid comments that did nothing to improve his temper.

He felt marginally better after his dousing. He could almost be thoughtful returning to the Inn, almost start figuring out what to do next.

As he looked things over again, it had to be said that the Inn looked normal apart from the smashed great window with the table in front of it, and the knocked-over flowerpots that stood by the door.

Damian straightened the one of these that wasn't broken and stood indecisively in the doorway, feeling utterly overwhelmed by the mess.

After far too long Zurannah appeared in the kitchen doorway opposite him. She regarded the room disapprovingly, clucked her tongue, and disappeared again. Damian jumped and started to clear the table nearest him for want of any better idea of where to start. He was fairly certain the whole thing was his fault.

He didn't get far, just a tray-full of crockery to the bar. He found himself sitting on a stool, staring at a pink and blue butterfly, wondering if this were the end of his hopes for adventure and friendship and his job all at once. Jullanar could hardly be happy with how the evening had turned out. And Fitzroy ... yesterday's behaviour had done nothing to assuage Damian's concerns. He looked queasily at the apparent forest inside the room.

He knew about magic. His mother had taught him what she knew, or at least the fundamentals of it. Real magic was not much accepted in Ixsaa, apart from what a handful of the students at the university got up to. Alezian always said they were just studying alchemy and dismissed any of it as *real* magic.

His mother could light candles ...

The butterflies fluttered around. This was *real* magic.

He was still sitting there when Jullanar came in. She offered him a cup of mint tea, which was kind of her, little though it did to assist him.

She didn't say anything, just leaned against the bar with her own cup of tea, taking in the mess.

After a bit, Jullanar said, "Where is Fitzroy?"

Damian spilled tea down his leg and bit back a curse. "I—I'm not certain."

"Oh," she said, and there was a pause. And then: "Do you think we should go find him?"

It felt as if his heart had started to beat again. He looked at Jullanar, blurry though her face was to him, and wondered ... He did not let himself wonder in words. He had to hold those close, tight in his heart, sheltered as a wildcat's newborn kitten.

(Once he had found a wildcat in the reed-plains, stretched out on a rocky outcropping in the sun. Damian had come close, and it had purred like the domestic cat of his childhood, and he had reached out so slowly, so gently, and stroked the wildcat's head.)

He swallowed, furious with himself at how close he was to tears.

"Yes," he said thickly, and had to cough and clear his throat. He looked around the disaster that was the Inn's taproom. He had a clear responsibility here ... and yet there was also the responsibility he felt (that he *had*) for his guest, strange and uncanny as he might be.

(If that *were* the Lord Phoenix, or the Calandran god Orophon, or— or anyone, what then? And if he weren't, if Fitzroy the Poet was simply another young man, a person like Damian or Jullanar, what then? Would Damian, lost and confused in a foreign land, not hope someone who had offered him hospitality would help him?)

"Yes," he said again, more clearly. "But I must see about ... this, first."

He gestured around the room. Jullanar hummed, then drank down her tea decisively. "Very good! My aunt will be here soon—she went to see Pelan Cadia. Let's see what we can get done before they get here."

Jullanar had not slept long, nor well, but once woken up with the crowing of the neighbour's rooster, she could not then return to sleep. She washed and dressed, and while the cook-fire got going, went outside for fresh water. The broken window of the Inn drew her attention, and after she'd filled up her water jug, she made mint tea enough to share.

Sure enough, Damian was sitting in the ruined taproom, with an uncharacteristically vague expression. For the first time Jullanar realized he was younger than she.

She set to work willingly enough, helping Damian right tables and picking up the broken shards of glasses and goblets. The room stank, and she thought sadly that this was probably why all those tract-writers were not *entirely* wrong in their admonitions against The Drink.

It had been such a *fun* evening until the crowd started breaking things.

They had not gotten far when Alezian and his friend showed up. Damian was inclined to be prickly, Jullanar could see as she returned from the kitchen with a broom, but his brother was surprisingly amiable.

"Well," the friend said, standing in the doorway with his arms on his hips. "What a mess!"

"Was anything stolen?" Alezian asked. "Or anyone hurt?"

"Bruises, one man knocked out," Damian replied brusquely. "Nothing stolen."

Both Alezian and his friend gave Damian an impressed glance Jullanar knew he didn't see. "Goodness," Alezian said softly. "Ema said you'd offered hospitality to a stranger? Is he around?"

Damian stopped in the middle of carrying a table across the room. He set it down with controlled motions, his fierce scowl directed down in something almost approaching shame. "No. We shall go look for him once we have cleaned up here."

There was a pause. Jullanar continued to sweep, watching as Alezian and his friend exchanged glances. She was too tired to deal with young men too full of themselves to help.

She felt guilty for the thought the next moment, when Alezian said, "We can work here, Dami, if you want to go find your friend."

Damian looked torn, but Jullanar was of the opinion that such helpfulness should be immediately accepted, and so she crossed the room and handed her broom to the friend. "Thank you," she said with as charming a smile as she could produce. "We are most grateful."

And without waiting another moment, she took Damian by the arm and led him out.

"And who is *she*?" she heard the friend ask Damian's brother, but she didn't hear Alezian's response past, "A stranger—"

No matter that.

They collected a reasonable bag of supplies from Pelan Maude—Jullanar had sensibly suggested that Fitzroy, at least, would likely be hungry when they found him—enough for all three of them and more, though Damian didn't feel like telling her it was far too much food.

Crossing the square to the north gate, they found the baker gossiping with a couple of local middle-aged women. Damian nodded stiffly at them when they nudged each other and laughed.

Jullanar said, "Did you see a young man? The black one? He was singing?"

The baker laughed. "Your friend, eh, Damian?"

Damian tried not to growl at him. He understood Jullanar's tactic—he did. There was no reason he couldn't follow suit. He cleared his throat. "I'm sorry about the noise last night. A drinking competition got out of control at the inn."

"Aye, it turned into a witch hunt."

One of the women shook her head censoriously. The other said, "I heard from Cotu that they built a bonfire up yonder."

Damian frowned. Jullanar was very tense beside him.

"I heard," the first woman said with a significant pause, "that the stranger turned into a bat and flew away."

Damian rather doubted this. Still—there was certainly something very *odd* about Fitzroy. Worrisomely so, in fact. He took a deep breath. "Who did you hear that from, Pelanna?"

She seemed marginally pleased by the honorific, her voice warming when she replied. "Glainor from the cheese shop."

"Thank you," he said, and went accordingly next door.

He bought a piece of hard cheese to go with their lunch, though he probably needn't have bothered. Glainor had been one of the more enthusiastic cheerers of the poet last night, and seemed now equally enthusiastic about telling his rapt customers about how they'd chased the witch three times widdershins around the fire—which anyone knew meant he was bound to jump in if he was a witch—but when push came to shove he'd spun magic (Glainor called it "a shroud of night") around him, leaped right over the fire, and disappeared until all that was left was a bat flying above the bonfire.

Damian had often noticed bats chasing insects attracted by firelight in Ixsaa. He pointed this out.

Glainor said, "Aye, you were much taken with him yesterday. Collecting all the foreigners, are you?" he added with a leer at Jullanar.

"She is to be a *Maiden Oracle*," Damian replied frigidly. "I offered the stranger my hospitality. It is my duty to find him. What field did you build the fire in?"

"Up past Pilli Palla. But I tell you, he turned into a bat and flew away. He could be back in the Pit by now—or roosting in the temple eaves—or gathering together other forces of darkness and gloom—"

"Thank you."

Jullanar didn't say anything as they exited the cheese shop and finally, finally, got out of the city. How Damian appreciated her quiet demeanour!

"We shall go to the field Glainor spoke of," he told her, "and see what we can find. Perhaps someone will still be there."

She nodded, and walked briskly. Damian strode beside her, feeling his tensions unwind in the fresh breeze of the morning.

The witch hunters had not been tidy: the trail of bottles, cloth, bits of buckles and trodden grass was evident. It led them across a pasture to the Pilli Palla bridge along the Saffronsands, through a trampled hedge, across a field in a wide swath of destroyed plants and into another bean field in fragrant bloom. There he found an old man in old-fashioned clothing, leaning on a stick and surveying a smouldering pile of cinders and charred wood.

"Good morning, sir," Damian said, more or less politely, halting.

Jullanar had stopped to pick something off the ground, and hurried up with it clenched in her hand. She smiled at the old man, who harrumphed.

"Half the bean crop ruined, and the year's wood half burnt. What a morning, what a day. Why not an army while the gods are at it? Or a giant? Or another century flood? We must be due one soon."

Damian drew in a deep breath. "The last one was only fifty years ago."

"And don't I remember it!" the old man said, rounding on him.

"Sir," Jullanar said hesitantly, which seemed to mollify him, or at least the old man's posture relaxed. "Sir, do you know what happened to the stranger they ran up here?"

"The beans were just coming into flower, too." The old spat accurately onto an ember, which sizzled. "Aye, strangers are bad news."

Jullanar shrank back slightly. Damian frowned. "It was locals who did this, sir."

The old man spat again. "I owned a hundred acres here before the Flood, and after it came the river took seventy-five of them with it, and gave me a hundred logs and five dead horses in return."

Damian didn't see how this statement had to do with anything. Probably Alezian was right about it always being about money. He sighed. "I'm sorry. Have you seen a black-skinned stranger hereabouts?"

"A pity!" The old man cackled. "That wood was worth more to a city under siege than fifty acres of swampy bottomland. You say it was locals, eh? You reckon they were drunk?"

"I know they were drunk. I'd been serving them at the Inn."

"What inn? Never the Thorn and Lantern, you couldn't fit that many inside. Or the Crossed Grapes—I was there last night."

Propping up the bar on one drink, no doubt. "The Rose and Phoenix, in the Greenmarket."

The old man spat. "There's a lot you don't know about the wide world, lad. Look to who stands to gain, is all I say. The river comes and the river goes, and the thing to look for is who's left standing in the mud, and who's standing richer when the tide goes down."

Damian hated gnomic utterances. He decided not to insist on an explanation, or point out that a witch hunt was not the same thing as a flood. The old man was old and to be respected, so he stifled his impatience, said, "Thank you, sir."

He withdrew a few feet away to examine the field, hoping he could figure out where Fitzroy might have gone.

The old man watched him critically. Damian felt foolish. He was skilled in the reed-plains, but he didn't *track* signs; he just understood how the wild things moved. He hoped Fitzroy had not turned into a bat but had instead dropped part of his outfit, or torn it, or fallen down and asleep in a puddle or something.

"Here," Jullanar said, coming over to him and showing him a small, heavy, golden thing.

Damian felt it in his hands: cool metal, etched with some design he could not see (could not see *without the spectacles*, which were back in his room at home), one end curved, the other full of small square flanges.

But he knew that shape. "A key?"

"It's made of gold," Jullanar said. "Or I think it is. And it's got the sun and the moon on it ... They are ... pictures from the ... from where I am from."

"This is his, you think?"

"Yes."

They both stood there. Damian gripped the key, wondering what it possibly opened, for such a strange and magical person as their quarry. The sky was clear, bar some high feathery clouds, and the wind blowing from the west. Even with the destruction, the bean-flowers scented the air with their sweet breath.

"Look," Jullanar said, pointing. "That white falcon is back."

Damian looked up, seeing the bird hovering not far above them. He glanced over, but the old man had stumped off, heading towards some tumbledown buildings in the middle distance. Pilli Palla, he guessed.

He hesitated, but surely Jullanar had shown herself a friend—had she not come this morning bearing mint tea, after all the trials of the night before? Had she not immediately begun to help him, and then come with him to find the stranger, Fitzroy? Had she not told *him*, Damian, the secret paths to her own far country?

Damian lifted his hand and whistled, and the falcon stooped down to land.

"His name," he said, "is Avandion. He is ... mine." He gave her a fierce stare. "He is not to be touched by others."

He could not say more than that. He did not have the words—not in Calandran, not even in Tanteyr—to explain what a satall was.

Damian did not know what a *soul* was, anyway, let alone how it could be that this falcon carried his. But that was what his mother said ... and it was true that Alezian's fine jay was as fond of brightly-shining things as his brother was himself. And their mother's great raven was wise ...

If they had lived in the mountains, in the old country, their satallir would live *with* them, in their homes, part of their lives. Since they did not, their satallir lived as the wild birds did, in the outskirts of the city, only occasionally to be met. Damian did not know what that could mean, either.

His mother's books might tell him, or his mother, if ever he dared ask her.

He had not dared to look at the Tanteyr books, even through the spectacles, for fear their words would still be as alien and hard to understand as they ever were.

"Avandion. The gyrfalcon," Jullanar murmured, and the falcon turned its head to regard her.

Damian hesitated a moment, another moment, and then he whispered to the falcon in Tanteyr. "Have you seen the stranger, the poet, the one full of magic? Where is he, our guest?"

The falcon hesitated a moment, and then rustled its wings. Damian stepped away from Jullanar so he could throw the bird into the sky. It flew up, up, up, in a widening gyre, blinding-white against the blue sky.

"He's so beautiful," Jullanar said, her voice thick. "Thank you, Damian."

Damian shivered, but it was—it was good, wasn't it, to share something so precious and private? It was not a weakness, no more than loving the beauties of the reed-plains and the wild things was.

Jullanar was silent, watchful. Damian gave her back the golden key, and she tucked it into the pocket of her skirt.

They watched the bird, the bean-flowers heady around them, the sun heavy on their shoulders. There was still that strange, thin, effervescence in the wind, a cool breath from the distant mountains, the glittering taste of magic.

Damian shivered again. Jullanar brushed his side with her elbow, though he was not sure if it were on purpose or simply because she had moved to follow the falcon's shifting location.

It was comforting, in its way. He did not step immediately away.

But it was still a relief when the bird suddenly slanted off to the north and west, then pulled to a hover. "There," he said, knowing he did not need to point, that Jullanar was watching, that she had *seen*. "That way."

CHAPTER TWENTY-SEVEN

IN WHICH JULLANAR AND DAMIAN FIND SOMETHING

Jullanar had no idea what the falcon meant to Damian, but there was something intensely *appropriate* about seeing the white bird on his wrist, the fierce dark eye with its golden ring staring deep into hers with what seemed to be an uncanny intelligence.

It gave her goosebumps, and then, when the bird clearly knew its own *name*—and then, when Damian murmured to the falcon in a mysterious other language—which sounded entirely unlike Calandran—and then launched the gyrfalcon into the air, and it went *looking*—

She had no words. None.

Damian gave her back the golden key, which was a heavy, cool, comforting weight in her hand, and she tucked it deep into her pocket where it would be safe, and then she followed where her friend and tutor led her, into the reeds, her stomach in her throat, her head dizzy, her heart thudding as if she'd been fencing with him all morning.

They found Fitzroy the Poet sitting with his arms wrapped around his knees, precariously balanced on a finger of orange sandstone that extended into the brown water of the Amberwells.

Extending, unfortunately, from the *northern* side of the river.

They had followed the nearly-invisible trails Damian knew, and were, therefore, on the other side of the stream. The poet was staring down at the brown water, and did not seem to see them.

"This is a difficulty," Damian said, scowling. "I shall have to get the boat."

"Is there no way around?" Jullanar asked. "He must have found some way across there himself."

"Unless he turned into a *galoma*," Damian returned sharply, then shook his head. "No, he went there, do you see?" He pointed to the left, where the Amberwells narrowed briefly before expanding into a wider river at the confluence of a dark orange stream. "That tree was above water before."

At first Jullanar could not see what he meant, but then she saw the broken log that had presumably formed a bridge. "Oh," she said. "I hope he didn't fall in."

"He got out," Damian said, unconcerned. "What matters is that he cannot swim, and this part of the stream is dangerous." He glared at the seemingly placid water. It was only ten or a dozen feet across, but that was too far for anyone but Damian to jump, Jullanar was quite sure.

She glanced at him, and then lifted her voice and called, "Fitzroy!" as loudly as she could.

The poet nearly fell of his stone, but scrambled to his feet to peer around his surroundings. Jullanar wondered if he were as nearsighted as Damian was the opposite, but when she waved Fitzroy waved back with great enthusiasm.

"Jullanar!" he cried happily. "You came to find me! I cannot get back across!"

"I know! We're working on it!"

Fitzroy gave her a brilliant smile and sat back down, his posture suddenly much more relaxed.

He *trusted* them, she realized. This stranger, this perfect stranger, who had fallen out of the sky and drunk more than anyone should rightly be able to hold, who had been run out of the city as a witch and ended up —here—

He *trusted* them.

Jullanar sniffled, touched, and then swallowed hard. "Perhaps I should wait here," she suggested to Damian. "You'll go faster without me, and I can talk to him."

Damian gave her an almost grateful look, and without further comment took five steps into the reeds and was gone.

Jullanar considered the situation, and especially the way Fitzroy was watching her every movement with an alert intensity, and carefully sat down on the ground. It wasn't too damp, fortunately, though she was sure she wouldn't enjoy cleaning her skirt afterwards. Still—standing for however long wasn't very appealing.

"Are you ... well?" she asked after a bit. They were not sitting quietly enough, and consequently were in a deep pool of silence, all the wild things hidden.

"I feel a bit odd," Fitzroy allowed, almost judiciously. She nodded, uncertain of what else to say to him, and after several minutes he said suddenly, "And you?"

"I'm fine, thank you," she replied automatically. "A little hungry, perhaps."

"Me, too," he agreed, as if this was a strange development. Perhaps it was.

Jullanar was still holding the sack of food, and she extracted a small pastry that seemed as if it would stand being thrown across the river. "Here," she said, and tossed it to him.

He fumbled the catch but managed not to completely destroy the pastry, and after examining it curiously, ate gladly. Jullanar followed suit, grateful she'd thought to bring anything and wishing she'd remembered to give some to Damian before he left.

After eating, Fitzroy brushed his fingers together and shifted position on his rock. He looked as if he were about to ask her something difficult, and she braced herself for questions about the riot and the bonfire and what all those Ixsaans had been shouting about witchcraft.

But what Fitzroy actually said was: "How did you come to be here?"

Jullanar opened her mouth to give him the same explanation she'd given her aunt, but then the thought of Damian's momentarily vulnerable expression as he called down his falcon from the sky and told her its name —the thought of the quiet places of the reeds—the thought of that silence, that gift of strength and *belief* that she, even she, could learn what Damian had to teach—

Fitzroy had *fallen out of the sky*. If she could not tell *him*, then who?

"I wanted to have an adventure," she said simply. "I wanted to be someone who *could* have an adventure."

Fitzroy looked at her solemnly, the brown water glinting with golden bubbles rising up between them. Jullanar wondered what he thought of her, this strange young woman sitting on the ground facing him.

Surely she wasn't any stranger than *him*, but then again ... She sighed, and smoothed out her skirt over her crossed legs. That probably wasn't true. Her family would definitely think *him* eccentric and *her* strange.

"This is like being inside a poem," Fitzroy said at length, smiling at her so engagingly Jullanar could only smile helplessly back.

"Any poem in particular?"

"*Larigor*," he said decisively. "The third book."

Jullanar had read *Larigor* at Madame Clancette's—how long ago that felt now!—they'd been supposed to study the first two books for the Entrance Examinations, but Jullanar had fallen in love with the poem—how could she not? It was about a young woman who had to set off to find her place in the world after her family was all killed by brigands in the mountains, during the course of which she met Ovanü, one of the brigands, and after declaring enmity they had been forced to work together and eventually become lifelong friends—

Book three was when they became friends, after the great tragic events of the first two books.

And Fitzroy was thinking of *that*.

She swallowed, and straightened her back, and said, with what she thought was a tolerable composure, "Did you read Orzon's translation, or the one by that scholar from Harktree, I forget his name?"

Fitzroy tilted his head, curiously. "Neither. I read it in the original."

Jullanar blinked at him. "You read Ferish?"

"Of course."

"Oh, of course," she said, because—because *of course* he was learned in languages; no doubt he'd had tutors from childhood. She smiled wanly at him. "We could only learn Old Shaian as an option in school."

He frowned; his frown was much less fierce than Damian's. "University, you mean?"

Where could he possibly be from, if he did not even know what a *school* was? (If he joked about children being pygmies ...) "No, before university." She smiled, a little self-deprecatingly. "I just finished going to Madame Clancette's Finishing School for Girls. Or have you been to university already? I was supposed to go this year."

Not that what she'd done instead was—she thought guiltily—*far* more interesting—

Fitzroy hummed. "I was taught at home." He said it easily, as if—well, he'd made no pretence of not being of a high rank, had he? Even tattered and muddy after his journey through the fens, his magenta and viridian clothes were still glorious. "I learned all the main languages of Astandalas," he went on, as if it were nothing remarkable at all. "Modern Shaian, Old Shaian, Ancient Shaian, Antique Shaian, Inshu, Qalan, Ferish, and Renvoonran, though my tutor said not many Voonrans speak it any more."

Jullanar stared at him. She'd not even *heard* of some of those languages before. "Oh."

"I can recite *Larigor* in Ferish," he offered, and when she nodded silently, did so at considerable length.

His voice was lovely, but then she'd thought that last night, hearing him sing.

And then, when he fell silent after the long passage, and Jullanar was staring dreamily at the flickering reflections of the sunlight on the water, half-listening to distant birds, wondering when Damian would return to fetch them, Fitzroy the poet said: "There should be more women who go on adventures, like Larigor. There are too many where the men get all the adventures while the women stay home and weave tapestries or practice brush painting or whatever. I'm sure that's all very good," he added when Jullanar glanced sharply at him, "but this is fun, too, isn't it?"

This. This right here, the two of them, sitting in a swamp after he'd been run out of a tavern, with a river between them.

"It's not much of an adventure," she said doubtfully. She'd always imagined true adventures to be full of—of action, of dragons and heroes, of gold and treasure, of dashing swordsmen and beautiful ladies—

Of poetry; of friendship; of the calluses forming on her hand from the sword she was learning to wield.

"Isn't it?" he replied, his face brightening. "I was lost, and you came to find me! It was a *quest*—what more of an adventure could you ask for? And next time we can go *together* to find something else!"

Jullanar swallowed again. Her throat felt as if there were an egg in it, pressing against her chest.

How could this *possibly* be true?

Had she accidentally summoned some spirit of magic, come to offer her all her most cherished dreams? (*I might be this*, he had said; *I might be that*. What *was* he, in truth?)

What cost would she have to pay for them?

There was always a cost. She knew that from every book she'd ever read, every tale she'd ever heard. She might not know it until the end, but there would be a cost.

"There's El Magar," she said, fighting for equilibrium. How could she feel this tumbled-over-and-around when she was sitting solidly on the ground, the damp earth pressing through her skirt, the air limpid on her skin? The brown-and-gold water, the ridiculously brightly-garbed young man across from her, the knowledge that Damian was somewhere in the reed-plains, coming for them like a hero out of a story—

She knew the cost, didn't she? In respectability, in homesickness, in *being acceptable*.

"She pretends to be a man," Fitzroy objected. "No, no," he went on, shaking his head. "You must go on adventures just as you are."

Jullanar remembered Marianne, thrusting those books on hydrology and river studies on her, praising her for her braveness and her willingness to stand against the 'men'. And Jullanar wasn't brave, not really, and her great stand was mostly in Marianne's mind—no doubt, she realized suddenly, because it was *Marianne* who wanted to study hydrology and what-have-you, those masculine subjects Mrs. Faraday did not entirely dismiss, but which would not be *acceptable* for her daughter to study.

Jullanar had already forfeited half her respectability, hadn't she, in choosing Galderon?

And the other half, it had to be said, in deciding not to return home, but to continue on, to press across the Border, to leave the Empire behind entirely.

She *could* have gone to Aunt Claudia in Kingsford. That would have been the *proper* thing to do.

She shivered hard, but she'd decided—already she had—each morning she went with Damian and let him show her another move with the sword, another form to practice—step by step, when she went to the tavern to translate, and found it *fun*—

She smiled at Fitzroy, trying to be as brave as Marianne thought her, as brave as she wanted to be, a woman Of Character. "Well," she said, not nonchalant but perhaps as close as she'd ever managed, "that depends on whether you're willing to come adventuring with Damian and *me*, doesn't it?"

Fitzroy gave her such a huge and brilliant grin than Jullanar was sure her heart actually stuttered. "I would be honoured and delighted and—and—and—" *He* stuttered to a halt, and then, in a quieter, simpler tone, said, "This is the best day of my life."

It was probably Jullanar's, too.

What matter if this was the end of her respectability? She'd never wanted that, had she? She'd wanted *friends*, and adventures, and to see what lay on the other side of the horizon, the Empire, the mountains.

"There'll be more and better days," she said, meaning it.

Damian ran through the reed-plains, all the cares and troubles of the night before, the morning, half his life, falling away into the quiet and the familiar strength of his body, capable of what he asked of it. The day had started off cool, but was growing warm as the sun crested noon. Not far above him, the falcon kept easy pace, its shadow always just ahead of his falling step.

Damian breathed deeply, and ran more easily than ever.

He found his boat where he'd left it the afternoon before, more or less cleaned of all the rainbow serpent's blood, and pushed off smartly into the streams that would lead him to the Amberwells. It might take him another hour to get to where he'd left Jullanar and Fitzroy, and another hour to return to the city—well, Alezian knew where they'd gone, and would tell their mother and Pelan Cadia and Pelan Maude if need be.

He didn't like rowing quite as much as running, but it was good to use his arms, his shoulders, to negotiate the bends and obstacles in the watercourses, to fall into that rhythm and imagine ...

Imagine *this*. That *this* was his life, that after all he the silent one was teaching someone else to speak, that she the foreigner was teaching him to see the familiar things of his life, and the both of them together had found that strange stranger who brought magic in his wake ...

He found himself humming, and after a while identified it as one of the songs Fitzroy had sung the night before. How strange, he thought, and smiled a little to himself as he rowed faster. How strange.

And—how nice.

AUTHOR'S NOTE

The Red Company have been longstanding companions of my imagination, and if you've read others of my books, you'll have seen them mentioned (and perhaps met one or two of them in other guises and periods). *Derring-Do for Beginners* begins the company (if not yet by name) and also the adventures. Look for the next book in the series in 2024.

Most of my other books take place long after the heyday of the Red Company, after the Fall of the Empire of Astandalas in a magical cataclysm. You might start with *Stargazy Pie* (Greenwing & Dart #1) or the standalone *In the Company of Gentlemen* for a bit more about Alinor, or *The Hands of the Emperor* (Lays of the Hearthfire #1) for a very different take on what happened after the Fall; all three of those books will give you an idea of what Jullanar and Damian and Fitzroy came to be and do.

In the meantime, you can keep up to date with my newsletter, talk about the characters and worlds in the fan-run Discord server, or simply check in on my website for all my other books.

For the newsletter: https://landing.mailerlite.com/webforms/landing/u8j8y4

For the Discord: https://discord.com/invite/bbXMcqehPs

For general news and announcements: www.victoriagoddard.ca